A CHRISTMAS

A CHRISTMAS CAROL

Charles Dickens

edited by Richard Kelly

broadview literary texts

National Library of Canada Cataloguing in Publication
Dickens, Charles, 1812-1870
    A Christmas carol / Charles Dickens ; edited by Richard Kelly.

(Broadview literary texts)
Includes bibliographical references.
isbn 1-55111-476-3

I. Kelly, Richard, 1937- .   II. Title.   III. Series.
PR4572.C45 2003   823'.8   C2003-900016-8

Broadview Press Ltd. is an independent, international publishing house, incorporated in 1985. Broadview believes in shared ownership, both with its employees and with the general public; since the year 2000 Broadview shares have traded publicly on the Toronto Venture Exchange under the symbol BDP.

We welcome comments and suggestions regarding any aspect of our publications–please feel free to contact us at the addresses below or at broadview@broadviewpress.com.

North America
PO Box 1243, Peterborough, Ontario, Canada K9J 7H5
3576 California Road, Orchard Park, NY, USA 14127
Tel: (705) 743-8990; Fax: (705) 743-8353
email: customerservice@broadviewpress.com

UK, Ireland, and continental Europe
Thomas Lyster Ltd., Units 3 & 4a, Old Boundary Way
Burscough Road, Ormskirk
Lancashire, L39 2YW
Tel: (01695) 575112; Fax: (01695) 570120
email: books@tlyster.co.uk

Australia and New Zealand
UNIREPS, University of New South Wales
Sydney, NSW, 2052
Tel: 61 2 9664 0999; Fax: 61 2 9664 5420
email: info.press@unsw.edu.au

www.broadviewpress.com

Broadview Press Ltd. gratefully acknowledges the financial support of the Government of Canada through the Book Publishing Industry Development Program for our publishing activities.
The interior of this book is printed on 100% recycled paper.

100%

Series editor: Professor L.W. Conolly
Advisory editor for this volume: Professor Eugene Benson
Text design and composition: George Kirkpatrick

PRINTED IN CANADA

Contents

Acknowledgments

In preparing this volume I am indebted to the work of many scholars and critics, especially Edgar Johnson, Michael Slater, Fred Kaplan, Peter Ackroyd, Ruth Glancy, Michael Hearn, Paul Davis, and Fred Guida. Edgar Johnson was the Chairman of the English Department at the City College of New York when I was an undergraduate there, and his compelling interest in and knowledge of the writings of Charles Dickens have left a life-long impression upon me. My thanks also to Florian Schweizer, Assistant Curator, The Dickens House Museum, London, and to Eugene Benson, Barbara Conolly, and Leonard Conolly for their many helpful suggestions and comments.

Introduction

The colorful details of Charles Dickens's evocation of Christmas reside not only in his books but have entered the popular imagination and influenced the manner in which many Western nations celebrate Christmas to this day. Dickens's vision of Christmas conjures up joyful family gatherings filled with the pleasures of the hearth: abundant food and drink, dancing and merry games, and generosity of spirit. His vision of this feast day, however, is a secularization of one of the most sacred days in the Christian calendar and has its roots in antiquity. During the Middle Ages Christianity appropriated many of the pagan rituals as part of its celebration of the birth of Christ. Both the ancient Roman ritual of Saturnalia—in honor of the god of agriculture—and the Germanic festival of Yule —in honor of the god Thor—enriched the customs and traditions of the Christian feast days. Christmas in medieval times was a twelve-day festival that took place in the household of a local lord. The burning of the Yule log, playing traditional games, and enjoying quantities of food and drink were all part of these celebratory days. By the middle of the seventeenth century, however, the pageantries of Christmastide were quelled under the influence of the Puritans. Until the beginning of the nineteenth century the celebration of Christmas seems to have been little observed. Writing in 1837, Thomas Hervey laments the passing of the Christmas traditions: "The revels of merry England are fast subsiding into silence, and her many customs wearing gradually away." He traces the neglect of these customs to the urbanization of England: "In fact, that social change which has enlarged and filled the towns at the expense of the country, which has annihilated the yeomanry of England, and drawn the estated gentleman from the shelter of his ancestral oaks, to live upon their produce in the haunts of dissipation, has been, in itself, the circumstance most unfavorable to the existence of many of [these customs], which delight in bye-ways and sheltered places, which had their appropriate homes in the old manor house or the baronial hall."[1]

It was not until the middle of the nineteenth century that the

---

1 *The Book of Christmas* (Chicago: Cuneo Press, 1951) 21.

revival of Christmas traditions began. William Sandys's *Selection of Christmas Carols, Ancient and Modern* (1833) and Thomas K. Hervey's *The Book of Christmas* (1837), a detailed account of Christmas traditions, aroused the nostalgia of urban Victorians. Shortly thereafter, Prince Albert introduced to England the German custom of decorating the Christmas tree; the singing of Christmas carols, which had all but disappeared at the turn of the century, began to thrive again; and the first Christmas card, which appeared in 1843, inspired a commercial tradition in England and America. It was the Christmas stories of Dickens, however, especially his 1843 masterpiece *A Christmas Carol*, that resurrected ancient traditions and celebrated anew the earthy appetites that define human life. Amid his scenes of genial family gatherings Dickens expresses a child-like abandon as the ordinary business of life gives way to eating plum puddings, drinking spiced wine, playing parlor games, dancing, and telling ghost stories at the fireside. He never allows the reader to forget, however, that the warm, colorful rooms of his Christmas merry-makers have a fragility and elusiveness about them: the wolfish twins of Ignorance and Want, as well as the specter of death, reside close by. *A Christmas Carol* is, indeed, a ghost story, a paradoxical mixture of light and darkness, joy and despair, warmth and cold, life and death.

Dickens's idea of Christmas may seem a far cry from the ancient rituals of the Saturnalia, but there are some interesting connections between the two. The period of what is popularly called the winter solstice has long been recognized as a period of great rejoicing. As the daylight hours gradually diminished after the summer solstice, leading to the longest night of the year in late December, people began to celebrate the expected return of longer days on or about December 22. The Roman Saturnalia, which occurred at this time, was a season of joyful celebration. Friends feasted with one another, wars were not declared, and executions were delayed. The hymns in honor of Saturn foreshadow the modern Christmas carols, and presents exchanged between friends anticipate the later exchange of Christmas gifts. Even the poor and slaves were recipients of favors in these ancient times, suggesting the good will that permeated the social classes on this occasion. A ruler was appointed to oversee the games held during the Saturnalia, a probable ancestor of the Christmas Prince, or Lord of Misrule, who presided over the Christmas games in more modern times. All of this to celebrate human nature's fundamental need for light, warmth, and the prospect of the land's rebirth. Indeed, in *A Christmas Carol* and other of his writings Dickens, in celebrating the death and renewal of the year, acknowledges his own rebirth and the prospect of his own mortality.

In describing the character of Ebenezer Scrooge, Dickens early on visualizes him as the embodiment of winter: "The cold within him froze his old features, nipped his pointed nose, shrivelled his cheek, stiffened his gait; made his eyes red, his thin lips blue; and spoke out shrewdly in his grating voice. A frosty rime was on his head, and on his eyebrows, and his wiry chin. He carried his own low temperature always about with him; he iced his office in the dog-days; and didn't thaw it one degree at Christmas" (p. 40). This same cold fills his dismal office, and the small fires in his room and that of Bob Cratchit emit little heat and less light. Scrooge's lodgings are also cold and dark: "darkness is cheap, and Scrooge liked it" (p. 49). By associating his character with images of winter and darkness, Dickens shows Scrooge to be at odds with the Christian sense of joy at the birth of Christ. Christmas is mere humbug to him; and like the cold and darkness of winter itself, Scrooge must thaw and give way to the generous warmth and bright celebrations of the Christmas season reflected in the people around him.

Describing Charles Dickens as "the man who invented Christmas," Byron Rogers writes: "In our dreams of the perfect pub it is always the 1830s, on the eve of the Railway Boom, with Christmas not far away. Christmas was never far away for him. It is there in his first book and in his last, and for him each year the deadline came for the Christmas story, something he was to ruefully call clearing 'the Christmas stone out of the road.' Look at the cards on your mantle piece. Those without robins or shepherds have coaches, inns, ladies in muffs and jolly men in Hessian boots, all these because a young man froze Christmas for us in the 1830s. He was able to do this because for reasons of his own he had largely invented it."[1] Indeed, the English writer Theodore Watts-Dunton claims to have

1   "The Man Who Invented Christmas," *Sunday Telegraph* (December 18, 1988): 16.

overheard this comment by a young female street vendor after Dickens's death in 1870: "'Dickens dead? Then will Father Christmas die too?'"[1]

While there are other authors before Dickens who celebrated the festive season, it was Dickens, above all, who superimposed his secular vision of this sacred holiday upon a welcoming public. Rogers states that Dickens was able to do this "for reasons of his own." Those reasons, central for understanding the immense power of *A Christmas Carol*, were stirred by several forces, including a profound humiliation in Dickens's childhood, his subsequent sympathy with the oppressed poor, especially children, during the heady capitalist decades of the 1830s and 1840s, and the Christmas tales of Washington Irving.

In 1824, when Charles was twelve years old, his father, John Dickens, was arrested for debt and locked away in the Marshalsea Prison. The family was devastated and had to sell many of their household possessions to make ends meet; Charles even had to pawn his collection of books to contribute some money to the dwindling family coffers. But worse was yet to come. Charles, who fostered dreams of a genteel and successful future, was taken out of school and sent to work in Warren's Blacking Warehouse, a shoe polish factory, where he pasted labels on blacking bottles. The factory was dark, filthy, and crawling with rats. Charles' sense of class and intellectual superiority made him feel uncomfortable working with the riverside boys, who referred to him as "the little gentleman." His family, meanwhile, had moved into the Marshalsea Prison with his father. Charles desperately wanted to continue with his schooling and to see his family reunited at home, but lack of money made that impossible. He took lodgings nearby and managed to visit his family twice a day. Filled with shame, anger and guilt, he began to have nervous fits that startled his young companions at the factory. John Dickens, upon receiving an inheritance, was released from prison after a period of three months, but he had Charles continue working in the warehouse long after his release, a decision that certainly must have wounded the boy even further.

1 Theodore Watts-Dunton, "Dickens and 'Father Christmas': A Yule-Tide Appeal for the Babes of Famine Street," *The Nineteenth Century and After* (December 1907) 1016.

Edmund Wilson points out that "one must realize that during those months [Charles] was in a state of complete despair. For the adult in desperate straits, it is almost always possible to imagine, if not to contrive, some way out; for the child, for whom love and freedom have inexplicably been taken away, no relief or release can be projected."[1] This trauma came at a critical time in his psychological development, and it was to inform and shape his entire writing career. Writes Dickens:

No words can express the secret agony of my soul as I sunk into this companionship; compared these everyday associates with those of my happier childhood; and felt my early hopes of growing up to be a learned and distinguished man crushed in my breast. The deep remembrance of the sense I had of being utterly neglected and hopeless; of the shame I felt in my position; of the misery it was to my young heart to believe that, day by day, what I had learned, and thought, and delighted in, and raised my fancy and my emulation up by, was passing away from me, never to be brought back any more; cannot be written. My whole nature was so penetrated with the grief and humiliation of such considerations, that even now, famous and caressed and happy, I often forget in my dreams that I have a dear wife and children; even that I am a man; and wander desolately back to that time of my life.[2]

It is interesting to note in this connection that Dickens's sensitivity was not always extended to those around him. A month after his wife, Catherine, gave birth to their son, Francis Jeffrey, Dickens wrote a letter to his friend, T.J. Thompson, in which he commented: "Kate is all right; and so, they tell me, is the Baby. But I decline (on principle) to look at the latter object."[3] Five months later

1   Edmund Wilson, The Wound and the Bow (London: Methuen, 1961) 6.
2   Quoted in Edgar Johnson, Charles Dickens, His Tragedy and Triumph, 2 vols. (New York: Simon and Schuster, 1952), vol. 1, 34.
3   The Letters of Charles Dickens, eds. Madeline House, Graham Storey, and Kathleen Tillotson (Oxford: Clarendon Press, 1974), vol. 4, 47. It is possible that this remark was made in a mock-serious tone, but given the financial and domestic difficulties Dickens was experiencing at the time, I suspect it was made in earnest.

Dickens and his family traveled to Italy, leaving Francis behind in the care of his maternal grandmother. The loving, self-sacrificing figure of Bob Cratchit may have been Dickens's idealized father, but perhaps there is something of Dickens himself in the person of the self-centered and cold-hearted Scrooge.

The elements of Dickens's childhood nightmare provide the gritty texture of *A Christmas Carol*: debt, poverty, hunger, isolation, ignorance, cruelty, cold, and the withholding of generosity and love. Through the power of fantasy Dickens reformulates his childhood humiliation. Although a vulnerable child, like Dickens, Tiny Tim has a loving father in Bob Cratchit. It is the unfeeling Scrooge, the economic paterfamilias, who parcels out a meager salary that keeps the Cratchit family in financial bondage. Yet, it is the same Scrooge who becomes Tim's "second father" at the end of the story, enabling the child to be restored to health and the family to a comfortable living. Dickens presents an idealized and sentimental portrait of the Cratchit family, one built upon love and affection, but without the good grace and generosity of Scrooge to restore their hope, Tiny Tim would be doomed. The emotional ambivalence that Dickens felt towards his father (a man to be at once demonized and loved), as well as Dickens's life-long insecurity about his finances, may well have influenced the creation of the two Scrooges of his tale.

Having experienced the humiliation of his father's imprisonment for debt, Dickens developed a keen interest in money and a profound awareness of the consequences of poverty. Despite the success of his early books and the money they earned him, Dickens was distraught over the poor sales of *Martin Chuzzlewit* at a time when his family's expenses were continuing to mount. To make matters worse, in June 1843 Dickens's publisher, Chapman and Hall, threatened to reduce his monthly income by fifty pounds if sales of future installments fell below a certain number. He had four small children and another on the way, his new residence in Devonshire Terrace was expensive to maintain, and his relatives were constantly asking him for loans. He began to search for a new source of income and finally settled upon the idea of writing a Christmas book, but this time, angered by his publisher's treatment, he determined to take more control over the book's production and sales.

Although the initial stimulus for writing a new work was financial, the idea for *A Christmas Carol* arose from Dickens's preoccupation in the early 1840s with issues of poverty, ignorance, and cruelty. In October 1843 he delivered a fund-raising speech at the Athenæum, a charitable institution for the Manchester working class. He declaimed upon the dangers of ignorance and destitution and praised the institution for attempting to educate the poor workers of the city. It was during his three-day stay in Manchester that Dickens, in the afterglow of his speech at the Athenæum, first conceived the notion of *A Christmas Carol*. His concern for the education of the poor had been heightened during the previous month when he visited the Ragged Schools of Field, which offered a basic education for the street urchins in this dismal section of London. He recorded his shocking discovery in a letter to Miss Burdett Coutts, a wealthy friend and philanthropist: "The school is held in three most wretched rooms on the first floor of a rotten house; every plank, and timber, and brick, and lath, and piece of plaster in which, shakes as you walk. One room is devoted to the girls: two to the boys. The former are much better-looking—I cannot say better dressed, for there is no such thing as dress among the seventy pupils; certainly not the elements of a whole suit of clothes, among them all. I have seldom seen, in all the strange and dreadful things I have seen in London and elsewhere, anything so shocking as the dire neglect of soul and body exhibited in these children." Although he urged Miss Coutts to help support the institution, Dickens expressed a quiet despair for its future: "My heart so sinks within me when I go into these scenes, that I almost lose the hope of ever seeing them changed."[1] Dickens later offered to write an account of the school for the *Edinburgh Review*, and although he never wrote the essay, the details of the misery he saw on his visit lingered in his mind and helped formulate the background of his *Carol*.

In addition to his efforts to aid in the education of the poor, Dickens became passionately involved in the issue of child labor in 1842. In that year appeared the first report of the Commission for Inquiring into the Employment and Condition of Children in Mines and Manufactories. The gruesome details of that report drove Dickens to visit Cornwall to see for himself the brutal working con-

---

1 *Letters of Charles Dickens*, vol. 3, 562, 564.

ditions that devastated the bodies and souls of small children—he actually descended into several of these tin and copper mines. One of the commissioners, Dr. Thomas Southwood Smith, who kept Dickens informed about the government's forthcoming second report, urged the author to support the commissioners' reports by writing about them. Dickens considered publishing a pamphlet entitled "An Appeal to the People of England on behalf of the Poor Man's Child," but like the piece for the *Edinburgh Review*, it was never written.

Instead of addressing the public through polemical essays and pamphlets, Dickens came to realize during his visit to Manchester in October that the best way to win the hearts and minds of his audience must be through a deeply felt narrative, a Christmas story, one that he had already outlined in *Pickwick Papers* in 1836. In that novel he told the tale of a misanthropic grave digger named Gabriel Grub, who is converted to benevolence and good deeds after being visited by goblins on Christmas Eve and shown frightening visions. Dickens was in the early stage of creating *A Christmas Carol* when he wrote to Southwood Smith in March of 1843 explaining why he never wrote the pamphlet: "Don't be frightened when I tell you, that since I wrote to you last, reasons have presented themselves for deferring the production of that pamphlet, until the end of the year. I am not at liberty to explain them further, just now; but *rest assured* that when you know them, and see what I do, and where, and how, you will certainly feel that a Sledge hammer has come down with twenty times the force—twenty thousand times the force—I could exert by following out my first idea."[1]

Upon returning to London, Dickens eagerly began writing his tale. Words flew from his pen, and before the end of November he had finished the manuscript. In January 1844 he wrote a letter to his friend, Cornelius Felton, a professor of Greek at Harvard University, that reveals the white heat of emotion with which he composed his story. He mailed a package to Felton and explained that "in that parcel you will find a Christmas Carol in Prose. Being a Ghost Story of Christmas by Charles Dickens. Over which Christmas Carol,

---

1   *Letters,* vol. 3, 461. (See also Appendix C.)

Charles Dickens wept, and laughed, and wept again, and excited himself in a most extraordinary manner, in the composition; and thinking whereof, he walked about the black streets of London, fifteen and twenty miles, many a night when all the sober folks had gone to bed."[1]

Chapman and Hall published the book on December 14, 1843. It was a handsomely designed little book in its crimson and gold binding, with four hand-colored illustrations by John Leech, the popular artist for *Punch* magazine. Dickens also appears to have recreated a Carolian Christmas in his personal life: "Such dinings, such dancings, such conjurings, such blindmans-buffings, such theatre-goings, such kissings-out of old years and kissings-in of new ones, never took place in these parts before." After the intense weeks spent at his writing desk, he re-enters the world in a burst of celebration: "But when it was done, I broke out like a Madman. And if you could have seen me at a children's party at Macreadys[2] the other night, going down a Country dance something longer than the Library at Cambridge with Mrs. M. you would have thought I was a country Gentleman of independent property, residing on a tip-top farm, with the wind blowing straight in my face every day."[3] He seems almost to have undergone a conversion similar to Scrooge's. As Monica Dickens observes, the book "changed his own nature, because he found that he believed in the moral as he gave it life."[4]

Because of his feud with his publisher over the small earnings from *Martin Chuzzlewit*, Dickens chose to pay all expenses for the publication of *A Christmas Carol* in order to receive the total profits. He hoped to earn at least £1,000 on the first 6000 copies, but his insistence upon an expensive binding and color illustrations diminished his earnings to a mere £230. His entire profit a year later was £744. In February of 1844 he wrote to his future biographer, John Foster, an account of his great disappointment: "Such a night as I have passed! I really believed I should never get up again, until I had

---

1   *Letters*, vol. 4, 2. (See also Appendix C.)
2   William Charles Macready (1793–1873), actor and theater manager.
3   *Letters*, vol. 4, 3.
4   Introduction, *A Christmas Carol, the Original Manuscript* (New York: Dover, 1967), xi.

passed through all the horrors of a fever. I found the *Carol* accounts awaiting me, and they were the cause of it.... What a wonderful thing it is, that such a great success should occasion me such intolerable anxiety and disappointment!"[1]

Dickens's anxiety over his finances, however, must have been alleviated somewhat by the warm reviews the book received. The *Athenaeum* proclaimed it "A tale to make the reader laugh and cry — open his hands, and open his heart to charity even towards the uncharitable,— wrought up with a thousand minute and tender touches of the true 'Boz' workmanship — a dainty dish to set before a King."[2] The poet and editor Thomas Hood wrote that "If Christmas, with its ancient and hospitable customs, its social and charitable observances, were in danger of decay, this is the book that would give them a new lease. The very name of the author predisposes one to the kindlier feelings; and a peep at the Frontispiece sets the animal spirits capering...."[3] Fellow novelist William Makepeace Thackeray declared the book "a national benefit, and to every man or woman who reads it a personal kindness. The last two people I heard speak of it were women; neither knew the other, or the author, and both said, by way of criticism, 'God bless him!'" As for Tiny Tim, Thackeray went on, "There is not a reader in England but that little creature will be a bond of union between the author and him; and he will say of Charles Dickens, as the woman just now, 'GOD BLESS HIM!' What a feeling is this for a writer to be able to inspire, and what a reward to reap!"[4]

The enthusiastic reviews and the popularity of the *Carol*, however, brought about a new financial problem for Dickens in the form of literary piracy. In January 1844, *Parley's Illuminated Library* published "A Christmas Ghost Story reoriginated from the original by Charles Dickens Esquire and analytically condensed for this work." Dickens was furious and fired off a letter to his solicitor Thomas Mitton: "I have not the least doubt that if these Vagabonds can be stopped, they must be. So let us go to work in such terrible earnest

---

1 *Letters*, vol. 4, 42. (See also Appendix C.)
2 Anon., *The Athenaeum* (December 23, 1843): 1127. (See also Appendix D.)
3 *The Works of Thomas Hood*, IX (London: Ward, Locke, & Co.: 1882-1884) 93. (See also Appendix D.)
4 "A Box of Novels," *Fraser's Magazine* (February 1844): 168-169. (See also Appendix D.)

that everything must tumble down before it.... Let us be *sledge-hammer* in this, or I shall be beset by hundreds of the same crew, when I come out with a long story."[1] Through his lawyer, Dickens filed affidavits against the "gang of Robbers," as he called them, and was confident that his chancery suits would bring about a just settlement. As the legal entanglements increased, however, the pirates declared bankruptcy. Since they had no assets Dickens had to pay all the expenses involved in the various suits he brought against them, a sum that amounted to nearly £700.

The legal and financial disappointments were very painful to Dickens because this book was especially dear to him. It embodied a compelling moral lesson of the magical powers of love and generosity that he wanted to proclaim to the world, a lesson he himself believed in (if he did not always practice it), and one which informed many of his subsequent novels. Scrooge's great gift, a second chance in which to live a good life, Dickens offered to all his readers caught up in selfish pursuits that blinded them to the needs of other people.

★   ★   ★

In creating *A Christmas Carol* Dickens gathered up the grim memories of his father's imprisonment, his depressing year in the blacking factory, his outrage over the condition of the poor and uneducated—especially the children working in the mines and industry—and fused these dark visions with the bright prospects of a Christmas celebration. He drew upon his earlier work, *Pickwick Papers*, to recreate the joyful scenes of dancing, singing, eating, and drinking that flesh out the good feelings of the holiday. Also in that novel Dickens has Mr. Wardle tell the party that it is customary for everyone to while away the time until midnight, when Christmas is ushered in, by playing games of forfeits or telling ghost stories. Mr. Wardle then relates the tale of a morose, lonely, and mean-spirited sexton named Gabriel Grub who, after being visited by a frightening group of goblins who show him the past and future, is transformed into an amiable man "who saw that men like himself, who snarled at the mirth

---

1   *Letters*, vol. 4 (January 7, 1844) 16. (See also Appendix C.)

and cheerfulness of others, were the foulest weeds on the fair surface of the earth." Unlike Scrooge, whose conversion is seen and welcomed by all around him, Gabriel could not bear the thought of returning to a place where his repentance would be scoffed at and his reformation disbelieved. He vanishes for ten years and returns "a ragged, contented, rheumatic old man."

Dickens's memorable descriptions of the Christmas scene in both *Pickwick Papers* and *A Christmas Carol* owe a great deal to the American writer, Washington Irving (1783-1859). At a New York dinner, hosted by Irving, Dickens amusingly revealed his devotion to the great American author: "I say, gentlemen, I do not go to bed two nights out of seven without taking Washington Irving under my arm upstairs to bed with me."[1] Irving traveled extensively throughout Europe recording his experiences in notebooks, and he was especially fond of England and its old world character. He spent a couple of years living in Birmingham, where he wrote some of his most famous stories, including *Bracebridge Hall* (1822), a blend of fact and fiction that centers on an old manor house, its residents and guests, and their elaborate parties and tales. The largesse of the English nobility and their ancient traditions held a fascination for the American author. Bracebridge Hall was modeled after Aston Hall, recently leased from Adam Bracebridge by James Watt, the son of the famous inventor and engineer. It was here that Irving enjoyed and later recorded the grand Christmas festivities and English rituals that had largely been abandoned. In the semi-feudal community of Dingley Dell in *Pickwick Papers*, Dickens's portrait of Mr. Wardle is designed after that of Irving's genial Squire Bracebridge. Irving's descriptions of the Bracebridge Hall Christmas celebrations, with their dancing, singing, games, tales, mistletoe, and holly, clearly helped to shape those seen in Dingley Dell, Mr. Fezziwig's ball, and at the home of Scrooge's nephew, Fred.

Irving's comment upon the short and cold winter days reflects the underlying reason for the conviviality that reaches back to the Saturnalia and forward to *A Christmas Carol*: "In the depth of winter, when nature lies despoiled of every charm, and wrapped in her shroud of sheeted snow, we turn for our gratifications to moral

---

1 Quoted in Fred Kaplan, *Dickens: a Biography* (New York: William Morrow, 1988) 133.

sources. The dreariness and desolation of the landscape, the short gloomy days and darksome nights, while they circumscribe our wanderings, shut in our feelings also from rambling abroad, and make us more keenly disposed for the pleasures of the social circle. Our thoughts are more concentrated; our friendly sympathies more aroused. We feel more sensibly the charm of each other's society, and are brought more closely together by dependence upon each other for enjoyment. Heart calleth unto heart; and we draw our pleasures from the deep wells of living kindness, which lie in the quiet recesses of our bosoms; and which, when resorted to, furnish forth the pure element of domestic felicity."[1] What could be more Dickensian than these words?

In addition to creating a powerful tension between the merriment of Irving's nostalgic account of Christmas with his own dark vision, shaped by his painful childhood memories and by his sympathy with the suffering of children brought on by the Industrial Revolution, Dickens changed the tradition of a twelve-day festival set in a manor house to a one-day celebration set in a city warehouse (Mr. Fezziwig's ball) and in the homes of middle and lower class families, namely those of Scrooge's nephew, Fred, and Bob Cratchit. As Paul Davis observes, "The *Carol* melded country customs and Christmas lore with a Londoner's vision to create a new Christmas story that was particularly attuned to the emergent urbanity of early Victorian England."[2]

Whereas Washington Irving discovers the ancient rituals of Christmas to be very much alive in the country mansion of Bracebridge Hall, Dickens relocates Christmas squarely in the heart of London. In place of Irving's idyllic, snow covered landscape with its quaint church, playful dogs, stage coaches crowded with Christmas fare and cheerful travelers, Dickens envelops his denizens of the city with a claustrophobic fog and bone-chilling cold, as if London was in the grip of a final ice age:

.... the fog and darkness thickened so, that people ran about with flaring links, proffering their services to go before horses

1   *Old Christmas* (Tarrytown, NY: Sleepy Hollow Restorations, 1977) 6-7.
2   *The Lives and Times of Ebenezer Scrooge* (New Haven: Yale University Press, 1990) 25.

in carriages, and conduct them on their way. The ancient tower of a church, whose gruff old bell was always peeping slily down at Scrooge out of a gothic window in the wall, became invisible, and struck the hours and quarters in the clouds, with tremulous vibrations afterwards, as if its teeth were chattering in its frozen head up there. The cold became intense. In the main street, at the corner of the court, some labourers were repairing the gas-pipes, and had lighted a great fire in the brazier, round which a party of ragged men and boys were gathered: warming their hands and winking their eyes before the blaze in rapture. The water-plug being left in solitude, its overflowings sullenly congealed, and turned to misanthropic ice. (pp. 45-46)

The cold and misanthropic atmosphere of London's streets, however, does not preclude the warmth of Christmas, albeit, on a less than manorial scale. The Ghost of Christmas Past conjures up the memory of Scrooge's old employer, Mr. Fezziwig, who converts his warehouse into a festive hall in which to celebrate Christmas: "Clear away. There is nothing they [Fezziwig's employees] wouldn't have cleared away, with old Fezziwig looking on. It was done in a minute. Every movable was packed off, as if it were dismissed from public life for evermore; the floor was swept and watered, the lamps were trimmed, fuel was heaped upon the fire; and the warehouse was as snug, and warm, and dry, and bright a ball-room, as you would desire to see upon a winter's night" (p. 69). The ledger books, the daily grind, and the cold give way to music, dance, games, food, and fellowship. Christmas, Dickens seems to be saying, can now be celebrated by anyone; its rituals and joys are no longer the exclusive province of the upper classes in their country estates, but can be found in a London warehouse or in a simple London home, such as that of the Cratchit family. At a time when the population of London was growing rapidly its inhabitants could look to *A Christmas Carol* for much needed inspiration during a period of great economic and social stress.

★   ★   ★

Scrooge is one of the great characters of English literature. A complex version of the stage villain of Victorian melodrama, he arouses a curious ambiguity in the reader's attitude towards him. How is it that this cruel, selfish old man has such an appeal to one's sympathy? Is it simply that he is transformed into a generous man at the story's end? Dickens manages the daunting task of presenting his hero in a manner that allows the reader to hiss the villain and relish his presence at the same time. He accomplishes this through the multi-nuanced voice of the narrator. As Michael Slater has observed, *A Christmas Carol* is "first and foremost a triumph of *tone*."[1]

The narrator opens his tale with the rather enigmatic sentence: "Marley was dead: to begin with." Shortly thereafter he begins to reinforce his opening comment: "The mention of Marley's funeral brings me back to the point I started from. There is no doubt that Marley was dead. This must distinctly be understood, or nothing wonderful can come of the story I am going to relate" (p. 39). Early on, then, the narrator makes it clear that this knowledge is prerequisite to a wondrous outcome of some sort. Like Mr. Wardle in *Pickwick Papers*, the narrator comes across as a genial, avuncular person eager to entertain his audience with a Christmas ghost story. He goes so far as to press his own ghostly presence on the reader. Upon being visited by the Ghost of Christmas Past, who draws aside Scrooge's bed curtains, Scrooge "found himself face to face with the unearthly visitor who drew them: as close to it as I am now to you, and I am standing in the spirit at your elbow" (p. 61). After engaging the reader with his personal charm and colloquial tone, the narrator begins developing the character of Scrooge: "Oh! but he was a tight-fisted hand at the grindstone, Scrooge! a squeezing, wrenching, grasping, scraping, clutching, covetous old sinner! Hard and sharp as flint, from which no steel had ever struck out generous fire; secret, and self-contained, and solitary as an oyster" (p. 40). There is a narrative joy in the outpouring of exclamation and hyperbole in this and other passages describing Scrooge. Even the simile "solitary as an oyster" lightens the tone and makes clear that yes, here is a villain, but one the reader is going to enjoy. Scrooge is shown to be so predictably miserly as to be comic. As Henri Bergson notes, in his essay

1   *The Christmas Books*, ed. Michael Slater (London: Penguin, 1971), vol. 1, xi.

"Laughter," humor arises when a person acts with a consistent machine-like predictability instead of with an uncalculated human suppleness.[1] Mention Christmas to Scrooge and the predicted response will be "Bah, humbug!" It is only later in the story that the reader is allowed to see the more human side of Scrooge that is elicited by the three Christmas spirits.

Scrooge's own dialogue frequently modulates the tone of the narrative. When he dismisses his genial nephew Fred with a brief condemnation of Christmas, he concludes with a spirited salvo of invective: "'If I could work my will ... every idiot who goes about with 'Merry Christmas,' on his lips, should be boiled with his own pudding, and buried with a stake of holly through his heart. He should!'" (p. 42) Articulate and grimly humorous, Scrooge maintains an equally imaginative and buoyant tone when he first meets Marley's ghost and explains why he doubts his senses: "'Because ... a little thing affects them. A slight disorder of the stomach makes them cheats. You may be an undigested bit of beef, a blot of mustard, a crumb of cheese, a fragment of an underdone potato. There's more of gravy than of grave about you, whatever you are!'" (p. 52)

At the end of Stave Three, however, the narrator adopts the stern tone of Dickens himself, as the Ghost of Christmas Present opens his robe and reveals the two children huddled beneath it. He addresses both Scrooge and all humanity in his speech: "They were a boy and a girl. Yellow, meagre, ragged, scowling, wolfish; but prostrate, too, in their humility. Where graceful youth should have filled their features out, and touched them with its freshest tints, a stale and shrivelled hand, like that of age, had pinched, and twisted them, and pulled them into shreds." The Ghost then issues his dreadful warning: "'They are Man's.... This boy is Ignorance. This girl is Want. Beware them both, and all of their degree, but most of all beware this boy, for on his brow I see that written which is Doom, unless the writing be erased'" (pp. 99-101). The ghastly apparitions in this somber passage appear to arise from the depths of Dickens's own unhappy childhood and his intimate knowledge of the Ragged Schools and the government reports on the abuse of children in the factories and mines.

---

1 Henri Bergson, "Laughter," *Comedy*, introd. by Wylie Sypher (New York: Doubleday, 1956).

In addition to his skillful modulation of the narrative tone, Dickens shapes the character of Scrooge by gradually unfolding details of his inner life. In Stave One he appears as a two-dimensional figure, a cold-hearted, selfish old man isolated from everyone around him. The appearance of Jacob Marley, however, initiates the transformation of Scrooge's character as he witnesses the horrid results of a life dedicated to money in the person of Marley, his old partner and alter-ego. The shock and fear that this visit instill in him lay the groundwork for the emotional transformation that follows upon his journey into the past.

The Ghost of Christmas Past serves as the catalyst that awakens Scrooge's childhood memories, conjuring up scenes that he had long suppressed through his single-minded devotion to money. As Edgar Johnson points out, these scenes further build the foundation for Scrooge's final redemption: "There have been readers who objected to Scrooge's conversion as too sudden and radical to be psychologically convincing. But this is to mistake a semi-serious fantasy for a piece of prosaic realism. Even so, the emotions in Scrooge to which the Ghosts appeal are no unsound means to the intended end: the awakened memories of a past when he had known gentler and warmer ties than any of his later years, the realization of his exclusion from all kindness and affection in others now, the fears of the future when he may be lonelier and more unloved still."[1]

Scrooge's memory of his early education reveals him to be a lonely child whose only companions appear to be characters from his favorite books (Dickens's childhood favorites, too), such as *The Arabian Nights*, and *Robinson Crusoe*. When Scrooge sees this solitary boy reading near a feeble fire, he sits down near him and weeps "to see his poor forgotten self as he had used to be" (p. 65). The next scene shows him alone again after all the other school children have gone home to enjoy the Christmas holidays. His young sister, Fan, however, comes to take him home, declaring, "Home, for good and all. Home for ever and ever. Father is so much kinder than he used to be, that home's like Heaven!" (p. 67) The following scene features Scrooge's former employer, Mr. Fezziwig, and his wondrous Christmas party. As Scrooge watches the dancing and singing and

---

1   *Charles Dickens: His Tragedy and Triumph*, vol. 1, 488.

games, "[h]is heart and soul were in the scene, and with his former self. He corroborated everything, remembered everything, enjoyed everything, and underwent the strangest agitation" (p. 71). The final memory Scrooge must face is that of Belle, the woman whose love he discarded in favor of financial gain. Intent on showing how Scrooge missed an opportunity of becoming a happily married man, Dickens presents a scene that clearly lies outside Scrooge's memory. The time is that of Christmas and Belle is married and has several children. As her husband returns home laden with Christmas presents, the children set upon him with glee and the domestic scene vibrates with good feeling. As he views the family that might have been his, Scrooge hears Belle's husband say that he looked into Scrooge's office earlier that day: "His partner lies upon the point of death, I hear; and there he sat alone. Quite alone in the world, I do believe" (p. 75). The pain of loss overcomes Scrooge and he attempts to extinguish the memories that the Ghost has awakened. He presses the extinguisher-cap down upon the head of the Ghost, darkens the scene, but fails to hide the light, which streams from under it.

All of these details of Scrooge's past rescue him from being merely the stage villain of the opening pages and show him to possess an emotional depth, a regret for lost opportunities, and a loneliness that stems from his childhood. When Fan comes to take him home for Christmas, her comment that "Father is so much kinder than he used to be" suggests that Scrooge's home life certainly was not the "heaven" that his sister now promises him. And so, the boy Scrooge appears as a lonely child whose only friends are characters from *The Arabian Nights* and *Robinson Crusoe*. Like Crusoe, Scrooge must create out of his isolation a small world for himself, his only tool being his imagination. In a sense, one might see Scrooge as the author of his own destiny. Out of the vivid memories of his past—a time of great sadness contrasted with moments of nostalgic happiness—Scrooge recreates himself in the present. In watching the loving Cratchit family gather for their Christmas meal, Scrooge's torment is to feel his exclusion from warm familial ties. Fan is long dead, and his only lifeline is her son, Fred, whose gracious Christmas invitations Scrooge has loudly rejected season after season. As the past and present intermingle, Scrooge's final vision, that of his own death, shapes the last chapter of his emotional life. But as Tennyson wrote,

"Men may rise on stepping-stones of their dead selves to higher things."

A *Christmas Carol* is built upon numerous contrasts: rich and poor, warmth and cold, plenty and hunger, family and loneliness, generosity and miserliness, affection and cruelty, dream and reality, freedom and compulsion, past and present, and present and future. Most of these opposing forces are recapitulated within the character of Scrooge himself. The cold-hearted, compulsive, lonely, miserly man, who eats his abstemious meal in the shadows, emerges from his dreams, memories, and fears to become a generous, fun-loving, warm, caring fatherly man. The texture of the story, rich with contrasting imagery, prepares the reader for Scrooge's conversion well in advance of the concluding chapter. While hardly a realistic tale — indeed, it resembles a fable with its cautionary note about human behavior — A *Christmas Carol* renders a powerful psychological account of the dangers of introspection and social withdrawal.

The three stages of Scrooge's conversion — the detailed memories of a lonely childhood, an awakened vision of the suffering and joys of those presently around him, and his fear of future loneliness and an awareness of his own mortality — combine to change him into a decent man, one who goes on to earn from those who knew him this crowning accolade: "it was always said of him, that he knew how to keep Christmas well, if any man alive possessed the knowledge" (p. 125). The reformation of Scrooge's character highlights one of the persistent themes in Dickens's novels. As George Orwell observes, "There is no clear sign that [Dickens] wants the existing order to be overthrown, or believes that it would make very much difference if it *were* overthrown. For in reality his target is not so much society as 'human nature.'" Orwell goes on to argue that Dickens was not a politician but a moralist: "He has no constructive suggestions, not even a clear grasp of the nature of the society he is attacking, only an emotional perception that something is wrong. All he can finally say is, 'Behave decently,' which, as I suggested earlier, is not necessarily so shallow as it seems."[1]

Dickens the moralist can be heard most clearly through the voices of Marley and the Ghost of Christmas Present. When Scrooge

---

1   George Orwell, *Dickens, Dali & Others* (New York: Harcourt Brace, 1946) 5, 71.

attempts to compliment Marley by declaring him "a good man of business," the Ghost cries out, "'Business! ... Mankind was my business. The common welfare was my business; charity, mercy, forbearance, and benevolence, were, all, my business. The dealings of my trade were but a drop of water in the comprehensive ocean of my business!'" (p. 56) Later, when Scrooge and the Ghost of Christmas Present watch the Cratchit family at their meal, the Ghost reminds Scrooge of his earlier Malthusian remark that by dying the poor will help to reduce the surplus population: "'Man,' said the Ghost, 'if man you be in heart, not adamant, forbear that wicked cant until you have discovered What the surplus is, and Where it is. Will you decide what men shall live, what men shall die? It may be, that in the sight of Heaven, you are more worthless and less fit to live than millions like this poor man's child. Oh God! to hear the Insect on the leaf pronouncing on the too much life among his hungry brothers in the dust!'" (p. 89)

★ ★ ★

It may be that most people know *A Christmas Carol* today not from Dickens's text but rather from one or more of the many television and motion picture productions based upon his story. Innovative adaptations have converted Dickens's Scrooge into a rich array of characters and animated figures. Among the many curious Scrooges are Mr. Magoo, Fred Flintstone, Beavis, and Scrooge McDuck. There have also been female Scrooges, such as Susan Lucci (*Ebbie*, 1995) and Cicily Tyson (*Ms. Scrooge*, 1997). Among the numerous classic films only a few stand out as having captured the essential Dickens: *Scrooge* (1935), with Seymour Hicks; *A Christmas Carol* (1938), with Reginald Owen; *Scrooge* (1951), with Alastair Sim; *Scrooge* (1970), with Albert Finney; and *A Christmas Carol* (1984), with George C. Scott.

Many critics have singled out the 1951 film with Alastair Sim as the best of the motion picture adaptations. This version, as Fred Guida points out, "like none before it, seeks to explain Ebenezer Scrooge" by focusing upon his past. "In dealing with Scrooge's past the film is ultimately, and quite simply, being faithful to the letter—and, even more so, to the implications—of Dickens's original text."[1] A few scenes not in Dickens's text are added to flesh out even further the sad consequences of Scrooge's actions in the past. The Ghost of Christmas Past, for example, carries Scrooge to his sister's deathbed, where he sees himself reject Fan's husband and baby and then angrily leave the room. Thinking her brother is still there, Fan says, "'Promise me you'll take care of my boy.'" Earlier in the film, during the visit to Scrooge's boyhood school, the Ghost of Christmas Past tells Scrooge that "your mother died in giving you life, for which your father never forgave you, as if you were to blame." In the text Dickens merely has Fan report to her brother that father "is so much kinder than he used to be." The film's psychological interpretation of Scrooge, however, does not seriously violate the spirit of the original story but expands upon an ambiguous line spoken by Fan in order to help one understand the root causes of Scrooge's complex misery.

Although Dickens took pains to control every aspect of *A Christmas Carol*, from details of the book's appearance and production to law suits against publishers who pirated his story, the world of the Victorian Scrooge has been appropriated by subsequent generations and reshaped into countless plays, motion pictures, television productions, operas, animated cartoons, and musicals. The text itself has been edited for children, illustrated by numerous different artists, and used as a springboard into fictional "prequels" and sequels. Literary purists might find many of these adaptations to be grotesque distortions of Dickens's text, but Paul Davis notes the inevitable consequences that follow upon the creation of a great work of literature: "Edward Wagenknecht characterized as a 'glaring example of critical irresponsibility' Edmund Wilson's speculation that after Christmas Scrooge reverts to his old self. 'We cannot follow Scrooge "beyond the frame of the story,"' Wagenknecht asserted, 'for the simple reason that beyond the frame of the story he does not exist.' The history of the *Carol* since 1843 would suggest otherwise, for Scrooge exists in the Anglo-American consciousness independent of his Dickensian origin. Dickens may have framed our thoughts and established the

---

1 *A Christmas Carol and its Adaptations* (Jefferson, NC: McFarland, 2000) 104.

broad outlines of the story, but the *Carol* is rewritten each Christmas, and Scrooge, an altered spirit, appears anew with each retelling."[1]

---

1 *The Lives and Times of Ebenezer Scrooge* (New Haven: Yale University Press, 1990) 15.

Charles Dickens: A Brief Chronology

1812   Born Feb. 7 Charles John Huffham Dickens at Portsmouth, second child and eldest son of John, a naval clerk, and Elizabeth Dickens.

1815   Family moves to London.

1817   Family moves to Sheerness and then to Chatham, Kent.

1822   Family (now six children) moves to London.

1824   Father imprisoned for three months for debt in the Marshalsea prison. Charles works at Warren's Blacking Warehouse. Begins school at Wellington House Academy.

1827   Enters solicitor's office as junior clerk.

1829   Becomes a freelance reporter at Doctors' Commons.

1831   Falls in love with Maria Beadnell. Appointed Parliamentary reporter.

1833   Stories appear in the *Monthly Magazine*.

1834   Becomes reporter on the *Morning Chronicle*.

1835   "Sketches of London" appear in the *Evening Chronicle*.

1836   *Sketches by Boz*. Marries Catherine Hogarth, daughter of editor of the *Evening Chronicle*. Lives at Furnival's Inn, London. Meets John Forster.

1837   *Pickwick Papers*. Edits *Bentley's Miscellany* for two years. Son born, first of ten children by Catherine Hogarth. Family moves to Doughty Street, London. Death of wife's sister, Mary Hogarth.

1838   *Oliver Twist*. Visits schools in Yorkshire in preparing to write *Nicholas Nickleby*.

1839   *Nicholas Nickleby*. Family moves to Devonshire Terrace, London.

1840   *Master Humphrey's Clock* appears weekly for some eighteen months.

1841   *The Old Curiosity Shop; Barnaby Rudge*.

1842   Visits America. *American Notes*.

1843   *A Christmas Carol*.

1844   *Martin Chuzzlewit; The Chimes* (a Christmas book). Family move to Genoa, Italy, for about a year.

1845   *The Cricket on the Hearth* (a Christmas book).

1846   Brief editorship of the *Daily News*. *Pictures from Italy*; *The Battle of Life* (a Christmas book).

1848   *Dombey and Son*; *The Haunted Man* (a Christmas book). Organizes and acts in private and charitable theatrical performances.

1850   Begins his weekly miscellany *Household Words*. *David Copperfield*.

1851   John Dickens dies.

1853   *Bleak House*. Tours Italy and Switzerland with Wilkie Collins.

1854   *Hard Times*.

1855   Moves to France with his family for almost a year.

1856   Buys Gad's Hill Place, Kent.

1857   *Little Dorrit*. Organizes and acts in charitable performances of *The Frozen Deep*, a melodrama by Wilkie Collins; falls in love with Ellen Ternan, a young actress in the company.

1858   *Reprinted Pieces* (articles from *Household Words*). Begins series of paid public readings. Separates from his wife.

1859   Breaks with Bradbury & Evans, buying out its share in *Household Words*, which was replaced by *All the Year Round*. *A Tale of Two Cities*.

1860   Sells Tavistock House and lives permanently at Gad's Hill Place.

1861   *The Uncommercial Traveller*, series of papers reprinted from *All the Year Round*, published in volume form. *Great Expectations*. Begins second series of public readings.

1863   Son Walter dies in India. Mother dies.

1865   *Our Mutual Friend*. "Dr Marigold's Prescriptions" appears in Christmas number *All the Year Round*.

1866   Begins third series of public readings.

1867   Begins six-month reading tour of USA. *No Thoroughfare*, with Wilkie Collins, published in *All the Year Round*.

1868   Begins fourth series of public readings (until 1869).

1870   Final season of public readings in London. First half of *The Mystery of Edwin Drood* issued in monthly parts and left incomplete. Dies at Gad's Hill Place and buried in Westminster Abbey.

A Note on the Text

The text of *A Christmas Carol* is that of the first edition, published by Chapman & Hall in 1843. There are a few minor variants in copies of the first edition. The copy reprinted here is based upon the facsimile of the volume that has the yellow end pages and the red-and-blue title page, with the date 1843. According to Edgar Johnson, it represents Dickens's own choice for all known copies he gave to his friends.

The spellings in this text have not been changed. Thus, "ankle," for example, is spelled "ancle" as well as "ankle"; "chestnuts" as "chesnuts" as well as "chestnuts." In later printings of the first edition "Stave I" is changed to "Stave One" and thereby brought into conformity with the other headings. Not until the second edition were most of the typographical errors corrected. Dickens's original manuscript is not always very easy to read. His many revisions on top of crossed-out passages are in a tiny script that at times is near impossible to read, which must certainly have added to the burden of typesetters and proof-readers. In addition, there are instances of Dickens's peculiarity in spelling, such as "recal" and "pannel," and his experimental use of dashes, colons, and semi-colons to enhance the speech rhythms he sought.

Dickens hired John Leech (1817-64), the popular artist for *Punch*, to illustrate the *Carol*. Dickens's costly plan called for three, full-page, hand-colored steel engravings and five textual woodcuts. The three colored full-page illustrations are "Mr. Fezziwig's Ball," "Scrooge's Third Visitor" (the Ghost of Christmas Present), and "The Last of the Spirits" (the Ghost of Christmas Yet To Come).

A CHRISTMAS CAROL

IN PROSE.

BEING

A Ghost Story of Christmas.

BY

CHARLES DICKENS

WITH ILLUSTRATIONS BY JOHN LEECH.

LONDON
CHAPMAN & HALL, 186, STRAND.

MDCCCXLIII.

PREFACE.

I HAVE endeavoured in this Ghostly little book, to raise the Ghost of an Idea, which shall not put my readers out of humour with themselves, with each other, with the season, or with me. May it haunt their houses pleasantly, and no one wish to lay it.

> Their faithful Friend and Servant,
> C.D.

December, 1843

A CHRISTMAS CAROL.

STAVE I.[1]

MARLEY'S GHOST.

MARLEY was dead: to begin with. There is no doubt whatever about that. The register of his burial was signed by the clergyman, the clerk, the undertaker, and the chief mourner. Scrooge signed it: and Scrooge's name was good upon 'Change,[2] for anything he chose to put his hand to. Old Marley was as dead as a door-nail.

Mind! I don't mean to say that I know, of my own knowledge, what there is particularly dead about a door-nail. I might have been inclined, myself, to regard a coffin-nail as the deadest piece of iron-mongery in the trade. But the wisdom of our ancestors is in the simile; and my unhallowed hands shall not disturb it, or the Country's done for. You will therefore permit me to repeat, emphatically, that Marley was as dead as a door-nail.

Scrooge knew he was dead? Of course he did. How could it be otherwise? Scrooge and he were partners for I don't know how many years. Scrooge was his sole executor, his sole administrator, his sole assign,[3] his sole residuary legatee,[4] his sole friend and sole mourner. And even Scrooge was not so dreadfully cut up by the sad event, but that he was an excellent man of business on the very day of the funeral, and solemnised it with an undoubted bargain.

The mention of Marley's funeral brings me back to the point I started from. There is no doubt that Marley was dead. This must be distinctly understood, or nothing wonderful can come of the story I am going to relate. If we were not perfectly convinced that Hamlet's Father died before the play began, there would be nothing more re-markable in his taking a stroll at night, in an easterly wind, upon his

---

1   A stave is a stanza of a poem or song. The term plays on the metaphor of Dickens's title, which suggests that his book is a song (carol) in prose and that the chapters are verses.
2   The Royal Exchange, the financial hub of London.
3   The person to whom the property of the deceased is assigned. Marley's only partner, Scrooge inherited his entire estate.
4   The person who receives the remainder of the estate after all payments of debt are satisfied.

own ramparts, than there would be in any other middle-aged gentleman rashly turning out after dark in a breezy spot — say Saint Paul's Churchyard for instance — literally to astonish his son's weak mind. Scrooge never painted out Old Marley's name. There it stood, years afterwards, above the warehouse door: Scrooge and Marley. The firm was known as Scrooge and Marley. Sometimes people new to the business called Scrooge Scrooge, and sometimes Marley, but he answered to both names: it was all the same to him.

Oh! But he was a tight-fisted hand at the grindstone, Scrooge! a squeezing, wrenching, grasping, scraping, clutching, covetous old sinner! Hard and sharp as flint, from which no steel had ever struck out generous fire; secret, and self-contained, and solitary as an oyster. The cold within him froze his old features, nipped his pointed nose, shrivelled his cheek, stiffened his gait; made his eyes red, his thin lips blue; and spoke out shrewdly in his grating voice. A frosty rime was on his head, and on his eyebrows, and his wiry chin. He carried his own low temperature always about with him; he iced his office in the dog-days; and didn't thaw it one degree at Christmas.

External heat and cold had little influence on Scrooge. No warmth could warm, nor wintry weather chill him. No wind that blew was bitterer than he, no falling snow was more intent upon its purpose, no pelting rain less open to entreaty. Foul weather didn't know where to have him.[1] The heaviest rain, and snow, and hail, and sleet, could boast of the advantage over him in only one respect. They often "came down"[2] handsomely, and Scrooge never did.

Nobody ever stopped him in the street to say, with gladsome looks, "My dear Scrooge, how are you? when will you come to see me?" No beggars implored him to bestow a trifle, no children asked him what it was o'clock, no man or woman ever once in all his life inquired the way to such and such a place, of Scrooge. Even the blindmen's dogs appeared to know him; and when they saw him coming on, would tug their owners into doorways and up courts; and then would wag their tails as though they said "no eye at all is better than an evil eye, dark master!"

---

1   The weather could not affect him.
2   Slang for "gave money."

But what did Scrooge care? It was the very thing he liked. To edge his way along the crowded paths of life, warning all human sympathy to keep its distance, was what the knowing ones call "nuts" to Scrooge.[1]

Once upon a time — of all the good days in the year, on Christmas Eve — old Scrooge sat busy in his counting-house. It was cold, bleak, biting weather: foggy withal: and he could hear the people in the court outside go wheezing up and down, beating their hands upon their breasts, and stamping their feet upon the pavement-stones to warm them. The city clocks had only just gone three, but it was quite dark already: it had not been light all day: and candles were flaring in the windows of the neighbouring offices, like ruddy smears upon the palpable brown air. The fog came pouring in at every chink and keyhole, and was so dense without, that although the court was of the narrowest, the houses opposite were mere phantoms. To see the dingy cloud come drooping down, obscuring everything, one might have thought that Nature lived hard by, and was brewing on a large scale.

The door of Scrooge's counting-house was open that he might keep his eye upon his clerk, who in a dismal little cell beyond, a sort of tank, was copying letters. Scrooge had a very small fire, but the clerk's fire was so very much smaller that it looked like one coal. But he couldn't replenish it, for Scrooge kept the coal-box in his own room; and so surely as the clerk came in with the shovel, the master predicted that it would be necessary for them to part. Wherefore the clerk put on his white comforter, and tried to warm himself at the candle, in which effort, not being a man of a strong imagination, he failed.

"A merry Christmas, uncle! God save you!" cried a cheerful voice. It was the voice of Scrooge's nephew, who came upon him so quickly that this was the first intimation he had of his approach.

"Bah!" said Scrooge, "Humbug!"

He had so heated himself with rapid walking in the fog and frost, this nephew of Scrooge's, that he was all in a glow; his face was ruddy and handsome; his eyes sparkled, and his breath smoked again.

---

1 Namely, gave pleasure to Scrooge.

"Christmas a humbug, uncle!" said Scrooge's nephew. "You don't mean that, I am sure."

"I do," said Scrooge. "Merry Christmas! what right have you to be merry? what reason have you to be merry? You're poor enough."

"Come, then," returned the nephew gaily. "What right have you to be dismal? what reason have you to be morose? You're rich enough."

Scrooge having no better answer ready on the spur of the moment, said, "Bah!" again; and followed it up with "Humbug."

"Don't be cross, uncle," said the nephew.

"What else can I be" returned the uncle, "when I live in such a world of fools as this? Merry Christmas! Out upon merry Christmas! What's Christmas time to you but a time for paying bills without money; a time for finding yourself a year older, and not an hour richer; a time for balancing your books and having every item in 'em through a round dozen of months presented dead against you? If I could work my will," said Scrooge, indignantly, "every idiot who goes about with 'Merry Christmas,' on his lips, should be boiled with his own pudding, and buried with a stake of holly through his heart. He should!"

"Uncle!" pleaded the nephew.

"Nephew!" returned the uncle, sternly, "keep Christmas in your own way, and let me keep it in mine."

"Keep it!" repeated Scrooge's nephew. "But you don't keep it."

"Let me leave it alone, then," said Scrooge. "Much good may it do you! Much good it has ever done you!"

"There are many things from which I might have derived good, by which I have not profited, I dare say," returned the nephew: "Christmas among the rest. But I am sure I have always thought of Christmas time, when it has come round—apart from the veneration due to its sacred name and origin, if anything belonging to it can be apart from that—as a good time: a kind, forgiving, charitable, pleasant time: the only time I know of, in the long calendar of the year, when men and women seem by one consent to open their shut-up hearts freely, and to think of people below them as if they really were fellow-passengers to the grave, and not another race of creatures bound on other journeys. And therefore, uncle, though it has never put a scrap of gold or silver in my pocket, I believe that it *has* done me good, and *will* do me good; and I say, God bless it!"

The clerk in the tank involuntarily applauded: becoming immediately sensible of the impropriety, he poked the fire, and extinguished the last frail spark for ever.

"Let me hear another sound from *you*" said Scrooge, "and you'll keep your Christmas by losing your situation. You're quite a powerful speaker, sir," he added, turning to his nephew. "I wonder you don't go into Parliament."

"Don't be angry, uncle. Come! Dine with us to-morrow."

Scrooge said that he would see him—yes, indeed he did. He went the whole length of the expression, and said that he would see him in that extremity first.

"But why?" cried Scrooge's nephew. "Why?"

"Why did you get married?" said Scrooge.

"Because I fell in love."

"Because you fell in love!" growled Scrooge, as if that were the only one thing in the world more ridiculous than a merry Christmas. "Good afternoon!"

"Nay, uncle, but you never came to see me before that happened. Why give it as a reason for not coming now?"

"Good afternoon," said Scrooge.

"I want nothing from you; I ask nothing of you; why cannot we be friends?"

"Good afternoon," said Scrooge.

"I am sorry, with all my heart, to find you so resolute. We have never had any quarrel, to which I have been a party. But I have made the trial in homage to Christmas, and I'll keep my Christmas humour to the last. So A Merry Christmas, uncle!"

"Good afternoon!" said Scrooge.

"And A Happy New Year!"

"Good afternoon!" said Scrooge.

His nephew left the room without an angry word, notwithstanding. He stopped at the outer door to bestow the greetings of the season on the clerk, who, cold as he was, was warmer than Scrooge; for he returned them cordially.

"There's another fellow," muttered Scrooge; who overheard him:

"my clerk, with fifteen shillings a week, and a wife and family, talking about a merry Christmas. I'll retire to Bedlam."[1]

This lunatic, in letting Scrooge's nephew out, had let two other people in. They were portly gentlemen, pleasant to behold, and now stood, with their hats off, in Scrooge's office. They had books and papers in their hands, and bowed to him.

"Scrooge and Marley's, I believe," said one of the gentlemen, referring to his list. "Have I the pleasure of addressing Mr. Scrooge, or Mr. Marley?"

"Mr. Marley has been dead these seven years," Scrooge replied. "He died seven years ago, this very night."

"We have no doubt his liberality is well represented by his surviving partner," said the gentleman, presenting his credentials.

It certainly was; for they had been two kindred spirits. At the ominous word "liberality," Scrooge frowned, and shook his head, and handed the credentials back.

"At this festive season of the year, Mr. Scrooge," said the gentleman, taking up a pen, "it is more than usually desirable that we should make some slight provision for the poor and destitute, who suffer greatly at the present time. Many thousands are in want of common necessaries; hundreds of thousands are in want of common comforts, sir."

"Are there no prisons?" asked Scrooge.

"Plenty of prisons," said the gentleman, laying down the pen again.

"And the Union workhouses?"[2] demanded Scrooge. "Are they still in operation?"

"They are. Still," returned the gentleman, "I wish I could say they were not."

"The Treadmill and the Poor Law are in full vigour, then?" said Scrooge.

"Both very busy, sir."

---

1 St. Mary's of Bethlehem in London, a hospital for the insane.
2 The Poor Law Amendment Act of 1834, which Dickens strongly opposed, divided England and Wales into twenty-one districts. Each district had a commissioner authorized to form "poor law unions" by grouping parishes together for administrative purposes and to build workhouses to contain the destitute. "Union" thus became synonymous with "workhouse."

"Oh I was afraid, from what you said at first, that something had occurred to stop them in their useful course," said Scrooge. "I'm very glad to hear it."

"Under the impression that they scarcely furnish Christian cheer of mind or body to the multitude," returned the gentleman, "a few of us are endeavouring to raise a fund to buy the Poor some meat and drink, and means of warmth. We choose this time, because it is a time, of all others, when Want is keenly felt, and Abundance rejoices. What shall I put you down for?"

"Nothing!" Scrooge replied.

"You wish to be anonymous?"

"I wish to be left alone," said Scrooge. "Since you ask me what I wish, gentlemen, that is my answer. I don't make merry myself at Christmas, and I can't afford to make idle people merry. I help to support the establishments I have mentioned: they cost enough: and those who are badly off must go there."

"Many can't go there; and many would rather die."

"If they would rather die," said Scrooge, "they had better do it, and decrease the surplus population.[1] Besides—excuse me—I don't know that."

"But you might know it," observed the gentleman.

"It's not my business," Scrooge returned. "It's enough for a man to understand his own business, and not to interfere with other people's. Mine occupies me constantly. Good afternoon, gentlemen!"

Seeing clearly that it would be useless to pursue their point, the gentlemen withdrew. Scrooge resumed his labours with an improved opinion of himself, and in a more facetious temper than was usual with him.

Meanwhile the fog and darkness thickened so, that people ran about with flaring links,[2] proffering their services to go before

---

1 The economist Thomas Malthus, in his book *An Essay on the Principle of Population* (1798), stirred up fear that England was destined to be overpopulated and outgrow its food supply unless proper measures were taken. He wrote chillingly of the poor, whom he considered expendable "surplus": "A man who is born into a world possessed, if he cannot get subsistence from his parents, on whom he has a just demand, and if society do not want his labour, has no claim of *right* to the smallest portion of food, and, in fact, has no business to be where he is. At nature's mighty feast there is no vacant cover for him. She tells him to be gone...."

2 Torches.

horses in carriages, and conduct them on their way. The ancient tower of a church, whose gruff old bell was always peeping slily down at Scrooge out of a gothic window in the wall, became invisible, and struck the hours and quarters in the clouds, with tremulous vibrations afterwards, as if its teeth were chattering in its frozen head up there. The cold became intense. In the main street, at the corner of the court, some labourers were repairing the gas-pipes, and had lighted a great fire in a brazier, round which a party of ragged men and boys were gathered: warming their hands and winking their eyes before the blaze in rapture. The water-plug being left in solitude, its overflowings sullenly congealed, and turned to misanthropic ice. The brightness of the shops where holly sprigs and berries crackled in the lamp-heat of the windows, made pale faces ruddy as they passed. Poulterers' and grocers' trades became a splendid joke: a glorious pageant, with which it was next to impossible to believe that such dull principles as bargain and sale had anything to do. The Lord Mayor, in the stronghold of the mighty Mansion House, gave orders to his fifty cooks and butlers to keep Christmas as a Lord Mayor's household should; and even the little tailor, whom he had fined five shillings on the previous Monday for being drunk and blood-thirsty in the streets, stirred up to-morrow's pudding in his garret, while his lean wife and the baby sallied out to buy the beef.

Foggier yet, and colder! Piercing, searching, biting cold. If the good Saint Dunstan[1] had but nipped the Evil Spirit's nose with a touch of such weather as that, instead of using his familiar weapons, then indeed he would have roared to lusty purpose. The owner of one scant young nose, gnawed and mumbled by the hungry cold as bones are gnawed by dogs, stooped down at Scrooge's keyhole to regale him with a Christmas carol: but at the first sound of—

> "God bless you merry gentleman!
> May nothing you dismay!"

---

1   Saint Dunstan (924-88), an English monk who was also a painter, jeweler, and blacksmith. According to legend, when tempted at his forge by the devil to lead a life of sinful pleasure, he seized the devil by the nose with a pair of red-hot pincers, causing him to cry out in pain so loudly that he could be heard miles away.

Scrooge seized the ruler with such energy of action, that the singer fled in terror, leaving the keyhole to the fog and even more congenial frost.

At length the hour of shutting up the counting-house arrived. With an ill-will Scrooge dismounted from his stool, and tacitly admitted the fact to the expectant clerk in the Tank, who instantly snuffed his candle out, and put on his hat.

"You'll want all day to-morrow, I suppose?" said Scrooge.

"If quite convenient, Sir."

"It's not convenient," said Scrooge, "and it's not fair. If I was to stop half-a-crown for it; you'd think yourself ill used, I'll be bound?"

The clerk smiled faintly.

"And yet," said Scrooge, "you don't think *me* ill-used, when I pay a day's wages for no work."

The clerk observed that it was only once a year. "A poor excuse for picking a man's pocket every twenty-fifth of December!" said Scrooge, buttoning his great-coat to the chin. "But I suppose you must have the whole day. Be here all the earlier next morning!"

The clerk promised that he would; and Scrooge walked out with a growl. The office was closed in a twinkling, and the clerk, with the long ends of his white comforter dangling below his waist (for he boasted no great-coat), went down a slide on Cornhill, at the end of a lane of boys, twenty times, in honour of its being Christmas-eve, and then ran home to Camden Town[1] as hard as he could pelt, to play at blindman's-buff.[2]

Scrooge took his melancholy dinner in his usual melancholy tavern; and having read all the newspapers, and beguiled the rest of the evening with his banker's-book, went home to bed. He lived in chambers which had once belonged to his deceased partner. They were a gloomy suite of rooms, in a lowering pile of building up a yard, where it had so little business to be, that one could scarcely help fancying it must have run there when it was a young house, playing at hide-and-seek with other houses, and have forgotten the

---

1 When Dickens was ten years old, he moved with his family to 16 Bayham Street, Camden Town, London. Dickens would later describe the area "as shabby, dingy, damp and mean a neighborhood as one would desire to see."

2 A popular parlor game in which the contestant is blindfolded and then must catch a guest and guess that person's name.

way out again. It was old enough now, and dreary enough, for nobody lived in it but Scrooge, the other rooms being all let out as offices. The yard was so dark that even Scrooge, who knew its every stone, was fain to grope with his hands. The fog and frost so hung about the black old gateway of the house, that it seemed as if the Genius of the Weather sat in mournful meditation on the threshold.

Now, it is a fact, that there was nothing at all particular about the knocker on the door, except that it was very large. It is also a fact, that Scrooge had seen it night and morning during his whole residence in that place; also that Scrooge had as little of what is called fancy about him as any man in the City of London, even including — which is a bold word — the corporation, aldermen, and livery. Let it also be borne in mind that Scrooge had not bestowed one thought on Marley, since his last mention of his seven-years' dead partner that afternoon. And then let any man explain to me, if he can, how it happened that Scrooge, having his key in the lock of the door, saw in the knocker, without its undergoing any intermediate process of change: not a knocker, but Marley's face.

Marley's face. It was not in impenetrable shadow as the other objects in the yard were, but had a dismal light about it, like a bad lobster in a dark cellar. It was not angry or ferocious, but looked at Scrooge as Marley used to look: with ghostly spectacles turned up upon its ghostly forehead. The hair was curiously stirred, as if by breath or hot-air; and though the eyes were wide open, they were perfectly motionless. That, and its livid colour, made it horrible; but its horror seemed to be, in spite of the face and beyond its control, rather than a part of its own expression.

As Scrooge looked fixedly at this phenomenon, it was a knocker again.

To say that he was not startled, or that his blood was not conscious of a terrible sensation to which it had been a stranger from infancy, would be untrue. But he put his hand upon the key he had relinquished, turned it sturdily, walked in, and lighted his candle.

He *did* pause, with a moment's irresolution, before he shut the door; and he *did* look cautiously behind it first, as if he half-expected to be terrified with the sight of Marley's pigtail sticking out into the hall. But there was nothing on the back of the door, except the screws and nuts that held the knocker on; so he said "Pooh, pooh!" and closed it with a bang.

The sound resounded through the house like thunder. Every room above, and every cask in the wine-merchant's cellars below, appeared to have a separate peal of echoes of its own. Scrooge was not a man to be frightened by echoes. He fastened the door, and walked across the hall, and up the stairs: slowly too: trimming his candle as he went.

You may talk vaguely about driving a coach-and-six up a good old flight of stairs, or through a bad young Act of Parliament; but I mean to say you might have got a hearse up that staircase, and taken it broadwise, with the splinter-bar[1] towards the wall, and the door towards the balustrades: and done it easy. There was plenty of width for that, and room to spare; which is perhaps the reason why Scrooge thought he saw a locomotive hearse going on before him in the gloom. Half a dozen gas-lamps out of the street wouldn't have lighted the entry too well, so you may suppose that it was pretty dark with Scrooge's dip.[2]

Up Scrooge went, not caring a button for that: darkness is cheap, and Scrooge liked it. But before he shut his heavy door, he walked through his rooms to see that all was right. He had just enough recollection of the face to desire to do that.

Sitting room, bed-room, lumber-room. All as they should be. Nobody under the table, nobody under the sofa; a small fire in the grate; spoon and basin ready; and the little saucepan of gruel (Scrooge had a cold in his head) upon the hob.[3] Nobody under the bed; nobody in the closet; nobody in his dressing-gown, which was hanging up in a suspicious attitude against the wall. Lumber-room as usual. Old fire-guard, old shoes, two fish-baskets, washing-stand on three legs, and a poker.

Quite satisfied, he closed his door, and locked himself in; double-locked himself in, which was not his custom. Thus secured against surprise, he took off his cravat; put on his dressing-gown and slip-

---

1 The crossbar in a carriage to support its springs.
2 A tallow candle.
3 A shelf at the back or side of a fireplace used to keep items warm.

pers, and his night-cap; and sat down before the fire to take his gruel.

It was a very low fire indeed; nothing on such a bitter night. He was obliged to sit close to it, and brood over it, before he could extract the least sensation of warmth from such a handful of fuel. The fire-place was an old one, built by some Dutch merchant long ago, and paved all round with quaint Dutch tiles, designed to illustrate the Scriptures. There were Cains and Abels; Pharaoh's daughters, Queens of Sheba, Angelic messengers descending through the air on clouds like feather-beds, Abrahams, Belshazzars, Apostles putting off to sea in butter-boats, hundreds of figures, to attract his thoughts; and yet that face of Marley, seven years dead, came like the ancient Prophet's rod, and swallowed up the whole.[1] If each smooth tile had been a blank at first, with power to shape some picture on its surface from the disjointed fragments of his thoughts, there would have been a copy of old Marley's head on every one.

"Humbug!" said Scrooge; and walked across the room.

After several turns, he sat down again. As he threw his head back in the chair, his glance happened to rest upon a bell, a disused bell, that hung in the room, and communicated for some purpose now forgotten with a chamber in the highest story of the building. It was with great astonishment, and with a strange, inexplicable dread, that as he looked, he saw this bell begin to swing. It swung so softly in the outset that it scarcely made a sound; but soon it rang out loudly, and so did every bell in the house.

This might have lasted half a minute, or a minute, but it seemed an hour. The bells ceased as they had begun, together. They were succeeded by a clanking noise, deep down below; as if some person were dragging a heavy chain over the casks in the wine-merchant's cellar. Scrooge then remembered to have heard that ghosts in haunted houses were described as dragging chains.

The cellar-door flew open with a booming sound, and then he heard the noise much louder, on the floors below; then coming up the stairs; then coming straight towards his door.

---

1   A reference to the Book of Exodus, which tells how Aaron's rod, after being transformed into a serpent, devoured the serpents produced by the Pharaoh's magicians.

"It's humbug still!" said Scrooge. "I won't believe it."

His colour changed though, when, without a pause, it came on through the heavy door, and passed into the room before his eyes. Upon its coming in, the dying flame leaped up, as though it cried "I know him! Marley's Ghost!" and fell again.

The same face: the very same. Marley in his pig-tail, usual waist-coat, tights, and boots; the tassels on the latter bristling, like his pig-tail, and his coat-skirts, and the hair upon his head. The chain he drew was clasped about his middle. It was long, and wound about him like a tail; and it was made (for Scrooge observed it closely) of cash-boxes, keys, padlocks, ledgers, deeds, and heavy purses wrought in steel. His body was transparent: so that Scrooge, observing him, and looking through his waistcoat, could see the two buttons on his coat behind.

Scrooge had often heard it said that Marley had no bowels,[1] but he had never believed it until now.

No, nor did he believe it even now. Though he looked the phantom through and through, and saw it standing before him; though he felt the chilling influence of its death-cold eyes; and marked the very texture of the folded kerchief bound about its head and chin, which wrapper he had not observed before: he was still incredulous, and fought against his senses.

"How now!" said Scrooge, caustic and cold as ever. "What do you want with me?"

"Much!"—Marley's voice, no doubt about it.

"Who are you?"

"Ask me who I *was*."

"Who *were* you then?" said Scrooge, raising his voice. "You're particular—for a shade." He was going to say "*to* a shade," but substituted this, as more appropriate.

"In life I was your partner, Jacob Marley."

"Can you—can you sit down?" asked Scrooge, looking doubtfully at him.

"I can."

---

1 The bowels were once thought of as the seat of compassion. Like Scrooge, Marley was viewed as a misanthrope.

"Do it then."

Scrooge asked the question, because he didn't know whether a ghost so transparent might find himself in a condition to take a chair; and felt that in the event of its being impossible, it might involve the necessity of an embarrassing explanation. But the ghost sat down on the opposite side of the fireplace, as if he were quite used to it.

"You don't believe in me," observed the Ghost.

"I don't," said Scrooge.

"What evidence would you have of my reality, beyond that of your senses?"

"I don't know," said Scrooge.

"Why do you doubt your senses?"

"Because," said Scrooge, "a little thing affects them. A slight disorder of the stomach makes them cheats. You may be an undigested bit of beef, a blot of mustard, a crumb of cheese, a fragment of an underdone potato. There's more of gravy than of grave about you, whatever you are!"

Scrooge was not much in the habit of cracking jokes, nor did he feel, in his heart, by any means waggish then. The truth is, that he tried to be smart, as a means of distracting his own attention, and keeping down his terror; for the spectre's voice disturbed the very marrow in his bones.

To sit, staring at those fixed, glazed eyes, in silence for a moment, would play, Scrooge felt, the very deuce with him. There was something very awful, too, in the spectre's being provided with an infernal atmosphere of its own. Scrooge could not feel it himself, but this was clearly the case; for though the Ghost sat perfectly motionless, its hair, and skirts, and tassels, were still agitated as by the hot vapour from an oven.

"You see this toothpick?" said Scrooge, returning quickly to the charge, for the reason just assigned; and wishing, though it were only for a second, to divert the vision's stony gaze from himself.

"I do," replied the Ghost.

"You are not looking at it," said Scrooge.

"But I see it," said the Ghost, "notwithstanding."

"Well!" returned Scrooge. "I have but to swallow this, and be for

John Leech

the rest of my days persecuted by a legion of goblins, all of my own creation. Humbug, I tell you — humbug!"

At this, the spirit raised a frightful cry, and shook its chain with such a dismal and appalling noise, that Scrooge held on tight to his chair, to save himself from falling in a swoon. But how much greater was his horror, when the phantom taking off the bandage round its head, as if it were too warm to wear in-doors, its lower jaw dropped down upon its breast![1]

Scrooge fell upon his knees, and clasped his hands before his face.

"Mercy!" he said. "Dreadful apparition, why do you trouble me?"

"Man of the worldly mind!" replied the Ghost, "do you believe in me or not?"

"I do," said Scrooge. "I must. But why do spirits walk the earth, and why do they come to me?"

"It is required of every man," the Ghost returned, "that the spirit within him should walk abroad among his fellow-men, and travel far and wide; and if that spirit goes not forth in life, it is condemned to do so after death. It is doomed to wander through the world — oh, woe is me! — and witness what it cannot share, but might have shared on earth, and turned to happiness!"

Again the spectre raised a cry, and shook its chain, and wrung its shadowy hands.

"You are fettered," said Scrooge, trembling. "Tell me why?"

"I wear the chain I forged in life," replied the Ghost. "I made it link by link, and yard by yard; I girded it on of my own free will, and of my own free will I wore it. Is its pattern strange to you?"

Scrooge trembled more and more.

"Or would you know," pursued the Ghost, "the weight and length of the strong coil you bear yourself? It was full as heavy and as long as this, seven Christmas Eves ago. You have laboured on it, since. It is a ponderous chain!"

Scrooge glanced about him on the floor, in the expectation of finding himself surrounded by some fifty or sixty fathoms of iron cable: but he could see nothing.

---

1 In order to keep the mouth of a corpse closed, morticians sometimes wrapped a cloth around its head and chin.

"Jacob," he said, imploringly. "Old Jacob Marley, tell me more. Speak comfort to me, Jacob."

"I have none to give," the Ghost replied. "It comes from other regions, Ebenezer Scrooge, and is conveyed by other ministers, to other kinds of men. Nor can I tell you what I would. A very little more, is all permitted to me. I cannot rest, I cannot stay, I cannot linger anywhere. My spirit never walked beyond our counting-house—mark me!—in life my spirit never roved beyond the narrow limits of our money-changing hole; and weary journeys lie before me!"

It was a habit with Scrooge, whenever he became thoughtful, to put his hands in his breeches pockets. Pondering on what the Ghost had said, he did so now, but without lifting up his eyes, or getting off his knees.

"You must have been very slow about it, Jacob," Scrooge observed, in a business-like manner, though with humility and deference.

"Slow!" the Ghost repeated.

"Seven years dead," mused Scrooge. "And travelling all the time?"

"The whole time," said the Ghost. "No rest, no peace. Incessant torture of remorse."

"You travel fast?" said Scrooge.

"On the wings of the wind," replied the Ghost.

"You might have got over a great quantity of ground in seven years," said Scrooge.

The Ghost, on hearing this, set up another cry, and clanked its chain so hideously in the dead silence of the night, that the Ward[1] would have been justified in indicting it for a nuisance.

"Oh! captive, bound, and double ironed," cried the phantom, "not to know, that ages of incessant labour by immortal creatures, for this earth must pass into eternity before the good of which it is susceptible is all developed. Not to know that any Christian spirit working kindly in its little sphere, whatever it may be, will find its mortal life too short for its vast means of usefulness. Not to know

---

1 A watchman who patrolled the streets of London at night.

that no space of regret can make amends for one life's opportunities misused! Yet such was I! Oh! such was I!"

"But you were always a good man of business, Jacob," faultered Scrooge, who now began to apply this to himself.

"Business!" cried the Ghost, wringing its hands again. "Mankind was my business. The common welfare was my business; charity, mercy, forbearance, and benevolence, were, all, my business. The dealings of my trade were but a drop of water in the comprehensive ocean of my business!"

It held up its chain at arm's length, as if that were the cause of all its unavailing grief, and flung it heavily upon the ground again.

"At this time of the rolling year," the spectre said, "I suffer most. Why did I walk through crowds of fellow-beings with my eyes turned down, and never raise them to that blessed Star which led the Wise Men to a poor abode? Were there no poor homes to which its light would have conducted *me*!"

Scrooge was very much dismayed to hear the spectre going on at this rate, and began to quake exceedingly.

"Hear me!" cried the Ghost. "My time is nearly gone."

"I will," said Scrooge. "But don't be hard upon me! Don't be flowery, Jacob! Pray!"

"How it is that I appear before you in a shape that you can see I may not tell. I have sat invisible beside you many and many a day."

It was not an agreeable idea. Scrooge shivered, and wiped the perspiration from his brow.

"That is no light part of my penance," pursued the Ghost. "I am here to-night to warn you, that you have yet a chance and hope of escaping my fate. A chance and hope of my procuring, Ebenezer."

"You were always a good friend to me," said Scrooge. "Thank'ee!"

"You will be haunted," resumed the Ghost, "by Three Spirits."

Scrooge's countenance fell almost as low as the Ghost's had done.

"Is that the chance and hope you mentioned, Jacob?" he demanded, in a faultering voice.

"It is."

"I—I think I'd rather not," said Scrooge.

"Without their visits," said the Ghost, "you cannot hope to shun the path I tread. Expect the first to-morrow, when the bell tolls one."

"Couldn't I take 'em all at once, and have it over, Jacob?" hinted Scrooge.

"Expect the second on the next night at the same hour. The third upon the next night[1] when the last stroke of twelve has ceased to vibrate. Look to see me no more; and look that, for your own sake, you remember what has passed between us!"

When it had said these words, the spectre took its wrapper from the table, and bound it round its head, as before. Scrooge knew this, by the smart sound its teeth made, when the jaws were brought together by the bandage. He ventured to raise his eyes again, and found his supernatural visitor confronting him in an erect attitude, with its chain wound over and about its arm.

The apparition walked backward from him; and at every step it took, the window raised itself a little, so that when the spectre reached it, it was wide open. It beckoned Scrooge to approach, which he did. When they were within two paces of each other, Marley's Ghost held up its hand, warning him to come no nearer. Scrooge stopped.

Not so much in obedience, as in surprise and fear: for on the raising of the hand, he became sensible of confused noises in the air; incoherent sounds of lamentation and regret; wailings inexpressibly sorrowful and self-accusatory. The spectre, after listening for a moment, joined in the mournful dirge; and floated out upon the bleak, dark night.

Scrooge followed to the window: desperate in his curiosity. He looked out.

The air was filled with phantoms, wandering hither and thither in restless haste, and moaning as they went. Every one of them wore chains like Marley's Ghost; some few (they might be guilty governments) were linked together; none were free. Many had been personally known to Scrooge in their lives. He had been quite famil-

---

1   The only way to explain the time puzzle here is to accept Scrooge's joyful declaration on Christmas Morning: "The Spirits have done it all in one night. They can do anything they like" (p. 119).

iar with one old ghost, in a white waistcoat, with a monstrous iron safe attached to its ancle, who cried piteously at being unable to assist a wretched woman with an infant, whom it saw below, upon a door-step. The misery with them all was, clearly, that they sought to interfere, for good, in human matters, and had lost the power for ever.

Whether these creatures faded into mist, or mist enshrouded them, he could not tell. But they and their spirit voices faded together; and the night became as it had been when he walked home.

Scrooge closed the window, and examined the door by which the Ghost had entered. It was double-locked, as he had locked it with his own hands, and the bolts were undisturbed. He tried to say "Humbug!" but stopped at the first syllable. And being, from the emotion he had undergone, or the fatigues of the day, or his glimpse of the Invisible World, or the dull conversation of the Ghost, or the lateness of the hour, much in need of repose; went straight to bed, without undressing, and fell asleep upon the instant.

STAVE TWO.

THE FIRST OF THE THREE SPIRITS.

WHEN Scrooge awoke, it was so dark, that looking out of bed, he could scarcely distinguish the transparent window from the opaque walls of his chamber. He was endeavouring to pierce the darkness with his ferret eyes, when the chimes of a neighbouring church struck the four quarters. So he listened for the hour.

To his great astonishment the heavy bell went on from six to seven, and from seven to eight, and regularly up to twelve; then stopped. Twelve! It was past two when he went to bed. The clock was wrong. An icicle must have got into the works. Twelve!

He touched the spring of his repeater,[1] to correct this most preposterous clock. Its rapid little pulse beat twelve; and stopped.

"Why, it isn't possible," said Scrooge, "that I can have slept through a whole day and far into another night. It isn't possible that anything has happened to the sun, and this is twelve at noon!"

The idea being an alarming one, he scrambled out of bed, and groped his way to the window. He was obliged to rub the frost off with the sleeve of his dressing-gown before he could see anything; and could see very little then. All he could make out was, that it was still very foggy and extremely cold, and that there was no noise of people running to and fro, and making a great stir, as there unquestionably would have been if night had beaten off bright day, and taken possession of the world. This was a great relief, because "three days after sight of this First of Exchange pay to Mr. Ebenezer Scrooge or his order," and so forth, would have become a mere United States' security[2] if there were no days to count by.

Scrooge went to bed again, and thought, and thought, and thought it over and over and over, and could make nothing of it. The more he thought, the more perplexed he was; and the more he

---

1 A watch or clock that can strike the hour and quarter hour.

2 During the 1830s individual states, without the support of the federal government, borrowed capital from foreign countries, especially England, to finance such public works as railways and canals. After a financial crisis in 1837, many states refused to pay their debts and thus lost credit worthiness abroad.

endeavoured not to think, the more he thought. Marley's Ghost bothered him exceedingly. Every time he resolved within himself, after mature inquiry, that it was all a dream, his mind flew back again, like a strong spring released, to its first position, and presented the same problem to be worked all through, "Was it a dream or not?"

Scrooge lay in this state until the chimes had gone three quarters more, when he remembered, on a sudden, that the Ghost had warned him of a visitation when the bell tolled one. He resolved to lie awake until the hour was past; and, considering that he could no more go to sleep than go to Heaven, this was perhaps the wisest resolution in his power.

The quarter was so long, that he was more than once convinced he must have sunk into a doze unconsciously, and missed the clock. At length it broke upon his listening ear.

"Ding, dong!"

"A quarter past," said Scrooge, counting.

"Ding, dong!"

"Half past!" said Scrooge.

"Ding, dong!"

"A quarter to it," said Scrooge.

"Ding, dong!"

"The hour itself," said Scrooge, triumphantly, "and nothing else!"

He spoke before the hour bell sounded, which it now did with a deep, dull, hollow, melancholy ONE. Light flashed up in the room upon the instant, and the curtains of his bed were drawn.

The curtains of his bed were drawn aside, I tell you, by a hand. Not the curtains at his feet, nor the curtains at his back, but those to which his face was addressed. The curtains of his bed were drawn aside; and Scrooge, starting up into a half-recumbent attitude, found himself face to face with the unearthly visitor who drew them: as close to it as I am now to you, and I am standing in the spirit at your elbow.

It was a strange figure — like a child: yet not so like a child as like an old man, viewed through some supernatural medium, which gave him the appearance of having receded from the view, and being diminished to a child's proportions. Its hair, which hung about its neck and down its back, was white as if with age; and yet the face had not a wrinkle in it, and the tenderest bloom was on the skin. The arms were very long and muscular; the hands the same, as if its hold were of uncommon strength. Its legs and feet, most delicately formed, were, like those upper members, bare. It wore a tunic of the purest white; and round its waist was bound a lustrous belt, the sheen of which was beautiful. It held a branch of fresh green holly in its hand; and, in singular contradiction of that wintry emblem, had its dress trimmed with summer flowers. But the strangest thing about it was, that from the crown of its head there sprung a bright clear jet of light, by which all this was visible; and which was doubtless the occasion of its using, in its duller moments, a great extinguisher for a cap, which it now held under its arm.

Even this, though, when Scrooge looked at it with increasing steadiness, was *not* its strangest quality. For as its belt sparkled and glittered now in one part and now in another, and what was light one instant, at another time was dark, so the figure itself fluctuated in its distinctness: being now a thing with one arm, now with one leg, now with twenty legs, now a pair of legs without a head, now a head without a body: of which dissolving parts, no outline would be visible in the dense gloom wherein they melted away. And in the very wonder of this, it would be itself again; distinct and clear as ever.

"Are you the Spirit, sir, whose coming was foretold to me?" asked Scrooge.

"I am!"

The voice was soft and gentle. Singularly low, as if instead of being so close beside him, it were at a distance.

"Who, and what are you?" Scrooge demanded.

"I am the Ghost of Christmas Past."

"Long past?" inquired Scrooge: observant of its dwarfish stature.

"No. Your past."

Perhaps, Scrooge could not have told anybody why, if anybody could have asked him; but he had a special desire to see the Spirit in his cap; and begged him to be covered.

"What!" exclaimed the Ghost, "would you so soon put out, with worldly hands, the light I give? Is it not enough that you are one of those whose passions made this cap, and force me through whole trains of years to wear it low upon my brow!"

Scrooge reverently disclaimed all intention to offend, or any knowledge of having wilfully "bonneted"[1] the Spirit at any period of his life. He then made bold to inquire what business brought him there.

"Your welfare!" said the Ghost.

Scrooge expressed himself much obliged, but could not help thinking that a night of unbroken rest would have been more conducive to that end. The Spirit must have heard him thinking, for it said immediately:

"Your reclamation, then. Take heed!"

It put out its strong hand as it spoke, and clasped him gently by the arm.

"Rise! and walk with me!"

It would have been in vain for Scrooge to plead that the weather and the hour were not adapted to pedestrian purposes; that bed was warm, and the thermometer a long way below freezing; that he was clad but lightly in his slippers, dressing-gown, and nightcap; and that he had a cold upon him at that time. The grasp, though gentle as a woman's hand, was not to be resisted. He rose: but finding that the Spirit made towards the window, clasped its robe in supplication.

"I am a mortal," Scrooge remonstrated, "and liable to fall."

"Bear but a touch of my hand there," said the Spirit, laying it upon his heart, "and you shall be upheld in more than this!"

As the words were spoken, they passed through the wall, and stood upon an open country road, with fields on either hand. The city had entirely vanished. Not a vestige of it was to be seen. The darkness and the mist had vanished with it, for it was a clear, cold, winter day, with snow upon the ground.

"Good Heaven!" said Scrooge, clasping his hands together, as he looked about him. "I was bred in this place. I was a boy here!"

The Spirit gazed upon him mildly. Its gentle touch, though it had been light and instantaneous, appeared still present to the old man's sense of feeling. He was conscious of a thousand odours floating in the air, each one connected with a thousand thoughts, and hopes, and joys, and cares long, long, forgotten!

---

1 To "bonnet" means to crush a person's hat down around his head as well as to snuff out a candle.

"Your lip is trembling," said the Ghost. "And what is that upon your cheek?"

Scrooge muttered, with an unusual catching in his voice, that it was a pimple; and begged the Ghost to lead him where he would.

"You recollect the way?" inquired the Spirit.

"Remember it!" cried Scrooge with fervour—"I could walk it blindfold."

"Strange to have forgotten it for so many years!" observed the Ghost. "Let us go on."

They walked along the road; Scrooge recognising every gate, and post, and tree; until a little market-town appeared in the distance, with its bridge, its church, and winding river. Some shaggy ponies now were seen trotting towards them with boys upon their backs, who called to other boys in country gigs and carts, driven by farmers. All these boys were in great spirits, and shouted to each other, until the broad fields were so full of merry music, that the crisp air laughed to hear it.

"These are but shadows of the things that have been," said the Ghost. "They have no consciousness of us."

The jocund travellers came on; and as they came, Scrooge knew and named them every one. Why was he rejoiced beyond all bounds to see them! Why did his cold eye glisten, and his heart leap up as they went past! Why was he filled with gladness when he heard them give each other Merry Christmas, as they parted at cross-roads and-bye ways, for their several homes! What was merry Christmas to Scrooge? Out upon merry Christmas! What good had it ever done to him?

"The school is not quite deserted," said the Ghost. "A solitary child, neglected by his friends, is left there still."

Scrooge said he knew it. And he sobbed.

They left the high-road, by a well remembered lane, and soon approached a mansion of dull red brick, with a little weathercock-surmounted cupola, on the roof, and a bell hanging in it. It was a large house, but one of broken fortunes; for the spacious offices were little used, their walls were damp and mossy, their windows broken, and their gates decayed. Fowls clucked and strutted in the stables; and the coach-houses and sheds were overrun with grass. Nor was it more retentive of its ancient state, within; for entering the dreary hall, and glancing through the open doors of many rooms, they found them poorly furnished, cold, and vast. There was an earthy savour in the air, a chilly bareness in the place, which associated itself somehow with too much getting up by candle-light, and not too much to eat.

They went, the Ghost and Scrooge, across the hall, to a door at the back of the house. It opened before them, and disclosed a long, bare, melancholy room, made barer still by lines of plain deal forms[1] and desks. At one of these a lonely boy was reading near a feeble fire; and Scrooge sat down upon a form, and wept to see his poor forgotten self as he had used to be.

Not a latent echo in the house, not a squeak and scuffle from the mice behind the panneling, not a drip from the half-thawed water-spout in the dull yard behind, not a sigh among the leafless boughs of one despondent poplar, not the idle swinging of an empty store-house door, no, not a clicking in the fire, but fell upon the heart of Scrooge with softening influence, and gave a freer passage to his tears.[2]

The Spirit touched him on the arm, and pointed to his younger self, intent upon his reading. Suddenly a man, in foreign garments: wonderfully real and distinct to look at: stood outside the window, with an axe stuck in his belt, and leading an ass laden with wood by the bridle.

"Why, it's Ali Baba!"[3] Scrooge exclaimed in ecstacy. "It's dear old honest Ali Baba! Yes, yes, I know! One Christmas time, when yonder solitary child was left here all alone, he *did* come, for the first time, just like that. Poor boy! And Valentine," said Scrooge, "and his wild brother, Orson;[4] there they go! And what's his name,[5] who was

---

1   Unfinished wooden school benches.
2   Dickens drew the details for the description of this house from Tennyson's poem "Mariana" (1830).
3   The hero of "Ali Baba and the Forty Thieves," one of the tales in The Arabian Nights.
4   The heroes of The History of Two Valyannte Brethern, Valentyne and Orson (1495), a French romance. At birth, the twins are separated. Orson is carried away by a bear and raised as a wild man. Valentine, on the other hand, becomes a knight of the French court. The brothers are eventually reunited.
5   Bedreddin Hassan, the hero of "Noureddin Ali of Cairo and his Son Bedreddin Hassan" in The Arabian Nights. The daughter of a vizier is promised in marriage to a sultan's hunch-backed groom. At the wedding, however, Bedreddin is carried to the palace by a genie,

put down in his drawers, asleep, at the Gate of Damascus; don't you see him! And the Sultan's Groom turned upside-down by the Genii; there he is upon his head! Serve him right. I'm glad of it. What business had *he* to be married to the Princess!"

To hear Scrooge expending all the earnestness of his nature on such subjects, in a most extraordinary voice between laughing and crying; and to see his heightened and excited face; would have been a surprise to his business friends in the city, indeed.

"There's the Parrot!"[1] cried Scrooge. "Green body and yellow tail, with a thing like a lettuce growing out of the top of his head; there he is! Poor Robin Crusoe, he called him, when he came home again after sailing round the island. 'Poor Robin Crusoe, where have you been, Robin Crusoe?' The man thought he was dreaming, but he wasn't. It was the Parrot, you know. There goes Friday, running for his life[2] to the little creek! Halloa! Hoop! Halloo!"

Then, with a rapidity of transition very foreign to his usual character, he said, in pity for his former self, "Poor boy!" and cried again.

"I wish," Scrooge muttered, putting his hand in his pocket, and looking about him, after drying his eyes with his cuff: "but it's too late now."

"What is the matter?" asked the Spirit.

"Nothing," said Scrooge. "Nothing. There was a boy singing a Christmas Carol at my door last night. I should like to have given him something: that's all."

The Ghost smiled thoughtfully, and waved its hand: saying as it did so, "Let us see another Christmas!"

Scrooge's former self grew larger at the words, and the room became a little darker and more dirty. The pannels shrunk, the windows cracked; fragments of plaster fell out of the ceiling, and the naked laths were shown instead; but how all this was brought about, Scrooge knew no more than you do. He only knew that it was quite

---

where he replaces the ugly fiancé, who is made by the spirits to hang upside-down during the wedding night. The genie, who must leave before sunrise, later drops Bedredden at the city gates of Damascus. Bedredden works as a cook for twelve years, but is finally restored to his wife and their son, born during his absence.

1   The talkative companion of Robinson Crusoe from Daniel Defoe's *The Life and Strange Adventures of Robinson Crusoe* (1719).

2   In *Robinson Crusoe* the native Friday flees his brother cannibals before they kill him.

correct; that everything had happened so; that there he was, alone again, when all the other boys had gone home for the jolly holidays. He was not reading now, but walking up and down despairingly. Scrooge looked at the Ghost, and with a mournful shaking of his head, glanced anxiously towards the door.

It opened; and a little girl, much younger than the boy, came darting in, and putting her arms about his neck, and often kissing him, addressed him as her "Dear, dear brother."

"I have come to bring you home, dear brother!" said the child, clapping her tiny hands, and bending down to laugh. "To bring you home, home, home!"

"Home, little Fan?"[1] returned the boy.

"Yes!" said the child, brimful of glee. "Home, for good and all. Home, for ever and ever. Father is so much kinder than he used to be, that home's like Heaven! He spoke so gently to me one dear night when I was going to bed, that I was not afraid to ask him once more if you might come home; and he said Yes, you should; and sent me in a coach to bring you. And you're to be a man!" said the child, opening her eyes, "and are never to come back here; but first, we're to be together all the Christmas long, and have the merriest time in all the world."

"You are quite a woman, little Fan!" exclaimed the boy.

She clapped her hands and laughed, and tried to touch his head; but being too little, laughed again, and stood on tiptoe to embrace him. Then she began to drag him, in her childish eagerness, towards the door; and he, nothing loth to go, accompanied her.

A terrible voice in the hall cried, "Bring down Master Scrooge's box, there!" and in the hall appeared the schoolmaster himself, who glared on Master Scrooge with a ferocious condescension, and threw him into a dreadful state of mind by shaking hands with him. He then conveyed him and his sister into the veriest old well of a shivering best-parlour that ever was seen, where the maps upon the wall, and the celestial and terrestrial globes in the windows, were waxy with cold. Here he produced a decanter of curiously light wine, and a block of curiously heavy cake, and administered instalments of those dainties to the young people: at the same time, sending out a

---

1 Fanny was the name of Dickens's elder sister.

meagre servant to offer a glass of "something" to the postboy, who answered that he thanked the gentleman, but if it was the same tap as he had tasted before, he had rather not. Master Scrooge's trunk being by this time tied on to the top of the chaise, the children bade the schoolmaster good-bye right willingly; and getting into it, drove gaily down the garden-sweep:[1] the quick wheels dashing the hoar-frost and snow from off the dark leaves of the evergreens like spray.

"Always a delicate creature, whom a breath might have withered," said the Ghost. "But she had a large heart!"

"So she had," cried Scrooge. "You're right. I'll not gainsay it, Spirit. God forbid!"

"She died a woman," said the Ghost, "and had, as I think, children."

"One child," Scrooge returned.

"True," said the Ghost. "Your nephew!"

Scrooge seemed uneasy in his mind; and answered briefly, "Yes."

Although they had but that moment left the school behind them, they were now in the busy thoroughfares of a city, where shadowy passengers passed and repassed; where shadowy carts and coaches battled for the way, and all the strife and tumult of a real city were. It was made plain enough, by the dressing of the shops, that here too it was Christmas time again; but it was evening, and the streets were lighted up.

The Ghost stopped at a certain warehouse door, and asked Scrooge if he knew it.

"Know it!" said Scrooge. "Was I apprenticed here?"

They went in. At sight of an old gentleman in a Welch wig,[2] sitting behind such a high desk, that if he had been two inches taller he must have knocked his head against the ceiling, Scrooge cried in great excitement:

"Why, it's old Fezziwig! Bless his heart; it's Fezziwig alive again!"

Old Fezziwig laid down his pen, and looked up at the clock, which pointed to the hour of seven. He rubbed his hands; adjusted his capacious waistcoat; laughed all over himself, from his shoes to

---

1 The curved area of the driveway.
2 A cap made of tightly twisted woolen yarn.

his organ of benevolence;[1] and called out in a comfortable, oily, rich, fat, jovial voice:

"Yo ho, there! Ebenezer! Dick!"

Scrooge's former self, now grown a young man, came briskly in, accompanied by his fellow-'prentice.

"Dick Wilkins, to be sure!" said Scrooge to the Ghost. "Bless me, yes. There he is. He was very much attached to me, was Dick. Poor Dick! Dear, dear!"

"Yo ho, my boys!" said Fezziwig. "No more work to-night. Christmas Eve, Dick. Christmas, Ebenezer! Let's have the shutters up," cried old Fezziwig, with a sharp clap of his hands, "before a man can say, Jack Robinson!"

You wouldn't believe how those two fellows went at it! They charged into the street with the shutters—one, two, three—had 'em up in their places—four, five, six—barred 'em and pinned 'em—seven, eight, nine—and came back before you could have got to twelve, panting like race-horses.

"Hilli-ho!" cried old Fezziwig, skipping down from the high desk, with wonderful agility. "Clear away, my lads, and let's have lots of room here! Hilli-ho, Dick! Chirrup, Ebenezer!"

Clear away! There was nothing they wouldn't have cleared away, or couldn't have cleared away, with old Fezziwig looking on. It was done in a minute. Every movable was packed off, as if it were dismissed from public life for evermore; the floor was swept and watered, the lamps were trimmed, fuel was heaped upon the fire; and the warehouse was as snug, and warm, and dry, and bright a ball-room, as you would desire to see upon a winter's night.

In came a fiddler with a music-book, and went up to the lofty desk, and made an orchestra of it, and tuned like fifty stomach-aches. In came Mrs. Fezziwig, one vast substantial smile. In came the three Miss Fezziwigs, beaming and loveable. In came the six young followers whose hearts they broke. In came all the young men and women employed in the business. In came the housemaid, with her cousin, the baker. In came the cook, with her brother's particular friend, the

---

1   According to Victorian phrenologists, one's moral and intellectual faculties could be assessed from the shape of the skull, which they divided into forty sections or "organs." The top of the forehead was the location of the "organ of benevolence."

milkman. In came the boy from over the way, who was suspected of not having board enough from his master; trying to hide himself behind the girl from next door but one, who was proved to have had her ears pulled by her Mistress. In they all came, one after another; some shyly, some boldly, some gracefully, some awkwardly, some pushing, some pulling; in they all came, anyhow and everyhow. Away they all went, twenty couple at once, hands half round and back again the other way; down the middle and up again; round and round in various stages of affectionate grouping; old top couple always turning up in the wrong place; new top couple starting off again, as soon as they got there; all top couples at last, and not a bottom one to help them. When this result was brought about, old Fezziwig, clapping his hands to stop the dance, cried out, "Well done!" and the fiddler plunged his hot face into a pot of porter,[1] especially provided for that purpose. But scorning rest upon his reappearance, he instantly began again, though there were no dancers yet, as if the other fiddler had been carried home, exhausted, on a shutter; and he were a bran-new man resolved to beat him out of sight, or perish.

There were more dances, and there were forfeits,[2] and more dances, and there was cake, and there was negus,[3] and there was a great piece of Cold Roast, and there was a great piece of Cold Boiled, and there were mince-pies, and plenty of beer. But the great effect of the evening came after the Roast and Boiled, when the fiddler (an artful dog, mind! The sort of man who knew his business better than you or I could have told it him!) struck up "Sir Roger de Coverley."[4] Then old Fezziwig stood out to dance with Mrs. Fezziwig. Top couple too; with a good stiff piece of work cut out for them; three or four and twenty pair of partners; people who were not to be trifled with; people who *would* dance, and had no notion of walking.

But if they had been twice as many: ah, four times: old Fezziwig would have been a match for them, and so would Mrs. Fezziwig. As to *her*, she was worthy to be his partner in every sense of the term. If

---

1 A dark bitter beer.
2 A popular parlor game in which a player is penalized for missing his turn.
3 A beverage made of wine, hot water, lemon juice, sugar, and nutmeg.
4 A country dance, similar to the Virginia reel.

that's not high praise, tell me higher, and I'll use it. A positive light appeared to issue from Fezziwig's calves. They shone in every part of the dance like moons. You couldn't have predicted, at any given time, what would become of 'em next. And when old Fezziwig and Mrs. Fezziwig had gone all through the dance; advance and retire, hold hands with your partner; bow and curtsey; corkscrew; thread-the-needle, and back again to your place; Fezziwig "cut"[1]—cut so deftly, that he appeared to wink with his legs, and came upon his feet again without a stagger.

When the clock struck eleven, this domestic ball broke up. Mr. and Mrs. Fezziwig took their stations, one on either side the door, and shaking hands with every person individually as he or she went out, wished him or her a Merry Christmas. When everybody had retired but the two 'prentices, they did the same to them; and thus the cheerful voices died away, and the lads were left to their beds; which were under a counter in the back-shop.

During the whole of this time, Scrooge had acted like a man out of his wits. His heart and soul were in the scene, and with his former self. He corroborated everything, remembered everything, enjoyed everything, and underwent the strangest agitation. It was not until now, when the bright faces of his former self and Dick were turned from them, that he remembered the Ghost, and became conscious that it was looking full upon him, while the light upon its head burnt very clear.

"A small matter," said the Ghost, "to make these silly folks so full of gratitude."

"Small!" echoed Scrooge.

The Spirit signed to him to listen to the two apprentices, who were pouring out their hearts in praise of Fezziwig: and when he had done so, said,

"Why! Is it not? He has spent but a few pounds of your mortal money: three or four, perhaps. Is that so much that he deserves this praise?"

"It isn't that," said Scrooge, heated by the remark, and speaking unconsciously like his former, not his latter, self. "It isn't that, Spirit.

---

1 Namely, upon springing into the air, Fezziwig rapidly twiddled his feet together before landing back on the floor.

He has the power to render us happy or unhappy; to make our service light or burdensome; a pleasure or a toil. Say that his power lies in words and looks; in things so slight and insignificant that it is impossible to add and count 'em up: what then? The happiness he gives, is quite as great as if it cost a fortune."

He felt the Spirit's glance, and stopped. "What is the matter?" asked the Ghost.

"Nothing particular," said Scrooge.

"Something, I think?" the Ghost insisted.

"No," said Scrooge, "No. I should like to be able to say a word or two to my clerk just now! That's all."

His former self turned down the lamps as he gave utterance to the wish; and Scrooge and the Ghost again stood side by side in the open air.

"My time grows short," observed the Spirit. "Quick!"

This was not addressed to Scrooge, or to any one whom he could see, but it produced an immediate effect. For again Scrooge saw himself. He was older now; a man in the prime of life. His face had not the harsh and rigid lines of later years; but it had begun to wear the signs of care and avarice. There was an eager, greedy, restless motion in the eye, which showed the passion that had taken root, and where the shadow of the growing tree would fall.

He was not alone, but sat by the side of a fair young girl in a mourning-dress: in whose eyes there were tears, which sparkled in the light that shone out of the Ghost of Christmas Past.

"It matters little," she said, softly. "To you, very little. Another idol has displaced me; and if it can cheer and comfort you in time to come, as I would have tried to do, I have no just cause to grieve."

"What Idol has displaced you?" he rejoined.

"A golden one."

"This is the even-handed dealing of the world!" he said. "There is nothing on which it is so hard as poverty; and there is nothing it professes to condemn with such severity as the pursuit of wealth!"

"You fear the world too much," she answered, gently. "All your other hopes have merged into the hope of being beyond the chance of its sordid reproach. I have seen your nobler aspirations fall off one by one, until the master-passion, Gain, engrosses you. Have I not?"

"What then?" he retorted. "Even if I have grown so much wiser, what then? I am not changed towards you."

She shook her head.

"Am I?"

"Our contract is an old one. It was made when we were both poor and content to be so, until, in good season, we could improve our worldly fortune by our patient industry. You *are* changed. When it was made, you were another man."

"I was a boy," he said impatiently.

"Your own feeling tells you that you were not what you are," she returned. "I am. That which promised happiness when we were one in heart, is fraught with misery now that we are two. How often and how keenly I have thought of this, I will not say. It is enough that I *have* thought of it, and can release you."

"Have I ever sought release?"

"In words. No. Never."

"In what, then?"

"In a changed nature; in an altered spirit; in another atmosphere of life; another Hope as its great end. In everything that made my love of any worth or value in your sight. If this had never been between us," said the girl, looking mildly, but with steadiness, upon him; "tell me, would you seek me out and try to win me now? Ah, no!"

He seemed to yield to the justice of this supposition, in spite of himself. But he said, with a struggle, "You think not."

"I would gladly think otherwise if I could," she answered, "Heaven knows! When *I* have learned a Truth like this, I know how strong and irresistible it must be. But if you were free to-day, to-morrow, yesterday, can even I believe that you would choose a dowerless girl—you who, in your very confidence with her, weigh everything by Gain: or, choosing her, if for a moment you were false enough to your one guiding principle to do so, do I not know that your repentance and regret would surely follow? I do; and I release you. With a full heart, for the love of him you once were."

He was about to speak; but with her head turned from him, she resumed.

"You may—the memory of what is past half makes me hope you

will—have pain in this. A very, very brief time, and you will dismiss the recollection of it, gladly, as an unprofitable dream, from which it happened well that you awoke. May you be happy in the life you have chosen!"

She left him; and they parted.

"Spirit!" said Scrooge, "show me no more! Conduct me home. Why do you delight to torture me?"

"One shadow more!" exclaimed the Ghost.

"No more!" cried Scrooge. "No more. I don't wish to see it. Show me no more!"

But the relentless Ghost pinioned him in both his arms, and forced him to observe what happened next.

They were in another scene and place: a room, not very large or handsome, but full of comfort. Near to the winter fire sat a beautiful young girl, so like the last that Scrooge believed it was the same, until he saw her, now a comely matron, sitting opposite her daughter. The noise in this room was perfectly tumultuous, for there were more children there, than Scrooge in his agitated state of mind could count; and, unlike the celebrated herd in the poem,[1] they were not forty children conducting themselves like one, but every child was conducting itself like forty. The consequences were uproarious beyond belief; but no one seemed to care; on the contrary, the mother and daughter laughed heartily, and enjoyed it very much; and the latter, soon beginning to mingle in the sports, got pillaged by the young brigands most ruthlessly. What would I not have given to be one of them! Though I never could have been so rude, no, no! I wouldn't for the wealth of all the world have crushed that braided hair, and torn it down; and for the precious little shoe, I wouldn't have plucked it off, God bless my soul! to save my life. As to measuring her waist in sport, as they did, bold young brood, I couldn't have done it; I should have expected my arm to have grown round it for a punishment, and never come straight again. And yet I should have dearly liked, I own, to have touched her lips; to have questioned her, that she might have opened them; to have looked upon the lashes of her downcast eyes, and never raised a blush; to have let loose waves

---

1 Wordsworth's "Written in March" (1802): "The cattle are grazing/ Their heads never raising;/ There are forty feeding like one!"

of hair, an inch of which would be a keepsake beyond price: in short, I should have liked, I do confess, to have had the lightest licence of a child, and yet been man enough to know its value.

But now a knocking at the door was heard, and such a rush immediately ensued that she with laughing face and plundered dress was borne towards it the centre of a flushed and boisterous group, just in time to greet the father, who, came home attended by a man laden with Christmas toys and presents. Then the shouting and the struggling, and the onslaught that was made on the defenceless porter! The scaling him, with chairs for ladders, to dive into his pockets, despoil him of brown-paper parcels, hold on tight by his cravat, hug him round the neck, pommel his back, and kick his legs in irrepressible affection! The shouts of wonder and delight with which the development of every package was received! The terrible announcement that the baby had been taken in the act of putting a doll's frying-pan into his mouth, and was more than suspected of having swallowed a fictitious turkey, glued on a wooden platter! The immense relief of finding this a false alarm! The joy, and gratitude, and ecstacy! They are all indescribable alike. It is enough that by degrees the children and their emotions got out of the parlour and by one stair at a time, up to the top of the house; where they went to bed, and so subsided.

And now Scrooge looked on more attentively than ever, when the master of the house, having his daughter leaning fondly on him, sat down with her and her mother at his own fireside; and when he thought that such another creature, quite as graceful and as full of promise, might have called him father, and been a spring-time in the haggard winter of his life, his sight grew very dim indeed.

"Belle," said the husband, turning to his wife with a smile, "I saw an old friend of yours this afternoon."

"Who was it?"

"Guess!"

"How can I? Tut, don't I know," she added in the same breath, laughing as he laughed. "Mr. Scrooge."

"Mr. Scrooge it was. I passed his office window; and as it was not shut up, and he had a candle inside, I could scarcely help seeing him. His partner lies upon the point of death, I hear; and there he sat alone. Quite alone in the world, I do believe."

"Spirit!" said Scrooge in a broken voice, "remove me from this place."

"I told you these were shadows of the things that have been," said the Ghost. "That they are what they are; do not blame me!"

"Remove me!" Scrooge exclaimed. "I cannot bear it!"

He turned upon the Ghost, and seeing that it looked upon him with a face, in which in some strange way there were fragments of all the faces it had shown him, wrestled with it.

"Leave me! Take me back. Haunt me no longer!"

In the struggle, if that can be called a struggle in which the Ghost with no visible resistance on its own part was undisturbed by any effort of its adversary, Scrooge observed that its light was burning high and bright; and dimly connecting that with its influence over him, he seized the extinguisher-cap, and by a sudden action pressed it down upon its head.

The Spirit dropped beneath it, so that the extinguisher covered its whole form; but though Scrooge pressed it down with all his force, he could not hide the light: which streamed from under it, in an unbroken flood upon the ground.

He was conscious of being exhausted, and overcome by an irresistible drowsiness; and, further, of being in his own bedroom. He gave the cap a parting squeeze, in which his hand relaxed; and had barely time to reel to bed, before he sank into a heavy sleep.

STAVE THREE.

THE SECOND OF THE THREE SPIRITS.

AWAKING in the middle of a prodigiously tough snore, and sitting up in bed to get his thoughts together, Scrooge had no occasion to be told that the bell was again upon the stroke of One. He felt that he was restored to consciousness in the right nick of time, for the especial purpose of holding a conference with the second messenger despatched to him through Jacob Marley's intervention. But finding that he turned uncomfortably cold when he began to wonder which of his curtains this new spectre would draw back, he put them every one aside with his own hands; and lying down again, established a sharp look-out all round the bed. For he wished to challenge the Spirit on the moment of its appearance, and did not wish to be taken by surprise and made nervous.

Gentlemen of the free-and-easy sort, who plume themselves on being acquainted with a move or two,[1] and being usually equal to the time-of-day,[2] express the wide range of their capacity for adventure by observing that they are good for anything from pitch-and-toss[3] to manslaughter; between which opposite extremes, no doubt, there lies a tolerably wide and comprehensive range of subjects. Without venturing for Scrooge quite as hardily as this, I don't mind calling on you to believe that he was ready for a good broad field of strange appearances, and that nothing between a baby and a rhinoceros would have astonished him very much.

Now, being prepared for almost anything, he was not by any means prepared for nothing; and, consequently, when the Bell struck One, and no shape appeared, he was taken with a violent fit of trembling. Five minutes, ten minutes, a quarter of an hour went by, yet nothing came. All this time, he lay upon his bed, the very core and centre of a blaze of ruddy light, which streamed upon it when the clock proclaimed the hour; and which being only light, was more alarming than a dozen ghosts, as he was powerless to make out what

---

1 Who pride themselves on their worldliness.
2 Prepared for whatever may happen.
3 A street gambling game.

it meant, or would be at; and was sometimes apprehensive that he might be at that very moment an interesting case of spontaneous combustion,[1] without having the consolation of knowing it. At last, however, he began to think—as you or I would have thought at first; for it is always the person not in the predicament who knows what ought to have been done in it, and would unquestionably have done it too—at last, I say, he began to think that the source and secret of this ghostly light might be in the adjoining room: from whence, on further tracing it, it seemed to shine. This idea taking full possession of his mind, he got up softly and shuffled in his slippers to the door.

The moment Scrooge's hand was on the lock, a strange voice called him by his name, and bade him enter. He obeyed.

It was his own room. There was no doubt about that. But it had undergone a surprising transformation. The walls and ceiling were so hung with living green,[2] that it looked a perfect grove, from every part of which, bright gleaming berries glistened. The crisp leaves of holly, mistletoe, and ivy reflected back the light, as if so many little mirrors had been scattered there; and such a mighty blaze went roaring up the chimney, as that dull petrifaction of a hearth had never known in Scrooge's time, or Marley's, or for many and many a winter season gone. Heaped up upon the floor, to form a kind of throne, were turkeys,[3] geese, game, poultry, brawn,[4] great joints of meat, sucking-pigs, long wreaths of sausages, mince-pies, plum-puddings, barrels of oysters, red-hot chesnuts, cherry-cheeked apples, juicy oranges, luscious pears, immense twelfth-cakes,[5] and seething bowls of punch, that made the chamber dim with their delicious steam. In easy state upon this couch, there sat a jolly Giant,[6] glorious to see; who bore a glowing torch, in shape not unlike Plenty's horn,

---

1 A medical myth in the early nineteenth century that held that the chemical elements of the human body could become so corrupted that the individual could suddenly be consumed in a self-generated conflagration.
2 Evergreens.
3 The Spanish took the domesticated turkey from Mexico to Europe about 1519. Turkeys were being bred in England by 1541, where they quickly became a popular holiday dish.
4 Traditional Christmas dish of boar's meat.
5 Large frosted, decorated cakes that are served on Twelfth Night.
6 Father Christmas, traditionally depicted as a pagan giant, dressed in a green, fur-lined robe and a crown of holly, carrying sprigs of mistletoe, a wassail bowl, and the yule log.

and held it up, high up, to shed its light on Scrooge, as he came peeping round the door.

"Come in!" exclaimed the Ghost. "Come in! and know me better, man!"

Scrooge entered timidly, and hung his head before this Spirit. He was not the dogged Scrooge he had been; and though its eyes were clear and kind, he did not like to meet them.

"I am the Ghost of Christmas Present," said the Spirit. "Look upon me!"

Scrooge reverently did so. It was clothed in one simple deep green robe, or mantle, bordered with white fur. This garment hung so loosely on the figure, that its capacious breast was bare, as if disdaining to be warded or concealed by any artifice. Its feet, observable beneath the ample folds of the garment, were also bare; and on its head it wore no other covering than a holly wreath set here and there with shining icicles. Its dark brown curls were long and free: free as its genial face, its sparkling eye, its open hand, its cheery voice, its unconstrained demeanour, and its joyful air. Girded round its middle was an antique scabbard; but no sword was in it, and the ancient sheath was eaten up with rust.

"You have never seen the like of me before!" exclaimed the Spirit.

"Never," Scrooge made answer to it.

"Have never walked forth with the younger members of my family; meaning (for I am very young) my elder brothers born in these later years?" pursued the Phantom.

"I don't think I have," said Scrooge. "I am afraid I have not. Have you had many brothers, Spirit?"

"More than eighteen hundred," said the Ghost.

"A tremendous family to provide for!" muttered Scrooge.

The Ghost of Christmas Present rose.

"Spirit," said Scrooge submissively, "conduct me where you will. I went forth last night on compulsion, and I learnt a lesson which is working now. To-night, if you have aught to teach me, let me profit by it."

"Touch my robe!"

Scrooge did as he was told, and held it fast. Holly, mistletoe, red berries, ivy, turkeys, geese, game, poultry, brawn, meat, pigs, sausages,

oysters, pies, puddings, fruit, and punch, all vanished instantly. So did the room, the fire, the ruddy glow, the hour of night, and they stood in the city streets on Christmas morning, where (for the weather was severe) the people made a rough, but brisk and not unpleasant kind of music, in scraping the snow from the pavement in front of their dwellings, and from the tops of their houses: whence it was mad delight to the boys to see it come plumping down into the road below, and splitting into artificial little snowstorms.

The house fronts looked black enough, and the windows blacker, contrasting with the smooth white sheet of snow upon the roofs, and with the dirtier snow upon the ground; which last deposit had been ploughed up in deep furrows by the heavy wheels of carts and waggons; furrows that crossed and re-crossed each other hundreds of times where the great streets branched off, and made intricate channels, hard to trace, in the thick yellow mud and icy water. The sky was gloomy, and the shortest streets were choked up with a dingy mist, half thawed half frozen, whose heavier particles descended in a shower of sooty atoms, as if all the chimneys in Great Britain had, by one consent, caught fire, and were blazing away to their dear hearts' content. There was nothing very cheerful in the climate or the town, and yet was there an air of cheerfulness abroad that the clearest summer air and brightest summer sun might have endeavoured to diffuse in vain.

For the people who were shovelling away on the house-tops were jovial and full of glee; calling out to one another from the parapets, and now and then exchanging a facetious snowball—better-natured missile far than many a wordy jest—laughing heartily if it went right, and not less heartily if it went wrong. The poulterers' shops were still half open, and the fruiterers' were radiant in their glory. There were great, round, pot-bellied baskets of chesnuts, shaped like the waistcoats of jolly old gentlemen, lolling at the doors, and tumbling out into the street in their apoplectic opulence. There were ruddy, brown-faced, broad-girthed Spanish Onions, shining in the fatness of their growth like Spanish Friars; and winking from their shelves in wanton slyness at the girls as they went by, and glanced demurely at the hung-up mistletoe. There were pears and apples, clustered high in blooming pyramids; there were bunches of grapes, made, in the shopkeepers' benevolence, to dangle from conspicuous hooks, that people's mouths might water gratis as they passed; were piles of filberts, mossy and brown, recalling, in their fragrance ancient walks among the woods, and pleasant shufflings ankle deep through withered leaves; there were Norfolk Biffins,[1] squab and swarthy, setting off the yellow of the oranges and lemons, and, in the great compactness of their juicy persons, urgently entreating and beseeching to be carried home in paper bags and eaten after dinner. The very gold and silver fish, set forth among these choice fruits in a bowl, though members of a dull and stagnant-blooded race, appeared to know that there was something going on; and, to a fish, went gasping round and round their little world in slow and passionless excitement.

The Grocers'! oh the Grocers'! nearly closed, with perhaps two shutters down, or one; but through those gaps such glimpses! It was not alone that the scales descending on the counter made a merry sound, or that the twine and roller parted company so briskly, or that the canisters were rattled up and down like juggling tricks, or even that the blended scents of tea and coffee were so grateful to the nose, or even that the raisins were so plentiful and rare, the almonds so extremely white, the sticks of cinnamon so long and straight, the other spices so delicious, the candied fruits so caked and spotted with molten sugar as to make the coldest lookers-on feel faint and subsequently bilious. Nor was it that the figs were moist and pulpy, or that the French plums blushed in modest tartness from their highly-decorated boxes, or that everything was good to eat and in its Christmas dress: but the customers were all so hurried and so eager in the hopeful promise of the day, that they tumbled up against each other at the door, clashing their wicker baskets wildly, and left their purchases upon the counter, and came running back to fetch them, and committed hundreds of the like mistakes in the best humour possible; while the Grocer and his people were so frank and fresh that the polished hearts with which they fastened their aprons behind might have been their own, worn outside for general inspection, and for Christmas daws to peck at if they chose.

But soon the steeples called good people all, to church and

---

1   Cooking apples from Norfolk, in eastern England, which have been baked slowly and are rusty red in color.

ıey came, flocking through the streets in their best
their gayest faces. And at the same time there
ɔres of bye streets, lanes, and nameless turnings,
ıle, carrying their dinners to the bakers' shops.[1]
poor revellers appeared to interest the Spirit very
ıd with Scrooge beside him in a baker's doorway,
and taking off the covers as their bearers passed, sprinkled incense on their dinners from his torch. And it was a very uncommon kind of torch, for once or twice when there were angry words between some dinner-carriers who had jostled with each other, he shed a few drops of water on them from it, and their good humour was restored directly. For they said, it was a shame to quarrel upon Christmas Day. And so it was! God love it, so it was!

In time the bells ceased, and the bakers' were shut up; and yet there was a genial shadowing forth of all these dinners and the progress of their cooking, in the thawed blotch of wet above each baker's oven; where the pavement smoked as if its stones were cooking too.

"Is there a peculiar flavour in what you sprinkle from your torch?" asked Scrooge.

"There is. My own."

"Would it apply to any kind of dinner on this day?" asked Scrooge.

"To any kindly given. To a poor one most."

"Why to a poor one most?" asked Scrooge.

"Because it needs it most."

"Spirit," said Scrooge, after a moment's thought, "I wonder you, of all the beings in the many worlds about us, should desire to cramp these people's opportunities of innocent enjoyment."

"I!" cried the Spirit.

"You would deprive them of their means of dining every seventh day,[2] often the only day on which they can be said to dine at all," said Scrooge. "Wouldn't you?"

---

1 Since bakers were legally forbidden to bake bread on Christmas day and Sundays, the poor would take their dinners on these days to the bakers in order to enjoy a hot meal.

2 In the name of religion, Sir Andrew Agnew several times between 1832 and 1837 introduced in the House of Commons a Sunday Observance Bill. The bill proposed not only to close the bakeries but to limit many of the recreations of the poor, while placing no restrictions on the wealthy.

"I!" cried the Spirit.

"You seek to close these places on the Seventh Day?" said Scrooge. "And it comes to the same thing."

"*I* seek!" exclaimed the Spirit.

"Forgive me if I am wrong. It has been done in your name, or at least in that of your family," said Scrooge.

"There are some upon this earth of yours," returned the Spirit, "who lay claim to know us, and who do their deeds of passion, pride, ill-will, hatred, envy, bigotry, and selfishness in our name; who are as strange to us and all our kith and kin, as if they had never lived. Remember that, and charge their doings on themselves, not us."

Scrooge promised that he would; and they went on, invisible, as they had been before, into the suburbs of the town. It was a remarkable quality of the Ghost (which Scrooge had observed at the baker's) that notwithstanding his gigantic size, he could accommodate himself to any place with ease; and that he stood beneath a low roof quite as gracefully and like a supernatural creature, as it was possible he could have done in any lofty hall.

And perhaps it was the pleasure the good Spirit had in showing off this power of his, or else it was his own kind, generous, hearty nature, and his sympathy with all poor men, that led him straight to Scrooge's clerk's; for there he went, and took Scrooge with him, holding to his robe; and on the threshold of the door the Spirit smiled, and stopped to bless Bob Cratchit's dwelling with the sprinklings of his torch. Think of that! Bob had but fifteen "Bob" a-week himself; he pocketed on Saturdays but fifteen copies of his Christian name; and yet the Ghost of Christmas Present blessed his four-roomed house!

Then up rose Mrs. Cratchit, Cratchit's wife, dressed out but poorly in a twice-turned gown, but brave in ribbons, which are cheap and make a goodly show for sixpence; and she laid the cloth, assisted by Belinda Cratchit, second of her daughters, also brave in ribbons; while Master Peter Cratchit plunged a fork into the saucepan of potatoes, and getting the corners of his monstrous shirt-collar (Bob's private property, conferred upon his son and heir in honour of the day) into his mouth, rejoiced to find himself so gallantly attired, and yearned to show his linen in the fashionable Parks. And now two smaller Cratchits, boy and girl, came tearing in, screaming that outside the baker's they had smelt the goose, and known it for their own; and basking in luxurious thoughts of sage-and-onion, these young Cratchits danced about the table, and exalted Master Peter Cratchit to the skies, while he (not proud, although his collars nearly choked him) blew the fire, until the slow potatoes bubbling up, knocked loudly at the saucepan-lid to be let out and peeled.

"What has ever got your precious father then," said Mrs. Cratchit. "And your brother, Tiny Tim; and Martha warn't as late last Christmas Day by half-an-hour!"

"Here's Martha, mother!" said a girl, appearing as she spoke.

"Here's Martha, mother!" cried the two young Cratchits. "Hurrah! There's *such* a goose, Martha!"

"Why, bless your heart alive, my dear, how late you are!" said Mrs. Cratchit, kissing her a dozen times, and taking off her shawl and bonnet for her, with officious zeal.

"We'd a deal of work to finish up last night," replied the girl, "and had to clear away this morning, mother!"

"Well! Never mind so long as you are come," said Mrs. Cratchit. "Sit ye down before the fire, my dear, and have a warm, Lord bless ye!"

"No no! There's father coming," cried the two young Cratchits, who were everywhere at once. "Hide Martha, hide!"

So Martha hid herself, and in came little Bob, the father, with at least three feet of comforter exclusive of the fringe, hanging down before him; and his thread-bare clothes darned up and brushed, to look seasonable; and Tiny Tim upon his shoulder. Alas for Tiny Tim, he bore a little crutch, and had his limbs supported by an iron frame!

"Why, where's our Martha?" cried Bob Cratchit looking round.

"Not coming," said Mrs. Cratchit.

"Not coming!" said Bob, with a sudden declension in his high spirits; for he had been Tim's blood horse[1] all the way from church, and had come home rampant. "Not coming upon Christmas Day!"

Martha didn't like to see him disappointed, if it were only in joke; so she came out prematurely from behind the closet door, and ran

---

1   A thoroughbred racehorse.

into his arms, while the two young Cratchits hustled Tiny Tim, and bore him off into the wash-house, that he might hear the pudding singing in the copper.[1]

"And how did little Tim behave?" asked Mrs. Cratchit, when she had rallied Bob on his credulity and Bob had hugged his daughter to his heart's content.

"As good as gold," said Bob, "and better. Somehow he gets thoughtful sitting by himself so much, and thinks the strangest things you ever heard. He told me, coming home, that he hoped the people saw him in the church, because he was a cripple, and it might be pleasant to them to remember upon Christmas Day, who made lame beggars walk and blind men see."

Bob's voice was tremulous when he told them this, and trembled more when he said that Tiny Tim was growing strong and hearty.

His active little crutch was heard upon the floor, and back came Tiny Tim before another word was spoken, escorted by his brother and sister to his stool beside the fire; and while Bob, turning up his cuffs—as if, poor fellow, they were capable of being made more shabby—compounded some hot mixture in a jug with gin and lemons, and stirred it round and round and put it on the hob to simmer; Master Peter and the two ubiquitous young Cratchits went to fetch the goose, with which they soon returned in high procession.

Such a bustle ensued that you might have thought a goose the rarest of all birds; a feathered phenomenon, to which a black swan was a matter of course: and in truth it was something very like it in that house. Mrs. Cratchit made the gravy (ready beforehand in a little saucepan) hissing hot; Master Peter mashed the potatoes with incredible vigour; Miss Belinda sweetened up the apple-sauce; Martha dusted the hot plates; Bob took Tiny Tim beside him in a tiny corner at the table; the two young Cratchits set chairs for everybody, not forgetting themselves, and mounting guard upon their posts, crammed spoons into their mouths, lest they should shriek for goose before their turn came to be helped. At last the dishes were set on, and grace was said. It was succeeded by a breathless pause, as Mrs. Cratchit, looking slowly all along the carving-knife, prepared to

---

1 A boiler, used mostly to clean clothes, but on this holiday it was reserved to cook the pudding, wrapped in a cloth.

plunge it in the breast; but when she did, and when the long expected gush of stuffing issued forth, one murmur of delight arose all
round the board, and even Tiny Tim, excited by the two young
Cratchits, beat on the table with the handle of his knife, and feebly
cried Hurrah!

There never was such a goose. Bob said he didn't believe there
ever was such a goose cooked. Its tenderness and flavour, size and
cheapness, were the themes of universal admiration. Eked out by the
apple-sauce and mashed potatoes, it was a sufficient dinner for the
whole family; indeed, as Mrs. Cratchit said with great delight (surveying one small atom of a bone upon the dish), they hadn't ate it all
at last! Yet every one had had enough, and the youngest Cratchits in
particular, were steeped in sage and onion to the eyebrows! But now,
the plates being changed by Miss Belinda, Mrs. Cratchit left the
room alone — too nervous to bear witnesses — to take the pudding
up, and bring it in.

Suppose it should not be done enough! Suppose it should break
in turning out! Suppose somebody should have got over the wall of
the back-yard, and stolen it, while they were merry with the goose: a
supposition at which the two young Cratchits became livid! All sorts
of horrors were supposed.

Hallo! A great deal of steam! The pudding was out of the copper.
A smell like a washing-day! That was the cloth. A smell like an eating-house, and a pastry cook's next door to each other, with a laundress's next door to that! That was the pudding. In half a minute
Mrs. Cratchit entered: flushed, but smiling proudly: with the pudding, like a speckled cannon-ball, so hard and firm, blazing in half of
half-a-quartern[1] of ignited brandy, and bedight[2] with Christmas
holly stuck into the top.

Oh, a wonderful pudding! Bob Cratchit said, and calmly too, that
he regarded it as the greatest success achieved by Mrs. Cratchit since
their marriage. Mrs. Cratchit said that now the weight was off her
mind, she would confess she had had her doubts about the quantity
of flour. Everybody had something to say about it, but nobody said
or thought it was at all a small pudding for a large family. It would

---

1   One-eighth of a pint.
2   An archaic term for *adorned*.

have been flat heresy to do so. Any Cratchit would have blushed to hint at such a thing.

At last the dinner was all done, the cloth was cleared, the hearth swept, and the fire made up. The compound in the jug being tasted and considered perfect, apples and oranges were put upon the table, and a shovel-full of chestnuts on the fire. Then all the Cratchit family drew round the hearth, in what Bob Cratchit called a circle, meaning half a one; and at Bob Cratchit's elbow stood the family display of glass; two tumblers, and a custard-cup without a handle.

These held the hot stuff from the jug, however, as well as golden goblets would have done; and Bob served it out with beaming looks, while the chestnuts on the fire sputtered and crackled noisily. Then Bob proposed:

"A Merry Christmas to us all, my dears. God bless us!"

Which all the family re-echoed.

"God bless us every one!" said Tiny Tim, the last of all.

He sat very close to his father's side, upon his little stool. Bob held his withered little hand in his, as if he loved the child, and wished to keep him by his side, and dreaded that he might be taken from him.

"Spirit," said Scrooge, with an interest he had never felt before, "tell me if Tiny Tim will live."

"I see a vacant seat," replied the Ghost, "in the poor chimney corner, and a crutch without an owner, carefully preserved. If these shadows remain unaltered by the Future, the child will die."

"No, no," said Scrooge. "Oh no, kind Spirit say he will be spared."

"If these shadows remain unaltered by the Future, none other of my race," returned the Ghost, "will find him here. What then? If he be like to die, he had better do it, and decrease the surplus population."

Scrooge hung his head to hear his own words quoted by the Spirit, and was overcome with penitence and grief.

"Man," said the Ghost, "if man you be in heart, not adamant, forbear that wicked cant until you have discovered What the surplus is, and Where it is. Will you decide what men shall live, what men shall die? It may be, that in the sight of Heaven, you are more worthless and less fit to live than millions like this poor man's child. Oh God! to hear the Insect on the leaf pronouncing on the too much life among his hungry brothers in the dust!"

Scrooge bent before the Ghost's rebuke, and trembling cast his eyes upon the ground. But he raised them speedily, on hearing his own name.

"Mr. Scrooge!" said Bob; "I'll give you Mr. Scrooge, the Founder of the Feast!"

"The Founder of the Feast indeed!" cried Mrs. Cratchit, reddening. "I wish I had him here. I'd give him a piece of my mind to feast upon, and I hope he'd have a good appetite for it."

"My dear," said Bob, "the children; Christmas Day."

"It should be Christmas Day, I am sure," said she, "on which one drinks the health of such an odious, stingy, hard, unfeeling man as Mr. Scrooge. You know he is, Robert! Nobody knows it better than you do, poor fellow!"

"My dear," was Bob's mild answer, "Christmas Day."

"I'll drink his health for your sake and the Day's," said Mrs. Cratchit, "not for his. Long life to him! A merry Christmas and a happy new year! — he'll be very merry and very happy, I have no doubt!"

The children drank the toast after her. It was the first of their proceedings which had no heartiness in it. Tiny Tim drank it last of all, but he didn't care twopence for it. Scrooge was the Ogre of the family. The mention of his name cast a dark shadow on the party, which was not dispelled for full five minutes.

After it had passed away, they were ten times merrier than before, from the mere relief of Scrooge the Baleful being done with. Bob Cratchit told them how he had a situation in his eye for Master Peter, which would bring in, if obtained, full five-and-sixpence weekly. The two young Cratchits laughed tremendously at the idea of Peter's being a man of business; and Peter himself looked thoughtfully at the fire from between his collars, as if he were deliberating what particular investments he should favour when he came into the receipt of that bewildering income. Martha, who was a poor apprentice at a milliner's, then told them what kind of work she had to do, and how many hours she worked at a stretch, and how she meant to lie a-bed to-morrow morning for a good long rest; to-morrow being a holiday she passed at home. Also how she had seen a countess and a lord some days before, and how the lord "was much about as tall as Peter;" at which Peter pulled up his collars so high that you couldn't have seen his head if you had been there. All this time the chesnuts and the jug went round and round; and bye and bye they had a song, about a lost child travelling in the snow, from Tiny Tim; who had a plaintive little voice, and sang it very well indeed.

There was nothing of high mark in this. They were not a handsome family; they were not well dressed; their shoes were far from being waterproof; their clothes were scanty; and Peter might have known, and very likely did, the inside of a pawnbroker's. But they were happy, grateful, pleased with one another, and contented with the time; and when they faded, and looked happier yet in the bright sprinklings of the Spirit's torch at parting, Scrooge had his eye upon them, and especially on Tiny Tim, until the last.

By this time it was getting dark, and snowing pretty heavily; and as Scrooge and the Spirit went along the streets, the brightness of the roaring fires in kitchens, parlours, and all sorts of rooms, was wonderful. Here, the flickering of the blaze showed preparations for a cosy dinner, with hot plates baking through and through before the fire, and deep red curtains, ready to be drawn, to shut out cold and darkness. There, all the children of the house were running out into the snow to meet their married sisters, brothers, cousins, uncles, aunts, and be the first to greet them. Here, again, were shadows on the window-blind of guests assembling; and there a group of handsome girls, all hooded and fur-booted, and all chattering at once, tripped lightly off to some near neighbour's house; where, wo[1] upon the single man who saw them enter   artful witches: well they knew it—in a glow!

But if you had judged from the numbers of people on their way to friendly gatherings, you might have thought that no one was at home to give them welcome when they got there, instead of every house expecting company, and piling up its fires half-chimney high. Blessings on it, how the Ghost exulted! How it bared its breadth of breast, and opened its capacious palm, and floated on, outpouring, with a generous hand, its bright and harmless mirth on everything

---

1   A variant spelling of *woe*.

within its reach! The very lamplighter, who ran on before dotting the dusky street with specks of light, and who was dressed to spend the evening somewhere, laughed out loudly as the Spirit passed: though little kenned[1] the lamplighter that he had any company but Christmas!

And now, without a word of warning from the Ghost, they stood upon a bleak and desert moor,[2] where monstrous masses of rude stone were cast about, as though it were the burial-place of giants; and water spread itself wheresoever it listed—or would have done so, but for the frost that held it prisoner; and nothing grew but moss and furze, and coarse, rank grass. Down in the west the setting sun had left a streak of fiery red, which glared upon the desolation for an instant, like a sullen eye, and frowning lower, lower, lower yet, was lost in the thick gloom of darkest night.

"What place is this?" asked Scrooge.

"A place where Miners live, who labour in the bowels of the earth," returned the Spirit. "But they know me. See!"

A light shone from the window of a hut, and swiftly they advanced towards it. Passing through the wall of mud and stone, they found a cheerful company assembled round a glowing fire. An old, old man and woman, with their children and their children's children, and another generation beyond that, all decked out gaily in their holiday attire. The old man, in a voice that seldom rose above the howling of the wind upon the barren waste, was singing them a Christmas song; it had been a very old song when he was a boy; and from time to time they all joined in the chorus. So surely as they raised their voices, the old man got quite blithe and loud; and so surely as they stopped, his vigour sank again.

The Spirit did not tarry here, but bade Scrooge hold his robe, and passing on above the moor, sped whither? Not to sea? To sea. To Scrooge's horror, looking back, he saw the last of the land, a frightful range of rocks, behind them; and his ears were deafened by the thundering of water, as it rolled, and roared, and raged among the

---

1 Knew.
2 The scene here is Cornwall. After reading in the Commissioner's Report, a graphic account of the abuse of children working in the Cornish tin mines, Dickens visited the dreary area and spent ten days there in 1842.

dreadful caverns it had worn, and fiercely tried to undermine the earth.

Built upon a dismal reef of sunken rocks, some league or so from shore, on which the waters chafed and dashed, the wild year through, there stood a solitary lighthouse. Great heaps of sea-weed clung to its base, and storm-birds—born of the wind one might suppose, as sea-weed of the water—rose and fell about it, like the waves they skimmed.

But even here, two men who watched the light had made a fire, that through the loophole in the thick stone wall shed out a ray of brightness on the awful sea. Joining their horny hands over the rough table at which they sat, they wished each other Merry Christmas in their can of grog;[1] and one of them: the elder, too, with his face all damaged and scarred with hard weather, as the figure-head of an old ship might be: struck up a sturdy song that was like a Gale in itself.

Again the Ghost sped on, above the black and heaving sea—on, on—until, being far away, as he told Scrooge, from any shore, they lighted on a ship. They stood beside the helmsman at the wheel, the look-out in the bow, the officers who had the watch; dark, ghostly figures in their several stations; but every man among them hummed a Christmas tune, or had a Christmas thought, or spoke below his breath to his companion of some bygone Christmas Day, with homeward hopes belonging to it. And every man on board, waking or sleeping, good or bad, had had a kinder word for another on that day than on any day in the year; and had shared to some extent in its festivities; and had remembered those he cared for at a distance, and had known that they delighted to remember him.

It was a great surprise to Scrooge, while listening to the moaning of the wind, and thinking what a solemn thing it was to move on through the lonely darkness over an unknown abyss, whose depths were secrets as profound as Death: it was a great surprise to Scrooge, while thus engaged, to hear a hearty laugh. It was a much greater surprise to Scrooge to recognise it as his own nephew's, and to find himself in a bright, dry, gleaming room, with the Spirit standing

---

1 A mixture of rum and water.

smiling by his side, and looking at that same nephew with approving affability!

"Ha, ha!" laughed Scrooge's nephew. "Ha, ha, ha!"

If you should happen, by any unlikely chance, to know a man more blest in a laugh than Scrooge's nephew, all I can say is, I should like to know him too. Introduce him to me, and I'll cultivate his acquaintance.

It is a fair, even-handed, noble adjustment of things, that while there is infection in disease and sorrow, there is nothing in the world so irresistibly contagious as laughter and good-humour. When Scrooge's nephew laughed in this way: holding his sides, rolling his head, and twisting his face into the most extravagant contortions: Scrooge's niece, by marriage, laughed as heartily as he. And their assembled friends being not a bit behindhand, roared out, lustily.

"Ha, ha! Ha, ha, ha, ha!"

"He said that Christmas was a humbug, as I live!" cried Scrooge's nephew. "He believed it too!"

"More shame for him, Fred!" said Scrooge's niece, indignantly. Bless those women; they never do anything by halves. They are always in earnest.

She was very pretty: exceedingly pretty. With a dimpled, surprised-looking, capital face; a ripe little mouth, that seemed made to be kissed—as no doubt it was; all kinds of good little dots about her chin, that melted into one another when she laughed; and the sunniest pair of eyes you ever saw in any little creature's head. Altogether she was what you would have called provoking, you know; but satisfactory, too. Oh, perfectly satisfactory!

"He's a comical old fellow," said Scrooge's nephew, "that's the truth; and not so pleasant as he might be. However, his offences carry their own punishment, and I have nothing to say against him."

"I'm sure he is very rich, Fred," hinted Scrooge's niece. "At least you always tell *me* so."

"What of that, my dear!" said Scrooge's nephew. "His wealth is of no use to him. He don't do any good with it. He don't make himself comfortable with it. He hasn't the satisfaction of thinking—ha, ha, ha!—that he is ever going to benefit Us with it."

"I have no patience with him," observed Scrooge's niece.

Scrooge's niece's sisters, and all the other ladies, expressed the same opinion.

"Oh, I have!" said Scrooge's nephew. "I am sorry for him; I couldn't be angry with him if I tried. Who suffers by his ill whims? Himself, always. Here, he takes it into his head to dislike us, and he won't come and dine with us. What's the consequence? He don't lose much of a dinner."

"Indeed, I think he loses a very good dinner," interrupted Scrooge's niece. Everybody else said the same, and they must be allowed to have been competent judges, because they had just had dinner; and, with the dessert upon the table, were clustered round the fire, by lamplight.

"Well! I am very glad to hear it," said Scrooge's nephew, "because I haven't any great faith in these young housekeepers. What do you say, Topper?"

Topper had clearly got his eye upon one of Scrooge's niece's sisters, for he answered that a bachelor was a wretched outcast, who had no right to express an opinion on the subject. Whereat Scrooge's niece's sister—the plump one with the lace tucker:[1] not the one with the roses—blushed.

"Do go on, Fred," said Scrooge's niece, clapping her hands. "He never finishes what he begins to say! He is such a ridiculous fellow!"

Scrooge's nephew revelled in another laugh, and as it was impossible to keep the infection off; though the plump sister tried hard to do it with aromatic vinegar;[2] his example was unanimously followed.

"I was only going to say," said Scrooge's nephew, "that the consequence of his taking a dislike to us, and not making merry with us, is, as I think, that he loses some pleasant moments, which could do him no harm. I am sure he loses pleasanter companions than he can find in his own thoughts, either in his mouldy old office, or his dusty chambers. I mean to give him the same chance every year, whether he likes it or not, for I pity him. He may rail at Christmas till he dies, but he can't help thinking better of it—I defy him—if he finds

---

1 A piece of linen or frill of lace worn by women around the neck and shoulders.
2 A perfumed liquid to ward off headaches.

me going there, in good temper, year after year, and saying Uncle Scrooge, how are you? If it only puts him in the vein to leave his poor clerk fifty pounds, that's something; and I think I shook him, yesterday."

It was their turn to laugh now, at the notion of his shaking Scrooge. But being thoroughly good-natured, and not much caring what they laughed at, so that they laughed at any rate, he encouraged them in their merriment, and passed the bottle, joyously.

After tea, they had some music. For they were a musical family, and knew what they were about, when they sung a Glee[1] or Catch,[2] I can assure you: especially Topper, who could growl away in the bass like a good one, and never swell the large veins in his forehead, or get red in the face over it. Scrooge's niece played well upon the harp; and played among other tunes a simple little air (a mere nothing: you might learn to whistle it in two minutes), which had been familiar to the child who fetched Scrooge from the boarding-school, as he had been reminded by the Ghost of Christmas Past. When this strain of music sounded, all the things that Ghost had shown him, came upon his mind; he softened more and more; and thought that if he could have listened to it often, years ago, he might have cultivated the kindnesses of life for his own happiness with his own hands, without resorting to the sexton's spade that buried Jacob Marley.

But they didn't devote the whole evening to music. After a while they played at forfeits; for it is good to be children sometimes, and never better than at Christmas, when its mighty Founder was a child himself. Stop! There was first a game at blindman's buff. Of course there was. And I no more believe Topper was really blind than I believe he had eyes in his boots. My opinion is, that it was a done thing between him and Scrooge's nephew; and that the Ghost of Christmas Present knew it. The way he went after that plump sister in the lace tucker, was an outrage on the credulity of human nature.

---

1   A musical composition, of English origin, for three or more voices (one voice to each part), set to words of any character, grave or gay, often consisting of two or more contrasted movements, and (in strict use) without accompaniment. (*OED*)
2   A short composition for three or more voices, which sing the same melody, the second singer beginning the first line as the first goes on to the second line, and so with each successive singer. (*OED*)

Knocking down the fire-irons, tumbling over the chairs, bumping up against the piano, smothering himself among the curtains, wherever she went, there went he. He always knew where the plump sister was. He wouldn't catch anybody else. If you had fallen up against him, as some of them did, and stood there; he would have made a feint of endeavouring to seize you, which would have been an affront to your understanding; and would instantly have sidled off in the direction of the plump sister. She often cried out that it wasn't fair; and it really was not. But when at last, he caught her; when, in spite of all her silken rustlings, and her rapid flutterings past him, he got her into a corner whence there was no escape; then his conduct was the most execrable. For his pretending not to know her; his pretending that it was necessary to touch her head-dress, and further to assure himself of her identity by pressing a certain ring upon her finger, and a certain chain about her neck; was vile, monstrous! No doubt she told him her opinion of it, when, another blindman being in office, they were so very confidential together, behind the curtains.

Scrooge's niece was not one of the blind-man's buff party, but was made comfortable with a large chair and a footstool, in a snug corner, where the Ghost and Scrooge were close behind her. But she joined in the forfeits, and loved her love to admiration with all the letters of the alphabet.[1] Likewise at the game of How, When, and Where,[2] she was very great, and to the secret joy of Scrooge's nephew, beat her sisters hollow: though they were sharp girls too, as Topper could have told you. There might have been twenty people there, young and old, but they all played, and so did Scrooge; for, wholly forgetting in the interest he had in what was going on, that his voice made no sound in their ears, he sometimes came out with his guess quite loud, and very often guessed right, too; for the sharpest needle, best Whitechapel, warranted not to cut in the eye, was not sharper than Scrooge: blunt as he took it in his head to be.

The Ghost was greatly pleased to find him in this mood, and

---

1 A parlor game in which each player completes a statement following the letters of the alphabet, as in "I love my love with an A because he is adorable."
2 A game in which each player in turn asks, "How do you like it?" "When do you like it?" and "Where do you like it?"

looked upon him with such favour that he begged like a boy to be allowed to stay until the guests departed. But this the Spirit said could not be done.

"Here's a new game," said Scrooge. "One half hour, Spirit, only one!" It was a Game called Yes and No, where Scrooge's nephew had to think of something, and the rest must find out what; he only answering to their questions yes or no as the case was. The brisk fire of questioning to which he was exposed, elicited from him that he was thinking of an animal, a live animal, rather a disagreeable animal, a savage animal, an animal that growled and grunted sometimes, and talked sometimes, and lived in London, and walked about the streets, and wasn't made a show of, and wasn't led by anybody,.and didn't live in a menagerie, and was never killed in a market, and was not a horse, or an ass, or a cow, or a bull, or a tiger, or a dog, or a pig, or a cat, or a bear. At every fresh question that was put to him, this nephew burst into a fresh roar of laughter; and was so inexpressibly tickled, that he was obliged to get up off the sofa and stamp. At last the plump sister, falling into a similar state, cried out:

"I have found it out! I know what it is, Fred! I know what it is!"

"What is it?" cried Fred.

"It's your Uncle Scro-o-o-o-oge!"

Which it certainly was. Admiration was the universal sentiment, though some objected that the reply to "Is it a bear?" ought to have been "Yes;" inasmuch as an answer in the negative was sufficient to have diverted their thoughts from Mr. Scrooge, supposing they had ever had any tendency that way.

"He has given us plenty of merriment, I am sure," said Fred, "and it would be ungrateful not to drink his health. Here is a glass of mulled wine ready to our hand at the moment; and I say 'Uncle Scrooge!'"

"Well! Uncle Scrooge!" they cried.

"A Merry Christmas and a happy New Year to the old man, whatever he is!" said Scrooge's nephew. "He wouldn't take it from me, but may he have it, nevertheless. Uncle Scrooge!"

Uncle Scrooge had imperceptibly become so gay and light of heart, that he would have pledged the unconscious company in return, and thanked them in an inaudible speech, if the Ghost had given him time. But the whole scene passed off in the breath of the last word spoken by his nephew; and he and the Spirit were again upon their travels.

Much they saw, and far they went, and many homes they visited, but always with a happy end. The Spirit stood beside sick beds, and they were cheerful; on foreign lands, and they were close at home; by struggling men, and they were patient in their greater hope; by poverty, and it was rich. In almshouse, hospital, and jail, in misery's every refuge, where vain man in his little brief authority had not made fast the door, and barred the Spirit out, he left his blessing, and taught Scrooge his precepts.

It was a long night, if it were only a night; but Scrooge had his doubts of this, because the Christmas Holidays appeared to be condensed into the space of time they passed together. It was strange, too, that while Scrooge remained unaltered in his outward form, the Ghost grew older, clearly older. Scrooge had observed this change, but never spoke of it, until they left a children's Twelfth Night party, when, looking at the Spirit as they stood together in an open place, he noticed that its hair was gray.

"Are spirits' lives so short?" asked Scrooge.

"My life upon this globe, is very brief," replied the Ghost. "It ends to-night."

"To-night!" cried Scrooge.

"To-night at midnight. Hark! The time is drawing near."

The chimes were ringing the three quarters past eleven at that moment.

"Forgive me if I am not justified in what I ask," said Scrooge, looking intently at the Spirit's robe, "but I see something strange, and not belonging to yourself, protruding from your skirts. Is it a foot or a claw!"

"It might be a claw, for the flesh there is upon it," was the Spirit's sorrowful reply. "Look here."

From the foldings of its robe, it brought two children; wretched, abject, frightful, hideous, miserable. They knelt down at its feet, and clung upon the outside of its garment.

"Oh, Man! look here. Look, look, down here!" exclaimed the Ghost.

They were a boy and girl. Yellow, meagre, ragged, scowling, wolfish; but prostrate, too, in their humility. Where graceful youth should

have filled their features out, and touched them with its freshest tints, a stale and shrivelled hand, like that of age, had pinched, and twisted them, and pulled them into shreds. Where angels might have sat enthroned, devils lurked, and glared out menacing. No change, no degradation, no perversion of humanity, in any grade, through all the mysteries of wonderful creation, has monsters half so horrible and dread.

Scrooge started back, appalled. Having them shown to him in this way, he tried to say they were fine children, but the words choked themselves, rather than be parties to a lie of such enormous magnitude.

"Spirit! are they yours?" Scrooge could say no more.

"They are Man's," said the Spirit, looking down upon them. "And they cling to me, appealing from their fathers. This boy is Ignorance. This girl is Want. Beware them both, and all of their degree, but most of all beware this boy, for on his brow I see that written which is Doom, unless the writing be erased. Deny it!" cried the Spirit, stretching out its hand towards the city. "Slander those who tell it ye! Admit it for your factious purposes, and make it worse! And bide the end!"

"Have they no refuge or resource?" cried Scrooge.

"Are there no prisons?" said the Spirit, turning on him for the last time with his own words. "Are there no workhouses?"

The bell struck twelve.

Scrooge looked about him for the Ghost, and saw it not. As the last stroke ceased to vibrate, he remembered the prediction of old Jacob Marley, and lifting up his eyes, beheld a solemn Phantom, draped and hooded, coming, like a mist along the ground, towards him.

STAVE FOUR.

THE LAST OF THE SPIRITS.

THE Phantom slowly, gravely, silently, approached. When it came near him, Scrooge bent down upon his knee; for in the very air through which this Spirit moved it seemed to scatter gloom and mystery.

It was shrouded in a deep black garment, which concealed its head, its face, its form, and left nothing of it visible save one outstretched hand. But for this it would have been difficult to detach its figure from the night, and separate it from the darkness by which it was surrounded.

He felt that it was tall and stately when it came beside him, and that its mysterious presence filled him with a solemn dread. He knew no more, for the Spirit neither spoke nor moved.

"I am in the presence of the Ghost of Christmas Yet To Come?" said Scrooge.

The Spirit answered not, but pointed downward[1] with its hand.

"You are about to show me shadows of the things that have not happened, but will happen in the time before us," Scrooge pursued. "Is that so, Spirit?"

The upper portion of the garment was contracted for an instant in its folds, as if the Spirit had inclined its head. That was the only answer he received.

Although well used to ghostly company by this time, Scrooge feared the silent shape so much that his legs trembled beneath him, and he found that he could hardly stand when he prepared to follow it. The Spirit paused a moment, as observing his condition, and giving him time to recover.

But Scrooge was all the worse for this. It thrilled him with a vague uncertain horror, to know that behind the dusky shroud there were ghostly eyes intently fixed upon him, while he, though he stretched his own to the utmost, could see nothing but a spectral hand and one great heap of black.

"Ghost of the Future!" he exclaimed, "I fear you more than any

---

1 An error in printing. Dickens's original manuscript has *onward*.

Spectre I have seen. But, as I know your purpose is to do me good, and as I hope to live to be another man from what I was, I am prepared to bear you company, and do it with a thankful heart. Will you not speak to me?"

It gave him no reply. The hand was pointed straight before them.

"Lead on!" said Scrooge. "Lead on! The night is waning fast, and it is precious time to me, I know. Lead on, Spirit!"

The Phantom moved away as it had come towards him. Scrooge followed in the shadow of its dress, which bore him up, he thought, and carried him along.

They scarcely seemed to enter the city; for the city rather seemed to spring up about them, and encompass them of its own act. But there they were, in the heart of it; on 'Change, amongst the merchants; who hurried up and down, and chinked the money in their pockets, and conversed in groups, and looked at their watches, and trifled thoughtfully with their great gold seals; and so forth, as Scrooge had seen them often.

The Spirit stopped beside one little knot of business men. Observing that the hand was pointed to them, Scrooge advanced to listen to their talk.

"No," said a great fat man with a monstrous chin, "I don't know much about it, either way. I only know he's dead."

"When did he die?" inquired another.

"Last night, I believe."

"Why, what was the matter with him?" asked a third, taking a vast quantity of snuff out of a very large snuff-box. "I thought he'd never die."

"God knows," said the first, with a yawn.

"What has he done with his money?" asked a red-faced gentleman with a pendulous excrescence on the end of his nose, that shook like the gills of a turkey-cock.

"I haven't heard," said the man with the large chin, yawning again. "Left it to his Company, perhaps. He hasn't left it to me. That's all [I][1] know."

This pleasantry was received with a general laugh.

"It's likely to be a very cheap funeral," said the same speaker; "for

---

1   The *I* was omitted in the first edition but appears in Dickens's original manuscript.

upon my life I don't know of anybody to go to it. Suppose we make up a party and volunteer?"

"I don't mind going if a lunch is provided," observed the gentleman with the excrescence on his nose. "But I must be fed, if I make one."

Another laugh.

"Well, I am the most disinterested among you, after all," said the first speaker, "for I never wear black gloves, and I never eat lunch. But I'll offer to go, if anybody else will. When I come to think of it, I'm not at all sure that I wasn't his most particular friend; for we used to stop and speak whenever we met. Bye, bye!"

Speakers and listeners strolled away, and mixed with other groups. Scrooge knew the men, and looked towards the Spirit for an explanation.

The Phantom glided on into a street. Its finger pointed to two persons meeting. Scrooge listened again, thinking that the explanation might lie here.

He knew these men, also, perfectly. They were men of business: very wealthy, and of great importance. He had made a point always of standing well in their esteem: in a business point of view, that is; strictly in a business point of view.

"How are you?" said one.

"How are you?" returned the other.

"Well!" said the first. "Old Scratch[1] has got his own at last, hey?"

"So I am told," returned the second. "Cold, isn't it?"

"Seasonable for Christmas time. You're not a skaiter,[2] I suppose?"

"No. No. Something else to think of. Good morning!"

Not another word. That was their meeting, their conversation, and their parting.

Scrooge was at first inclined to be surprised that the Spirit should attach importance to conversations apparently so trivial; but feeling assured that they must have some hidden purpose, he set himself to consider what it was likely to be. They could scarcely be supposed to have any bearing on the death of Jacob, his old partner, for that

---

1 A nickname for the devil.
2 In the 1868 edition Dickens changed this unusual spelling to the more conventional *skater*.

was Past, and this Ghost's province was the Future. Nor could he think of any one immediately connected with himself, to whom he could apply them. But nothing doubting that to whomsoever they applied they had some latent moral for his own improvement, he resolved to treasure up every word he heard, and everything he saw; and especially to observe the shadow of himself when it appeared. For he had an expectation that the conduct of his future self would give him the clue he missed, and would render the solution of these riddles easy.

He looked about in that very place for his own image; but another man stood in his accustomed corner, and though the clock pointed to his usual time of day for being there, he saw no likeness of himself among the multitudes that poured in through the Porch. It gave him little surprise, however; for he had been revolving in his mind a change of life, and thought and hoped he saw his new-born resolutions carried out in this.

Quiet and dark, beside him stood the Phantom, with its outstretched hand. When he roused himself from his thoughtful quest, he fancied from the turn of the hand, and its situation in reference to himself, that the Unseen Eyes were looking at him keenly. It made him shudder, and feel very cold.

They left the busy scene, and went into an obscure part of the town, where Scrooge had never penetrated before, although he recognised its situation, and its bad repute. The ways were foul and narrow; the shops and houses wretched; the people half-naked, drunken, slipshod, ugly. Alleys and archways, like so many cesspools, disgorged their offences of smell, and dirt, and life, upon the straggling streets; and the whole quarter reeked with crime, with filth, and misery.

Far in this den of infamous resort, there was a low-browed, beetling[1] shop, below a pent-house roof, where iron, old rags, bottles, bones, and greasy offal, were bought. Upon the floor within, were piled up heaps of rusty keys, nails, chains, hinges, files, scales, weights, and refuse iron of all kinds. Secrets that few would like to scrutinise were bred and hidden in mountains of unseemly rags, masses of cor-

---

1 Overhanging.

rupted fat, and sepulchres of bones.[1] Sitting in among the wares he dealt in, by a charcoal-stove, made of old bricks, was a gray-haired rascal, nearly seventy years of age; who had screened himself from the cold air without, by a frousy curtaining of miscellaneous tatters, hung upon a line; and smoked his pipe in all the luxury of calm retirement.

Scrooge and the Phantom came into the presence of this man, just as a woman with a heavy bundle slunk into the shop. But she had scarcely entered, when another woman, similarly laden, came in too; and she was closely followed by a man in faded black, who was no less startled by the sight of them, than they had been upon the recognition of each other. After a short period of blank astonishment, in which the old man with the pipe had joined them, they all three burst into a laugh.

"Let the charwoman alone to be the first!" cried she who had entered first. "Let the laundress alone to be the second; and let the undertaker's man alone to be the third. Look here, old Joe, here's a chance! If we haven't all three met here without meaning it!"

"You couldn't have met in a better place," said old Joe, removing his pipe from his mouth. "Come into the parlour. You were made free of it long ago, you know; and the other two an't strangers. Stop till I shut the door of the shop. Ah! How it skreeks! There an't such a rusty bit of metal in the place as its own hinges, I believe; and I'm sure there's no such old bones here, as mine. Ha, ha! We're all suitable to our calling, we're well matched. Come into the parlour. Come into the parlour."

The parlour was the space behind the screen of rags. The old man raked the fire together with an old stair-rod, and having trimmed his smoky lamp (for it was night), with the stem of his pipe, put it in his mouth again.

While he did this, the woman who had already spoken threw her bundle on the floor and sat down in a flaunting manner on a stool; crossing her elbows on her knees, and looking with a bold defiance at the other two.

---

1   The small, foul-smelling rag-and-bottle shops, as they were called, purchased rags, bottles, bones, and grease drippings.

"What odds then![1] What odds, Mrs. Dilber?" said the woman. "Every person has a right to take care of themselves. *He* always did!" "That's true, indeed!" said the laundress. "No man more so."

"Why, then, don't stand staring as if you was afraid, woman; who's the wiser? We're not going to pick holes in each other's coats,[2] I suppose?"

"No, indeed!" said Mrs. Dilber and the man together. "We should hope not."

"Very well, then!" cried the woman. "That's enough. Who's the worse for the loss of a few things like these? Not a dead man, I suppose."

"No, indeed," said Mrs. Dilber, laughing.

"If he wanted to keep 'em after he was dead, a wicked old screw,"[3] pursued the woman, "why wasn't he natural in his lifetime? If he had been, he'd have had somebody to look after him when he was struck with Death, instead of lying gasping out his last there, alone by himself."

"It's the truest word that ever was spoke," said Mrs. Dilber. "It's a judgment on him."

"I wish it was a little heavier one," replied the woman; "and it should have been, you may depend upon it, if I could have laid my hands on anything else. Open that bundle, old Joe, and let me know the value of it. Speak out plain. I'm not afraid to be the first, nor afraid for them to see it. We knew pretty well that we were helping ourselves, before we met here, I believe. It's no sin. Open the bundle, Joe."

But the gallantry of her friends would not allow of this; and the man in faded black, mounting the breach first, produced *his* plunder. It was not extensive. A seal or two, a pencil-case, a pair of sleeve-buttons, and a brooch of no great value, were all. They were severally examined and appraised by old Joe, who chalked the sums he was disposed to give for each upon the wall, and added them up into a total when he found that there was nothing more to come.

---

1   What does it matter?
2   Argue with one another.
3   Old miser.

"That's your account," said Joe, "and I wouldn't give another six-pence, if I was to be boiled for not doing it. Who's next?"

Mrs. Dilber was next. Sheets and towels, a little wearing apparel, two old-fashioned silver teaspoons, a pair of sugar-tongs, and a few boots. Her account was stated on the wall in the same manner.

"I always give too much to ladies. It's a weakness of mine, and that's the way I ruin myself," said old Joe. "That's your account. If you asked me for another penny, and made it an open question, I'd repent of being so liberal, and knock off half-a-crown."

"And now undo *my* bundle, Joe," said the first woman.

Joe went down on his knees for the greater convenience of open-ing it, and having unfastened a great many knots, dragged out a large and heavy roll of some dark stuff.

"What do you call this?" said Joe. "Bed-curtains!"

"Ah!" returned the woman, laughing and leaning forward on her crossed arms. "Bed-curtains!"

"You don't mean to say you took 'em down, rings and all, with him lying there?" said Joe.

"Yes I do," replied the woman. "Why not?"

"You were born to make your fortune," said Joe, "and you'll cer-tainly do it."

"I certainly shan't hold my hand, when I can get anything in it by reaching it out, for the sake of such a man as He was, I promise you, Joe," returned the woman coolly. "Don't drop that oil upon the blankets, now."

"His blankets?" asked Joe.

"Whose else's do you think?" replied the woman. "He isn't likely to take cold without 'em, I dare say."

"I hope he didn't die of anything catching? Eh?" said old Joe, stopping in his work, and looking up.

"Don't you be afraid of that," returned the woman. "I an't so fond of his company that I'd loiter about him for such things, if he did. Ah! You may look through that shirt till your eyes ache; but you won't find a hole in it, nor a threadbare place. It's the best he had, and a fine one too. They'd have wasted it, if it hadn't been for me."

"What do you call wasting of it?" asked old Joe.

"Putting it on him to be buried in, to be sure," replied the woman with a laugh. "Somebody was fool enough to do it, but I took it off again. If calico an't good enough for such a purpose, it isn't good enough for anything. It's quite as becoming to the body. He can't look uglier than he did in that one."

Scrooge listened to this dialogue in horror. As they sat grouped about their spoil, in the scanty light afforded by the old man's lamp, he viewed them with a detestation and disgust, which could hardly have been greater, though they had been obscene demons, marketing the corpse itself.

"Ha, ha!" laughed the same woman, when old Joe, producing a flannel bag with money in it, told out their several gains upon the ground. "This is the end of it, you see! He frightened every one away from him when he was alive, to profit us when he was dead! Ha, ha, ha!"

"Spirit!" said Scrooge, shuddering from head to foot. "I see, I see. The case of this unhappy man might be my own. My life tends that way, now. Merciful Heaven, what is this!"

He recoiled in terror, for the scene had changed, and now he almost touched a bed: a bare, uncurtained bed: on which, beneath a ragged sheet, there lay a something covered up, which, though it was dumb, announced itself in awful language.

The room was very dark, too dark to be observed with any accuracy, though Scrooge glanced round it in obedience to a secret impulse, anxious to know what kind of room it was. A pale light, rising in the outer air, fell straight upon the bed; and on it, plundered and berett, unwatched, unwept, uncared for, was the body of this man.

Scrooge glanced towards the Phantom. Its steady hand was pointed to the head. The cover was so carelessly adjusted that the slightest raising of it, the motion of a finger upon Scrooge's part, would have disclosed the face. He thought of it, felt how easy it would be to do, and longed to do it; but had no more power to withdraw the veil than to dismiss the spectre at his side.

Oh cold, cold, rigid, dreadful Death, set up thine altar here, and dress it with such terrors as thou hast at thy command: for this is thy dominion! But of the loved, revered, and honoured head, thou canst not turn one hair to thy dread purposes, or make one feature odious.

It is not that the hand is heavy and will fall down when released; it is not that the heart and pulse are still; but that the hand was open, generous, and true; the heart brave, warm, and tender; and the pulse a man's. Strike, Shadow, strike! And see his good deeds springing from the wound, to sow the world with life immortal!

No voice pronounced these words in Scrooge's ears, and yet he heard them when he looked upon the bed. He thought, if this man could be raised up now, what would be his foremost thoughts? Avarice, hard dealing, griping cares? They have brought him to a rich end, truly!

He lay, in the dark empty house, with not a man, a woman, or a child, to say he was kind to me in this or that, and for the memory of one kind word I will be kind to him. A cat was tearing at the door, and there was a sound of gnawing rats beneath the hearth-stone. What *they* wanted in the room of death, and why they were so restless and disturbed, Scrooge did not dare to think.

"Spirit!" he said, "this is a fearful place. In leaving it, I shall not leave its lesson, trust me. Let us go!"

Still the Ghost pointed with an unmoved finger to the head.

"I understand you," Scrooge returned, "and I would do it, if I could. But I have not the power, Spirit. I have not the power."

Again it seemed to look upon him.

"If there is any person in the town, who feels emotion caused by this man's death," said Scrooge quite agonized, "show that person to me, Spirit, I beseech you!"

The phantom spread its dark robe before him for a moment, like a wing; and withdrawing it, revealed a room by daylight, where a mother and her children were.

She was expecting some one, and with anxious eagerness; for she walked up and down the room; started at every sound; looked out from the window; glanced at the clock; tried, but in vain, to work with her needle; and could hardly bear the voices of the children in their play.

At length the long-expected knock was heard. She hurried to the door, and met her husband; a man whose face was care-worn and depressed, though he was young. There was a remarkable expression in it now; a kind of serious delight of which he felt ashamed, and which he struggled to repress.

He sat down to the dinner that had been hoarding[1] for him by the fire; and when she asked him faintly what news (which was not until after a long silence), he appeared embarrassed how to answer.

"Is it good," she said, "or bad?" — to help him.

"Bad," he answered.

"We are quite ruined?"

"No. There is hope yet, Caroline."

"If *he* relents," she said, amazed, "there is! Nothing is past hope, if such a miracle has happened."

"He is past relenting," said her husband. "He is dead."

She was a mild and patient creature if her face spoke truth; but she was thankful in her soul to hear it, and she said so, with clasped hands. She prayed forgiveness the next moment, and was sorry; but the first was the emotion of her heart.

"What the half-drunken woman whom I told you of last night, said to me, when I tried to see him and obtain a week's delay; and what I thought was a mere excuse to avoid me; turns out to have been quite true. He was not only very ill, but dying, then."

"To whom will our debt be transferred?"

"I don't know. But before that time we shall be ready with the money; and even though we were not, it would be bad fortune indeed to find so merciless a creditor in his successor. We may sleep to-night with light hearts, Caroline!"

Yes. Soften it as they would, their hearts were lighter. The children's faces hushed, and clustered round to hear what they so little understood, were brighter; and it was a happier house for this man's death! The only emotion that the Ghost could show him, caused by the event, was one of pleasure.

"Let me see some tenderness connected with a death," said Scrooge; "or that dark chamber, Spirit, which we left just now, will be for ever present to me."

The Ghost conducted him through several streets familiar to his feet; and as they went along, Scrooge looked here and there to find himself, but nowhere was he to be seen. They entered poor Bob Cratchit's house; the dwelling he had visited before; and found the mother and the children seated round the fire.

---

1 Kept warm for him by the fire.

Quiet. Very quiet. The noisy little Cratchits were as still as statues in one corner, and sat looking up at Peter, who had a book before him. The mother and her daughters were engaged in sewing. But surely they were very quiet!

"'And He took a child, and set him in the midst of them.'"

Where had Scrooge heard those words? He had not dreamed them. The boy must have read them out, as he and the Spirit crossed the threshold. Why did he not go on?

The mother laid her work upon the table, and put her hand up to her face.

"The colour hurts my eyes," she said.

The colour?[1] Ah, poor Tiny Tim!

"They're better now again," said Cratchit's wife. "It makes them weak by candle-light; and I wouldn't show weak eyes to your father when he comes home, for the world. It must be near his time."

"Past it rather," Peter answered, shutting up his book. "But I think he's walked a little slower than he used, these few last evenings, mother."

They were very quiet again. At last she said, and in a steady cheerful voice, that only faultered once:

"I have known him walk with—I have known him walk with Tiny Tim upon his shoulder, very fast indeed."

"And so have I," cried Peter. "Often."

"And so have I!" exclaimed another. So had all.

"But he was very light to carry," she resumed, intent upon her work, "and his father loved him so, that it was no trouble—no trouble. And there is your father at the door!"

She hurried out to meet him; and little Bob in his comforter—he had need of it, poor fellow—came in. His tea was ready for him on the hob, and they all tried who should help him to it most. Then the two young Cratchits got upon his knees and laid, each child a little cheek, against his face, as if they said, "Don't mind it, father. Don't be grieved!"

Bob was very cheerful with them, and spoke pleasantly to all the family. He looked at the work upon the table, and praised the indus-

---

1   Mrs. Cratchit and her daughters are sewing their mourning clothes in preparation for Tiny Tim's death. In the manuscript Dickens had written *black* but then crossed it out.

try and speed of Mrs. Cratchit and the girls. They would be done long before Sunday he said.

"Sunday! You went to-day then, Robert?" said his wife.

"Yes, my dear," returned Bob. "I wish you could have gone. It would have done you good to see how green a place it is. But you'll see it often. I promised him that I would walk there on a Sunday. My little, little child!" cried Bob. "My little child!"

He broke down all at once. He couldn't help it. If he could have helped it, he and his child would have been farther apart perhaps than they were.

He left the room, and went up stairs into the room above, which was lighted cheerfully, and hung with Christmas. There was a chair set close beside the child, and there were signs of some one having been there, lately. Poor Bob sat down in it, and when he had thought a little and composed himself, he kissed the little face. He was reconciled to what had happened, and went down again quite happy.

They drew about the fire, and talked; the girls and mother working still. Bob told them of the extraordinary kindness of Mr. Scrooge's nephew, whom he had scarcely seen but once, and who, meeting him in the street that day, and seeing that he looked a little — "just a little down you know" said Bob, enquired what had happened to distress him. "On which," said Bob, "for he is the pleasantest-spoken gentleman you ever heard, I told him. 'I am heartily sorry for it, Mr. Cratchit,' he said, 'and heartily sorry for your good wife.' By the bye, how he ever knew that, I don't know."

"Knew what, my dear?"

"Why, that you were a good wife," replied Bob.

"Everybody knows that!" said Peter.

"Very well observed, my boy!" cried Bob. "I hope they do. 'Heartily sorry,' he said, 'for your good wife. If I can be of service to you in any way,' he said, giving me his card, 'that's where I live. Pray come to me.' Now, it wasn't," cried Bob, "for the sake of anything he might be able to do for us, so much as for his kind way, that this was quite delightful. It really seemed as if he had known our Tiny Tim, and felt with us."

"I'm sure he's a good soul!" said Mrs. Cratchit.

"You would be surer of it, my dear," returned Bob, "if you saw and spoke to him. I shouldn't be at all surprised, mark what I say, if he got Peter a better situation."

"Only hear that, Peter," said Mrs. Cratchit.

"And then," cried one of the girls, "Peter will be keeping company with some one, and setting up for himself."

"Get along with you!" retorted Peter, grinning.

"It's just as likely as not," said Bob, "one of these days; though there's plenty of time for that, my dear. But however and whenever we part from one another, I am sure we shall none of us forget poor Tiny Tim—shall we—or this first parting that there was among us?"

"Never, father!" cried they all.

"And I know," said Bob, "I know, my dears, that when we recollect how patient and how mild he was; although he was a little, little child; we shall not quarrel easily among ourselves, and forget poor Tiny Tim in doing it."

"No, never, father!" they all cried again.

"I am very happy," said little Bob, "I am very happy!"

Mrs. Cratchit kissed him, his daughters kissed him, the two young Cratchits kissed him, and Peter and himself shook hands. Spirit of Tiny Tim, thy childish essence was from God!

"Spectre," said Scrooge, "something informs me that our parting moment is at hand. I know it, but I know not how. Tell me what man that was whom we saw lying dead?"

The Ghost of Christmas Yet To Come conveyed him, as before— though at a different time, he thought: indeed, there seemed no order in these latter visions, save that they were in the Future—into the resorts of business men, but showed him not himself. Indeed, the Spirit did not stay for anything, but went straight on, as to the end just now desired, until besought by Scrooge to tarry for a moment.

"This court," said Scrooge, "through which we hurry now, is where my place of occupation is, and has been for a length of time. I see the house. Let me behold what I shall be, in days to come."

The Spirit stopped; the hand was pointed elsewhere.

"The house is yonder," Scrooge exclaimed. "Why do you point away?"

The inexorable finger underwent no change. Scrooge hastened to the window of his office, and looked in. It was an office still, but not his. The furniture was not the same, and the figure in the chair was not himself. The Phantom pointed as before.

He joined it once again, and wondering why and whither he had gone, accompanied it until they reached an iron gate. He paused to look round before entering.

A churchyard. Here, then, the wretched man whose name he had now to learn, lay underneath the ground. It was a worthy place. Walled in by houses; overrun by grass and weeds, the growth of vegetation's death, not life; choked up with too much burying; fat with repleted appetite. A worthy place!

The Spirit stood among the graves, and pointed down to One. He advanced towards it trembling. The Phantom was exactly as it had been, but he dreaded that he saw new meaning in its solemn shape.

"Before I draw nearer to that stone to which you point," said Scrooge, "answer me one question. Are these the shadows of the things that Will be, or are they shadows of the things that May be, only?"

Still the Ghost pointed downward to the grave by which it stood.

"Men's courses will foreshadow certain ends, to which, if persevered in, they must lead," said Scrooge. "But if the courses be departed from, the ends will change. Say it is thus with what you show me!"

The Spirit was immovable as ever.

Scrooge crept towards it, trembling as he went; and following the finger, read upon the stone of the neglected grave his own name, EBENEZER SCROOGE.

"Am *I* that man who lay upon the bed?" he cried, upon his knees.

The finger pointed from the grave to him, and back again.

"No, Spirit! Oh no, no!"

The finger still was there.

"Spirit!" he cried, tight clutching at its robe, "hear me! I am not the man I was. I will not be the man I must have been but for this intercourse. Why show me this, if I am past all hope?" For the first time the hand appeared to shake.

"Good Spirit," he pursued, as down upon the ground he fell

before it: "Your nature intercedes for me, and pities me. Assure me that I yet may change these shadows you have shown me, by an altered life!"

The kind hand trembled.

"I will honour Christmas in my heart, and try to keep it all the year. I will live in the Past, the Present, and the Future. The Spirits of all Three shall strive within me. I will not shut out the lessons that they teach. Oh, tell me I may sponge away the writing on this stone!"

In his agony, he caught the spectral hand. It sought to free itself, but he was strong in his entreaty, and detained it. The Spirit, stronger yet, repulsed him.

Holding up his hands in one last prayer to have his fate reversed, he saw an alteration in the Phantom's hood and dress. It shrunk, collapsed, and dwindled down into a bedpost.

STAVE FIVE.

THE END OF IT.

YES! and the bedpost was his own. The bed was his own, the room was his own. Best and happiest of all, the Time before him was his own, to make amends in!

"I will live in the Past, the Present, and the Future!" Scrooge repeated, as he scrambled out of bed. "The Spirits of all Three shall strive within me. Oh Jacob Marley! Heaven, and the Christmas Time be praised for this! I say it on my knees, old Jacob; on my knees!"

He was so fluttered and so glowing with his good intentions, that his broken voice would scarcely answer to his call. He had been sobbing violently in his conflict with the Spirit, and his face was wet with tears.

"They are not torn down," cried Scrooge, folding one of his bed-curtains in his arms, "they are not torn down, rings and all. They are here: I am here: the shadows of the things that would have been, may be dispelled. They will be. I know they will!"

His hands were busy with his garments all this time: turning them inside out, putting them on upside down, tearing them, mislaying them, making them parties to every kind of extravagance.

"I don't know what to do!" cried Scrooge, laughing and crying in the same breath; and making a perfect Laocoön[1] of himself with his stockings. "I am as light as a feather, I am as happy as an angel. I am as merry as a school-boy. I am as giddy as a drunken man. A merry Christmas to everybody! A happy New Year to all the world. Hallo here! Whoop! Hallo!"

He had frisked into the sitting-room, and was now standing there: perfectly winded.

"There's the saucepan that the gruel was in!" cried Scrooge, starting off again, and frisking round the fire-place. "There's the door, by

---

1 Laocoön and his two sons were crushed to death by sea serpents because Laocoön offend-ed Athena by attempting to convince his countrymen not to drag the wooden horse into Troy. The allusion conjures up a mock-heroic image of Scrooge caught up in the coils of his stockings.

which the Ghost of Jacob Marley entered! There's the corner where the Ghost of Christmas Present, sat! There's the window where I saw the wandering Spirits! It's all right, it's all true, it all happened. Ha ha ha!"

Really, for a man who had been out of practice for so many years, it was a splendid laugh, a most illustrious laugh. The father of a long, long, line of brilliant laughs!

"I don't know what day of the month it is!" said Scrooge. "I don't know how long I've been among the Spirits. I don't know anything. I'm quite a baby. Never mind. I don't care. I'd rather be a baby. Hallo! Whoop! Hallo here!"

He was checked in his transports by the churches ringing out the lustiest peals he had ever heard. Clash, clang, hammer, ding, dong, bell. Bell, dong, ding, hammer, clang, clash! Oh, glorious, glorious!

Running to the window, he opened it, and put out his head. No fog, no mist; clear, bright, jovial, stirring, cold; cold, piping for the blood to dance to; Golden sunlight; Heavenly sky; sweet fresh air; merry bells. Oh, glorious. Glorious!

"What's to-day?" cried Scrooge, calling downward to a boy in Sunday clothes, who perhaps had loitered in to look about him.

"Eh?" returned the boy, with all his might of wonder.

"What's to-day, my fine fellow?" said Scrooge.

"To-day!" replied the boy. "Why, CHRISTMAS DAY."

"It's Christmas Day!" said Scrooge to himself. "I haven't missed it. The Spirits have done it all in one night. They can do anything they like. Of course they can. Of course they can. Hallo, my fine fellow!"

"Hallo!" returned the boy.

"Do you know the Poulterer's, in the next street but one, at the corner?" Scrooge inquired.

"I should hope I did," replied the lad.

"An intelligent boy!" said Scrooge. "A remarkable boy! Do you know whether they've sold the prize Turkey that was hanging up there? Not the little prize Turkey: the big one?"

"What, the one as big as me?" returned the boy.

"What a delightful boy!" said Scrooge. "It's a pleasure to talk to him. Yes, my buck!"

"It's hanging there now," replied the boy.

"Is it?" said Scrooge. "Go and buy it."

"Walk-ER!"[1] exclaimed the boy.

"No, no," said Scrooge, "I am in earnest. Go and buy it, and tell 'em to bring it here, that I may give them the direction where to take it. Come back with the man, and I'll give you a shilling. Come back with him in less than five minutes, and I'll give you half-a-crown!"

The boy was off like a shot. He must have had a steady hand at a trigger who could have got a shot off half so fast.

"I'll send it to Bob Cratchit's!" whispered Scrooge, rubbing his hands, and splitting with a laugh. "He sha'n't know who sends it. It's twice the size of Tiny Tim. Joe Miller[2] never made such a joke as sending it to Bob's will be!"

The hand in which he wrote the address was not a steady one, but write it he did, somehow, and went down stairs to open the street door, ready for the coming of the poulterer's man. As he stood there, waiting his arrival, the knocker caught his eye.

"I shall love it, as long as I live!" cried Scrooge, patting it with his hand. "I scarcely ever looked at it before. What an honest expression it has in its face! It's a wonderful knocker!—Here's the Turkey. Hallo! Whoop! How are you! Merry Christmas!"

It *was* a Turkey! He never could have stood upon his legs, that bird. He would have snapped 'em short off in a minute, like sticks of sealing-wax.

"Why, it's impossible to carry that to Camden Town," said Scrooge. "You must have a cab."

The chuckle with which he said this, and the chuckle with which he paid for the Turkey, and the chuckle with which he paid for the cab, and the chuckle with which he recompensed the boy, were only to be exceeded by the chuckle with which he sat down breathless in his chair again, and chuckled till he cried.

Shaving was not an easy task, for his hand continued to shake very much; and shaving requires attention, even when you don't dance while you are at it. But if he had cut the end of his nose off, he would have put a piece of sticking-plaister over it, and been quite satisfied.

---

1   A Cockney expression of disbelief or surprise.
2   Joe Miller was a comic actor (1684-1738) whose jokes were collected by John Mottley in *Joe Miller's Jests* (1739).

He dressed himself "all in his best," and at last got out into the streets. The people were by this time pouring forth, as he had seen them with the Ghost of Christmas Present; and walking with his hands behind him, Scrooge regarded every one with a delighted smile. He looked so irresistibly pleasant, in a word, that three or four good-humoured fellows said, "Good morning, sir! A merry Christmas to you!" And Scrooge said often afterwards, that of all the blithe sounds he had ever heard, those were the blithest in his ears.

He had not gone far, when coming on towards him he beheld the portly gentleman, who had walked into his counting-house the day before and said, "Scrooge and Marley's, I believe?" It sent a pang across his heart to think how this old gentleman would look upon him when they met; but he knew what path lay straight before him, and he took it.

"My dear sir," said Scrooge, quickening his pace, and taking the old gentleman by both his hands. "How do you do? I hope you succeeded yesterday. It was very kind of you. A merry Christmas to you, sir!"

"Mr. Scrooge?"

"Yes," said Scrooge. "That is my name, and I fear it may not be pleasant to you. Allow me to ask your pardon. And will you have the goodness" — here Scrooge whispered in his ear.

"Lord bless me!" cried the gentleman, as if his breath were gone. "My dear Mr. Scrooge, are you serious?"

"If you please," said Scrooge. "Not a farthing less. A great many back-payments are included in it, I assure you. Will you do me that favour?"

"My dear sir," said the other, shaking hands with him. "I don't know what to say to such munifi—"

"Don't say anything, please," retorted Scrooge. "Come and see me. Will you come and see me?"

"I will!" cried the old gentleman. And it was clear he meant to do it.

"Thank 'ee," said Scrooge. "I am much obliged to you. I thank you fifty times. Bless you!"

He went to church, and walked about the streets, and watched the people hurrying to and fro, and patted children on the head, and questioned beggars, and looked down into the kitchens of houses, and up to the windows; and found that everything could yield him pleasure. He had never dreamed that any walk—that anything—could give him so much happiness. In the afternoon, he turned his steps towards his nephew's house.

He passed the door a dozen times, before he had the courage to go up and knock. But he made a dash, and did it:

"Is your master at home, my dear?" said Scrooge to the girl. Nice girl! Very.

"Yes, sir."

"Where is he, my love?" said Scrooge.

"He's in the dining-room, sir, along with mistress. I'll show you up stairs, if you please."

"Thank'ee. He knows me," said Scrooge, with his hand already on the dining-room lock. "I'll go in here, my dear."

He turned it gently, and sidled his face in, round the door. They were looking at the table (which was spread out in great array); for these young housekeepers are always nervous on such points, and like to see that everything is right.

"Fred!" said Scrooge.

Dear heart alive, how his niece by marriage started! Scrooge had forgotten, for the moment, about her sitting in the corner with the footstool, or he wouldn't have done it, on any account.

"Why bless my soul!" cried Fred, "who's that?"

"It's I. Your uncle Scrooge. I have come to dinner. Will you let me in, Fred?"

Let him in! It is a mercy he didn't shake his arm off. He was at home in five minutes. Nothing could be heartier. His niece looked just the same. So did Topper when *he* came. So did the plump sister, when *she* came. So did every one when *they* came. Wonderful party, wonderful games, wonderful unanimity, won-der-ful happiness!

But he was early at the office next morning. Oh he was early there. If he could only be there first, and catch Bob Cratchit coming late! That was the thing he had set his heart upon.

And he did it; yes he did! The clock struck nine. No Bob. A quarter past. No Bob. He was full eighteen minutes and a half, behind his time. Scrooge sat with his door wide open, that he might see him come into the Tank.

His hat was off, before he opened the door; his comforter too. He was on his stool in a jiffy; driving away with his pen, as if he were trying to overtake nine o'clock.

"Hallo!" growled Scrooge, in his accustomed voice as near as he could feign it. "What do you mean by coming here at this time of day?"

"I'm very sorry, sir," said Bob. "I am behind my time."

"You are?" repeated Scrooge. "Yes. I think you are. Step this way, if you please."

"It's only once a year, sir," pleaded Bob, appearing from the Tank. "It shall not be repeated. I was making rather merry yesterday, sir."

"Now, I'll tell you what, my friend," said Scrooge, "I am not going to stand this sort of thing any longer. And therefore," he continued, leaping from his stool, and giving Bob such a dig in the waistcoat that he staggered back into the Tank again: "and therefore I am about to raise your salary!"

Bob trembled, and got a little nearer to the ruler. He had a momentary idea of knocking Scrooge down with it; holding him; and calling to the people in the court for help and a strait-waistcoat.[1]

"A merry Christmas, Bob!" said Scrooge, with an earnestness that could not be mistaken, as he clapped him on the back. "A merrier Christmas, Bob, my good fellow, than I have given you, for many a year! I'll raise your salary, and endeavour to assist your struggling family, and we will discuss your affairs this very afternoon, over a Christmas bowl of smoking bishop,[2] Bob! Make up the fires, and buy another coal-scuttle before you dot another i, Bob Cratchit!"

Scrooge was better than his word. He did it all, and infinitely more; and to Tiny Tim, who did NOT die, he was a second father.[3] He became as good a friend, as good a master, and as good a man, as the good old city knew, or any other good old city, town, or borough, in the good old world. Some people laughed to see the alteration in him, but he let them laugh, and little heeded them; for he

1 Strait-jacket.

2 A Christmas punch made by pouring hot red wine over ripe bitter oranges, and then adding sugar, cloves, and cinnamon. The name of the drink comes from its purple color, like that of a bishop's cassock.

3 "And to Tiny Tim, who did NOT die, he was a second father" does not appear in the original manuscript. Dickens made the last-minute addition apparently to clarify the fate of Tiny Tim and to demonstrate the power of Scrooge's beneficence.

was wise enough to know that nothing ever happened on this globe, for good, at which some people did not have their fill of laughter in the outset; and knowing that such as these would be blind anyway, he thought it quite as well that they should wrinkle up their eyes in grins, as have the malady in less attractive forms. His own heart laughed: and that was quite enough for him.

He had no further intercourse with Spirits, but lived upon the Total Abstinence Principle,[1] ever afterwards; and it was always said of him, that he knew how to keep Christmas well, if any man alive possessed the knowledge. May that be truly said of us, and all of us! And so, as Tiny Tim observed, God Bless Us, Every One!

THE END

---

1   A pun, suggesting his abstinence from alcoholic and supernatural spirits.

Appendix A: Reflections on Christmas

1. Washington Irving, from *The Sketch Book* (1819-20)

CHRISTMAS EVE.

It was a brilliant moonlight night, but extremely cold; our chaise whirled rapidly over the frozen ground; the post-boy smacked his whip incessantly, and a part of the time his horses were on a gallop. "He knows where he is going," said my companion, laughing, "and is eager to arrive in time for some of the merriment and good cheer of the servants' hall. My father, you must know, is a bigoted devotee of the old school, and prides himself upon keeping up something of old English hospitality. He is a tolerable specimen of what you will rarely meet with now-a-days in its purity, the old English country gentleman; for our men of fortune spend so much of their time in town, and fashion is carried so much into the country, that the strong rich peculiarities of ancient rural life are almost polished away. My father, however, from early years, took honest Peacham[1] for his text book, instead of Chesterfield:[2] he determined, in his own mind, that there was no condition more truly honourable and enviable than that of a country gentleman on his paternal lands, and, therefore, passes the whole of his time on his estate. He is a strenuous advocate for the revival of the old rural games and holiday observances, and is deeply read in the writers, ancient and modern, who have treated on the subject. Indeed, his favourite range of reading is among the authors who flourished at least two centuries since; who, he insists, wrote and thought more like true Englishmen than any of their successors. He even regrets sometimes that he had not been born a few centuries earlier, when England was itself, and had its peculiar manners and customs. As he lives at some distance from the main road, in rather a lonely part of the country, without any rival gentry near him, he has that most enviable of all blessings to an Englishman, an opportunity of indulging the bent of his own humour without molestation. Being representative of the oldest family in the neighbourhood, and a great part of the peasantry being his tenants, he is much looked up to, and, in general, is known simply by the appellation of 'The Squire;' a title which has been accorded to the head of the

---

1 Henry Peacham (1576-1643), author of *The Compleat Gentleman* (1622), in which he offers his vision of the ideal Englishman.
2 Philip Dormer Stanhope, fourth Earl of Chesterfield (1694-1773), author of *Letters to His Son* (1774), a work filled with worldly advice originally designed for the education of his illegitimate son, Philip Stanhope.

family since time immemorial. I think it best to give you these hints about my worthy old father, to prepare you for any little eccentricities that might otherwise appear absurd."

★　　★　　★

The family meeting was warm and affectionate; as the evening was far advanced, the Squire would not permit us to change our travelling dresses, but ushered us at once to the company, which was assembled in a large old-fashioned hall. It was composed of different branches of a numerous family connection, where there were the usual proportion of old uncles and aunts, comfortably married dames, superannuated spinsters, blooming country cousins, half-fledged striplings, and bright-eyed boarding-school hoydens. They were variously occupied; some at a round game of cards; others conversing around the fireplace; at one end of the hall was a group of the young folks, some nearly grown up, others of a more tender and budding age, fully engrossed by a merry game; and a profusion of wooden horses, penny trumpets, and tattered dolls, about the floor, showed traces of a troop of little fairy beings, who having frolicked through a happy day, had been carried off to slumber through a peaceful night.

While the mutual greetings were going on between Bracebridge and his relatives, I had time to scan the apartment. I have called it a hall, for so it had certainly been in old times, and the Squire had evidently endeavoured to restore it to something of its primitive state. Over the heavy projecting fireplace was suspended a picture of a warrior in armour, standing by a white horse, and on the opposite wall hung helmet, buckler, and lance. At one end an enormous pair of antlers were inserted in the wall, the branches serving as hooks on which to suspend hats, whips, and spurs; and in the corners of the apartment were fowling-pieces, fishing-rods, and other sporting implements. The furniture was of the cumbrous workmanship of former days, though some articles of modern convenience had been added, and the oaken floor had been carpeted; so that the whole presented an odd mixture of parlour and hall.

The grate had been removed from the wide overwhelming fireplace, to make way for a fire of wood, in the midst of which was an enormous log glowing and blazing, and sending forth a vast volume of light and heat; this I understood was the Yule-log, which the Squire was particular in having brought in and illumined on a Christmas eve, according to ancient custom.

It was really delightful to see the old Squire seated in his hereditary elbow-chair by the hospitable fireside of his ancestors, and looking around him like the sun of a system, beaming warmth and gladness to every heart.

Even the very dog that lay stretched at his feet, as he lazily shifted his position and yawned, would look fondly up in his master's face, wag his tail against the floor, and stretch himself again to sleep, confident of kindness and protection. There is an emanation from the heart in genuine hospitality which cannot be described, but is immediately felt, and puts the stranger at once at his ease. I had not been seated many minutes by the comfortable hearth of the worthy cavalier before I found myself as much at home as if I had been one of the family.

Supper was announced shortly after our arrival. It was served up in a spacious oaken chamber, the panels of which shone with wax, and around which were several family portraits decorated with holly and ivy. Beside the accustomed lights, two great wax tapers, called Christmas candles, wreathed with greens, were placed on a highly-polished buffet among the family plate. The table was abundantly spread with substantial fare; but the Squire made his supper of frumenty, a dish made of wheat cakes boiled in milk with rich spices, being a standing dish in old times for Christmas eve. I was happy to find my old friend, minced-pie, in the retinue of the feast; and finding him to be perfectly orthodox, and that I need not be ashamed of my predilection, I greeted him with all the warmth wherewith we usually greet an old and very genteel acquaintance.

The mirth of the company was greatly promoted by the humours of an eccentric personage whom Mr. Bracebridge always addressed with the quaint appellation of Master Simon. He was a tight brisk little man, with the air of an arrant old bachelor. His nose was shaped like the bill of a parrot; his face slightly pitted with the small-pox, with a dry perpetual bloom on it, like a frost-bitten leaf in autumn. He had an eye of great quickness and vivacity, with a drollery and lurking waggery of expression that was irresistible. He was evidently the wit of the family, dealing very much in sly jokes and inuendoes with the ladies, and making infinite merriment by harpings upon old themes; which, unfortunately, my ignorance of the family chronicles did not permit me to enjoy. It seemed to be his great delight during supper to keep a young girl next him in a continual agony of stifled laughter, in spite of her awe of the reproving looks of her mother, who sat opposite. Indeed, he was the idol of the younger part of the company, who laughed at everything he said or did, and at every turn of his countenance. I could not wonder at it; for he must have been a miracle of accomplishments in their eyes. He could imitate Punch and Judy;[1] make an old woman of his hand, with the assistance of a burnt cork and pocket-hand-

---

1 A English puppet play, popular with children, especially at Christmas time. Punch, a hunchback with a hook nose, is the quarrelsome husband of Judy, his nagging wife, whom he often beats with a stick.

kerchief: and cut an orange into such a ludicrous caricature, that the young folks were ready to die with laughing.

I was let briefly into his history by Frank Bracebridge. He was an old bachelor of a small independent income, which by careful management was sufficient for all his wants. He revolved through the family system like a vagrant comet in its orbit; sometimes visiting one branch, and sometimes another quite remote; as is often the case with gentlemen of extensive connections and small fortunes in England. He had a chirping buoyant disposition, always enjoying the present moment; and his frequent change of scene and company prevented his acquiring those rusty unaccommodating habits with which old bachelors are so uncharitably charged. He was a complete family chronicle, being versed in the genealogy, history, and intermarriages of the whole house of Bracebridge, which made him a great favourite with the old folks; he was a beau of all the elder ladies and superannuated spinsters, among whom he was habitually considered rather a young fellow, and he was a master of the revels among the children; so that there was not a more popular being in the sphere in which he moved than Mr. Simon Bracebridge. Of late years he had resided almost entirely with the Squire, to whom he had become a factotum, and whom he particularly delighted by jumping with his humour in respect to old times, and by having a scrap of an old song to suit every occasion. We had presently a specimen of his last-mentioned talent; for no sooner was supper removed, and spiced wines and other beverages peculiar to the season introduced, than Master Simon was called on for a good old Christmas song. He bethought himself for a moment, and then, with a sparkle of the eye, and a voice that was by no means bad, excepting that it ran occasionally into a falsetto, like the notes of a split reed, he quavered forth a quaint old ditty,—

> Now Christmas is come,
> Let us beat up the drum,
> And call all our neighbours together;
> And when they appear,
> Let us make them such cheer,
> As will keep out the wind and the weather, etc.

The supper had disposed every one to gaiety, and an old harper was summoned from the servants' hall, where he had been strumming all the evening, and to all appearance comforting himself with some of the Squire's home-brewed. He was a kind of hanger-on, I was told, of the establishment, and though ostensibly a resident of the village, was oftener to be found in the Squire's kitchen than his own home, the old gentleman being fond of the sound of "harp in hall."

The dance, like most dances after supper, was a merry one; some of the older folks joined in it, and the Squire himself figured down several couples with a partner with whom he affirmed he had danced at every Christmas for nearly half-a-century. Master Simon, who seemed to be a kind of connecting link between the old times and the new, and to be withal a little antiquated in the taste of his accomplishments, evidently piqued himself on his dancing, and was endeavouring to gain credit by the heel and toe, rigadoon,[1] and other graces of the ancient school; but he had unluckily assorted himself with a little romping girl from boarding-school, who, by her wild vivacity, kept him continually on the stretch, and defeated all his sober attempts at elegance;—such are the ill-assorted matches to which antique gentlemen are unfortunately prone!

★   ★   ★

The party now broke up for the night with the kind-hearted old custom of shaking hands. As I passed through the hall, on the way to my chamber, the dying embers of the *Yule-log* still sent forth a dusky glow; and had it not been the season when "no spirit dares stir abroad," I should have been half tempted to steal from my room at midnight, and peep whether the fairies might not be at their revels about the hearth.

My chamber was in the old part of the mansion, the ponderous furniture of which might have been fabricated in the days of the giants. The room was panneled with cornices of heavy carved-work, in which flowers and grotesque faces were strangely intermingled; and a row of black-looking portraits stared mournfully at me from the walls. The bed was of rich though faded damask, with a lofty tester, and stood in a niche opposite a bow-window. I had scarcely got into bed when a strain of music seemed to break forth in the air just below the window. I listened, and found it proceeded from a band, which I concluded to be the waits[2] from some neighbouring village. They went round the house, playing under the windows. I drew aside the curtains, to hear them more distinctly. The moonbeams fell through the upper part of the casement, partially lighting up the antiquated apartment. The sounds, as they receded, became more soft and aerial, and seemed to accord with quiet and moonlight. I listened and listened—they became more and more tender and remote, and, as they gradually died away, my head sank upon the pillow and I fell asleep.

---

1   A lively dance with a jumping step, popular in the seventeenth and eighteenth centuries.
2   Christmas carolers.

CHRISTMAS DAY.

[After attending a country church service, Irving and the Squire begin their return to Bracebridge Hall.]

On our way homeward his heart seemed overflowing with generous and happy feelings. As we passed over a rising ground which commanded something of a prospect, the sounds of rustic merriment now and then reached our ears; the Squire paused for a few moments, and looked around with an air of inexpressible benignity. The beauty of the day was of itself sufficient to inspire philanthropy. Notwithstanding the frostiness of the morning, the sun in his cloudless journey had acquired sufficient power to melt away the thin covering of snow from every southern declivity, and to bring out the living green which adorns an English landscape even in mid-winter. Large tracts of smiling verdure contrasted with the dazzling white-ness of the shaded slopes and hollows. Every sheltered bank, on which the broad rays rested, yielded its silver rill of cold and limpid water, glittering through the dripping grass; and sent up slight exhalations to contribute to the thin haze that hung just above the surface of the earth. There was something truly cheering in this triumph of warmth and verdure over the frosty thraldom of winter: it was, as the Squire observed, an emblem of Christmas hospitality, breaking through the chills of ceremony and selfish-ness, and thawing every heart into a flow. He pointed with pleasure to the indications of good cheer reeking from the chimneys of the comfortable farm-houses and low thatched cottages. "I love," said he, "to see this day well kept by rich and poor; it is a great thing to have one day in the year, at least, when you are sure of being welcome wherever you go, and of having, as it were, the world all thrown open to you; and I am almost disposed to join with Poor Robin, in his malediction of every churlish enemy to this honest festival: —

"Those who at Christmas do repine,
And would fain hence despatch him,
May they with old Duke Humphry dine,[1]
Or else may Squire Ketch[2] catch 'em."

---

1 To have no dinner to go to. Humphrey, Duke of Gloucester, son of Henry IV, was renowned for his hospitality. At his death it was reported that a monument would be erected to him in St. Paul's, but his body was interred at St. Albans. When the prome-naders left for dinner, the poor stay-behinds who had no dinner used to say to the gay sparks who asked if they were going, that they would stay a little longer and look for the monument of the "good duke."

2 John Ketch (d. 1686), commonly known as Jack Ketch, was a famous executioner.

The Squire went on to lament the deplorable decay of the games and amusements which were once prevalent at this season among the lower orders, and countenanced by the higher: when the old halls of castles and manor-houses were thrown open at daylight; when the tables were covered with brawn, and beef, and humming ale; when the harp and the carol resounded all day long, and when rich and poor were alike welcome to enter and make merry. "Our old games and local customs," said he, "had a great effect in making the peasant fond of his home, and the promotion of them by the gentry made him fond of his lord. They made the times merrier, and kinder, and better; and I can truly say, with one of our old poets,—

> "I like them well—the curious preciseness
> And all-pretended gravity of those
> That seek to banish hence these harmless sports,
> Have thrust away much ancient honesty."

"The nation," continued he, "is altered; we have almost lost our simple true-hearted peasantry. They have broken asunder from the higher classes, and seem to think their interests are separate. They have become too knowing, and begin to read newspapers, listen to alehouse politicians, and talk of reform. I think one mode to keep them in good humour in these hard times would be for the nobility and gentry to pass more time on their estates, mingle more among the country people, and set the merry old English games going again."

Such was the good Squire's project for mitigating public discontent; and, indeed, he had once attempted to put his doctrine in practice, and a few years before had kept open house during the holidays in the old style. The country people, however, did not understand how to play their parts in the scene of hospitality; many uncouth circumstances occurred; the manor was overrun by all the vagrants of the country, and more beggars drawn into the neighbourhood in one week than the parish officers could get rid of in a year. Since then, he had contented himself with inviting the decent part of the neighbouring peasantry to call at the hall on Christmas day, and distributing beef, and bread, and ale, among the poor, that they might make merry in their own dwellings.

★   ★   ★

THE CHRISTMAS DINNER.

The dinner was served up in the great hall, where the Squire always held his Christmas banquet. A blazing crackling fire of logs had been heaped on to warm the spacious apartment, and the flame went sparkling and wreathing up the wide-mouthed chimney. The great picture of the crusader and his white horse had been profusely decorated with greens for the occasion; and holly and ivy had likewise been wreathed round the helmet and weapons on the opposite wall, which I understood were the arms of the same warrior. I must own, by the by, I had strong doubts about the authenticity of the painting and armour as having belonged to the crusader, they certainly having the stamp of more recent days; but I was told that the painting had been so considered time out of mind; and that as to the armour, it had been found in a lumber room, and elevated to its present situation by the Squire, who at once determined it to be the armour of the family hero; and as he was absolute authority on all such subjects in his own household, the matter had passed into current acceptation. A sideboard was set out just under this chivalric trophy, on which was a display of plate that might have vied (at least in variety) with Belshazzar's[1] parade of the vessels of the temple; "flagons, cans, cups, beakers, goblets, basins, and ewers;" the gorgeous utensils of good companionship, that had gradually accumulated through many generations of jovial housekeepers. Before these stood the two Yule candles beaming like two stars of the first magnitude; other lights were distributed in branches, and the whole array glittered like a firmament of silver.

We were ushered into this banqueting scene with the sound of minstrelsy, the old harper being seated on a stool beside the fireplace, and twanging his instrument with a vast deal more power than melody. Never did Christmas board display a more goodly and gracious assemblage of countenances: those who were not handsome were, at least, happy; and happiness is a rare improver of your hard-favoured visage.

★   ★   ★

When the cloth was removed, the butler brought in a huge silver vessel of rare and curious workmanship, which he placed before the Squire. Its appearance was hailed with acclamation; being the Wassail Bowl, so renowned in Christmas festivity. The contents had been prepared by the Squire himself; for it was a beverage in the skilful mixture[2] of which he particularly prided himself; alleging that it was too abstruse and complex for the comprehension of an ordinary servant. It was a potation, indeed, that might well make the heart of a toper[3] leap within him; being composed of

---

1   Son of Nebuchadnezzar and the last king of Babylon.
2   Usually made of ale or wine spiced with roasted apples, nutmeg, sugar, toast, and ginger.
3   A heavy drinker.

the richest and raciest wines, highly spiced and sweetened, with roasted apples bobbing about the surface.

The old gentleman's whole countenance beamed with a serene look of indwelling delight, as he stirred this mighty bowl. Having raised it to his lips, with a hearty wish of a merry Christmas to all present, he sent it brimming round the board, for every one to follow his example, according to the primitive style pronouncing it "the ancient fountain of good feeling, where all hearts met together."

There was much laughing and rallying as the honest emblem of Christmas joviality circulated, and was kissed rather coyly by the ladies. When it reached Master Simon he raised it in both hands, and with the air of a boon companion struck up an old Wassail chanson:

> The browne bowle,
> The merry browne bowle,
> As it goes round about-a,
> Fill
> Still,
> Let the world say what it will,
> And drink your fill all out-a.

> The deep canne,
> The merry deep canne,
> As thou dost freely quaff-a,
> Sing,
> Fling,
> Be as merry as a king,
> And sound a lusty laugh-a.[1]

*   *   *

After the dinner-table was removed, the hall was given up to the younger members of the family, who, prompted to all kind of noisy mirth by the Oxonian and Master Simon, made its old walls ring with their merriment, as they played at romping games. I delight in witnessing the gambols of children, and particularly at this happy holiday-season, and could not help stealing out of the drawing-room on hearing one of their peals of laughter. I found them at the game of blindman's buff. Master Simon, who was the leader of their revels, and seemed on all occasions to fulfil the office of that

---

1   From "Poor Robin's Almanack." [Irving's note]

ancient potentate, the Lord of Misrule,[1] was blinded in the midst of the hall. The little beings were as busy about him as the mock fairies about Falstaff; pinching him, plucking at the skirts of his coat, and tickling him with straws. One fine blue-eyed girl of about thirteen, with her flaxen hair all in beautiful confusion, her frolic face in a glow, her frock half torn off her shoulders, a complete picture of a romp, was the chief tormentor; and from the slyness with which Master Simon avoided the smaller game, and hemmed this wild little nymph in corners, and obliged her to jump shrieking over chairs, I suspected the rogue of being not a whit more blinded than was convenient.

When I returned to the drawing-room, I found the company seated round the fire, listening to the parson, who was deeply ensconced in a high-backed oaken chair, the work of some cunning artificer of yore, which had been brought from the library for his particular accommodation. From this venerable piece of furniture, with which his shadowy figure and dark weazen face so admirably accorded, he was dealing forth strange accounts of the popular superstitions and legends of the surrounding country, with which he had become acquainted in the course of his antiquarian researches. I am half inclined to think that the old gentleman was himself somewhat tinctured with superstition, as men are very apt to be who live a recluse and studious life in a sequestered part of the country, and pore over black-letter tracts, so often filled with the marvellous and supernatural. He gave us several anecdotes of the fancies of the neighbouring peasantry, concerning the effigy of the crusader which lay on the tomb by the church altar. As it was the only monument of the kind in that part of the country, it had always been regarded with feelings of superstition by the goodwives of the village. It was said to get up from the tomb and walk the rounds of the churchyard in stormy nights, particularly when it thundered; and one old woman, whose cottage bordered on the churchyard, had seen it, through the windows of the church, when the moon shone, slowly pacing up and down the aisles. It was the belief that some wrong had been left unredressed by the deceased, or some treasure hidden, which kept the spirit in a state of trouble and restlessness. Some talked of gold and jewels buried in the tomb, over which the spectre kept watch; and there was a story current of a sexton in old times who endeavoured to break his way to the coffin at night; but just as he reached it, received a violent blow from the marble hand of the effigy, which stretched him senseless on the pavement. These tales were often laughed at by some of the sturdier among the rustics, yet when night came

---

1 The title "Lord of Misrule" stems from earlier centuries when a special officer was designated to preside over the Christmas festivities. He is also sometimes called "Abbot of Misrule" or "Master of Merry Disports."

on, there were many of the stoutest unbelievers that were shy of venturing alone in the footpath that led across the churchyard.

*   *   *

[Master Simon, an elderly bachelor and the wit of the family, conceives the idea of a Christmas mummery, a burlesque imitation of an ancient masque, in which the guests dress up in elaborate costumes and proceed to promenade and dance.]

Master Simon covered himself with glory by the stateliness with which, as Ancient Christmas, he walked a minuet with the peerless, though giggling, Dame Mince-Pie. It was followed by a dance of all the characters, which, from its medley of costumes, seemed as though the old family portraits had skipped down from their frames to join in the sport. Different centuries were figuring at cross hands and right and left; the dark ages were cutting pirouettes and rigadoons; and the days of Queen Bess jigging merrily down the middle, through a line of succeeding generations.

The worthy Squire contemplated these fantastic sports, and this resurrection of his old wardrobe, with the simple relish of childish delight. He stood chuckling and rubbing his hands, and scarcely hearing a word the parson said, notwithstanding that the latter was discoursing most authentically on the ancient and stately dance at the Paon, or Peacock, from which he conceived the minuet to be derived. For my part, I was in a continual excitement, from the varied scenes of whim and innocent gaiety passing before me. It was inspiring to see wild-eyed frolic and warmhearted hospitality breaking out from among the chills and glooms of winter, and old age throwing off his apathy, and catching once more the freshness of youthful enjoyment. I felt also an interest in the scene, from the consideration that these fleeting customs were posting fast into oblivion, and that this was, perhaps, the only family in England in which the whole of them were still punctiliously observed. There was a quaintness, too, mingled with all this revelry, that gave it a peculiar zest: it was suited to the time and place; and as the old Manor House almost reeled with mirth and wassail, it seemed echoing back the joviality of long-departed years.

[Source: *Old Christmas* (Tarrytown, NY: Sleepy Hollow Restorations, 1977) 43-45; 54-67; 72-74; 105-10; 121-23; 132-35; 142-47; 154-57.]

2. Charles Dickens, "A Christmas Dinner" (1836)

CHRISTMAS TIME! THAT MAN MUST BE A MISANTHROPE indeed, in whose breast something like a jovial feeling is not roused—in whose mind some pleasant associations are not awakened—by the recurrence of Christmas. There are people who will tell you that Christmas is not to them what it used to be; that each succeeding Christmas has found some cherished hope, or happy prospect, of the year before, dimmed or passed away; that the present only serves to remind them of reduced circumstances and straitened incomes—of the feasts they once bestowed on hollow friends, and of the cold looks that meet them now, in adversity and misfortune. Never heed such dismal reminiscences. There are few men who have lived long enough in the world, who cannot call up such thoughts any day in the year. Then do not select the merriest of the three hundred and sixty-five for your doleful recollections, but draw your chair nearer the blazing fire—fill the glass and send round the song—and if your room be smaller than it was a dozen years ago, or if your glass be filled with reeking punch, instead of sparkling wine, put a good face on the matter, and empty it offhand, and fill another, and troll off the old ditty you used to sing, and thank God it's no worse. Look on the merry faces of your children (if you have any) as they sit round the fire. One little seat may be empty;[1] one slight form that gladdened the father's heart, and roused the mother's pride to look upon, may not be there. Dwell not upon the past; think not that one short year ago, the fair child now resolving into dust, sat before you, with the bloom of health upon its cheek and the gaiety of infancy in its joyous eye. Reflect upon your present blessings—of which every man has many—not your misfortunes, of which all men have some. Fill your glass again, with a merry face and contented heart. Our life on it, but your Christmas shall be merry, and your new year a happy one!

Who can be insensible to the out-pourings of good feeling, and the honest interchange of affectionate attachment, which abound at this season of the year? A Christmas family-party! We know nothing in nature more delightful! There seems a magic in the very name of Christmas. Petty jealousies and discords are forgotten; social feelings are awakened, in bosoms to which they have long been strangers; father and son, or brother and sister, who have met and passed with averted gaze, or a look of cold recognition, for months before, proffer and return the cordial embrace, and bury their

---

1   Dickens echoes this passage a decade later in *A Christmas Carol*. While visiting the Cratchit home with Scrooge, the Ghost of Christmas Present foretells the likely fate of Tiny Tim: "I see a vacant seat ... in the poor chimney corner, and a crutch without an owner, carefully preserved."

past animosities in their present happiness. Kindly hearts that have yearned towards each other, but have been withheld by false notions of pride and self-dignity, are again reunited, and all is kindness and benevolence! Would that Christmas lasted the whole year through (as it ought), and that the prejudices and passions which deform our better nature, were never called into action among those to whom they should ever be strangers!

The Christmas family-party that we mean, is not a mere assemblage of relations, got up at a week or two's notice, originating this year, having no family precedent in the last, and not likely to be repeated in the next. No. It is an annual gathering of all the accessible members of the family, young or old, rich or poor; and all the children look forward to it, for two months beforehand, in a fever of anticipation. Formerly it was held at grandpapa's; but grandpapa getting old, and grandmamma getting old too, and rather infirm, they have given up housekeeping, and domesticated themselves with uncle George; so, the party always takes place at uncle George's house, but grandmamma sends in most of the good things, and grandpapa always *will* toddle down, all the way to Newgate-market, to buy the turkey, which he engages a porter to bring home behind him in triumph, always insisting on the man's being rewarded with a glass of spirits, over and above his hire, to drink "a merry Christmas and a happy new year" to aunt George. As to grandmamma, she is very secret and mysterious for two or three days before-hand, but not sufficiently so to prevent rumours getting afloat that she has purchased a beautiful new cap with pink ribbons for each of the servants, together with sundry books, and pen-knives, and pencil-cases, for the younger branches; to say nothing of divers secret additions to the order originally given by aunt George at the pastry-cook's, such as another dozen of mince pies for the dinner, and a large plum-cake for the children.

On Christmas-eve, grandmamma is always in excellent spirits, and after employing all the children during the day, in stoning the plums, and all that, insists, regularly every year, on uncle George coming down into the kitchen, taking off his coat, and stirring the pudding for half an hour or so, which uncle George good-humouredly does to the vociferous delight of the children and servants. The evening concludes with a glorious game of blind-man's buff, in an early stage of which grandpapa takes great care to be caught, in order that he may have an opportunity of displaying his dexterity.

On the following morning, the old couple, with as many of the children as the pew will hold, go to church in great state: leaving aunt George at home dusting decanters and filling castors, and uncle George carrying bottles into the dining-parlour, and calling for corkscrews, and getting into everybody's way.

When the church-party return to lunch, grandpapa produces a small sprig of mistletoe from his pocket, and tempts the boys to kiss their little cousins under it—a proceeding which affords both the boys and the old gentleman unlimited satisfaction, but which rather outrages grandmamma's ideas of decorum, until grandpapa says, that when he was just thirteen years and three months old *he* kissed grandmamma under a mistletoe too, on which the children clap their hands, and laugh very heartily, as do aunt George and uncle George; and grandmamma looks pleased, and says, with a benevolent smile, that grandpapa was an impudent young dog, on which the children laugh very heartily again, and grandpapa more heartily than any of them.

But all these diversions are nothing to the subsequent excitement when grandmamma in a high cap, and slate-coloured silk gown; and grandpapa with a beautifully plaited shirt-frill, and white neckerchief; seat themselves on one side of the drawing-room fire, with uncle George's children and little cousins innumerable, seated in the front, waiting the arrival of the expected visitors. Suddenly a hackney-coach is heard to stop, and uncle George who has been looking out of the window, exclaims, "Here's Jane!" on which the children rush to the door, and helter-skelter down stairs; and uncle Robert and aunt Jane, and the dear little baby, and the nurse, and the whole party, are ushered up stairs amidst tumultuous shouts of "Oh, my!" from the children, and frequently repeated warnings not to hurt baby from the nurse. And grandpapa takes the child, and grandmamma kisses her daughter, and the confusion of this first entry has scarcely subsided, when some other aunts and uncles with more cousins arrive, and the grown-up cousins flirt with each other, and so do the little cousins too, for that matter, and nothing is to be heard but a confused din of talking, laughing, and merriment.

A hesitating double knock at the street-door, heard during a momentary pause in the conversation, excites a general inquiry of "Who's that?" and two or three children, who have been standing at the window, announce in a low voice, that it's "poor aunt Margaret." Upon which, aunt George leaves the room to welcome the new comer; and grandmamma draws herself up, rather stiff and stately; for Margaret married a poor man without her consent, and poverty not being a sufficient weighty punishment for her offence, has been discarded by her friends, and debarred the society of her dearest relatives. But Christmas has come round, and the unkind feelings that have struggled against better dispositions during the year, have melted away before its genial influence, like half-formed ice beneath the morning sun. It is not difficult in a moment of angry feeling for a parent to denounce a disobedient child; but, to banish her at a period of general good will and hilarity, from the hearth, round which she has sat on so many anniversaries of the same day, expanding by slow degrees from infancy to girlhood, and then bursting, almost imperceptibly, into a woman, is widely different. The air of conscious rectitude, and cold forgiveness, which the old lady has assumed, sits ill upon her; and when the poor girl is led in by her sister, pale in looks and broken in hope—not from poverty, for that she could bear, but from the consciousness of undeserved neglect, and unmerited unkindness—it is easy to see how much of it is assumed. A momentary pause succeeds; the girl breaks suddenly from her sister and throws herself, sobbing, on her mother's neck. The father steps hastily forward, and takes her husband's hand. Friends crowd round to offer their hearty congratulations, and happiness and harmony again prevail.

As to the dinner, it's perfectly delightful—nothing goes wrong, and everybody is in the very best of spirits, and disposed to please and be pleased. Grandpapa relates a circumstantial account of the purchase of the turkey, with a slight digression relative to the purchase of previous turkeys, on former Christmas-days, which grandmamma corroborates in the minutest particular. Uncle George tells stories, and carves poultry, and takes wine, and jokes with the children at the side-table, and winks at the cousins that are making love, or being made love to, and exhilarates everybody with his good humour and hospitality; and when, at last, a stout servant staggers in with a gigantic pudding, with a sprig of holly in the top, there is such a laughing, and shouting, and clapping of little chubby hands, and kicking up of fat dumpy legs, as can only be equalled by the applause with which the astonishing feat of pouring lighted brandy into mince-pies, is received by the younger visitors. Then the dessert!—and the wine!—and the fun! Such beautiful speeches, and such songs, from aunt Margaret's husband, who turns out to be such a nice man, and so attentive to grandmamma! Even grandpapa not only sings his annual song with unprecedented vigour, but on being honoured with an unanimous encore, according to annual custom, actually comes out with a new one which nobody but grandmamma ever heard before; and a young scape-grace of a cousin, who has been in some disgrace with the old people, for certain heinous sins of omission and commission—neglecting to call, and persisting in drinking Burton ale—astonishes everybody into convulsions of laughter by volunteering the most extraordinary comic songs that ever were heard. And thus the evening passes, in a strain of rational good-will and cheerfulness, doing more to awaken the sympathies of every member of the party in behalf of his neighbour, and to perpetuate their good feeling, during the ensuing year, than half the homilies that have ever been written, by half the Divines that have ever lived.

[Source: Sketches by Boz, vol. 22, The Nonesuch Dickens (Bloomsbury, London: Nonesuch Press, 1937-38) 218-22.]

3. Charles Dickens, from *The Posthumous Papers of the Pickwick Club* (1836-37)

A good-humoured Christmas Chapter, containing an Account of a Wedding, and some other Sports besides; which, although in their way even as Good Customs as Marriage itself, are not quite so religiously kept up, in these Degenerate Times.

As brisk as bees, if not altogether as light as fairies, did the four Pickwickians assemble on the morning of the twenty second day of December, in the year of grace in which these, their faithfully recorded adventures, were undertaken and accomplished. Christmas was close at hand, in all his bluff and hearty honesty; it was the season of hospitality, merriment, and open-heartedness; the old year was preparing, like an ancient philosopher, to call his friends around him, and amid the sound of feasting and revelry to pass gently and calmly away. Gay and merry was the time; and right gay and merry were at least four of the numerous hearts that were gladdened by its coming.

And numerous indeed are the hearts to which Christmas brings a brief season of happiness and enjoyment. How many families whose members have been dispersed and scattered, far and wide, in the restless struggles of life, are then reunited, and meet once again in that happy state of companionship, and mutual goodwill, which is a source of such pure and unalloyed delight, and one so incompatible with the cares and sorrows of the world, that the religious belief of the most civilized nations, and the rude traditions of the roughest savages, alike number it among the first joys of a future condition of existence, provided for the blest and happy! How many old recollections and how many dormant sympathies does Christmas time awaken!

We write these words now, many miles distant from the spot at which, year after year, we met on that day, a merry and joyous circle. Many of the hearts that throbbed so gayly then have ceased to beat; many of the looks that shone so brightly then have ceased to glow; the hands we grasped have grown cold; the eyes we sought have hid their lustre in the grave, and yet the old house, the room, the merry voices and smiling faces, the jest, the laugh, the most minute and trivial circumstances connected with those happy meetings, crowd upon our mind at each recurrence of the season, as if the last assemblage had been but yesterday! Happy, happy Christmas, that can win us back to the delusions of our childish days; that can recall to the old man the pleasures of his youth; and transport the sailor and the traveller thousands of miles away, back to his own fireside and his quiet home!

But we are so taken up, and occupied, with the good qualities of this saint Christmas that we are keeping Mr. Pickwick and his friends waiting in the cold, on the outside of the Muggleton coach; which they have just attained, well wrapped up in greatcoats, shawls, and comforters. The portmanteaus and carpet-bags have been stowed away, and Mr. Weller and the guard are endeavouring to insinuate into the fore-boot a huge codfish several sizes too large for it; which is snugly packed up, in a long brown basket, with a layer of straw over the top; and which has been left to the last, in order that he may repose in safety on the half-dozen barrels of real native oysters, all the property of Mr. Pickwick, which have been arranged in regular order at the bottom of the receptacle. The interest displayed in Mr. Pickwick's countenance is most intense, as Mr. Weller and the guard try to squeeze the codfish into the boot, first head first, and then tail first, and then top upward, and then bottom upward, and then sidewise, and then longwise, all of which artifices the implacable codfish sturdily resists, until the guard accidentally hits him in the very middle of the basket, whereupon he suddenly disappears into the boot, and with him the head and shoulders of the guard himself, who, not calculating upon so sudden a cessation of the passive resistance of the codfish, experiences a very unexpected shock, to the unsmotherable delight of all the porters and bystanders. Upon this, Mr. Pickwick smiles with great good-humour, and drawing a shilling from his waistcoat pocket, begs the guard, as he picks himself out of the boot, to drink his health in a glass of hot brandy-and-water; at which the guard smiles, too, and Messrs. Snodgrass, Winkle, and Tupman, all smile in company. The guard and Mr. Weller disappear for five minutes; most probably to get the hot brandy and-water, for they smell very strongly of it when they return; the coachman mounts to the box, Mr. Weller jumps up behind, the Pickwickians pull their coats round their legs, and their shawls over their noses; the helpers pull the horse-cloths off, the coachman shouts out a cheery "All right," and away they go.

★   ★   ★

[The Pickwickians arrive at Dingley Dell, where they are guests of the hospitable Mr. Wardle.]

From the centre of the ceiling of this kitchen old Wardle had just suspended, with his own hands, a huge branch of mistletoe, and this same branch of mistletoe instantaneously gave rise to a scene of general and most delightful struggling and confusion; in the midst of which, Mr. Pickwick, with a gallantry that would have done honour to a descendant of Lady Tollimglower herself, took the old lady by the hand, led her beneath the mystic branch, and saluted her in all courtesy and decorum. The old lady submitted to this piece of practical politeness with all the dignity which befitted so important and serious a solemnity, but the younger ladies, not being so thoroughly imbued with a superstitious veneration for the custom; or imagining that the value of a salute is very much enhanced if it cost a little trouble to obtain it; screamed and struggled, and ran into corners, and threatened and remonstrated, and did everything but leave the room, until some of the less adventurous gentlemen were on the point of desisting, when they all at once found it useless to resist any longer, and submitted to be kissed with a good grace. Mr. Winkle kissed the young lady with the black eyes, and Mr. Snodgrass kissed Emily, and Mr. Weller, not being particular about the form of being under the mistletoe, kissed Emma and the other female servants, just as he caught them. As to the poor relations, they kissed everybody, not even excepting the plainer portion of the young lady visitors, who, in their excessive confusion, ran right under the mistletoe, as soon as it was hung up, without knowing it! Wardle stood with his back to the fire, surveying the whole scene, with the utmost satisfaction; and the fat boy took the opportunity of appropriating to his own use and summarily devouring, a . particularly fine mince pie, that had been carefully put by for somebody else.

Now, the screaming had subsided, and faces were in a glow, and curls in a tangle, and Mr. Pickwick, after kissing the old lady as before-mentioned, was standing under the mistletoe, looking with a very pleased countenance on all that was passing around him, when the young lady with the black eyes, after a little whispering with the other young ladies, made a sudden dart forward, and putting her arm round Mr. Pickwick's neck, saluted him affectionately on the left cheek; and before Mr. Pickwick distinctly knew what was the matter, he was surrounded by the whole body and kissed by every one of them.

It was a pleasant thing to see Mr. Pickwick in the centre of the group, now pulled this way, and then that, and first kissed on the chin, and then on the nose, and then on the spectacles; and to hear the peals of laughter which were raised on every side; but it was a still more pleasant thing to see Mr. Pickwick, blinded shortly afterward with a silk handkerchief, falling up against the wall, and scrambling into corners, and going through all the mysteries of blindman's buff, with the utmost relish for the game, until at last he caught one of the poor relations, and then had to evade the blindman himself, which he did with a nimbleness and agility that elicited the admiration and applause of all beholders. The poor relations caught the people who they thought would like it; and when the game flagged, got caught themselves. When they were all tired of blindman's buff, there was a great game at snapdragon,[1] and when fingers enough were burned with that, and all the raisins were gone, they sat down by the huge fire of blazing

---

1   A game in which raisins are plucked from burning brandy and quickly eaten.

logs, to a substantial supper, and a mighty bowl of wassail, something smaller than an ordinary washhouse copper, in which the hot apples were hissing and bubbling with a rich look, and a jolly sound, that were perfectly irresistible.

"This," said Mr. Pickwick, looking round him, "this is, indeed, comfort."

"Our invariable custom," replied Mr. Wardle. "Everybody sits down with us on Christmas Eve, as you see them now — servants and all; and here we wait, until the clock strikes twelve, to usher Christmas in, and beguile the time with forfeits and old stories. Trundle, my boy, rake up the fire."

Up flew the bright sparks in myriads as the logs were stirred. The deep red blaze sent forth a rich glow that penetrated into the furthest corner of the room and cast its cheerful tint on every face.

"Come," said Wardle, "a song—a Christmas song! I'll give you one, in default of a better."

"Bravo!" said Mr. Pickwick.

"Fill up," cried Wardle. "It will be two hours, good, before you see the bottom of the bowl through the deep rich colour of the wassail; fill up all round, and now for the song."

Thus saying, the merry old gentleman, in a good, sound, sturdy voice, commenced without more ado: [Sings a long song called "A Christmas Carol"].

This song was tumultuously applauded—for friends and dependents make a capital audience—and the poor relations, especially, were in perfect ecstasies of rapture. Again was the fire replenished, and again went the wassail round.

"How it snows!" said one of the men, in a low tone.

"Snows, does it?" said Wardle.

"Rough, cold night, sir," replied the man; "and there's a wind got up that drifts it across the fields in a thick white cloud."

"What does Jem say?" inquired the old lady. "There ain't anything the matter, is there?"

"No, no, mother," replied Wardle; "he says there's a snow-drift, and a wind that's piercing cold. I should know that, by the way it rumbles in the chimney."

"Ah!" said the old lady, "there was just such a wind, and just such a fall of snow, a good many years back, I recollect—just five years before your poor father died. It was a Christmas Eve, too; and I remember that on that very night he told us the story about the goblins that carried away old Gabriel Grub."

"The story about what?" said Mr. Pickwick.

"Oh, nothing—nothing," replied Wardle. "About an old sexton, that the good people down here suppose to have been carried away by goblins."

"Suppose!" ejaculated the old lady. "Is there anybody hardy enough to disbelieve it? Suppose! Haven't you heard, ever since you were a child, that he *was* carried away by the goblins, and don't you know he was?"

"Very well, mother, he was, if you like," said Wardle, laughing. "He *was* carried away by goblins, Pickwick; and there's an end of the matter."

"No, no," said Mr. Pickwick, "not an end of it, I assure you; for I must hear how, and why, and all about it."

Wardle smiled, as every head was bent forward to hear; and filling out the wassail with no stinted hand, nodded a health to Mr. Pickwick, and began as follows: —

"In an old abbey town, down in this part of the country, a long, long while ago — so long, that the story must be a true one, because our great grandfathers implicitly believed it — there officiated as sexton and gravedigger in the churchyard, one Gabriel Grub. It by no means follows that because a man is a sexton, and constantly surrounded by emblems of mortality, therefore he should be a morose and melancholy man; your undertakers are the merriest fellows in the world; and I once had the honour of being on intimate terms with a mute, who, in private life and off duty, was as comical and jocose a little fellow as ever chirped out a devil-may-care song, without a hitch in his memory, or drained off the contents of a good stiff glass without stopping for breath. But, notwithstanding these precedents to the contrary, Gabriel Grub was an ill-conditioned, cross-grained, surly fellow — a morose and lonely man, who consorted with nobody but himself, and an old wicker bottle which fitted into his large deep waistcoat pocket — and who eyed each merry face, as it passed him by, with such a deep scowl of malice and ill-humour as it was difficult to meet without feeling something the worse for.

"A little before twilight, one Christmas Eve, Gabriel shouldered his spade, lighted his lantern, and betook himself toward the old churchyard; for he had got a grave to finish by next morning, and, feeling very low, he thought it might raise his spirits, perhaps, if he went on with his work at once. As he went his way, up the ancient street, he saw the cheerful light of the blazing fires gleam through the old casements, and heard the loud laugh and the cheerful shouts of those who were assembled around them; he marked the bustling preparations for next day's cheer, and smelled the numerous savoury odours consequent thereupon, as they steamed up from the kitchen windows in clouds. All this was gall and wormwood to the heart of Gabriel Grub; and when groups of children bounded out of the houses, tripped across the road, and were met, before they could knock at the opposite door, by half a dozen curly-headed little rascals who crowded round them as they flocked upstairs to spend the evening in their Christmas games, Gabriel smiled grimly, and clutched the handle of his spade with a firmer grasp as he thought of measles, scarlet fever, thrush, whooping-cough, and a good many other sources of consolation besides.

"In this happy frame of mind, Gabriel strode along—returning a short sullen growl to the good-humoured greetings of such of his neighbours as now and then passed him—until he turned into the dark lane which led to the churchyard. Now, Gabriel had been looking forward to reaching the dark lane, because it was, generally speaking, a nice, gloomy, mournful place, into which the townspeople did not much care to go, except in broad daylight, and when the sun was shining; consequently, he was not a little indignant to hear a young urchin roaring out some jolly song about a merry Christmas in this very sanctuary, which had been called Coffin Lane ever since the days of the old abbey, and the time of the shaven-headed monks. As Gabriel walked on, and the voice drew nearer, he found it proceeded from a small boy, who was hurrying along to join one of the little parties in the old street, and who, partly to keep himself company, and partly to prepare himself for the occasion, was shouting out the song at the highest pitch of his lungs. So Gabriel waited until the boy came up, and then dodged him into a corner, and rapped him over the head with his lantern, five or six times, to teach him to modulate his voice. And as the boy hurried away with his hand to his head, singing quite a different sort of tune, Gabriel Grub chuckled very heartily to himself, and entered the churchyard, locking the gate behind him.

"He took off his coat, put down his lantern, and getting into the unfinished grave, worked at it for an hour or so with right good will. But the earth was hardened with the frost, and it was no very easy matter to break it up, and shovel it out; and although there was a moon, it was a very young one, and shed little light upon the grave, which was in the shadow of the church. At any other time, these obstacles would have made Gabriel Grub very moody and miserable, but he was so well pleased with having stopped the small boy's singing, that he took little heed of the scanty progress he had made, and looked down into the grave, when he had finished work for the night, with grim satisfaction; murmuring as he gathered up his things:

> Brave lodgings for one, brave lodgings for one,
> A few feet of cold earth, when life is done;
> A stone at the head, a stone at the feet,
> A rich, juicy meal for the worms to eat:
> Rank grass over head, and damp clay around,
> Brave lodgings for one, these, in holy ground!

"'Ho! ho!' laughed Gabriel Grub, as he sat himself down on a flat tomb-stone, which was a favourite resting-place of his, and drew forth his wicker bottle. 'A coffin at Christmas! A Christmas Box! Ho! ho! ho!'

"'Ho! ho! ho!' repeated a voice which sounded close behind him.

"Gabriel paused in some alarm, in the act of raising the wicker bottle to his lips, and looked round. The bottom of the oldest grave about him was not more still and quiet than the churchyard in the pale moonlight. The cold hoarfrost glistened on the tombstones, and sparkled like rows of gems among the stone carvings of the old church; the snow lay hard and crisp upon the ground, and spread over the thickly strewn mounds of earth so white and smooth a cover that it seemed as if corpses lay there, hidden only by their winding sheets. Not the faintest rustle broke the profound tran-quillity of the solemn scene. Sound itself appeared to be frozen up, all was so cold and still.

"'It was the echoes,' said Gabriel Grub, raising the bottle to his lips again.

"'It was *not*,' said a deep voice.

"Gabriel started up, and stood rooted to the spot with astonishment and terror; for his eyes rested on a form that made his blood run cold.

"Seated on an upright tombstone, close to him, was a strange, unearthly figure, whom Gabriel felt at once was no being of this world. His long fan-tastic legs, which might have reached the ground, were cocked up, and crossed after a quaint, fantastic fashion; his sinewy arms were bare; and his hands rested on his knees. On his short, round body he wore a close cover-ing, ornamented with small slashes; a short cloak dangled at his back; the collar was cut into curious peaks, which served the goblin in lieu of ruff or neckerchief; and his shoes curled up at the toes into long points. On his head he wore a broad brimmed sugar-loaf hat, garnished with a single feather. The hat was covered with the white frost; and the goblin looked as if he had sat on the same tombstone very comfortably for two or three hundred years. He was sitting perfectly still; his tongue was put out, as if in derision; and he was grinning at Gabriel Grub with such a grin as only a goblin could call up.

"'It was *not* the echoes,' said the goblin.

"Gabriel Grub was paralysed, and could make no reply.

"'What do you do here on Christmas Eve?' said the goblin, sternly.

"'I came to dig a grave, sir,' stammered Gabriel Grub.

"'What man wanders among graves and churchyards on such a night as this?' cried the goblin.

"'Gabriel Grub! Gabriel Grub!' screamed a wild chorus of voices that seemed to fill the churchyard. Gabriel looked fearfully round—nothing was to be seen.

"'What have you got in that bottle?' said the goblin.

"'Hollands,[1] sir,' replied the sexton, trembling more than ever; for he had bought it of the smugglers and he thought that perhaps his questioner might be in the excise department of the goblins.

"'Who drinks Hollands alone, and in a churchyard, on such a night as this?' said the goblin.

"'Gabriel Grub! Gabriel Grub!' exclaimed the wild voices again.

"The goblin leered maliciously at the terrified sexton, and then raising his voice, exclaimed:

"'And who, then, is our fair and lawful prize?'

"To this inquiry the invisible chorus replied, in a strain that sounded like the voices of many choristers singing to the mighty swell of the old church organ—a strain that seemed borne to the sexton's ears upon a wild wind, and to die away as it passed onward—but the burden of the reply was still the same, 'Gabriel Grub! Gabriel Grub!'

"The goblin grinned a broader grin than before, as he said, 'Well, Gabriel, what do you say to this?'

"The sexton gasped for breath.

"'What do you think of this, Gabriel?' said the goblin, kicking up his feet in the air on either side of the tombstone, and looking at the turned up points with as much complacency as if he had been contemplating the most fashionable pair of Wellingtons in all Bond Street.

"'It's—it's—very curious, sir,' replied the sexton, half dead with fright; 'very curious, and very pretty, but I think I'll go back and finish my work, sir, if you please.'

"'Work!' said the goblin; 'what work?'

"'The grave, sir; making the grave,' stammered the sexton.

"'Oh, the grave, eh?' said the goblin; 'who makes graves at a time when all other men are merry, and takes a pleasure in it?'

"Again the mysterious voices replied, 'Gabriel Grub! Gabriel Grub!'

"'I'm afraid my friends want you, Gabriel,' said the goblin, thrusting his tongue further into his cheek than ever—and a most astonishing tongue it was—'I'm afraid my friends want you, Gabriel,' said the goblin.

"'Under favour, sir,' replied the horror-stricken sexton, 'I don't think they can, sir; they don't know me, sir; I don't think the gentlemen have ever seen me, sir.'

"'Oh, yes, they have,' replied the goblin; 'we know the man with the sulky face and the grim scowl, that came down the street to-night, throwing his evil looks at the children, and grasping his burying spade the tighter. We know the man who struck the boy in the envious malice of his heart,

[1] Gin.

because the boy could be merry and he could not. We know him, we know him.'

"Here the goblin gave a loud shrill laugh, which the echoes returned twenty-fold; and throwing his legs up in the air, stood upon his head, or rather upon the very point of his sugar-loaf hat, on the narrow edge of the tombstone; whence he threw a summerset with extraordinary agility, right to the sexton's feet, at which he planted himself in the attitude in which tailors generally sit upon the shop-board.

"'I—I—am afraid I must leave you, sir,' said the sexton, making an effort to move.

"'Leave us!' said the goblin, 'Gabriel Grub going to leave us. Ho! ho! ho!'

"As the goblin laughed, the sexton observed, for one instant, a brilliant illumination within the windows of the church, as if the whole building were lighted up; it disappeared, the organ pealed forth a lively air, and whole troops of goblins, the very counterpart of the first one, poured into the churchyard, and began playing at leap-frog with the tombstones; never stopping for an instant to take breath, but 'overing' the highest among them, one after the other, with the most marvellous dexterity. The first goblin was a most astonishing leaper, and none of the others could come near him; even in the extremity of his terror the sexton could not help observing that while his friends were content to leap over the common-sized gravestones, the first one took the family vaults, iron railings and all, with as much ease as if they had been so many street posts.

"At last the game reached to a most exciting pitch; the organ played quicker and quicker; and the goblins leaped faster and faster; coiling themselves up, rolling head over heels upon the ground, and bounding over the tombstones like footballs. The sexton's brain whirled round with the rapidity of the motion he beheld, and his legs reeled beneath him as the spirits flew before his eyes; when the goblin king, suddenly darting toward him, laid his hand upon his collar, and sank with him through the earth.

"When Gabriel Grub had had time to fetch his breath, which the rapidity of his descent had for the moment taken away, he found himself in what appeared to be a large cavern, surrounded on all sides by crowds of goblins, ugly and grim; in the centre of the room, on an elevated seat, was stationed his friend of the churchyard; and close beside him stood Gabriel Grub himself, without the power of motion.

"'Cold to-night,' said the king of the goblins, 'very cold. A glass of something warm, here!'

"At this command, half-a-dozen officious goblins, with a perpetual smile upon their faces, whom Gabriel Grub imagined to be courtiers, on that account, hastily disappeared, and presently returned with a goblet of liquid fire, which they presented to the king.

"'Ah!' cried the goblin, whose cheeks and throat were transparent, as he tossed down the flame, 'this warms one, indeed! Bring a bumper of the same for Mr. Grub.'

"It was in vain for the unfortunate sexton to protest that he was not in the habit of taking anything warm at night; one of the goblins held him while another poured the blazing liquid down his throat; the whole assembly screeched with laughter as he coughed and choked, and wiped away the tears which gushed plentifully from his eyes, after swallowing the burning draught.

"'And now,' said the king, fantastically poking the taper corner of his sugar-loaf hat into the sexton's eye, and thereby occasioning him the most exquisite pain; 'and now show the man of misery and gloom a few of the pictures from our great storehouse!'

"As the goblin said this, a thick cloud which obscured the remoter end of the cavern rolled gradually away, and disclosed, apparently at a great distance, a small and scantily furnished, but neat and clean apartment. A crowd of little children were gathered round a bright fire, clinging to their mother's gown, and gambolling around her chair. The mother occasionally rose, and drew aside the window-curtain, as if to look for some expected object; a frugal meal was ready spread upon the table; and an elbow-chair was placed near the fire. A knock was heard at the door; the mother opened it, and the children crowded round her, and clapped their hands for joy as their father entered. He was wet and weary, and shook the snow from his garments, as the children crowded round him, and seizing his cloak, hat, stick, and gloves, with busy zeal, ran with them from the room. Then, as he sat down to his meal before the fire, the children climbed about his knee, and the mother sat by his side, and all seemed happiness and comfort.

"But a change came upon the view, almost imperceptibly. The scene was altered to a small bedroom, where the fairest and youngest child lay dying; the roses had fled from his cheek and the light from his eye; and even as the sexton looked upon him with an interest he had never felt or known before, he died. His young brothers and sisters crowded round his little bed, and seized his tiny hand, so cold and heavy; but they shrunk back from its touch, and looked with awe on his infant face; for calm and tranquil as it was, and sleeping in rest and peace as the beautiful child seemed to be, they saw that he was dead, and they knew that he was an Angel looking down upon, and blessing them from a bright and happy heaven.

"Again the light cloud passed across the picture, and again the subject changed. The father and mother were old and helpless now, and the number of those about them was diminished more than half; but content and cheerfulness sat on every face, and beamed in every eye, as they crowded round the fireside, and told and listened to old stories of earlier and bygone days. Slowly and peacefully the father sank into the grave, and, soon after, the sharer of all his cares and troubles followed him to a place of rest. The few who yet survived them, knelt by their tomb, and watered the green turf which covered it with their tears; then rose, and turned away; sadly and mournfully, but not with bitter cries or despairing lamentations, for they knew that they should one day meet again; and once more they mixed with the busy world, and their content and cheerfulness were restored. The cloud settled upon the picture, and concealed it from the sexton's view.

"'What do you think of *that*?' said the goblin, turning his large face toward Gabriel Grub.

"Gabriel murmured out something about its being very pretty, and looked somewhat ashamed, as the goblin bent his fiery eyes upon him.

"'*You* a miserable man!' said the goblin, in a tone of excessive contempt. 'You!' He appeared disposed to add more, but indignation choked his utterance, so he lifted up one of his very pliable legs, and flourishing it above his head a little, to insure his aim, administered a good sound kick to Gabriel Grub; immediately after which, all the goblins in waiting crowded round the wretched sexton, and kicked him without mercy; according to the established and invariable custom of courtiers upon earth, who kick whom royalty kicks, and hug whom royalty hugs.

"'Show him some more!' said the king of the goblins.

"At these words, the cloud was again dispelled, and a rich and beautiful landscape was disclosed to view—there is just such another, to this day, within half a mile of the old abbey town. The sun shone from out the clear blue sky, the water sparkled beneath his rays, and the trees looked greener, and the flowers more gay, beneath his cheering influence. The water rippled on with a pleasant sound; the trees rustled in the light wind that murmured among their leaves; the birds sang upon the boughs; and the lark caroled on high her welcome to the morning. Yes, it was morning; the bright, balmy morning of summer; the minutest leaf, the smallest blade of grass, was instinct with life. The ant crept forth to her daily toil, the butterfly fluttered and basked in the warm rays of the sun; myriads of insects spread their transparent wings, and revelled in their brief but happy existence. Man walked forth, elated with the scene; and all was brightness and splendour.

"'*You* a miserable man!' said the king of the goblins, in a more contemptuous tone than before. And again the king of the goblins gave his leg a flourish; again it descended on the shoulders of the sexton; and again the attendant goblins imitated the example of their chief.

"Many a time the cloud went and came, and many a lesson it taught to Gabriel Grub, who, although his shoulders smarted with pain from the frequent applications of the goblin's feet, looked on with an interest that nothing could diminish. He saw that men who worked hard, and earned their scanty bread with lives of labour, were cheerful and happy; and that to the most ignorant, the sweet face of Nature was a never-failing source of cheerfulness and joy. He saw those who had been delicately nurtured, and tenderly brought up, cheerful under privations, and superior to suffering, that would have crushed many of a rougher grain, because they bore within their own bosoms the materials of happiness, contentment, and peace. He saw that women, the tenderest and most fragile of all God's creatures, were the oftenest superior to sorrow, adversity, and distress; and he saw that it was because they bore, in their own hearts, an inexhaustible well-spring of affection and devotion. Above all, he saw that men like himself, who snarled at the mirth and cheerfulness of others, were the foulest weeds on the fair surface of the earth; and, setting all the good of the world against the evil, he came to the conclusion that it was a very decent and respectable sort of world, after all. No sooner had he formed it, than the cloud which had closed over the last picture seemed to settle on his senses, and lull him to repose. One by one the goblins faded from his sight; and as the last one disappeared, he sunk to sleep.

"The day had broken when Gabriel Grub awoke, and found himself lying, at full length, on the flat gravestone in the churchyard, with the wicker bottle lying empty by his side, and his coat, spade, and lantern, all well whitened by the last night's frost, scattered on the ground. The stone on which he had first seen the goblin seated stood bolt upright before him, and the grave at which he had worked, the night before, was not far off. At first, he began to doubt the reality of his adventures, but the acute pain in his shoulders when he attempted to rise assured him that the kicking of the goblins was certainly not ideal. He was staggered again by observing no traces of footsteps in the snow on which the goblins had played at leap-frog with the gravestones, but he speedily accounted for this circumstance when he remembered that, being spirits, they would leave no visible impression behind them. So, Gabriel Grub got on his feet as well as he could, for the pain in his back; and brushing the frost off his coat, put it on, and turned his face toward the town.

"But he was an altered man, and he could not bear the thought of returning to a place where his repentance would be scoffed at and his refor-mation disbelieved.[1] He hesitated for a few moments; and then turned away to wander where he might, and seek his bread elsewhere.

"The lantern, the spade, and the wicker bottle were found, that day, in the churchyard. There were a great many speculations about the sexton's fate, at first, but it was speedily determined that he had been carried away by the goblins; and there were not wanting some very credible witnesses

---

1 Unlike Scrooge, who "little heeded" those who laughed at his transformation.

who had distinctly seen him whisked through the air on the back of a chestnut horse blind of one eye, with the hind-quarters of a lion, and the tail of a bear. At length all this was devoutly believed; and the new sexton used to exhibit to the curious, for a trifling emolument, a good-sized piece of the church weathercock which had been accidentally kicked off by the aforesaid horse in his aerial flight, and picked up by himself in the church-yard, a year or two afterward.

"Unfortunately, these stories were somewhat disturbed by the unlooked-for reappearance of Gabriel Grub himself, some ten years afterward, a ragged, contented, rheumatic old man. He told his story to the clergyman, and also to the mayor; and in course of time it began to be received, as a matter of history, in which form it has continued down to this very day. The believers in the weathercock tale, having misplaced their confidence once, were not easily prevailed upon to part with it again, so they looked as wise as they could, shrugged their shoulders, touched their foreheads, and murmured something about Gabriel Grub having drunk all the Hollands, and then fallen asleep on the flat tombstone; and they affected to explain what he supposed he had witnessed in the goblin's cavern, by saying that he had seen the world, and grown wiser. But this opinion, which was by no means a popular one at any time, gradually died off; and be the matter how it may, as Gabriel Grub was afflicted with rheumatism to the end of his days, this story has at least one moral, if it teach no better one — and that is, that if a man turn sulky and drink by himself at Christmas time, he may make up his mind to be not a bit the better for it; let the spirits be never so good, or let them be even as many degrees beyond proof as those which Gabriel Grub saw in the goblin's cavern."

[Source: *The Posthumous Papers of the Pickwick Club*, vol. 20, *The Nonesuch Dickens* (Bloomsbury, London: Nonesuch Press, 1937-1938) 372-74; 389-403.]

4. Thomas K. Hervey, from *The Book of Christmas. Descriptions of the customs, ceremonies, traditions, superstitions, fun, feeling and festivities of the Christmas Season* (1837)

[Thomas Hervey (1799-1859) was a poet, critic, and book reviewer. A frequent contributor to the *Athenaeum*, from 1830, he became its editor in 1846 until 1853. His *Book of Christmas*, published in 1837 and illustrated by Robert Seymour (the first illustrator of Dickens's *Pickwick Papers*), was a seminal work in recalling the Christmas rituals and traditions of the past for the Victorians. It seems likely that Dickens was familiar with this fascinating book.]

To the philosophic inquirer, few things are more important in the annals of nations than their festivals, their anniversaries, and their public celebrations of all kinds. In nothing is their peculiar character more strikingly exhibited. They show a people in its undress, acting upon its impulses, and separated from the conventions and formalities of its every-day existence. We may venture to say that could we, in the absence of every other record, be furnished with a complete account of the festivals, traditions, and anniversaries of any given nation now extinct, not only might a correct estimate be therefrom made of their progress in morals and civilization, but a conjectural history of their doings be hazarded, which should bear a closer resemblance to the facts than many an existing history constructed from more varied materials.

For these reasons—and some others, which are more personal and less philosophical—we love all old traditions and holiday customs. Like honest Sir Andrew Aguecheek,[1] we "delight in masques and revels, sometimes altogether." Many a happy chance has conducted us unpremeditatedly into the midst of some rustic festival, whose recollection is amongst our pleasant memories yet,—and many a one have we gone venturously forth to seek,—when we dwelt in the more immediate neighborhood of the haunts to which, one by one, these traditionary observances are retiring before the face of civilization. The natural tendency of time to obliterate ancient customs and silence ancient sports, is too much promoted by the utilitarian spirit of the day; and they who would have no man enjoy without being able to give a reason for the enjoyment which is in him, are robbing life of half its beauty and some of its virtues. If the old festivals and hearty commemorations in which our land was once so abundant—and which obtained for her, many a long day since, the name of "merrie England"— had no other recommendation than their convivial character, the community of enjoyment which they imply, they would on that account alone be worthy of all promotion, as an antidote to the cold and selfish spirit which is tainting the life-blood and freezing the pulses of society. "'Tis good to be merry and wise;" but the wisdom which eschews mirth, and holds the time devoted to it as so much wasted by being taken from the schoolmaster, is very questionable wisdom in itself, and assuredly not made to promote the happiness of nations. We love all commemorations. We love these anniversaries, for their own sakes, and for their uses. We love those Lethes[2] of an hour which have a virtue beyond their gift of oblivion, and while they furnish a temporary forgetfulness of many of the ills of life, revive the memory

---

1   The companion of Sir Toby Belch in Shakespeare's *Twelfth Night*. Aguecheek is a foolish knight whose hopeless pursuit of Olivia makes him a laughing stock.
2   In Greek mythology, the river of forgetfulness.

of many a past enjoyment, and reawaken many a slumbering affection. We love those milestones on the journey of life beside which man is called upon to pause, and take a reckoning of the distance he has passed, and of that which he may have yet to go. We love to reach those free, open spaces at which the cross-roads of the world converge, and where we are sure to meet, as at a common rendezvous, with travellers from its many paths. We love to enter those houses of refreshment by the way-side of existence, where we know we shall encounter with other wayfarers like ourselves,—perchance with friends long separated, and whom the chances of the world keep far apart,—and whence, after a sweet communion and lusty festival and needful rest, we may go forth upon our journey new fortified against its accidents, and strengthened for its toils. We love those festivals which have been made, as Washington Irving says, "the season for gathering together of family connections, and drawing closer again those bonds of kindred hearts which the cares and pleasures and sorrows of the world are continually operating to cast loose; of calling back the children of a family who have launched forth in life and wandered widely asunder, once more to assemble about the paternal hearth, that rallying place of the affections, there to grow young and loving again among the endearing mementos of childhood." Above all, we love those seasons ("for pity is not common!" says the old ballad) which call for the exercise of a general hospitality, and give the poor man his few and precious glimpses of a plenty which, as the world is managed, his toil cannot buy; which shelter the houseless wanderer, and feed the starving child, and clothe the naked mother, and spread a festival for all,—those seasons which in their observance by our ancestors, kept alive, by periodical reawakenings, that flame of charity which thus had scarcely time wholly to expire during all the year. We love all which tends to call man from the solitary and chilling pursuit of his own separate and selfish views into the warmth of a common sympathy, and within the bands of a common brotherhood. We love these commemorations, as we have said, for themselves; we love them for their uses; and still more we love them for the memories of our boyhood! Many a bright picture do they call up in our minds, and in the minds of most who have been amongst their observers; for with these festivals of the heart are inalienably connected many a memory for sorrow or for joy, many a scene of early love, many a merry meeting which was yet the last, many a parting of those who shall part no more, many a joyous group composed of materials which separated only too soon and shall never be put together again on earth, many a lost treasure and many a perished hope....

Of all the festivals which crowd the Christian calendar there is none that exercises an influence so strong and universal as that of Christmas; and those varied superstitions, and quaint customs, and joyous observances, which once abounded throughout the rural districts of England, are at no period of the year so thickly congregated or so strongly marked as at this season of unrestrained festivity and extended celebration. The reasons for this are various and very obvious. In the case of a single celebration, which has to support itself by its own solitary influence long, perchance, after the feeling in which it originated has ceased to operate, whose significance is perhaps dimly and more dimly perceived (through the obscurity of a distance, year after year receding further into shadow) by its own unaided and unreflected light, the chances are many that the annually increasing neglect into which its observance is likely to fall, shall finally consign it to an entire obliteration. But a cluster of festivals, standing in a proximate order of succession, at once throwing light upon each other and illustrated by a varied and numerous host of customs, traditions, and ceremonies,—of which, as in a similar cluster of stars, the occasional obscuration of any one or more would not prevent their memory being suggested and their place distinctly indicated by the others,—present greatly multiplied probabilities against their existence being ever entirely forgotten or their observation wholly discontinued. The arrangement by which a series of celebrations—beautiful in themselves, and connected with the paramount event in which are laid the foundations of our religion—are made to fall at a period otherwise of very solemn import (from its being assumed as the close of the larger of those revolutions of time into which man measures out the span of his transitory existence), and the chance which has brought down to the same point and thrown together the traces of customs and superstitions both of a sacred and secular character, uniting with the crowd of Catholic observances, off-shoots from the ancient Saturnalia,[1] remains of old Druidical[2] rites, and glimpses into the mythology of the Northern nations, have written a series of hieroglyphics upon that place of the calendar, which, if they cannot be deciphered in every part, are still, from their number and juxtaposition, never likely to be overlooked.

But though these causes are offered as accounting for the preservation of many customs which, without them, would long since have passed into oblivion, which exist by virtue of the position they occupy on the calendar,

---

1　The ancient Roman seven-day festival of Saturn, which began on December 17.
2　The Druids were an order of priests in ancient Gaul and Britain who appear in Welsh and Irish legend as prophets and sorcerers.

yet the more conspicuous celebrations of this season need no such aid and no such arguments. Nothing can be added to their intrinsic interest, and they are too closely connected with the solemn warnings of man's temporal destiny, and linked with the story of his eternal hopes, ever to lose any portion of that influence, a share of which (without thereby losing, as light is communicated without diminution) they throw over all the other celebrations that take shelter under their wing.

In every way, and by many a tributary stream, are the holy and beneficent sentiments which belong to the period increased and refreshed. Beautiful feelings, too apt to fade within the heart of man amid the chilling influences of worldly pursuit, steal out beneath the sweet religious warmth of the season, and the pure and holy amongst the hopes of earth assemble, to place themselves under the protection of that eternal hope whose promise is now, as it were, yearly renewed. Amid the echoes of that song which proclaimed peace on earth and good-will towards men, making no exclusions, and dividing them into no classes, rises up a dormant sense of universal brotherhood in the heart; and something like a distribution of the good things of the earth is suggested in favor of those, destitute here, who are proclaimed as joint participators in the treasure thus announced from heaven. At no other period of the year are the feeling of a universal benevolence and the sense of a common Adam so widely awakened; at no season is the predominant spirit of selfishness so effectually rebuked; never are the circles of love so largely widened.

The very presence of a lengthened festivity—for festivity can never be *solitary*—would, apart from its sacred causes, promote these wholesome effects. The extended space of time over which this festival is spread, the protracted holiday which it creates, points it out for the gathering together of distant friends whom the passing nature of an occasional and single celebration would fail to collect from their scattered places of the world. By this wise and beautiful arrangement the spell of home is still made to cast its sweet and holy influence along the sterile regions as along the bright places of afterlife, and from the dark valleys and the sunny hilltops of the world to call back alike the spoiled of fortune and the tired and travel-stained to refresh themselves again and again at the fountain of their calmer hopes and purer feelings. A wise and beautiful arrangement this would be, in whatever season of the year it might be placed! Wise and beautiful is any institution which sets up a rallying-place for the early affections and re-awakens the sacred sympathies of youth,—which, from that wellhead of purity and peace, sends forth, as it were, a little river of living waters, to flow with revivifying freshness and soothing murmur along the wastes and wildernesses of after years; which makes of that spring-time of the heart a reservoir of balm, to which in hours of sorrow it can return for joy, and in years

"In furry pall yclad,
His brows enwreathed with holly never sere,
Old Christmas comes to close the wained year."

[Original illustration by Robert Seymore from Thomas K. Hervey's *The Book of Christmas*. By depicting Old Christmas riding a goat and carrying the wassail bowl and gifts, Seymore draws upon Scandanavian folklore in which the god Thor, as the Yule Elf, has his carriage drawn through the sky by two magical goats as he visits folk to bestow gifts and receive his traditional offering of porridge.]

of guilt for regeneration; and which, like the widow's cruse of oil, wasteth not in all the ages of the mind's dearth. But how greatly are the wisdom and the beauty of this arrangement increased by the sacred season at which it been placed! Under the sanctions of religion the covenants of the heart are renewed. Upon the altars of our faith the lamps of the spirit are rekindled. The loves of earth seem to have met together at the sound of the "glad tidings" of the season, to refresh themselves for the heaven which those tidings proclaim.

★   ★   ★

But there is yet another reason, in aid of those which we have enumerated, accounting for an observance of the Christmas festivities more universal, and a preservation of its traditions more accurate and entire, than are bestowed in England upon the festival customs of any other period of the year. This reason, which might not at first view seem so favorable to that end as in truth it is, is to be found in the outward and natural aspects of the season. We have been watching the year through the period of its decline, are arrived at the dreary season of its old age, and stand near the edge of its grave. We have seen the rich sunshines and sweet but mournful twilights of autumn, with their solemn inspirations, give place to the short days and gloomy evenings which usher in the coming solstice. One by one the fair faces of the flowers have departed from us, and the sweet murmuring of "shallow rivers, by whose falls melodious birds sing madrigals," has been exchanged for the harsh voice of the swollen torrent and the dreary music of winds that "rave through the naked tree." ...

The halcyon days, which sometimes extend their southern influence even to our stern climate, and carry an interval of gloomy calm into the heart of this dreary month, have generally ere its close given place to the nipping frosts and chilling blasts of mid-winter. "Out of the South" hath come "the whirlwind, and cold out of the North." The days have dwindled to their smallest stature, and the long nights, with their atmosphere of mist, shut in and circumscribe the wanderings of man. Clouds and shadows surround us. The air has lost its rich echoes, and the earth its diversified aspects; and to the immediate threshold of the house of feasting and merriment we have travelled through those dreary days which are emphatically called "the dark days before Christmas."

★   ★   ★

The feelings excited by this dreary period of transition, and by the desolate aspect of external things to which it has at length brought us, would seem, at first view, to be little in harmony with a season of festival, and peculiarly unpropitious to the claims of merriment. And yet it is precisely this joyless condition of the natural world which drives us to take refuge in our moral resources, at the same time that it furnishes us with the leisure necessary for their successful development. The spirit of cheerfulness which, for the blessing of man, is implanted in his nature, deprived of the many issues by which, at other seasons, it walks abroad and breathes amid the sights and sounds of Nature, is driven to its own devices for modes of manifestation, and takes up its station by the blazing hearth. In rural districts, the varied occupations which call the sons of labor abroad into the fields are suspended by the austerities of the time; and to the cottage of the poor man has come a season of temporal repose, concurrently with the falling of that period which seals anew for him, as it were, the promises of an eternal rest. At no other portion of the year, could a feast of equal duration find so many classes of men at leisure for its reception.

> "With his ice, and snow, and rime,
> Let bleak winter sternly come!
> There is not a sunnier clime
> Than the love-lit winter home."

Amid the comforts of the fireside, and all its sweet companionships and cheerful inspirations, there is something like the sense of a triumph obtained over the hostilities of the season. Nature, which at other times promotes the expansion of the feelings and contributes to the enjoyments of man, seems here to have promulgated her fiat against their indulgence; and there is a kind of consciousness of an inner world created, in evasion of her law,—a tract won by the genius of the affections from the domain of desolation, spots of sunshine planted by the heart in the very bosom of shadow, a pillar of fire lit up in the darkness. And thus the sensation of a respite from toil, the charms of renewed companionship, the consciousness of a general sympathy of enjoyment running along all the links of the social chain, and the contrasts established within to the discomforts without, are all components of that propitious feeling to which the religious spirit of the season, and all its quaint and characteristic observances, make their appeal.

There is, too (connected with these latter feelings, and almost unacknowledged by the heart of man), another moral element of that cheerful sentiment which has sprung up within it. It consists in the prospect, even at this distant and gloomy period, of a coming spring. This is peculiarly the season of looking forward. Already, as it were, the infant face of the new year is perceived beneath the folds of the old one's garment. The business of the present year has terminated, and along the night which has succeeded to its season of labor have been set up a series of illuminations, which, we know, will be extinguished only that the business of another seed-time may begin.

Neither, amid all its dreary features, is the *natural* season without its own picturesque beauty, nor even entirely divested of all its summer indications of a living loveliness, or all suggestions of an eternal hope. Not only hath it the peculiar beauties of old age, but it hath besides lingering traces of that beauty which old age hath not been able wholly to extinguish, and which comes finely in aid of the moral hints and religious hopes of the season.

The former—the graces which are peculiar to the season itself—exist in many a natural aspect and grotesque effect, which is striking both for the variety it offers and for its own intrinsic loveliness.... The white mantle which the earth occasionally puts on with the rapidity of a spell, covering, in the course of a night and while we have slept, the familiar forms with a sort of strangeness that makes us feel as if we had awakened in some new and enchanted land; the fantastic forms assumed by the drifting snow; the wild and fanciful sketching of old winter upon the "frosty pane;" the icicles that depend like stalactites from every projection, and sparkle in the sun like jewels of the most brilliant water; and, above all, the featherly investiture of the trees above alluded to, by which their minute tracery is brought out with a richness shaming the carving of the finest chisel,—are amongst the features which exhibit the inexhaustible fertility of Nature in the production of striking and beautiful effects.

★   ★   ★

One of the most striking signs of the season, and which meets the eye in all directions, is that which arises out of the ancient and still familiar practice of adorning our houses and churches with evergreens during the continuance of this festival. The decorations of our mantel-pieces, and in many places of our windows, the wreaths which ornament our lamps and Christmas candles, the garniture of our tables, are alike gathered from the hedges and winter gardens; and in the neighborhood of every town and village the traveller may meet with some such sylvan procession as is here represented, or some group of boys returning from the woods laden with their winter greenery, and like the sturdy ambassador in the plate, engaged in what we have heard technically called "bringing home Christmas." This symptom of the approaching festivity is mentioned by Gay[1] in his "Trivia": —

---

1   John Gay (1685-1732), English poet and dramatist.

Bringing home Christmas

[Original illustration by Robert Seymore from Thomas K. Hervey's *The Book of Christmas.*]

"When Rosemary and Bays, the poet's crown,
Are bawl'd in frequent cries through all the town,
Then judge the festival of Christmass near,—
Christmass, the joyous period of the year!
Now with bright holly all the temples strow;
With Lawrel green, and sacred Misletoe."

The practice of these decorations, which is recommended to modern times by its own pleasantness and natural beauty, is of very high antiquity, and has been ascribed by various writers to various sources. They who are desirous of tracing a Christian observance to a Christian cause remind us of those figurative expressions in the prophets which speak of the Messiah as the "Branch of righteousnes," etc., and describe by natural allusions the fertility which should attend his coming. "The Lord shall comfort Zion," says Isaiah: "he will comfort all her waste places; and he will make her wilderness like Eden, and her desert like the garden of the Lord." Again, "The glory of Lebanon shall come unto thee, the fir tree, the pine tree, and the box together, to beautify the place of my sanctuary; and I will make the place of my feet glorious." And Nehemiah, on an occasion of rejoicing, orders the people, after the law of Moses, to "go forth unto the mount and fetch olive branches, and pine branches, and myrtle branches, and palm branches, and branches of thick trees," and to make booths thereof, "every one upon the roof of his house, and in their courts, and in the courts of the house of God," and in the streets; "and all the congregation of them that were come again out of the captivity" sat under these booths, "and there was very great gladness." A writer in the "Gentleman's Magazine" asks if this custom may not be referred, as well as that of the palms on Palm Sunday, to that passage in the Scripture account of Christ's entry into Jerusalem which states that the multitude "cut down branches from the trees, and strawed them in the way."

The practice, however, of introducing flowers and branches amongst the tokens of festivity seems, and very naturally, to have existed universally and at all times. It was, as we know, a pagan manifestation of rejoicing and worship, and is forbidden on that express ground in early councils of the Christian Church. Hone, in his "Every-Day Book,"[1] quotes Polydore Virgil[2] to the effect that "trymming of the temples with hangynges, flowres, boughes,

---

1   William Hone (1780-1842), an English writer and bookseller. His *Every-Day Book* (1826-27) was a popular compilation of miscellaneous information about customs and manners.

2   A sixteenth-century Italian historian and humanist whose *Anglicae historicae libri XXVI* was the first critical history of England.

and garlondes, was taken of the heathen people, whiche decked their idols and houses with suche array;" and it came under the list of abominations denounced by the Puritans for the same reason. The practice was also in use amongst the nations both of Gothic and Celtic origin; and Brand[1] quotes from Dr. Chandler's "Travels in Greece"[2] a very beautiful superstition, mentioned as the reason of this practice, amongst the votaries of Druidism. "The houses," he says, "were decked with evergreens in December, that the sylvan spirits might repair to them and remain unnipped with frost and cold winds until a milder season had renewed the foliage of their darling abodes."

In England the practice, whencesoever derived, has existed from the very earliest days, and, in spite of outcry and prohibition, has come down in full vigor to our own. In former times, as we learn from Stow,[3] in his "Survey of London," not only were our houses and churches decorated with evergreens, but also the conduits, standards, and crosses in the streets; and in our own day they continue to form a garniture not only of our temples and our houses, but constitute a portion of the striking display made at this festive season in our markets and from the windows of our shops. Holly forms a decoration of the shambles, and every tub of butter has a sprig of rosemary in its breast.

The plants most commonly in use for this purpose appear to have generally been the holly, the ivy, the laurel, the rosemary, and the mistletoe; although the decorations were by no means limited to these materials. Brand expresses some surprise at finding cypress included in the list, as mentioned in the tract called "Round about our Coal-Fire," and observes that he "should as soon have expected to have seen the yew as the cypress used on this joyful occasion." The fact, however, is that yew is frequently mentioned amongst the Christmas decorations, as well as box, pine, fir, and indeed the larger part of the Christmas plants which we have enumerated in a former chapter. The greater number of these appear to have been so used, not on account of any mystic meanings supposed to reside therein, but simply for the sake of their greenery or of their rich berries. Stow speaks of the houses being decked with "whatsover the year afforded to be green;" and Sandys observes that "at present great variety is observed in decorating our houses and buildings, and many flowers are introduced that were unknown to our ancestors, but whose varied colors add to the cheer-

1 John Brand (1744-1806), antiquary.
2 Richard Chandler (1738-1810), classical antiquary and traveler. His *Travels* was published in 1775 and 1776.
3 John Stow (1525?-1605), English chronicler and antiquary. His *Survey of London* appeared in 1598.

ful effect; as the chrysanthemum, satin-flower, etc., mingling with the red berry of the holly and the mystic mistletoe. In the West of England," he adds, "the myrtle and laurustinum form a pleasing addition." There is a very beautiful custom which we find mentioned in connection with the subject of evergreens as existing at this season of the year in some parts of Germany and Sicily. A large bough is set up in the principal room, the smaller branches of which are hung with little presents suitable to the different members of the household. "A good deal of innocent mirth and spirit of courtesy," it is observed, "is produced by this custom."

★   ★   ★

The reverence of the mistletoe among the Ancient Britons appears, however, to have been limited to that which grew upon the oak; whereas the *Viscum album*, or common mistletoe,—the sight of whose pearly berries brings the flush into the cheek of the maiden of modern days,—may be gathered besides from the old apple-tree, the hawthorn, the lime-tree, and the Scotch or the silver fir. Whether there remain any traces of the old superstitions which elevated it into a moral or a medical amulet,—beyond that which is connected with the custom alluded to in the opening of our remarks upon this plant, and represented, by our artist here,—we know not. We should, however, be very sorry to see any light let in amongst us which should fairly rout a belief connected with so agreeable a privilege as this. That privilege, as all our readers know, consists in the right to kiss any female who may be caught under the mistletoe-bough,—and, we may hope, will continue, for its own pleasantness, even if the superstition from which it springs should be finally lost. This superstition arose, clearly enough, out of the old mystic character of the plant in question, and erects it into a charm, the neglect of which exposes to the imminent danger of all the evils of old-maidenism. For, according to Archbishop Nares,[1] the tradition is, "that the maid who was not kissed under it, at Christmas, would not be married in that year,"—by which, we presume, the Archdeacon means in the following year. Accordingly, a branch of this parasitical plant was hung (formerly with great state, but now it is generally suspended with much secrecy) either from the centre of the roof, or over the door,—and we recommend this latter situation to our readers, both as less exposed to untimely observation, and because every maiden who joins the party must of necessity do so by passing under it. We learn from Brand that the ceremony was not duly performed unless a berry was plucked off with each kiss. This berry, it is stated by other authorities, was to be presented for good luck to the maiden

---

1   Robert Nares (1753-1829), philologist and literary scholar.

kissed; and Washington Irving adds that "when the berries are all plucked, the privilege ceases." If this be so, it behooves the maidens of a household to take good care that the branch provided for the occasion shall be as well furnished with these pearly tokens as the feast is likely to be with candidates for the holy state of matrimony. The practice is still of very common observance in kitchens and servants' halls, particularly in the country. But, as we have hinted, we have met with it (and so, we dare say, have most of our readers) in higher scenes; and many a merry laugh have we heard ring from beneath the mistletoe bough. There are lips in the world that we would gladly meet there in this coming season.

[Source: Thomas K. Hervey. *The Book of Christmas. Descriptions of the customs, ceremonies, traditions, superstitions, fun, feeling and festivities of the Christmas Season* (Chicago: The Cuneo Press, 1951) 15-20; 135-39; 146-48; 149-52; 178-83; 196-99.]

5. John Calcott Horsley/Sir Henry Cole: The First Christmas Card

[John Calcott Horsley, a London illustrator, designed the first Christmas card in 1843. He was commissioned by Sir Henry Cole, a wealthy businessman, whose many ventures left him little time to write the numerous personal Christmas greetings he needed to send to friends and professional associates. Cole was responsible for modernizing the British postal system, managing the construction of the Albert Hall, and planning for the Great Exhibition of 1851. He later became the first director of the South Kensington Museum, subsequently renamed the Victoria and Albert Museum in 1899. Cole was also a writer and publisher of books and journals. Under the pen-name of Felix Summerly he wrote several books about art collections and architecture.

He commissioned Horsley to illustrate a family Christmas scene for the card comprised of three panels. In the center there is a family of three generations celebrating the festive season with drink and food. (The British Temperance Movement was not pleased with that portion of the design.) The side panels depict a man feeding the hungry and a woman clothing the naked. By surrounding the image of a genial family-gathering enjoying wine, food, and fellowship with images of the poor being sustained by generous, moral people, this Christmas card parallels in theme much of Dickens's *A Christmas Carol*, both of which interestingly appeared in 1843.

Cole had 1000 copies of the card printed by a lithographic process and hand-coloring. The message reads simply "A Merry Christmas and A Happy New Year to You." Sold at one shilling each, the cards were an early commercial success. Within the next several years, many upper-class families began to have their own Christmas cards lithographed. By the 1870s the cost of postage became low enough to entice the masses of Victorians to join in the Christmas card adventure.]

6. Charles Dickens, "A Christmas Tree" (1850)

I have been looking on, this evening, at a merry company of children assembled round that pretty German toy, a Christmas Tree.[1] The tree was planted in the middle of a great round table, and towered high above their heads. It was brilliantly lighted by a multitude of little tapers; and everywhere sparkled and glittered with bright objects. There were rosy-cheeked dolls, hiding behind the green leaves; there were real watches (with movable hands, at least, and an endless capacity of being wound up) dangling from innumerable twigs; there were French-polished tables, chairs, bedsteads, wardrobes, eight-day clocks, and various other articles of domestic furniture (wonderfully made, in tin, at Wolverhampton), perched among the boughs, as if in preparation for some fairy housekeeping; there were jolly, broad-faced little men, much more agreeable in appearance than many real men—and no wonder, for their heads took off, and showed them to be full of sugar-plums; there were fiddles and drums; there were tambourines, books, work-boxes, paint-boxes, sweetmeat-boxes, peep-show boxes, all

---

1 The Christmas tree was introduced into England in 1841 by Prince Albert.

kinds of boxes; there were trinkets for the elder girls, far brighter than any grown-up gold and jewels; there were baskets and pincushions in all devices; there were guns, swords, and banners; there were witches standing in enchanted rings of pasteboard, to tell fortunes; there were teetotums, humming-tops, needle-cases, pen-wipers, smelling-bottles, conversation-cards, bouquet-holders; real fruit, made artificially dazzling with gold leaf; imitation apples, pears, and walnuts, crammed with surprises; in short, as a pretty child, before me, delightedly whispered to another pretty child, her bosom friend, "There was everything, and more." This motley collection of odd objects clustering on the tree like magic fruit, and flashing back the bright looks directed towards it from every side—some of the diamond-eyes admiring it were hardly on a level with the table, and a few were languishing in timid wonder on the bosoms of pretty mothers, aunts, and nurses—made a lively realisation of the fancies of childhood; and set me thinking how all the trees that grow, and all the things that come into existence on the earth, have their wild adornments at that well-remembered time.

Being now at home again, and alone, the only person in the house awake, my thoughts are drawn back, by a fascination which I do not care to resist, to my own childhood. I begin to consider what do we all remember best upon the branches of the Christmas Tree of our own young Christmas days, by which we climbed to real life.

Straight, in the middle of the room, cramped in the freedom of its growth by no encircling walls or soon-reached ceiling, a shadowy tree arises; and, looking up into the dreamy brightness of its top—for I observe in this tree the singular property that it appears to grow downward towards the earth—I look into my youngest Christmas recollections!

All toys at first, I find. Up yonder, among the green holly and red berries, is the Tumbler, with his hands in his pockets, who wouldn't lie down, but whenever he was put upon the floor, persisted in rolling his fat body about, until he rolled himself still, and brought those lobster eyes of his to bear upon me—when I affected to laugh very much, but in my heart of hearts was extremely doubtful of him. Close beside him is that infernal snuff-box, out of which there sprang a demoniacal Counsellor in a black gown, with an obnoxious head of hair, and a red cloth mouth, wide open, who was not to be endured on any terms, but could not be put away either; for he used suddenly, in a highly magnified state, to fly out of Mammoth Snuff-boxes in dreams, when least expected. Nor is the frog with cobbler's wax on his tail, far off; for there was no knowing where he wouldn't jump; and when he flew over the candle, and came upon one's hand with that spotted back—red on a green ground—he was horrible. The cardboard lady in a blue-silk skirt, who was stood up against the candlestick to dance, and whom I see on the same branch, was milder, and was beautiful; but I can't say as much for the larger cardboard man, who used to be hung against the wall and pulled by string; there was a sinister expression in that nose of his; and when he got his legs round his neck (which he very often did), he was ghastly, and not a creature to be alone with.

When did that dreadful Mask first look at me? Who put it on, and why was I so frightened that the sight of it is an era in my life? It is not a hideous visage in itself; it is even meant to be droll; why then were its stolid features so intolerable? Surely not because it hid the wearer's face. An apron would have done as much; and though I should have preferred even the apron away, it would not have been absolutely insupportable, like the mask? Was it the immovability of the mask? The doll's face was immovable, but I was not afraid of *her*. Perhaps that fixed and set change coming over a real face, infused into my quickened heart some remote suggestion and dread of the universal change that is to come on every face, and make it still? Nothing reconciled me to it. No drummers, from whom proceeded a melancholy chirping on the turning of a handle; no regiment of soldiers, with a mute band, taken out of a box, and fitted, one by one, upon a stiff and lazy little set of lazy-tongs; no old woman, made of wires and a brown-paper composition, cutting up a pie for two small children; could give me a permanent comfort, for a long time. Nor was it any satisfaction to be shown the Mask, and see that it was made of paper, or to have it locked up and be assured that no one wore it. The mere recollection of that fixed face, the mere knowledge of its existence anywhere, was sufficient to wake me in the night all perspiration and horror, with, "O I know it's coming! O the mask!"

I never wondered what the dear old donkey with the panniers — there he is! — was made of then! His hide was real to the touch, I recollect. And the great black horse with the round red spots all over him — the horse that I could even get upon — I never wondered what had brought him to that strange condition, or thought that such a horse was not commonly seen at Newmarket.[1] The four horses of no colour, next to him, that went into the wagon of cheeses, and could be taken out and stabled under the piano, appear to have bits of fur-tippet for their tails, and other bits for their manes, and to stand on pegs instead of legs, but it was not so when they were brought home for a Christmas present. They were all right, then; neither was their harness unceremoniously nailed into their chests, as appears to be the case now. The tinkling works of the music-cart, I *did* find out, to be made of quill toothpicks and wire; and I always thought that little tumbler in his shirt sleeves, perpetually swarming up one side of a wooden frame, and coming down, head foremost, on the other, rather a weak-mind-

---

[1] A race course.

ed person—though good-natured; but the Jacob's Ladder,[1] next him, made of little squares of red wood, that went flapping and clattering over one another, each developing a different picture, and the whole enlivened by small bells, was a mighty marvel and a great delight.

· Ah! The Doll's house!—of which I was not proprietor, but where I visited. I don't admire the Houses of Parliament half so much as that stone-fronted mansion with real glass windows, and door-steps, and a real balcony—greener than I ever see now, except at watering-places; and even they afford but a poor imitation. And though it *did* open all at once, the entire house-front (which was a blow, I admit, as cancelling the fiction of a staircase), it was but to shut it up again, and I could believe. Even open, there were three distinct rooms in it: a sitting-room and bedroom, elegantly furnished, and, best of all, a kitchen, with uncommonly soft fire-irons, a plentiful assortment of diminutive utensils—oh, the warming-pan!—and a tin man-cook in profile, who was always going to fry two fish. What Barmecide justice[2] have I done to the noble feasts wherein the set of wooden platters figured, each with its own peculiar delicacy, as a ham or turkey, glued tight on to it, and garnished with something green, which I recollect as moss! Could all the Temperance Societies of these later days, united, give me such a tea-drinking as I have had through the means of yonder little set of blue crockery, which really would hold liquid (it ran out of the small wooden cask, I recollect, and tasted of matches), and which made tea, nectar. And if the two legs of the ineffectual little sugar-tongs did tumble over one another, and want purpose, like Punch's hands,[3] what does it matter? And if I did once shriek out, as a poisoned child, and strike the fashionable company with consternation, by reason of having drunk a little teaspoon, inadvertently dissolved in hot tea, I was never the worse for it, except by a powder!

Upon the next branches of the tree, lower down, hard by the green roller and miniature gardening-tools, how thick the books begin to hang. Thin books, in themselves, at first, but many of them, and with deliciously smooth covers of bright red or green. What fat black letters to begin with! "A was an archer, and shot at a frog."[4] Of course he was. He was an apple pie also, and there he is! He was a good many things in his time, was A, and so were most of his friends, except X, who had so little versatility, that I

---

1 A child's toy, still sold today, named after the biblical ladder connecting earth and heaven in Jacob's dream.
2 In *The Arabian Nights* Prince Barmecide invites a beggar to a great feast that turns out to be illusory.
3 In the Punch and Judy puppet shows Punch must strike blows with his stick tucked under his arms, since his puppet hands are of little use.
4 References to the nineteenth-century alphabet books for children.

never knew him to get beyond Xerxes or Xantippe—like Y, who was always confined to a Yacht or a Yew Tree; and Z condemned forever to be a Zebra or a Zany. But, now, the very tree itself changes, and becomes a bean-stalk—the marvellous bean-stalk up which Jack climbed to the Giant's house! And now, those dreadfully interesting, double-headed giants, with their clubs over their shoulders, begin to stride along the boughs in a perfect throng, dragging knights and ladies home for dinner by the hair of their heads. And Jack—how noble, with his sword of sharpness, and his shoes of swiftness! Again those old meditations come back upon me as I gaze up at him; and I debate within myself whether there was more than one Jack (which I am loth to believe possible), or only one genuine original admiral Jack, who achieved all the recorded exploits.

Good for Christmas time is the ruddy colour of the cloak, in which— the tree making a forest of itself for her to trip through, with her basket— Little Red Riding-Hood comes to me one Christmas Eve to give me information of the cruelty and treachery of that dissembling wolf who ate her grandmother, without making any impression on his appetite, and then ate her, after making that ferocious joke about his teeth. She was my first love. I felt that if I could have married Little Red Riding-Hood, I should have known perfect bliss. But it was not to be; and there was nothing for it but to look out the Wolf in the Noah's Ark there, and put him late in the procession on the table, as a monster who was to be degraded. Oh, the wonderful Noah's Ark! It was not found seaworthy when put in a washing-tub, and the animals were crammed in at the roof, and needed to have their legs well shaken down before they could be got in, even there—and then, ten to one, but they began to tumble out the door, which was but imperfectly fastened with a wire latch—but what was *that* against it? Consider the noble fly, a size or two smaller than the elephant: the lady-bird, the butterfly—all triumphs of art! Consider the goose, whose feet were so small, and whose balance was so indifferent, that he usually tumbled forward, and knocked down all the animal creation. Consider Noah and his family, like idiotic tobacco-stoppers; and how the leopard stuck to warm little fingers; and how the tails of the larger animals used gradually to resolve themselves into frayed bits of string!

Hush! Again a forest, and somebody up in a tree—not Robin Hood, not Valentine,[1] not the Yellow Dwarf (I have passed him and all Mother Bunch's wonders, without mention),[2] but an Eastern King[3] with a glittering

---

1   The hero of the fifteenth-century romance *Valentine and Orson*, a popular children's book.
2   Characters from a seventeenth-century fairy tale by Comtesse Marie Catherine D'Aulnoy.
3   Shahriyar, the husband of Sheherazade, who beguiles him with stories that comprise *The Arabian Nights*.

scimitar and turban. By Allah! two Eastern Kings, for I see another looking over his shoulder! Down upon the grass, at the tree's foot, lies the full length of a coal-black Giant, stretched asleep, with his head in a lady's lap; and near them is a glass box, fastened with four locks of shining steel, in which he keeps the lady prisoner when he is awake. I see the four keys at his girdle now. The lady makes signs to the two kings in the tree, who softly descend. It is the setting-in of the bright Arabian Nights.

Oh, now all common things become uncommon and enchanted to me! All lamps are wonderful, all rings are talismans. Common flower-pots are full of treasure, with a little earth scattered on the top; trees are for Ali Baba[1] to hide in; beefsteaks are to throw down into the Valley of Diamonds,[2] that the precious stones may stick to them, and be carried by the eagles to their nests, whence the traders, with loud cries, will scare them. Tarts are made, according to the recipe of the Vizier's son of Bussorah,[3] who turned pastrycook after he was set down in his drawers at the gate of Damascus; cobblers are all Mustaphas,[4] and in the habit of sewing up people cut into four pieces, to whom they are taken blindfold.

Any iron ring let into stone is the entrance to a cave which only waits for the magician, and the little fire, and the necromancy, that will make the earth shake.[5] All the dates imported come from the same tree as that unlucky date with whose shell the merchant knocked out the eye of the genie's invisible son.[6] All olives are of the stock of that fresh fruit, concerning which the Commander of the Faithful[7] overheard the boy conduct the fictitious trial of the fraudulent olive merchant; all apples are akin to the apple purchased (with two others) from the Sultan's gardener for three se-

---

1   The hero of "Ali Baba and the Forty Thieves," one of the tales in *The Arabian Nights*.
2   In *The Arabian Nights* Sinbad the Sailor visits the Valley of the Diamonds, where merchants throw meat to adhere to the diamonds so that vultures upon flying out of the valley retrieve the diamonds.
3   In *The Arabian Nights* tale "The Story of Nur-ed-din and his son, and of Shems-ed-din and his Daughter" Hasan, the son of Nur-ed-din, attempts to save Shems-ed-din's daughter from marriage to a hunchback, but he is taken by genies to the gates of Damascus. He reconciles with his widowed mother (who earlier opposed the marriage), becomes a pastrycook, and later wins his bride.
4   In "Ali Baba and the Forty Thieves" Mustaphas is a cobbler who sews together the dismembered body of Ali Baba's brother. He is blindfolded to prevent him from identifying the body.
5   In "The Story of Aladdin" a magician builds a fire and makes the earth shake, revealing a stone with a brass ring. Aladdin removes the stone and goes into a cave containing the magic lamp.
6   In "The Merchant and the Genie" (*The Arabian Nights*) the merchant accidentally kills the genie's son with the shell of a date.
7   Haround Alraschid, the Caliph of Baghdad, in "The Story of Ali Cogia, A Merchant of Baghdad" (*The Arabian Nights*).

quins, and which the tall black slave stole from the child.[1] All dogs are associated with the dog, really a transformed man, who jumped upon the baker's counter, and put his paw on the piece of bad money. All rice recalls the rice which the awful lady, who was a ghoule, could only peck by grains, because of her nightly feasts in the burial-place. My very rocking-horse—there he is, with his nostrils turned completely inside-out, indicative of Blood!—should have a peg in his neck, by virtue thereof to fly away with me, as the wooden horse did with the Prince of Persia, in the sight of all his father's Court.

Yes, on every object that I recognise among those upper branches of my Christmas Tree, I see this fairy light! When I wake in bed, at daybreak, on the cold, dark winter mornings, the white snow dimly beheld, outside, through the frost on the window-pane, I hear Dinarzade.[2] "Sister, sister, if you are yet awake, I pray you finish the history of the Young King of the Black Islands." Scheherazade replies, "If my lord the Sultan will suffer me to live another day, sister, I will not only finish that, but tell you a more wonderful story yet." Then the gracious Sultan goes out, giving no orders for the execution, and we all three breathe again.

At this height of my tree I begin to see, cowering among the leaves—it may be born of turkey, or of pudding, or mince pie, or of these many fancies, jumbled with Robinson Crusoe[3] on his desert island, Philip Quarll[4] among the monkeys, Sanford and Merton[5] with Mr. Barlow, Mother Bunch, and the Mask—or it may be the result of indigestion, assisted by imagination and over-doctoring—a prodigious nightmare. It is so exceedingly indistinct that I don't know why it's frightful—but I know it is. I can only make out that it is an immense array of shapeless things, which appear to be planted on a vast exaggeration of the lazy-tongs that used to bear the toy soldiers, and to be slowly coming close to my eyes, and receding to an immeasurable distance. When it comes closest, it is worst. In connection with it I descry remembrances of winter nights incredibly long; of being

---

1   In "The Story of Three Apples" (*The Arabian Nights*) a man buys three apples for his sick wife. His child takes one that is then stolen by a slave. The slave later meets the man and tells him that he got the apple from his lover. In a jealous rage the man returns home and kills his wife, only to learn the truth later from his child.

2   Dinarzade, the sister of Sheherazade, who, along with the Sultan, listens to her sister's many tales.

3   *The Life and Strange Surprizing Adventures of Robinson Crusoe of York, Mariner* (1719) by Daniel Defoe.

4   The hero of the novel *The Hermit* (1727), a work similar to *Robinson Crusoe*, and generally attributed to Peter Longueville (Edward Dorrington, pseudonym).

5   *The History of Sandford and Merton, A Work Intended for the Use of Children* (1783-89) by Thomas Day. Mr. Barlow is a tutor whose pedantry, along with the good example of Harry Sandford, helps to correct the misbehavior of the arrogant Tommy Merton.

sent early to bed, as a punishment for some small offence, and waking in two hours, with a sensation of having been asleep two nights; of the laden hopelessness of morning ever dawning; and the oppression of a weight of remorse.

And now, I see a wonderful row of little lights rise smoothly out of the ground, before a vast green curtain. Now, a bell rings—a magic bell, which still sounds in my ears unlike all other bells—and music plays, amidst a buzz of voices, and a fragrant smell of orange-peel and oil. Anon, the magic bell commands the music to cease, and the great green curtain rolls itself up majestically, and The Play begins! The devoted dog of Montargis[1] avenges the death of his master, foully murdered in the Forest of Bondy; and a humourous Peasant with a red nose and a very little hat, whom I take from this hour forth to my bosom as a friend (I think he was a Waiter or an Hostler at a village Inn, but many years have passed since he and I have met), remarks that the sassigassity of that dog is indeed surprising; and ever-more this jocular conceit will live in my remembrance fresh and unfading, overtopping all possible jokes, unto the end of time. Or now, I learn with bitter tears how poor Jane Shore,[2] dressed all in white, and with her brown hair hanging down, went starving through the streets; or how George Barnwell[3] killed the worthiest uncle that ever man had, and was afterwards so sorry for it that he ought to have been let off. Comes swift to comfort me, the Pantomime[4]—stupendous Phenomenon!—when Clowns are shot from loaded mortars into the great chandelier, bright constellation that it is; when Harlequins, covered all over with scales of pure gold, twist and sparkle, like amazing fish; when Pantaloon (whom I deem it no irreverence to compare in my own mind to my grandfather) puts red-hot pokers in his pocket, and cries, "Here's somebody coming!" or taxes the Clown with petty larceny, by saying, "Now, I sawed you do it!" When Everything is capable, with the greatest of ease, of being changed into Anything; and "Nothing is, but thinking makes it so." Now, too, I perceive my first experience of the dreary sensation—often to return in after-life—of being unable, next day, to get back to the dull, settled world, of wanting to live forever in the bright atmosphere I have quitted; of doting on the little Fairy, with the wand like a celestial Barber's Pole, and pining for a Fairy immor-

---

1 *The Dog of Montargis* (author unknown) was a popular play in London early in the century. It was first produced at the Theatre Royal, Drury Lane, in 1828.
2 *Jane Shore* (1714), a play by Nicholas Rowe. Jane was made to do public penance for sorcery.
3 *The London Merchant, or the History of George Barnwell* (1731) a play by George Lillo. Under the influence of his lover, Barnwell robs his master and murders his uncle.
4 Some standard figures from this popular form of theater include Harlequin, his beloved Columbine, her father Pantaloon, and the beleaguered Clown.

tality along with her. Ah! she comes back, in many shapes, as my eye wanders down the branches of my Christmas Tree, and goes as often, and has never yet stayed by me!

Out of this delight springs the toy theatre—there it is, with its familiar proscenium, and ladies in feathers, in the boxes!—and all its attendant occupation with paste and glue and gum, and water colours, in the getting up of The Miller and his Men,[1] and Elizabeth, or the Exile of Siberia.[2] In spite of a few besetting accidents and failures (particularly an unreasonable disposition in the respectable Kelmar, and some others, to become faint in the legs, and double up, at exciting points of the drama), a teeming world of fancies so suggestive and all-embracing, that, far below it on my Christmas Tree, I see dark, dirty, real Theatres in the daytime, adorned with these associations as with the freshest garlands of the rarest flowers, and charming me yet.

But hark! The Waits[3] are playing, and they break my childish sleep! What images do I associate with the Christmas music as I see them set forth on the Christmas Tree? Known before all the others, keeping far apart from all the others, they gather round my little bed. An angel, speaking to a group of shepherds in a field; some travellers, with eyes uplifted, following a star; a baby in a manger; a child in a spacious temple, talking with grave men; a solemn figure, with a mild and beautiful face, raising a dead girl by the hand; again, near a city gate, calling back the son of a widow, on his bier, to life; a crowd of people looking through the opened roof of a chamber where he sits, and letting down a sick person on a bed, with ropes; the same, in a tempest, walking on the water to a ship; again, on a sea-shore, teaching a great multitude; again, with a child upon his knee, and other children round; again, restoring sight to the blind, speech to the dumb, hearing to the deaf, health to the sick, strength to the lame, knowledge to the ignorant; again, dying upon a cross, watched by armed soldiers, a thick darkness coming on, the earth beginning to shake, and only one voice heard. "Forgive them, for they know not what they do!"

Still, on the lower and maturer branches of the Tree, Christmas associations cluster thick. School-books shut up; Ovid and Virgil[4] silenced; the Rule of Three,[5] with its cool impertinent enquiries, long disposed of; Terence and Plautus[6] acted no more, in an arena of huddled desks and forms,

---

1   The Miller and his Men (1813), a play by Isaac Pocock. Imprisoned in a mill by the villain, Kelmar, the heroine is rescued by her lover.
2   The Exiles of Siberia (1806), by Marie Cottin, a French writer.
3   Folk who celebrate Christmas by playing music and singing outdoors at night.
4   Roman poets.
5   A means of discovering the fourth term of a proportion when three are stated.
6   Roman playwrights.

all chipped, and notched, and inked; cricket-bats, stumps, and balls, left higher up, with the smell of trodden grass and the softened noise of shouts in the evening air; the tree is still fresh, still gay. If I no more come home at Christmas time, there will be girls and boys (thank Heaven!) while the World lasts; and they do! Yonder they dance and play upon the branches of my Tree, God bless them, merrily, and my heart dances and plays too!

And I do come home at Christmas. We all do, or we all should. We all come home, or ought to come home, for a short holiday — the longer, the better — from the great boarding-school, where we are forever working at our arithmetical slates, to take, and give a rest. As to going a visiting, where can we not go, if we will; where have we not been, when we would; starting our fancy away from our Christmas Tree!

Away into the winter prospect. There are many such upon the Tree! On, by low-lying misty grounds, through fens and fogs, up long hills, winding dark as caverns between thick plantations, almost shutting out the sparkling stars; so, out on broad heights, until we stop at last, with sudden silence, at an avenue. The gate-bell has a deep, half-awful sound in the frosty air; the gate swings open on its hinges; and, as we drive up to the great house, the glancing lights grow larger in the windows, and the opposing rows of trees seem to fall solemnly back on either side, to give us place. At intervals, all day, a frightened hare has shot across this whitened turf; or the distant clatter of a herd of deer trampling the hard frost, has, for the minute, crushed the silence too. Their watchful eyes beneath the fern may be shining now, if we could see them, like the icy dewdrops on the leaves; but they are still, and all is still. And so, the lights growing larger, and the trees falling back before us, and closing up again behind us, as if to forbid retreat, we come to the house.

There is probably a smell of roasted chestnuts and other good comfortable things all the time, for we are telling Winter Stories — Ghost Stories, or more shame for us — round the Christmas fire; and we have never stirred, except to draw a little nearer to it. But, no matter for that. We came to the house, and it is an old house, full of great chimneys where wood is burnt on ancient dogs upon the hearth, and grim portraits (some of them with grim legends, too) lower distrustfully from the oaken panels of the walls. We are a middle-aged nobleman, and we make a generous supper with our host and hostess and their guests — it being Christmas time, and the old house full of company — and then we go to bed. Our room is a very old room. It is hung with tapestry. We don't like the portrait of a cavalier in green, over the fireplace. There are great black beams in the ceiling, and there is a great black bedstead, supported at the foot by two great black figures, who seem to have come off a couple of tombs in the old baronial church in the park, for our particular accommodation. But we are not a superstitious nobleman, and we don't mind. Well! we dismiss our servant, lock the door, and sit before the fire in our dressing-gown, musing about a great many things. At length we go to bed. Well! we can't sleep. We toss and tumble, and can't sleep. The embers on the hearth burn fitfully and make the room look ghostly. We can't help peeping out over the counterpane, at the two black figures and the cavalier—that wicked-looking cavalier—in green. In the flickering light, they seem to advance and retire; which, though we are not by any means a superstitious nobleman, is not agreeable. Well! we get nervous—more and more nervous. We say, "This is very foolish, but we can't stand this; we'll pretend to be ill, and knock up somebody." Well! we are just going to do it, when the locked door opens, and there comes in a young woman, deadly pale, and with long fair hair, who glides to the fire, and sits down in the chair we have left there, wringing her hands. Then we notice that her clothes are wet. Our tongue cleaves to the roof of our mouth, and we can't speak; but we observe her accurately. Her clothes are wet; her long hair is dabbled with moist mud; she is dressed in the fashion of two hundred years ago; and she has at her girdle a bunch of rusty keys. Well! there she sits, and we can't even faint, we are in such a state about it. Presently she gets up, and tries all the locks in the room with the rusty keys, which won't fit one of them; then she fixes her eyes on the portrait of the cavalier in green, and says, in a low, terrible voice, "The stags know it!" After that, she wrings her hands again, passes the bedside, and goes out at the door. We hurry on our dressing-gown, seize our pistols (we always travel with pistols), and are following, when we find the door locked. We turn the key, look out into the dark gallery; no one there. We wander away, and try to find our servant. Can't be done. We pace the gallery till daybreak; then return to our deserted room, fall asleep, and are awakened by our servant (nothing ever haunts *him*) and the shining sun. Well! we make a wretched breakfast, and all the company say we look queer. After breakfast, we go over the house with our host, and then we take him to the portrait of the cavalier in green, and then it all comes out. He was false to a young housekeeper once attached to that family, and famous for her beauty, who drowned herself in a pond, and whose body was discovered, after a long time, because the stags refused to drink of the water. Since which, it has been whispered that she traverses the house at midnight (but goes especially to that room where the cavalier in green was wont to sleep), trying the old locks with the rusty keys. Well! we tell our host of what we have seen, and a shade comes over his features, and he begs it may be hushed up; and so it is. But it's all true; and we said so, before we died (we are dead now) to many responsible people.

There is no end to the old houses, with resounding galleries, and dismal state-bed-chambers, and haunted wings shut up for many years, through which we may ramble, with an agreeable creeping up our back, and encounter any number of ghosts, but (it is worthy of remark perhaps) reducible to a very few general types and classes; for, ghosts have little originality, and "walk" in a beaten track. Thus, it comes to pass, that a certain room in a certain old hall, where a certain bad lord, baronet, knight, or gentleman, shot himself, has certain planks in the floor from which the blood *will not* be taken out. You may scrape and scrape, as the present owner has done, or plane and plane, as his father did, or scrub and scrub, as his grandfather did, or burn and burn with strong acids, as his great-grandfather did, but there the blood will still be—no redder and no paler—no more and no less—always just the same. Thus, in such another house there is a haunted door, that never will keep open; or another door that never will keep shut; or a haunted sound of a spinning-wheel, or a hammer, or a footstep, or a cry, or a sigh, or a horse's tramp, or the rattling of a chain. Or else, there is a turret-clock, which, at the midnight hour, strikes thirteen when the head of the family is going to die; or a shadowy, immovable black carriage which at such a time is always seen by somebody, waiting near the great gates in the stable-yard. Or thus, it came to pass how Lady Mary went to pay a visit at a large wild house in the Scottish Highlands, and, being fatigued with her long journey, retired to bed early, and innocently said, next morning, at the breakfast-table, "How odd, to have so late a party last night, in this remote place, and not to tell me of it, before I went to bed!" Then, every one asked Lady Mary what she meant? Then Lady Mary replied, "Why, all night long, the carriages were driving round and round the terrace, underneath my window!" Then the owner of the house turned pale, and so did his Lady, and Charles Macdoodle of Macdoodle signed to Lady Mary to say no more, and every one was silent. After breakfast, Charles Macdoodle told Lady Mary that it was a tradition in the family that those rumbling carriages on the terrace betokened death. And so it proved, for two months afterwards, the lady of the mansion died. And Lady Mary, who was a Maid of Honour at Court, often told this story to the old Queen Charlotte; by this token that the old King[1] always said, "Eh, eh? What, what? Ghosts, ghosts? No such thing, no such thing!" And never left off saying so, until he went to bed.

Or, a friend of somebody's whom most of us know, when he was a young man at college, had a particular friend, with whom he made the compact that, if it were possible for the Spirit to return to this earth after its separation from the body, he of the twain who first died should reappear to the other. In course of time, this compact was forgotten by our friend; the two young men having progressed in life, and taken diverging paths that

---

[1]   Queen Charlotte (1744-1818), queen consort of George III (1738-1820).

were wide asunder. But one night, many years afterwards, our friend being in the North of England, and staying for the night in an inn, on the Yorkshire Moors, happened to look out of bed; and there, in the moonlight, leaning on a bureau near the window, steadfastly regarding him, saw his old college friend! The appearance being solemnly addressed, replied, in a kind of whisper, but very audibly, "Do not come near me. I am dead. I am here to redeem my promise. I come from another world, but may not disclose its secrets!" Then, the whole form becoming paler, melted as it were, into the moonlight, and faded away.

Or, there was the daughter of the first occupier of the picturesque Elizabethan house, so famous in our neighbourhood. You have heard about her? No! Why, *she* went out one summer evening, at twilight, when she was a beautiful girl, just seventeen years of age, to gather flowers in the garden; and presently came running, terrified, into the hall to her father, saying, "Oh, dear father, I have met myself!" He took her in his arms, and told her it was fancy, but she said, "Oh, no! I met myself in the broad walk, and I was pale and gathering withered flowers, and I turned my head, and held them up!" And that night she died, and a picture of her story was begun, though never finished, and they say it is somewhere in the house to this day, with its face to the wall.

Or, the uncle of my brother's wife was riding home on horseback, one mellow evening at sunset, when, in a green lane close to his own house, he saw a man standing before him, in the very centre of the narrow way. "Why does that man in the cloak stand there!" he thought. "Does he want me to ride over him?" But the figure never moved. He felt a strange sensation at seeing it so still, but slackened his trot and rode forward. When he was so close to it, as almost to touch it with his stirrup, his horse shied, and the figure glided up the bank, in a curious, unearthly manner—backward, and without seeming to use its feet—and was gone. The uncle of my brother's wife, exclaiming, "Good Heaven! It's my cousin Harry, from Bombay!" put spurs to his horse, which was suddenly in a profuse sweat, and, wondering at such strange behaviour, dashed round to the front of his house. There he saw the same figure, just passing in at the long French window of the drawing-room, opening on the ground. He threw his bridle to a servant, and hastened in after it. His sister was sitting there, alone. "Alice, where's my cousin Harry?.... Your cousin Harry, John?.... Yes. From Bombay. I met him in the lane just now, and saw him enter here, this instant." Not a creature had been seen by any one; and in that hour and minute, as it afterwards appeared, this cousin died in India.

Or, it was a certain sensible, old maiden lady, who died at ninety-nine, and retained her faculties to the last, who really did see the Orphan Boy; a story which has often been incorrectly told, but of which the real truth is this—because it is, in fact, a story belonging to our family—and she was a connection of our family. When she was about forty years of age, and still an uncommonly fine woman (her lover died young, which was the reason why she never married, though she had many offers), she went to stay at a place in Kent, which her brother, an Indian Merchant, had newly bought. There was a story that this place had once been held in trust, by the guardian of a young boy: who was himself the next heir, and who killed the young boy by harsh and cruel treatment. She knew nothing of that. It has been said that there was a Cage in her bed-room in which the guardian used to put the boy. There was no such thing. There was only a closet. She went to bed, made no alarm whatever in the night, and in the morning said composedly to her maid when she came in, "Who is the pretty forlorn-looking child who has been peeping out of that closet all night?" The maid replied by giving a loud scream, and instantly decamping. She was surprised; but she was a woman of remarkable strength of mind, and she dressed herself and went down-stairs, and closeted herself with her brother. "Now, Walter," she said, "I have been disturbed all night by a pretty forlorn-looking boy, who has been constantly peeping out of that closet in my room, which I can't open. This is some trick." "I am afraid not, Charlotte," said he, "for it is the legend of the house. It is the Orphan Boy. What did he do?" "He opened the door softly," said she, "and peeped out. Sometimes, he came a step or two into the room. Then I called to him, to encourage him, and he shrunk, and shuddered, and crept in again, and shut the door." "The closet has no communication, Charlotte," said her brother, "with any other part of the house, and it's nailed up." This was undeniably true, and it took two carpenters a whole forenoon to get it open for examination. Then she was satisfied that she had seen the Orphan Boy. But, the wild and terrible part of the story is, that he was also seen by three of her brother's sons, in succession, who all died young. On the occasion of each child being taken ill, he came home in a heat, twelve hours before, and said, Oh, mamma, he had been playing under a particular oak tree, in a certain meadow, with a strange boy—a pretty, forlorn-looking boy, who was very timid, and made signs! From fatal experience, the parents came to know that this was the Orphan Boy, and that the course of that child whom he chose for his little playmate was surely ruin.

Legion is the name of the German castles, where we sit up alone to wait for the Spectre—where we are shown into a room, made comparatively cheerful for our reception—where we glance round at the shadows, thrown on the blank walls by the crackling fire—where we feel very lonely when the village innkeeper and his pretty daughter have retired, after laying down a fresh store of wood upon the hearth, and setting forth on the small table such supper-cheer as a cold roast capon, bread, grapes, and a flask of old Rhine wine—where the reverberating doors close on their retreat, one after another, like so many peals of sullen thunder—and where, about the small hours of the night, we come into the knowledge of divers supernatural mysteries. Legion is the name of the haunted German students, in whose society we draw yet nearer to the fire, while the schoolboy in the corner opens his eyes wide and round, and flies off the footstool he has chosen for his seat, when the door accidentally blows open. Vast is the crop of such fruit, shining on our Christmas Tree; in blossom, almost at the very top; ripening all down the boughs!

Among the later toys and fancies hanging there—as idle often and less pure—be the images once associated with the sweet old Waits, the softened music in the night, ever unalterable! Encircled by the social thoughts of Christmas time, still let the benignant figure of my childhood stand unchanged! In every cheerful image and suggestion that the season brings, may the bright star that rested above the poor roof be the star of all the Christian world! A moment's pause, O vanishing tree, of which the lower boughs are dark to me as yet, and let me look once more! I know there are blank spaces on thy branches, where eyes that I have loved, have shone and smiled; from which they are departed. But, far above, I see the raiser of the dead girl, and the Widow's Son; and God is good! If Age be hiding for me in the unseen portion of thy downward growth, oh! may I, with a grey head, turn a child's heart to that figure yet, and a child's trustfulness and confidence!

Now, the tree is decorated with bright merriment, and song, and dance, and cheerfulness. And they are welcome. Innocent and welcome be they ever held, beneath the branches of the Christmas Tree, which cast no gloomy shadow! But, as it sinks into the ground, I hear a whisper going through the leaves. "This, in commemoration of the law of love and kindness, mercy and compassion. This, in remembrance of Me!"[1]

[Source: *Reprinted Pieces*, vol. 21, *The Nonesuch Dickens* (Bloomsbury, London: Nonesuch Press, 1937-38) 262-77.]

7. Charles Dickens, "What Christmas Is, As We Grow Older" (1851)

Time was, with most of us, when Christmas Day encircling all our limited world like a magic ring, left nothing out for us to miss or seek; bound together all our home enjoyments, affections, and hopes; grouped everything and every one around the Christmas fire; and made the little picture shining in our bright young eyes, complete.

---

1   An allusion to Christ's statement at the Last Supper.

Time came, perhaps, all so soon, when our thoughts over leaped that narrow boundary; when there was some one (very dear, we thought then, very beautiful, and absolutely perfect) wanting to the fulness of our happiness; when we were wanting too (or we thought so, which did just as well) at the Christmas hearth by which that some one sat; and when we intertwined with every wreath and garland of our life that some one's name.

That was the time for the bright visionary Christmases which have long arisen from us to show faintly, after summer rain, in the palest edges of the rainbow! That was the time for the beatified enjoyment of the things that were to be, and never were, and yet the things that were so real in our resolute hope that it would be hard to say, now, what realities achieved since, have been stronger!

What! Did that Christmas never really come when we and the priceless pearl who was our young choice were received, after the happiest of totally impossible marriages, by the two united families previously at daggers — drawn on our account? When brothers and sisters-in-law who had always been rather cool to us before our relationship was effected, perfectly doted on us, and when fathers and mothers overwhelmed us with unlimited incomes? Was that Christmas dinner never really eaten, after which we arose, and generously and eloquently rendered honour to our late rival, present in the company, then and there exchanging friendship and forgiveness, and founding an attachment, not to be surpassed in Greek or Roman story, which subsisted until death? Has that same rival long ceased to care for that same priceless pearl, and married for money, and become usurious? Above all, do we really know, now, that we should probably have been miserable if we had won and worn the pearl, and that we are better without her?

That Christmas when we had recently achieved so much fame; when we had been carried in triumph somewhere, for doing something great and good; when we had won an honoured and ennobled name, and arrived and were received at home in a shower of tears of joy; is it possible that *that* Christmas has not come yet?

And is our life here, at the best, so constituted that, pausing as we advance at such a noticeable mile-stone in the track as this great birthday, we look back on the things that never were, as naturally and full as gravely as on the things that have been and are gone, or have been and still are? If it be so, and so it seems to be, must we come to the conclusion that life is little better than a dream, and little worth the loves and strivings that we crowd into it?

No! Far be such miscalled philosophy from us, dear Reader, on Christmas Day! Nearer and closer to our hearts be the Christmas spirit, which is the spirit of active usefulness, perseverance, cheerful discharge of duty, kindness and forbearance! It is in the last virtues especially, that we are, or should be, strengthened by the unaccomplished visions of our youth; for, who shall say that they are not our teachers to deal gently even with the impalpable nothings of the earth!

Therefore, as we grow older, let us be more thankful that the circle of our Christmas associations and of the lessons that they bring, expands! Let us welcome every one of them, and summon them to take their places by the Christmas hearth.

Welcome, old aspirations, glittering creatures of an ardent fancy, to your shelter underneath the holly! We know you, and have not outlived you yet. Welcome, old projects and old loves, however fleeting, to your nooks among the steadier lights that burn around us. Welcome, all that was ever real to our hearts; and for the earnestness that made you real, thanks to Heaven! Do we build no Christmas castles in the clouds now? Let our thoughts, fluttering like butterflies among these flowers of children, bear witness! Before this boy, there stretches out a Future, brighter than we ever looked on in our old romantic time, but bright with honour and with truth. Around this little head on which the sunny curls lie heaped, the graces sport, as prettily, as airily, as when there was no scythe within the reach of Time to shear away the curls of our first-love. Upon another girl's face near it—placider but smiling bright—a quiet and contented little face, we see Home fairly written. Shining from the word, as rays shine from a star, we see how, when our graves are old, other hopes than ours are young, other hearts than ours are moved; how other ways are smoothed; how other happiness blooms, ripens, and decays—no, not decays, for other homes and other bands of children, not yet in being nor for ages yet to be, arise, and bloom and ripen to the end of all!

Welcome, everything! Welcome, alike what has been, and what never was, and what we hope may be, to your shelter underneath the holly, to your places round the Christmas fire, where what is sits open-hearted! In yonder shadow, do we see obtruding furtively upon the blaze, an enemy's face? By Christmas Day we do forgive him! If the injury he has done us may admit of such companionship, let him come here and take his place. If otherwise, unhappily, let him go hence, assured that we will never injure nor accuse him.

On this day we shut out Nothing!

"Pause," says a low voice. "Nothing? Think!"

"On Christmas Day, we will shut out from our fireside, Nothing."

"Not the shadow of a vast City where the withered leaves are lying deep?" the voice replies. "Not the shadow that darkens the whole globe? Not the shadow of the City of the Dead?"

Not even that. Of all days in the year, we will turn our faces towards that City upon Christmas Day, and from its silent hosts bring those we loved, among us. City of the Dead, in the blessed name wherein we are gathered together at this time, and in the Presence that is here among us according to the promise, we will receive, and not dismiss, thy people who are dear to us! Yes. We can look upon these children angels that alight, so solemnly, so beautifully among the living children by the fire, and can bear to think how they departed from us. Entertaining angels unawares, as the Patriarchs did, the playful children are unconscious of their guests; but we can see them— can see a radiant arm around one favourite neck, as if there were a tempting of that child away. Among the celestial figures there is one, a poor mis-shapen boy[1] on earth, of a glorious beauty now, of whom his dying mother said it grieved her much to leave him here, alone, for so many years as it was likely would elapse before he came to her—being such a little child. But he went quickly, and was laid upon her breast, and in her hand she leads him.

There was a gallant boy, who fell, far away, upon a burning sand beneath a burning sun, and said, "Tell them at home, with my last love, how much I could have wished to kiss them once, but that I died contented and had done my duty!" Or there was another, over whom they read the words, "Therefore we commit his body to the deep," and so consigned him to the lonely ocean and sailed on. Or there was another, who lay down to his rest in the dark shadow of great forests, and, on earth, awoke no more. O shall they not, from sand and sea and forest, be brought home at such a time!

There was a dear girl—almost a woman—never to be one—who made a mourning Christmas in a house of joy, and went her trackless way to the silent City. Do we recollect her, worn out, faintly whispering what could not be heard, and falling into that last sleep for weariness? O look upon her now! O look upon her beauty, her serenity, her changeless youth, her happiness! The daughter of Jairus[2] was recalled to life, to die; but she, more blest, has heard the same voice, saying unto her, "Arise for ever!"

We had a friend who was our friend from early days, with whom we often pictured the changes that were to come upon our lives, and merrily imagined how we would speak, and walk, and think, and talk, when we came to be old. His destined habitation in the City of the Dead received him in his prime. Shall he be shut out from our Christmas remembrance? Would his love have so excluded us? Lost friend, lost child, lost parent, sister, brother, husband, wife, we will not so discard you! You shall hold your cherished places in our Christmas hearts, and by our Christmas fires; and in

---

1 Harry Burnett, the crippled son of Dickens's sister Fanny, who died in September 1848. Her son died four months later.
2 In the gospel of Saint Mark, the story of Jairus, a ruler in the synagogue, whose daughter is restored to life by Jesus.

the season of immortal hope, and on the birthday of immortal mercy, we will shut out Nothing!

The winter sun goes down over town and village; on the sea it makes a rosy path, as if the Sacred tread were fresh upon the water. A few more moments, and it sinks, and night comes on, and lights begin to sparkle in the prospect. On the hill-side beyond the shapelessly-diffused town, and in the quiet keeping of the trees that gird the village-steeple, remembrances are cut in stone, planted in common flowers, growing in grass, entwined with lowly brambles around many a mound of earth. In town and village, there are doors and windows closed against the weather, there are flaming logs heaped high, there are joyful faces, there is healthy music of voices. Be all ungentleness and harm excluded from the temples of the Household Gods, but be those remembrances admitted with tender encouragement! They are of the time and all its comforting and peaceful reassurances; and of the history that re-united even upon earth the living and the dead; and of the broad beneficence and goodness that too many men have tried to tear to narrow shreds.

[Source: *Charles Dickens: Christmas Stories*, ed. Ruth Glancy (London: J.M. Dent, 1966) 19-23. Originally published in December 1851 in *Household Words*.]

Appendix B: Child Labor, Education, and the Workhouse

1. From Report of the Children's Employment Commission (1842)

[In October 1840, the British government set up a commission to investigate the employment and condition of the children of the poorer classes in mines, collieries, and various branches of trade and manufacture. The first report, issued in 1842 and numbering thousands of pages, presented in meticulous detail a devastating account of the horrific abuse of children. These investigations contributed to the gradual improvement of the working conditions of children and women through such legislation as the 1847 Factory Act, which regulated industrial labor. Horne's report, along with the "Blue Book" reports of the other commissioners, helped to fuel the protest literature of such authors as Benjamin Disraeli, Elizabeth Gaskell, Elizabeth Barrett Browning (her Cry of the Children was a powerful indictment of child labor abuses), and Charles Dickens.

The full reports are available in the British Parliamentary Papers, 15 vols. (Irish University Press: Shannon, 1968-69).

The following essay by Richard Henry Horne, one of the appointed sub-commissioners, captures the essence of these lengthy government reports through his judicious selection of details from the various investigators, and, as one who had a significant hand in the investigations himself, he ably frames the discussion with his own sense of outrage. Horne was a poet, critic, and editor who contributed to Dickens's Daily News and Household Words. By publishing his essay on the commissioners' report in the popular Illuminated Magazine, edited by Douglas Jerrold, the radical contributor to Punch and a popular playwright, he could be assured of reaching a large and sympathetic audience of influential people.

Dickens found the commissioners' report so disturbing that he visited the mines in Cornwall to witness for himself the inhumane conditions of the children working there. One of the commissioners urged Dickens to write about the appalling conditions of the children and helped him to monitor the progress of the government's second report, which was published in 1843. Dickens planned to write a pamphlet entitled "An Appeal to the People of England, on behalf of the Poor Man's Child" but the pamphlet never materialized. Fortuitously, however, Dickens's appeal found expression in A Christmas Carol, through which it left an indelible mark on the conscience of the age.

Internal references in the report have been omitted.]

Children's Employment Commission.

First Report of the Commissioners, On Mines; Second Report, On Trades and Manufactures; Appendices (Containing Reports and Evidence from the Assistant Commissioners). Folio. 4 Vols. 1842-3.

By R.H. Horne.

IT is an unalterable decree of nature that man, to maintain a healthful condition of body or mind, must *work*; but there is no decree in nature that man should be a slave. Born for no despotism, his faculties not given him to be narrowed and abused, and the light of heaven being his simple right — no king of armies has a greater — the life-long confinement to hard labour, like a criminal without crime, the homicidal field of war, the degradation of the galleys, the mine or the reeking factory, are the sheer invention of his fellow-men, the vicious power and knowledge that master his vice and ignorance, or his industrious poverty and weakness in the social scale. To labour hard is honourable; to earn the needful daily bread by the sweat of the brow — that bread which is never given without that sweat to those who are hungry — can never be a disgrace to the earner; but when the honest working-man is treated like a beast, and his wife and children like the commonest cattle, then, indeed, is it time for his countrymen to bethink them of their boasted freedom, their excellent institutions, and the Christianity of the owners of the soil. But beneath this depth of degradation a lower deep is yet to be found. In what dark pit of coal or stone? — in what unwholesome factory? — in what smoky, squalid field or hovel? In the mind — in that abject condition which has no sense of its abjectness, no care to be otherwise: which can make no struggle to emancipate itself, but *will* make a struggle, if emancipated, to return to its darkness and its chain; an abject condition in which a father and a mother shall forget the common ties of nature, and sell their children to the worst slavery, even during their tender years.

To the honour of the late Government, which, at the instigation of Lord Ashley,[1] originated the Children's Employment Commission, and to the honour of the present Government, which gave so immediate an attention to the able and profoundly-moving appeal of that benevolent nobleman, a rapid legislation took place with reference to the women and girls employed in mines and collieries, together with the premature and excessive labour of children. No sooner were these evils fully made known and

---

1 Anthony Ashley Cooper, 7th Earl of Shaftesbury, on 7 June 1842 moved "An Act to prohibit the Employment of Women and Girls in Mines and Collieries, to regulate the Employment of Boys, and make Provisions for the Safety of Persons working therein."

attested—through the very careful and freely-condensed report of the Central Board of Commissioners, compiled from the voluminous reports and evidence of the Assistant-Commissioners, who had personally visited the several districts—than a bill was passed tending greatly to ameliorate them. It is true that Lord Ashley's bill aimed at higher things than the House of Lords could tolerate, and it was mutilated accordingly to fit their lordships' minds; but to the honour of human nature, though opposed to the financial interests of many extensive proprietors, a bill did pass, whereby no child under ten years of age is allowed to work in a mine, and no woman or girl, of whatever age. This law came into operation on the 1st of March.

But observe what the very next session—that is, the present—develops! Petitions are poured in from mining and factory districts, praying to have all the good undone before its natural effect has had any time to operate. In some districts the most effectual means were taken to prevent the wholesome operation of the bill. The bill recommended the gradual removal of female labourers from the mines previous to the 1st of March; and in Scotland, where the greatest abuses in the mines were discovered, the proprietors, in general, reserved all their female labourers to be let loose on the same day. Of course they had no other occupation at hand; of course neither habit nor understanding, nor domestic position, enabled them to say to their husbands, fathers, and brothers—"Do not get drunk twice a week, but work instead." The consequences were certain; these petitions are the second feature of those consequences; the first has already fallen, in various forms and degrees, upon the unfortunate women and girls. The proprietors wished to keep the women and girls because they got them cheaper than the men, and because they would do more humiliating drudgery, and in more noxious and slushy places than the men. But if any one entertains a doubt as to whether all these poor women and girls should be sacrificed to these few interests of property, it is easy to settle that question. Let us begin by quoting the words of an eyewitness, one of the Assistant-Commissioners, describing a coal-pit in the east of Scotland, where the workings are from 100 to 200 yards from the main roads, and where, throughout that distance, and through dark, steep, narrow passages, from only 22 to 28 inches in height, children and young persons of both sexes had to crawl, dragging after them a load of coal of 3 cwt.[1]

"The danger and the difficulties," observes the Sub-Commissioner, "of dragging on roads, dipping from one foot in three to one foot in six, may be more easily conceived than explained; and the state which females are in after pulling like horses through these holes—their perspiration, their

---

1   1 cwt (a hundredweight) equals 112 pounds.

exhaustion, and very frequently even their tears, it is painful in the extreme to witness; yet, when the work is done, they return to it with a vigour which is surprising, considering how inwardly they hate it." Of the seventy of the labour performed by young women in these pits, the account of her work given by Margaret Hipps may serve as an example.

Margaret Hipps, 17 years old, putter, Stoney Rigg Colliery, Stirling-shire: — "My employment, after reaching the wall-face, is to fill a bogie,[1] or slype, with 2.5 to 3 cwt. of coal. I then hook it on to my chain, and drag it through the seam, which is 26 to 28 inches high, till I get to the main road—a good distance, probably 200 to 400 yards. The pavement I drag over is wet, and I am obliged at all times to crawl on hands and feet, with my bogie hung to the chain and ropes. It is sad sweating and sore fatiguing work, and frequently maims the women." ...

The persons employed in coal-bearing are almost always girls and women. Boys are sometimes engaged in the same labour, but that is com-paratively rare. The coal-bearers have to carry coal on their backs in unrailed roads, or up ladders or turnpike stairs, with burdens varying from .75 cwt. to 3 cwt. The Sub-Commissioner represents this labourer as "a cruel slaving revolting to humanity;" yet he found engaged in this labour a child, a beautiful girl, only six years old, whose age he ascertained, carrying in the pit a half cwt. of coals, and regularly making with this load fourteen long and toilsome journeys a day.

Margaret Leveston, six years old, coal-bearer: — "Been down at coal-carrying six weeks; makes ten to fourteen rakes a day; carries full 56 lbs. of coal in a wooden backit. The work is na guid; it is so very sair. I work with sister Jessie and mother; dinna ken the time we gang; it is gai dark." ...

The degraded condition of the children and young persons employed in mines was rendered the more apparent to comprehension by the introduc-tion of certain diagrams and sketches, made on the spot by the Assistant-Commissioners. The sight of them caused great commiseration among all those who could feel for poor people; and great annoyance and disgust to the fine senses of all those who could not, or would not. Lord London-derry[2] declared that the sketches were offensive—made him quite sick—and were "calculated to inflame the passions." The passions—what pas-sions? The passions of pity and indignation. True, the sketches were often "disgusting;" but for that very reason the cause, not the explanatory sketch-es, should be removed. ...

The importance will be perceived of keeping the doors [of the mine

---

1   A heavy wooden cart or truck.
2   Charles William Vane, 3rd Marquis of Londonderry, who owned vast coalfields in Durham, was the main opponent of the Bill.

shafts] shut which prevent the passage of the air from one main-way to another, before it has traversed the whole extent of the mine; and as these doors require to be frequently opened, to allow the passage of the loaded corvus, or small carts, which convey the coal towards the shaft, some means are necessary to provide for their immediately closing again. It will scarcely be believed that this important trust, on which depends the lives of the colliers and the property of the owners, was found by the Commissioners to be universally intrusted to the youngest children in the mine. Little creatures, almost always under eight years of age, often five and six, of both sexes, were found placed at these air-doors for twelve or more hours consecutively, in darkness, their sole employment being to attend to these doors. These poor infants are called "trappers."

The trappers sit in a little hole scooped out for them in the side of the gates behind each door, where they sit with a string in their hands attached to the door, and pull it open the moment they hear the corves (*i.e.* carriages for conveying the coal) at hand, and the moment it has passed they let the door fall to, which it does of its own weight. If anything impedes the shutting of the door they remove it, or, if unable to do so, run to the nearest man to get him to do it for them. They have nothing else to do; but, as their office must be performed from the repassing of the first to the passing of the last corve during the day, they are in the pit the whole time it is worked, frequently above 12 hours a day. They sit, moreover, in the dark, often with a damp floor to stand on, and exposed necessarily to drafts. It is a most painful thing to contemplate the dull dungeon-like life these little creatures are doomed to spend,— a life, for the most part, passed in solitude, damp, and darkness. They are allowed no light; but sometimes a good-natured collier will bestow a little bit of candle on them as a treat. On one occasion, as I was passing a little trapper, he begged me for a little grease from my candle. I found that the poor child had scooped out a hole in a great stone, and, having obtained a wick, had manufactured a rude sort of lamp; and that he kept it going as well as he could by begging contributions of melted tallow from the candles of any Samaritan passers by. To be in the dark, in fact, seemed to be the great grievance with all of them....

John Saville, seven years old, collier's boy at the Soap Pit, Sheffield: — "I stand and open and shut the door. I'm generally in the dark, and sit me down against the door. I stop 12 hours in the pit. I never see daylight now, except on Sundays. I fell asleep one day, and a corve ran over my leg and made it smart. They'd squeeze me against the door if I fall to sleep again." — Sarah Gooder, aged eight years: — "I'm a trapper in the Gauber Pit. I have to trap without a light; and I'm scared. I go at four and sometimes half-past three in the morning, and come out at five and half-past. I never go to sleep. Sometimes I sing when I've light, but not in the dark; I dare not sing then. I don't like being in the pit. I am very sleepy when I go sometimes in the morning." ...

[Richard] Ayton's[1] description of the trappers is as follows: —

One class of sufferers in the mine moved my compassion more than any other: a number of children who attend at the doors to open them when the horses pass through, and who, in this duty, are compelled to linger through their lives in silence, solitude and darkness, for sixpence a day. When I first came to one of these doors, I saw it open without perceiving by what means, till, looking behind it, I beheld a miserable little wretch steading without a light, silent and motionless, and resembling, in the abjectness of its condition, *some reptile peculiar to the place, rather than a human creature.* On speaking to it I was touched with the patience and uncomplaining meekness with which it submitted to its horrible imprisonment, and the little sense that it had of the barbarity of its unnatural parents. Few of the children thus inhumanly sacrificed were more than eight years old, and *several were considerably less,* and had barely strength sufficient to perform the office that was required from them. On their first introduction into the mine the poor little victims struggle and scream with terror at the darkness; but there are found people brutal enough to force them to compliance, and after a few trials they become tame and spiritless, and yield themselves up, at least without noise and resistance, to any cruel slavery that it pleases their masters to impose upon them. In the winter time they never see daylight except on a Sunday, for it has been discovered that they can serve for thirteen hours a day without perishing; and they are pitilessly compelled to such a term of solitary confinement, with as little consideration for the injury that they suffer, as is felt for the hinges and pulleys of the doors at which they attend.

The next species of employment to which children are put in the mines, as soon as they are strong enough, is that of dragging the loaded corves from the workings to the foot of the shaft. In some districts this is done by fixing a girdle round the naked waist, to which a chain from the corve is hooked and passed between the legs, and the boys or girls crawl on their hands and knees, drawing the corve full of coal after them. This is called "drawing by girdle and chain." In other districts the same kind of work is done by pushing with the head and hands from behind. This is called "putting," or "hurrying." ...

The printed evidence of the Children, taken from various districts, will show the severe pain which this mode of labour inflicts. They attest that the girdle and chain frequently rub the skin off them, make blisters "as large

---

1 Horne quotes from the essayist Richard Aytoun (1786–1823).

as shillings, and half-crowns," and otherwise injure the boys and girls. They get no rest all day, unless for a few moments at a time, and in general "only when something is the matter with the engine." The *human* engine, it will be perceived, is treated without any such consideration, though there is continually something the matter with it. The galling modes of work are various: —

Katharine Logan, 16 years old, Coal-putter: — "Began to work at coal-carrying more than five years since; *works in harness* now; draws backwards, with face to the tubs; the ropes and chains go under pit-clothes; it is o'er sair work, especially when we crawl."

Rosa Lucas, aged 18, Lamberhead Green: — "Do you find it very hard work?" "Yes, it is very hard work for a woman. I have been so tired many a time that I could scarcely wash myself. I could scarcely ever wash myself at night, I was so tired; and I felt very dull and stiff when I set off in the morning." — James Crabtree, aged 15, Mr. Dearden's, near Todmorden: — "Is it hard work for the lads in winter?" — "My brother falls asleep before his supper, and the little lass that helps him is often very tired." — Peter Gaskell, Mr. Lancaster's, near Worsley: — "Has four sisters, and they have all worked in the pits; one of them works in the pits now; she sometimes complains of the severity of her work. Three years ago, when they had very hard work, I used to hear her complain of the boils on her back, *and her legs were all eaten by the water;* she had to go through water to her work; she used to go about four or five o'clock in the morning, and stay till three or four in the afternoon, just as she was wanted; I have known her to be that tired at night that she would go to sleep before she had anything to eat." ...

In this district (the West Riding of Yorkshire) girls are almost universally employed as trappers and hurriers in common with boys. The girls employed as hurriers are of all ages, from seven to twenty-one; they commonly work quite naked down to the waist. The boys of similar ages who work with them are also naked down to the waist, and both (for the garment is pretty much the same in both) are dressed, as far as they are dressed at all, in a loose pair of trousers, seldom whole in either sex. In many of the collieries, as has been already stated, the adult colliers, whom these girls serve, work perfectly naked....

The second Report of this Commission contains a series of facts with regard to the Trades and Manufactures, no less startling, and equally unknown to the public at large. Foremost stand the disclosures relating to the system of apprenticeship; and as it is to be hoped that the Legislature will extend its consideration to the abuses which exist in the trades and manufactures, it is very important that public sympathy should be aroused on this subject....

In all cases the children, of whatever age, are bound till they attain the age of twenty-one years. If the child be only seven years of age, the period of servitude remains the same, however simple the process or nature of the trade to be learnt. During the first year or two, if the apprentice be very young, he is merely used to run errands, do dirty house-hold work, nurse infants, &c.

If the master die before the apprentice attain the age of twenty-one years, the apprentice is equally bound as the servant of his deceased master's heirs, executors, administrators, and assigns—in fact, the apprentice is part of the deceased master's goods and chattels. Whoever, therefore, may carry on the trade, he is the servant of such person or persons until his manumission is obtained by reaching his one-and-twentieth year. The apprentice has no regular pocket-money allowed him by the master. Sometimes a few halfpence are given to him. An apprentice of eighteen or nineteen years of age often has 2d. or 3d. a week given him, but never as a rightful claim.

Wolverhampton may be described as the capital of a region, the surface of which is covered with cinders, varied here and there by tall chimneys vomiting smoke and flame, and at longer intervals by congregations of dingy, mean-looking houses, which, when they have become sufficiently numerous, are called towns. The "landscape" round Bilston is literally "as black as a hat;" and a tree that appears here and there, bears a close resemblance to those odd-looking brush-machines that are used to sweep chimneys. Coseley, near Sedgley, is absolutely a town of black chimneys, varying in height, from two or three feet to upwards of 100 feet, all situated in a low hallow, and vomiting thick sooty wreaths of swift-ascending smoke. But, in other respects, a yet more extraordinary place is Willenhall, a kind of detached branch of Wolverhampton, at the distance of about three miles from its parent place, and containing only five or six individuals who are not engaged in the peculiar trade of the town. The small masters there work from 16 to 18 hours a day—sometimes more—and their apprentices, of whatever age, all work the same time. Many of the small masters idle away Monday and Tuesday in the public-houses, and are often unfit for work on Wednesday morning. But as they live from week to week, a certain amount of work must be done, so that there are no bounds to the drudgery at the latter end of the week, in all of which the children must share so long as they are able to stand or hold a file. The consequences of such a life to the apprentices may be, in part, conjectured; to the adults it speedily induces various kinds of disease, deformity, and premature death.

Among other witnesses, the Superintendent Registrar states that in those trades, particularly in which the work is by the piece, the growth of the children is injured; that in these cases more especially their strength is over-taxed for profit. One of the constables of the town says that "there are examples without number in the place of deformed men and boys; their backs, or their legs, and often both, grow wrong—the backs grow out and the legs grow in at the knees—hump-backed and knock-kneed. There is most commonly only one leg turned in,—a K leg; it is occasioned by standing all day for years filing at a vice; the hind leg grows in—the leg that is hindermost. Thinks that among the adults of the working classes of Willenhall, whose work is all forging and filing, one-third of the number are afflicted with hernia," &c....

As to the food of great numbers of the apprentices of these towns, the statements are incontrovertibly supported:—

That "offal meat is continually sold by the small masters, who feed their apprentices with it; that cows, calves, sheep, and pigs, that die, no matter from what cause, are bought by butchers, and are sold in the market; and that there are butchers who deal exclusively in diseased meat. It is further stated in evidence that horse-flesh is often sold for beef-steaks, and that bad fish is frequently purchased for the use of the apprentices, producing bowel-complaints and other disease."

Overwhelming evidence corroborates this disgusting fact. Mr. Henry Nicholls Payne, superintendent-registrar of Wolverhampton, says—

"The food of the children is not of a sufficiently good quality; inferior meat is often given them; calves which come prematurely into the world find a ready sale by candlelight in the markets, together with very bad beef of old cows which it was necessary to kill hastily, or which are sometimes dead before they come into the hands of the butcher; and all these are frequently purchased for apprenticed children. This, of course, is not the case with all masters, some of them being careful to supply proper provisions—they would be disgusted at the meat which is thus purchased by so many."...

The clothing, or rather the thin tatters, of numbers of the apprentices, their meagre bodies and stunted stature, space will not allow to be described. But the appalling part of the picture yet remains to be disclosed. These poor boys, helpless orphans as most of them are, without friend to appeal to, or law to protect them, are, in many cases, treated by their masters with a degree of brutality which would be incredible, were it not attested by so many witnesses in the printed evidence.

In Sedgley they are sometimes struck with a red-hot iron, and burnt and bruised simultaneously; sometimes they have "a flash of lightning" sent at them. When a bar of iron is drawn white-hot from the forge it emits fiery particles, which the man commonly flings in a shower upon the ground by a swing of his arm, before placing the bar upon the anvil. This shower is sometimes directed at the boy. It may come over his hands and face, his naked arms, or on his breast. If his shirt be open in front, which is usually the case, the red-hot particles are lodged therein, and he has to shake them out as fast as he can. In Darlaston, however, the children appear to be very little beaten, and in Bilston there were only a few instances of cruel treatment: "the boys are kicked and cuffed abundantly, but not with any vicious or cruel intention, and only with an idea that this is getting the work done." In Wednesbury the treatment is better than in any other town in the district. The boys are not generally subject to any severe corporal chastisement, though a few cases of ill-treatment occasionally occur. "A few months ago an adult workman broke a boy's arm by a blow with a piece of iron; the boy went to school till his arm got well; his father and mother thought it a good opportunity to give him some schooling."

But the class of children in this district the most abused and oppressed are the apprentices, and particularly those who are bound to the small masters among the locksmiths, key and bolt makers, screw makers, &c. Even among these smaller masters, there are respectable and humane men, who do not suffer any degree of poverty to render them brutal; but many of these men treat their apprentices not so much with neglect and harshness, as with ferocious violence: the result of unbridled passions, excited often by ardent spirits, acting on bodies exhausted by over-work, and on minds which have never received the slightest moral or religious culture, and which, therefore, never exercise the smallest moral or religious restraint.

Evidence from all classes, masters, journeymen, residents, magistrates, clergymen, constables, and, above all, from the mouths of the poor oppressed sufferers themselves, is adduced to a heart-breaking extent. The public has been excited to pity by Dickens's picture of Smike[1]—in Willenhall, there are many Smikes.

★ ★ ★, aged sixteen: — "His master stints him from six in the morning till ten and sometimes eleven at night, as much as ever he can do; and if he don't do it, his master gives him no supper, and gives him a good hiding, sometimes with a big strap, sometimes with a big stick. His master has cut his head open five times—once with a key and twice with a lock; knocked the corner of a lock into his head twice—once with an iron belt, and once with an iron shut—a thing that runs into the staple. His master's name is _____, of Little London. There is another apprentice besides him, who is treated just as bad." —★ ★ ★, aged fifteen: — "Works at knob-locks with _____. Is a fellow-apprentice with ____ ____. Lives in the house of his master. Is beaten by his master, who hits him sometimes with his fists, and sometimes with the file-haft, and sometimes with a stick—it's no matter what when he's a bit cross; sometimes hits him with the locks; has cut his head open four or five times; so he has his fellow apprentice's head. Once, when he cut his head open with a key, thinks half a pint of blood run

---

1   A slow-witted and abused boy in Squeers' Dotheboys Hall, in Dickens's *Nicholas Nickleby*.

off him." —★ ★ ★, aged fourteen: — "Has been an in-door apprentice three years. Has no wages; nobody gets any wages for him. Has to serve till he is twenty-one. His master behaves very bad. His mistress behaves worst, like a devil; she beats him; knocks his head against the wall. His master goes out a-drinking, and when he comes back, if anything's gone wrong that he (the boy) knows nothing about, he is beat all the same."—★ ★ ★, aged sixteen: — "His master sometimes hits him with his fist, sometimes kicks him; gave him the black eye he has got; beat him in bed while he was asleep, at five in the morning, because he was not up to work. He came upstairs and set about him—set about him with his fist. Has been over to the public office, Brummagem, to complain; took a note with him, which was written for him; his brother gave it to the public office there, but they would not attend to it; they said they could do no good; and gave the note back. He had been beaten at that time with a whip-handle—it made wales all down his arms and back and all; everybody he showed it to said it was scandalous. Wishes he could be released from his master, 'who's never easy but when he's a-beating of me. Never has enough to eat at no time; ax him for more, he won't gie it me.'"…

It is admissible that in the process of these investigations my sympathies were chiefly attracted by those who most needed legislative interference and help, and, consequently, my Reports have displayed more consideration towards the poorest classes of operatives than many of their employers have been pleased to approve. I have been angrily accused by some of the latter, or their friends, of writing one-sided Reports, and the letters of complaint against me have, no doubt, been well intended. It was not the express business of this Commission to be complimentary, or I could have found various things to enlarge upon with admiration; nor have I ever failed to make all due and honourable exceptions. These exceptions are the light side of the picture, and would also be one-sided, i.e., one of the true sides;—the dark side is equally true, and only seems exaggerated because most dwelt upon, with a view to the amelioration of those who are suffering in the shade.

[Source: *The Illuminated Magazine*, ed. Douglas Jerrold, 4 vols. (London: Published for the proprietors, 1843–45); vol. 1 (May, 1843): 45–53.]

2. From Charles Dickens's speech at the First Annual Soirée of the Athenaeum: Manchester (October 5, 1843)

[The Athenaeum was a charitable institution for the Manchester working class. It was during his three-day visit to Manchester that Dickens, caught up in issues of the poor reflected in his speech, conceived the idea for *A Christmas Carol*.]

....You are perfectly well aware, I have no doubt, that the Athenæum was projected at a time when commerce was in a vigorous and flourishing condition, and when those classes of society to which it particularly addresses itself were fully employed, and in the receipt of regular incomes. A season of depression almost without parallel ensued, and large numbers of young men employed in warehouses and offices suddenly found their occupation gone, and themselves reduced to very straightened and penurious circumstances. This altered state of things led, as I am told, to the compulsory withdrawal of many of the members, to a proportionate decrease in the expected funds, and to the incurrence of a debt of £3,000. By the very great zeal and energy of all concerned, and by the liberality of those to whom they applied for help, that debt is now in rapid course of being discharged. [*Great applause.*] A little more of the same indefatigable exertion on the one hand, and a little more of the same community of feeling upon the other, and there will be no such thing; the figures will be blotted out for good and all; and, from that time, the Athenæum may be said to belong to you and to your heirs for ever. [*Loud applause.*]

But, ladies and gentlemen, at all times, now in its most thriving, and in its least flourishing condition—here, with its cheerful rooms, its pleasant and instructive lectures, its improving library of six thousand volumes; its opportunities of discussion and debate, of healthful bodily exercise, and, though last not least (for by this I set great store, as a very novel and excellent provision) its opportunities of blameless rational enjoyment [*hear, hear*]—here it is, open to every youth and man in this great town, accessible to every being in this vast hive, who, for all these benefits, and the inestimable ends to which they lead, can set aside one sixpence weekly. [*Hear, hear, and applause.*] I do look upon the reduction of the subscription to that amount, and upon the fact that the number of members has considerably more than doubled within the last twelve months, as strides in the path of the very best civilization, and chapters of rich promise in the history of mankind. [*Applause.*]

I do not know, ladies and gentlemen, whether, at this time of day and with such a prospect before us, we need trouble ourselves very much to rake up the ashes of the dead-and-gone objections,—the palsied, halting, blind, deaf, everything but dumb objections, that were wont to be urged by men of all parties against institutions such as this whose interests we are met to promote; but their philosophy was always to be summed up in the unmeaning application of one short sentence. How often have we heard, from that large class of men, wise in their generation, who would really seem to be born and bred for no other purpose than to pass into currency counterfeit and mischievous scraps of wisdom, as it is the sole pursuit of some other criminals to utter base coin,—how often have we heard from them as an all-convincing and self-evident argument, that 'A little learning is a dangerous thing'? [*Hear, hear.*] Why, a little hanging was considered a very dangerous thing, according to the same authorities [*laughter*], with this difference, that because a little hanging was dangerous, we had a great deal of it; and because a little learning was dangerous, we were to have none at all. [*Applause and laughter.*] Why, when I hear such cruel absurdities gravely reiterated, I do sometimes begin to doubt whether the parrots of society are not more pernicious to its interests than its birds of prey. I should be glad to hear such people's estimate of the comparative danger of 'a little learning' and a vast amount of ignorance [*hear, hear*]; I should be glad to know which they consider the most prolific parent of misery and crime. [*Hear, hear, and applause.*] Descending a little lower in the social scale, I should be glad to assist them in their calculations, by carrying them into certain jails and nightly refuges I know of, where my own heart dies within me when I see thousands of immortal creatures condemned, without alternative or choice, to tread, not what our great poet calls 'the primrose path to the everlasting bonfire,' but one of jagged flints and stones, laid down by brutal ignorance, and held together like the solid rocks by years of this most wicked axiom. [*Great applause.*]

Would we know from any honourable body of merchants, upright in deed and thought, whether they would rather have ignorant or enlightened persons in their employment, we have their answer in this building; we have their answer in this company; we have it emphatically given in the munificent generosity of your own merchants of Manchester, of all sects and kinds, when this establishment was first proposed. [*Applause.*] But, ladies and gentlemen, are the advantages derivable by the people from institutions such as this, only of a negative character? If a little learning be an innocent thing, has it no distinct, wholesome, and immediate influence upon the mind? [*Hear, hear.*] The old doggerel rhyme, so often written in the beginning of books, says that

When house and lands are gone and spent,
Then learning is most excellent.

But I should be strongly disposed to reform that adage, and say that

Though house and lands be never got,
Learning can give what they can not.

[*Hear, hear, and applause.*] And this I know, that the first un-purchaseable blessing earned by every man who makes an effort to improve himself in such a place as the Athenæum is self-respect [*hear*]—an inward dignity of character which once acquired and righteously maintained, nothing, no, not the hardest drudgery, nor the direst poverty, can vanquish. [*Applause.*] Though he should find it hard for a season even to keep the wolf of hunger from his door, let him but once have chased the dragon of ignorance from his hearth, and self-respect and hope are left him. [*Applause.*] You could no more deprive him of those sustaining qualities by loss or destruction of his worldly goods, than you could, by plucking out his eyes, take from him an internal consciousness of the bright glory of the sun. [*Loud applause*] ...

The more a man who improves his leisure in such a place learns, the better, gentler, kinder man he must become. [*Hear, hear.*] When he knows how much great minds have suffered for the truth in every age and time, and to what dismal persecutions opinion has been exposed, he will become more tolerant of other men's belief in all matters, and will incline more leniently to their sentiments when they chance to differ from his own. [*Hear, hear.*] Understanding that the relations between himself and his employers involve a mutual duty and responsibility, he will discharge his part of the implied contract cheerfully, faithfully, and honourably; for the history of every useful life warns him to shape his course in that direction.

The benefits he acquires in such a place are not of a selfish kind, but extend themselves to his home, and to those whom it contains. Something of what he hears or reads within such walls can scarcely fail to become at times a topic of discourse by his own fireside, nor can it ever fail to lead to larger sympathies with men, and to a higher veneration for the great Creator of all the wonders of this universe. [*Applause.*] It appeals to his home and his homely feeling in other ways; for at certain times he carries there his wife and daughter, or his sister, or, possibly, some bright-eyed acquaintance of a more tender description. [*Hear, hear.*] Judging from what I see before me, I think it is very likely [*applause*]; I am sure I would if I could. [*Laughter and applause.*] He takes her there to enjoy a pleasant evening, to be gay and happy. Or, sometimes, it is possible he may happen to date his tenderness from the Athenæum. [*Laughter.*] I think that it is a very excellent thing, too, and not the least among the advantages of the institution. [*Hear, hear.*] In any case I am quite sure that the number of bright eyes and beaming faces which grace this meeting tonight by their presence, will never be among the least of its excellences in my recollection. [*Applause.*]

Ladies and gentlemen, I shall not easily forget this scene, the pleasing task your favour has devolved upon me, or the strong and inspiring confirmation I have tonight, of all the hopes and reliances I have ever placed upon institutions of this nature. In the literary point of view—in their bearings upon literature—I regard them as of great importance, deeming that the more intelligent and reflective society in the mass becomes, and the more readers there are, the more distinctly writers of all kinds will be able to throw themselves upon the truthful feeling of the people, and the more honoured and the more useful literature must be. [*Applause.*] At the same time, I must confess that, if there had been an Athenæum, and the people had been readers years ago, some leaves of dedication in your library, of praise of patrons which was very cheaply bought, very dearly sold, and very marketably haggled for by the groat, would be blank leaves, and posterity might probably have lacked the information that certain monsters of virtue ever had existence. [*Hear.*] But it is upon a much better and wider scale; it is, let me say it once again, in the effect of such institutions as these upon the great social system, and the peace and happiness of mankind, that I delight to contemplate them [*applause*]; and, in my heart, I am quite certain that long after this institution, and others of the same nature, have crumbled into dust, the noble harvest of the seed sown in them will shine out brightly in the wisdom, the mercy, and the forbearance of another race. [*Loud applause.*]

[Source: *The Speeches of Charles Dickens*, ed. K.J. Fielding (Oxford: Clarendon Press, 1960) 45–50.]

3. Charles Dickens, "A Walk in the Workhouse" (1850)

[The 1834 Poor Law Amendment Act proposed that all 15,000 parishes in England and Wales form into Poor Law Unions, each with its own workhouse and supervised by a local Board of Guardians. Under the new Act, the threat of the Union workhouse was intended to act as a deterrent to the able-bodied pauper. In fact, it removed the dole that supplemented wages, broke up homes, and forced into the workhouse the old, the infirm, the orphaned, unmarried mothers, the physically and mentally ill— along with the idle, drunkards, and prostitutes.

These grim institutions stirred dark memories in Dickens who, as a child, visited his parents in the Marshalsea debtors' prison. In *Oliver Twist* (1838) Dickens depicts the cruelty imposed upon children in the workhouse. A few years later, in *A Christmas Carol*, he has Scrooge refuse to make a donation to charity and glibly defer to the workhouse as the appropriate agent to accommodate the poor.

In the following essay, written seven years after *A Christmas Carol*, Dickens continues his attack upon the savage treatment of the poor in the union workhouses.]

On a certain Sunday, I formed one of the congregation assembled in the chapel of a large metropolitan Workhouse. With the exception of the clergyman and clerk, and a very few officials, there were none but paupers present. The children sat in the galleries; the women in the body of the chapel, and in one of the side aisles; the men in the remaining aisle. The service was decorously performed, though the sermon might have been much better adapted to the comprehension and to the circumstances of the hearers. The usual supplications were offered, with more than the usual significancy in such a place, for the fatherless children and widows, for all sick persons and young children, for all that were desolate and oppressed, for the comforting and helping of the weak-hearted, for the raising-up of them that had fallen; for all that were in danger, necessity, and tribulation. The prayers of the congregation were desired "for several persons in the various wards dangerously ill;" and others who were recovering returned their thanks to Heaven.

Among this congregation, were some evil-looking young women, and beetle-browed young men; but not many — perhaps that kind of characters kept away. Generally, the faces (those of the children excepted) were depressed and subdued, and wanted colour. Aged people were there, in every variety. Mumbling, blear-eyed, spectacled, stupid, deaf, lame; vacantly winking in the gleams of sun that now and then crept in through the open doors, from the paved yard; shading their listening ears, or blinking eyes, with their withered hands; poring over their books, leering at nothing, going to sleep, crouching and drooping in corners. There were weird old women, all skeleton within, all bonnet and cloak without, continually wiping their eyes with dirty dusters of pocket-handkerchiefs; and there were ugly old crones, both male and female, with a ghastly kind of contentment upon them which was not at all comforting to see. Upon the whole, it was the dragon, Pauperism, in a very weak and impotent condition; toothless, fangless, drawing his breath heavily enough, and hardly worth chaining up.

When the service was over, I walked with the humane and conscientious gentleman whose duty it was to take that walk, that Sunday morning, through the little world of poverty enclosed within the workhouse walls. It was inhabited by a population of some fifteen hundred or two thousand paupers, ranging from the infant newly born or not yet come into the pauper world, to the old man dying on his bed.

In a room opening from a squalid yard, where a number of listless women were lounging to and fro, trying to get warm in the ineffectual sunshine of the tardy May morning—in the "Itch Ward," not to compromise the truth—a woman such as HOGARTH[1] has often drawn, was hurriedly getting on her gown before a dusty fire. She was the nurse, or

---

1   William Hogarth (1697-1764), a British artist whose satirical paintings dramatized the contrast between luxury and squalor in society.

wardswoman, of that insalubrious department—herself a pauper—flabby, raw-boned, untidy—unpromising and coarse of aspect as need be. But, on being spoken to about the patients whom she had in charge, she turned round, with her shabby gown half on, half off, and fell a crying with all her might. Not for show, not querulously, not in any mawkish sentiment, but in the deep grief and affliction of her heart; turning away her dishevelled head: sobbing most bitterly, wringing her hands, and letting fall abundance of great tears, that choked her utterance. What was the matter with the nurse of the itch-ward? Oh, "the dropped child" was dead! Oh, the child that was found in the street, and she had brought up ever since, had died an hour ago, and see where the little creature lay, beneath this cloth! The dear, the pretty dear!

The dropped child seemed too small and poor a thing for Death to be in earnest with, but Death had taken it; and already its diminutive form was neatly washed, composed, and stretched as if in sleep upon a box. I thought I heard a voice from Heaven saying, It shall be well for thee, O nurse of the itch-ward, when some less gentle pauper does those offices to thy cold form, that such as the dropped child are the angels who behold my Father's face!

In another room, were several ugly old women crouching, witch-like, round a hearth, and chattering and nodding, after the manner of the monkeys. "All well here? And enough to eat?" A general chattering and chuckling; at last an answer from a volunteer. "Oh yes, gentleman! Bless you, gentleman! Lord bless the Parish of St. So-and-So! It feed the hungry, sir, and give drink to the thusty, and it warm them which is cold, so it do, and good luck to the parish of St. So-and-So, and thankee, gentleman!" Elsewhere, a party of pauper nurses were at dinner. "How do YOU get on?" "Oh pretty well, sir! We works hard, and we lives hard—like the sodgers!"[1]

In another room, a kind of purgatory or place of transition, six or eight noisy madwomen were gathered together, under the superintendence of one sane attendant. Among them was a girl of two or three and twenty, very prettily dressed, of most respectable appearance and good manners, who had been brought in from the house where she had lived as domestic servant (having, I suppose, no friends), on account of being subject to epileptic fits, and requiring to be removed under the influence of a very bad one. She was by no means of the same stuff, or the same breeding, or the same experience, or in the same state of mind, as those by whom she was surrounded; and she pathetically complained that the daily association and the nightly noise made her worse, and was driving her mad—which was perfectly evident. The case was noted for inquiry and redress, but she said she had already been there for some weeks.

---

1   Soldiers.

If this girl had stolen her mistress's watch, I do not hesitate to say she would have been infinitely better off. We have come to this absurd, this dangerous, this monstrous pass, that the dishonest felon is, in respect of cleanliness, order, diet, and accommodation, better provided for, and taken care of, than the honest pauper.

And this conveys no special imputation on the workhouse of the parish of St. So-and-So, where, on the contrary, I saw many things to commend. It was very agreeable, recollecting that most infamous and atrocious enormity committed at Tooting[1]—an enormity which, a hundred years hence, will still be vividly remembered in the bye-ways of English life, and which has done more to engender a gloomy discontent and suspicion among many thousands of the people than all the Chartist leaders[2] could have done in all their lives—to find the pauper children in this workhouse looking robust and well, and apparently the objects of very great care. In the Infant School—a large, light, airy room at the top of the building—the little creatures, being at dinner, and eating their potatoes heartily, were not cowed by the presence of strange visitors, but stretched out their small hands to be shaken, with a very pleasant confidence. And it was comfortable to see two mangy pauper rocking-horses rampant in a corner. In the girls' school, where the dinner was also in progress, everything bore a cheerful and healthy aspect. The meal was over, in the boys' school, by the time of our arrival there, and the room was not yet quite rearranged; but the boys were roaming unrestrained about a large and airy yard, as any other schoolboys might have done. Some of them had been drawing large ships upon the schoolroom wall; and if they had a mast with shrouds and stays set up for practice (as they have in the Middlesex House of Correction), it would be so much the better. At present, if a boy should feel a strong impulse upon him to learn the art of going aloft, he could only gratify it, I presume, as the men and women paupers gratify their aspirations after better board and lodging, by smashing as many workhouse windows as possible, and being promoted to prison.

In one place, the Newgate of the Workhouse, a company of boys and youths were locked up in a yard alone; their day-room being a kind of kennel where the casual poor used formerly to be littered down at night. Divers of them had been there some long time. "Are they never going away?" was the natural inquiry. "Most of them are crippled, in some form

---

1 Peter Drouet, in charge of the union workhouse in Tooting, was found guilty of manslaughter in 1849, after four children in his care died of cholera. The children were starved, poorly clothed, and lived in quarters described as "mephitic," the air reeking of carbonic acid.

2 Political reformers, chiefly workingmen, active in England from 1838 to 1848.

or other," said the Wardsman, "and not fit for anything." They slunk about, like dispirited wolves or hyaenas; and made a pounce at their food when it was served out, much as those animals do. The big-headed idiot shuffling his feet along the pavement, in the sunlight outside, was a more agreeable object everyway.

Groves of babies in arms; groves of mothers and other sick women in bed; groves of lunatics; jungles of men in stone-paved down-stairs day-rooms, waiting for their dinners; longer and longer groves of old people, in up-stairs Infirmary wards, wearing out life, God knows how — this was the scenery through which the walk lay, for two hours. In some of these latter chambers, there were pictures stuck against the wall, and a neat display of crockery and pewter on a kind of sideboard; now and then it was a treat to see a plant or two; in almost every ward there was a cat.

In all of these Long Walks of aged and infirm, some old people were bedridden, and had been for a long time; some were sitting on their beds half-naked; some dying in their beds; some out of bed, and sitting at a table near the fire. A sullen or lethargic indifference to what was asked, a blunted sensibility to everything but warmth and food, a moody absence of complaint as being of no use, a dogged silence and resentful desire to be left alone again, I thought were generally apparent. On our walking into the midst of one of these dreary perspectives of old men, nearly the following little dialogue took place, the nurse not being immediately at hand:

"All well here?"

No answer. An old man in a Scotch cap sitting among others on a form at the table, eating out of a tin porringer, pushes back his cap a little to look at us, claps it down on his forehead again with the palm of his hand, and goes on eating.

"All well here?" (repeated).

No answer. Another old man sitting on his bed, paralytically peeling a boiled potato, lifts his head and stares.

"Enough to eat?"

No answer. Another old man, in bed, turns himself and coughs.

"How are YOU to-day?" To the last old man.

That old man says nothing; but another old man, a tall old man of very good address, speaking with perfect correctness, comes forward from some-where, and volunteers an answer. The reply almost always proceeds from a volunteer, and not from the person looked at or spoken to.

"We are very old, sir," in a mild, distinct voice. "We can't expect to be well, most of us."

"Are you comfortable?"

"I have no complaint to make, sir." With a half shake of his head, a half shrug of his shoulders, and a kind of apologetic smile.

"Enough to eat?"

"Why, sir, I have but a poor appetite," with the same air as before; "and yet I get through my allowance very easily."

"But," showing a porringer with a Sunday dinner in it; "here is a portion of mutton, and three potatoes. You can't starve on that?"

"Oh dear no, sir," with the same apologetic air. "Not starve."

"What do you want?"

"We have very little bread, sir. It's an exceedingly small quantity of bread."

The nurse, who is now rubbing her hands at the questioner's elbow, interferes with, "It ain't much raly, sir. You see they've only six ounces a day, and when they've took their breakfast, there CAN only be a little left for night, sir." Another old man, hitherto invisible, rises out of his bed-clothes, as out of a grave, and looks on.

"You have tea at night?" The questioner is still addressing the well-spoken old man.

"Yes, sir, we have tea at night."

"And you save what bread you can from the morning, to eat with it?"

"Yes, sir—if we can save any."

"And you want more to eat with it?"

"Yes, sir." With a very anxious face.

The questioner, in the kindness of his heart, appears a little discomposed, and changes the subject.

"What has become of the old man who used to lie in that bed in the corner?"

The nurse don't remember what old man is referred to. There has been such a many old men. The well-spoken old man is doubtful. The spectral old man who has come to life in bed, says, "Billy Stevens." Another old man who has previously had his head in the fireplace, pipes out,

"Charley Walters."

Something like a feeble interest is awakened. I suppose Charley Walters had conversation in him.

"He's dead," says the piping old man.

Another old man, with one eye screwed up, hastily displaces the piping old man, and says.

"Yes! Charley Walters died in that bed, and—and—"

"Billy Stevens," persists the spectral old man.

"No, no! and Johnny Rogers died in that bed, and—and—they're both on 'em dead—and Sam'l Bowyer;" this seems very extraordinary to him; "he went out!"

With this he subsides, and all the old men (having had quite enough of it) subside, and the spectral old man goes into his grave again, and takes the shade of Billy Stevens with him.

As we turn to go out at the door, another previously invisible old man, a hoarse old man in a flannel gown, is standing there, as if he had just come up through the floor.

"I beg your pardon, sir, could I take the liberty of saying a word?"

"Yes, what is it?"

"I am greatly better in my health, sir; but what I want, to get me quite round," with his hand on his throat, "is a little fresh air, sir. It has always done my complaint so much good, sir. The regular leave for going out, comes round so seldom, that if the gentlemen, next Friday, would give me leave to go out walking, now and then—for only an hour or so, sir!—"

Who could wonder, looking through those weary vistas of bed and infirmity, that it should do him good to meet with some other scenes, and assure himself that there was something else on earth? Who could help wondering why the old men lived on as they did; what grasp they had on life; what crumbs of interest or occupation they could pick up from its bare board; whether Charley Walters had ever described to them the days when he kept company with some old pauper woman in the bud, or Billy Stevens ever told them of the time when he was a dweller in the far-off foreign land called Home!

The morsel of burnt child, lying in another room, so patiently, in bed, wrapped in lint, and looking steadfastly at us with his bright quiet eyes when we spoke to him kindly, looked as if the knowledge of these things, and of all the tender things there are to think about, might have been in his mind as if he thought, with us, that there was a fellow-feeling in the pauper nurses which appeared to make them more kind to their charges than the race of common nurses in the hospitals—as if he mused upon the Future of some older children lying around him in the same place, and thought it best, perhaps, all things considered, that he should die—as if he knew, without fear, of those many coffins, made and unmade, piled up in the store below—and of his unknown friend, "the dropped child," calm upon the box-lid covered with a cloth. But there was something wistful and appealing, too, in his tiny face, as if, in the midst of all the hard necessities and incongruities he pondered on, he pleaded, in behalf of the helpless and the aged poor, for a little more liberty—and a little more bread.

[Source: *Reprinted Pieces*, vol. 21, *The Nonesuch Dickens* (Bloomsbury, London: Nonesuch Press, 1937-38) 200-06. Originally published on 25 May, 1850, in *Household Words*.]

Appendix C: From Letters of Charles Dickens

To The editor of the *Morning Chronicle*,
25 July 1842
Monday morning, July 25, 1842

Sir,

As the Mines and Collieries Bill[1] will be committed in the House of Lords to-night; or, in other words, as it will arrive to-night at that stage in which the tender mercies of the Colliery Lords will so distort and maim it, that its relations and friends elsewhere will be sorely puzzled to know it again when it is returned to them, I venture to trouble you with a few remarks upon the subject. From its first public exposition it has had such ready sympathy from you, and has received such able and manly support in your journal, that I offer no apology for this intrusion on your time and space.

That for very many years these mines and all belonging to them, as they have been out of sight in the dark earth, have been utterly out of legislative mind; that for so many years all considerations of humanity, policy, social virtue, and common decency, have been left rotting at the pit's mouth, with other disregarded dunghill matter from which lordly colliers could extract no money; that for very many years, a state of things has existed in these places, in the heart and core of a Christian country, which, if it had been discovered by mariners or missionaries in the Sandwich Islands, would have made the fortune of two quarto volumes, filled the whole bench of bishops with emotion, and nerved to new and mighty projects the Society for the Propagation of the Gospel in Foreign Parts, is well known to every one. That the evidence taken by the commissioners wrought (as well it might) an extraordinary impression on the public mind, from the first moment of its diffusion;[2] that the bill founded upon it, passed the House of Commons with the hearty consent of all parties, and the ready union of all interests; that the people of every class, and their representatives of every class, were no sooner made acquainted with the evil, than they hastened to apply the remedy, are recent and notorious facts. It was reserved for the House of

---

1 "An Act to prohibit the Employment of Women and Girls in Mines and Collieries, to regulate the employment of Boys, and make Provisions for the Safety of Persons working therein."

2 The First Report of the Children's Employment Commission, published in May 1842, focused upon the abusive working conditions for women and children in the mines and collieries.

Lords alone to discover that this kind of legislation was very bad and odious, and would never do.[1] Let us see on what grounds.

It is an interference with the rights of labour, because it proposes to banish women from the mines. It proceeds on insufficient evidence, because the witnesses were not upon oath. The sub-commissioners who examined the witnesses did so improperly. Nobody knows how or why — but somebody says so. To these formidable heads of objection Lord Londonderry[2] adds (with true Lord Londonderry naïveté) that the prints[3] upon their lordships' table are excessively disgusting. Wherefore, he argues, (with true Lord Londonderry logic) that the parties who originated them are excessively hypocritical.

In addition to these grounds of opposition, it was stoutly contended by their collier lordships that there are no grievances, no discomforts, no miseries whatever, in the mines; that all labourers in mines are perpetually singing and dancing, and festively enjoying themselves; in a word, that they lead such rollicking and roystering lives that it is well they work below the surface of the earth, or society would be deafened by their shouts of merriment. This is humorous, but not new. Exactly the same things have been said of slavery, factory-work, Irish destitution, and every other grade of poverty, neglect, oppression, and distress. There is a kind of opposition to truth, which may be called the out-and-out, or whole-hog opposition. It stops at nothing, and recognises no middle course. Show beyond all dispute, and the remotest possibility of doubt, that any class of persons are in especial need of legislative protection and assistance, and opponents of this stamp will instantly arise, and meet you with the assertion, not that that class are moderately well off, or have an average amount of comfort; but that of all earthly ranks and conditions, theirs is the most surpassingly and exquisitely desirable. Now, happiness capers and sings on a slave plantation, making it an Eden of ebony. Now, she dwelleth in a roofless cabin, with potatoes thrice a week, buttermilk o' Sundays, a pig in the parlour, a fever in the dungheap, seven naked children on the damp earth-floor, and a wife newly delivered of an eighth, upon a door, brought from the nearest hut that boasts one — five miles off. Now, she rambles through a refreshing grove of steam engines, at midnight, with a Manchester child, patting him occasionally on the head with a billy-roller.[4] And now she sits down in the

---

1 Several members of the House of Lords were mine owners and vigorously opposed the Bill, but it finally passed with numerous amendments.
2 See p. 190, n.2.
3 Drawings presented by the Commissioners that depicted the abominable working conditions in the mines.
4 An instrument to punish children.

dark, a thousand feet below the level of the sea, passing the livelong day beside a little trapper six years old.[1] If I were not this great peer, quoth Lord Londonderry, I would be that small trapper. If I were not a lord, doomed unhappily in my high place to preserve a solemn bearing, for the wonder and admiration of mankind, and hold myself aloof from innocent sports, I would be a jolly little trapper. Oh, for the cindery days of trapper infancy! The babes in the wood had a rich and cruel uncle. When were the children in the coals ever murdered for their inheritance? Jolly, jolly trappers!

It is an interference with the rights of labour to exclude women from the mines—women who work by the side of naked men—(daughters often do this beside their own fathers)—and harnessed to carts in a most revolting and disgusting fashion, by iron chains. Is it among the rights of labour to blot out from that sex all form and stamp, and character of womanhood—to predestine their neglected offspring, from the hour of their conception in the womb, to lives of certain sin and suffering, misery and crime—to divest them of all knowledge of home, and all chance of womanly influence in the humble sphere of a poor peasant's hearth—to make them but so many weaker men, saving in respect of their more rapid and irresistible opportunities of being brutalised themselves, and of brutalizing others; and their capacity of breeding for the scaffold and the gaol? When we talk of "rights of labour," do we picture to ourselves a hideous phantom whispering discontent in the depths of pits and mines, sharpening the Chartist's pike by stealth, and skulking from the farmer's rick-yard? Or are we men, possessing the common average of reason bestowed by God upon the descendants of Adam, who well know that what these lords proclaim to be the rights of labour are its wrongs? Who well know that the opposition to this vital clause originates with men who stand, it may be almost said, upon their trial—who in any other tribunal would be heard with caution and distrust; and could not sit upon the jury, far less carry in their pockets friendly verdicts from absent jurymen, by the score! To speak more plainly yet, do we not know, right well, that the real leader of the opposition to this very clause is himself the owner of the worst-conducted mine in that worst district of Scotland; who has at this moment 400 women in his weekly pay and service. And is there a man alive (out of the House of Lords) who does not read in this phrase "rights of labour," fears of possible claims for higher wages from the men, when the women no longer prostitute all the faculties of their minds and bodies to the degrading work they have pursued too long? Who does not see upon its face distinctly pictured apprehensions of a

---

1   The youngest children were employed to open and close the doors (traps) for the coal carriages.

louder cry for bread? The mining labourers, with no complaint or hope of change, are bound to work, from year to year, and from age to age, their fingers to the bone; to turn their women into men, and children into devils; and do all this to live. These are the "rights of labour" with your collier lords! ...

In these times, when so wide a gulf has opened between the rich and poor, which, instead of narrowing, as all good men would have it, grows broader daily; it is most important that all ranks and degrees of people should understand whose hands are stretched out to separate these two great divisions of society each of whom, for its strength and happiness, and the future existence of this country, as a great and powerful nation, is dependent on the other. Therefore it is that I implore your readers closely to watch the fate of this measure, which has for its sole object the improvement of the condition and character of one great class of hewers of wood and drawars [sic.] of water, whose lives, at the very best, must be fraught with danger, toil, and hardship; to compare the fate of this bill in the House of Lords, with its reception by the country, and its progress through the House of Commons, and to bestow their best attention on the debate of this night.

                                                                                                       B.[1]
To Dr. Southwood Smith[2]
Address: Dr. Southwood Smith | New Broad Street | City

                                                    Devonshire Terrace | Sixth March 1843.
My Dear Dr. Smith

I sent a message across the way today, begging you, in case you should come to the Sanatorium, to call on me, if convenient. My reason was this;—I am so perfectly stricken down by the blue book[3] you have sent me, that I think (as soon as I shall have done my month's work) of writing, and bringing out, a very cheap pamphlet, called "An appeal to the People of England, on behalf of the Poor Man's Child" — with my name attached, of course. I should be very glad to take counsel with you in the matter, and to

---

1   This signature may stand for "Boz," the pseudonym Dickens used in his *Sketches by Boz* (1836, 1837).
2   Southwood Smith, one of the four Commissioners responsible for the Second Report of the Children's Employment Commission.
3   So called because of the color of its covers, the blue book was the Second Report of the Children's Employment Commission, published in February 1843. This report focused upon the trades and manufactures. The First Report studied conditions in the mines and collieries.

receive any suggestions from you, in reference to it. Suppose I were to call on you one evening in the course of ten days or so, what would be the most likely hour to find you at home?

In haste | Always Faithfully | Your friend
Charles Dickens

To Dr. Southwood Smith, 10 March 1843
Address: Dr. Southwood Smith | 36 New Broad Street | City.

Devonshire Terrace | Tenth March 1843.
My Dear Dr. Smith

Don't be frightened when I tell you, that since I wrote to you last, reasons have presented themselves for deferring the production of that pamphlet, until the end of the year. I am not at liberty to explain them further, just now; but *rest assured* that when you know them, and see what I do, and where, and how, you will certainly feel that a Sledge hammer has come down with twenty times the force—twenty thousand times the force—I could exert by following out my first idea. Even so recently as when I wrote to you the other day, I had not contemplated the means I shall now, please God, use. But they have been suggested to me, and I have girded myself for their seizure—as you shall see in due time.[1]

If you will allow our tete a tete, and projected conversation on the subject, still to come off, I will write to you, as soon as I see my way to the end of my Month's work.

Always Faithfully Yours
Charles Dickens

To Macvey Napier,[2] 24 October 1843
Address: Professor Napier | Muirestone House | Mid-Calder | by Edinburgh.

Devonshire Terrace | Twenty Fourth October 1843
My Dear Sir.

I am extremely sorry to find that my proposal puts you to any inconve-

---

1   It appears that Dickens was at this time considering the most effective way of responding to the horrors of the Second Report, which he was finally to formulate in *A Christmas Carol.* His depiction of the wretched children, Ignorance and Want, revealed beneath the robes of the Spirit of Christmas Present, certainly carries the impact of the "Sledge hammer."

2   Napier was the editor of the *Edinburgh Review.*

nience; but the fault is really not mine. You wrote me in answer to my letter, that you were much oppressed by matter of all kinds and from a variety of distinguished sources (as I can readily understand)—but would "*endeavour*" to find room for me in the January Number. I immediately resolved not to give you that trouble, but to write the paper at my leisure, and send it to you for the Number following—really meaning to be considerate, and to meet your views, as I understood them. And I thought the postponement, rather advantageous than otherwise, as the mention of the subject in the Queen's Speech, or the omission of it, would be alike a good reason for taking it up afresh. Accordingly I plunged headlong into a little scheme[1] I had held in abeyance during the interval which had elapsed between my first letter and your answer; set an artist[2] at work upon it; and put it wholly out of my own power to touch the Edinburgh subject until after Christmas is turned. For carrying out the notion I speak of, and being punctual with Chuzzlewit,[3] will occupy every moment of my working time, up to the Christmas Holidays.[4]

I hope you will see how this has come to pass; and that I acted *on your letter, distinctly.*

I did not fail to give your message to Hood,[5] who thanks you very much, and greatly regrets having missed you.

My Dear Sir | Faithfully Yours always
Charles Dickens

To Charles Mackay,[6] 19 December 1843
| Devonshire Terrace | York Gate Regents Park

Nineteenth December 1843.
My Dear Mackay.

Believe me that your pleasure in the Carol, so earnestly and spontaneously expressed, gives me real gratification of heart. It has delighted me very much. I am sure you feel it; that your praise is manly and generous; and well worth having. Thank you heartily.

I was very much affected by the little Book myself; in various ways, as I wrote it; and had an interest in the idea, which made me reluctant to lay it

---

1 This is the first certain reference to *A Christmas Carol.*
2 John Leech (1817-64), who did the illustrations for the *Carol.*
3 Dickens published his novel *The Life and Adventures of Martin Chuzzlewit* in monthly parts (1843-44), and then as a book in 1844.
4 Dickens finished the *Carol* on December 2.
5 Thomas Hood (1799-1845), author and editor.
6 As sub-editor of the *Morning Chronicle*, Mackay, a poet and journalist, was the likely reviewer of Dickens's book.

aside for a moment. Your allusion to that inexorable Pot, tempts me into saying that the Subscription was large, and the demand great.

I shall not forget your note, easily.

Always Faithfully Yours
Charles Dickens

To Thomas Mitton,[1] 27 December 1843
Devonshire Terrace, | Twenty-Seventh December, 1843

My dear Mitton,

You will be glad to hear that I had a note from C and H[2] on the twenty-fourth to say that the Carol was then in its Sixth Thousand; and that as the orders were coming in fast from town and country, it would soon be necessary to reprint. I am very glad you saw the children the other day, and made them so happy. I have much to say in reference to your note of last Friday, but cannot say it better perhaps than when France draws nearer to us. I shall see you within a day or two.

Ever faithfully | Charles Dickens

To C.C. Felton,[3] 2 January 1844

Address: By The January Cunard Steamer | Professor Felton | Cambridge | Massachusetts | United States.

Devonshire Terrace London | Second January 1844

My very dear Felton.

You are a Prophet, and had best retire from business straightway. Yesterday Morning, New Year's Day, when I had walked into my little work room after breakfast, and was looking out of window at the Snow in the Garden—not seeing it particularly well in consequence of some staggering suggestions of last night's Punch and Turkey whereby I was beset—the Postman came to the door with a knock for which I damned him from my heart. Seeing your hand upon the cover of a letter which he brought, I immediately blessed him—presented him with a Glass of Whisky—inquired after his family (they are all well)—and opened the despatch, with a moist and oystery twinkle in my eye. And on the very day from which the new year dates, I read your New Year congratulations, as punctually as if you lived in the next house. — Why don't you!

---

1 Mitton was Dickens's solicitor.
2 Chapman and Hall, Dickens's publisher.
3 Cornelius Conway Felton, Professor of Greek at Harvard University.

Now, if instantly on the receipt of this, you will send a free and independent citizen down to the Cunard Wharf at Boston, you will find that Captain Hewett of the Britannia Steam Ship *(my* ship) has a small parcel for Professor Felton of Cambridge; and in that parcel you will find a Christmas Carol in Prose. Being a Ghost Story of Christmas by Charles Dickens. Over which Christmas Carol, Charles Dickens wept, and laughed, and wept again, and excited himself in a most extraordinary manner, in the composition; and thinking whereof, he walked about the black streets of London, fifteen and twenty miles, many a night when all the sober folks had gone to bed. He don't like America, I am told, but he has some friends there, as dear to him as any in England; so you may read it safely. Its success is most prodigious. And by every post, all manner of strangers write all manner of letters to him about their homes and hearths, and how this same Carol is read aloud there, and kept on a very little shelf by itself. Indeed it is the greatest success as I am told, that this Ruffian and Rascal has ever achieved.

Forster[1] is out again—and if he don't go in again after the manner in which we have been keeping Christmas, he must be very strong indeed. Such dinings, such dancings, such conjurings, such blindmans-buffings, such theatre-goings, such kissings-out of old years and kissings-in of new ones, never took place in these parts before. To keep the Chuzzlewit going, and do this little book, the Carol, in the odd times between two parts of it, was, as you may suppose, pretty tight work. But when it was done, I broke out like a Madman. And if you could have seen me at a children's party at Macreadys[2] the other night, going down a Country dance something longer than the Library at Cambridge with Mrs. M. you would have thought I was a country Gentleman of independent property, residing on a tip-top farm, with the wind blowing straight in my face every day....

The Proscribed One

Oh breathe not his name[3]

To Laman Blanchard,[4] 4 January 1844

Devonshire Terrace | Fourth January 1844.

My Dear Blanchard

I cannot thank you enough for the beautiful manner, and the true spirit

---

1 John Forster (1812-76), literary and dramatic critic for the *Examiner*, a friend of Dickens and later his official biographer. He had recently recovered from an illness that kept him home.
2 William Charles Macready (1793-1873), actor and theater manager.
3 A line from Thomas Moore's *Irish Melodies*, a joking reference to the hostile criticism that *Martin Chuzzlewit* received in America.
4 Samuel Laman Blanchard (1804-45), a journalist.

of friendship, in which you have noticed my Carol. But I *must* thank you, because you have filled my heart up to the brim, and it is running over. You meant to give me great pleasure, my dear fellow, and you have done it. The tone of your elegant and fervent praise has touched me in the tenderest place. I cannot write about it; and as to talking of it, I could no more do that, than a dumb man. I have derived inexpressible gratification from what I know and feel was a labour of love on your part. And I can never forget it.

When I think it likely that I may meet you (perhaps at Ainsworth's[1] on Friday?) I shall slip a Carol into my pocket, and ask you to put it among your books for my sake. You will never like it the less for having made it the means of so much happiness to me.

Always My Dear Blanchard | Faithfully Your friend
Charles Dickens

To Thomas Mitton, 7 January 1844

Devonshire Terrace. | Seventh January 1844
Sunday Night.

My Dear Mitton.

I received the enclosed letter from Bradburys, *and* the enclosed yellow book[2] on Saturday afternoon at about Four o'Clock.

I have not the least doubt that if these Vagabonds[3] can be stopped, they must be. So let us go to work in such terrible earnest that everything must tumble down before it.

First, register the copyright as mine.

Secondly, will you get an *immediate* opinion from some man, learned in Injunction matters? If he be a man who has a taste for Literature besides, so much the better. Should it be favorable, let us instantly apply for an injunction or their second number will be out. If we could have a conversation with the Counsel, it would be well that I, who know the original book, should be present. And I certainly would be in court too, as I know the V.C.[4] and would wish to shew that I have a strong feeling in the matter.

I shall not leave home all the morning: expecting a summons from you. I have written on a piece of paper, and slipped into the yellow book, a few

---

1 William Harrison Ainsworth (1805-82), novelist and editor.
2 A piracy of *A Christmas Carol* entitled "A Christmas Ghost Story Re-originated from the original by Charles Dickens Esquire and analytically condensed expressly for this work," which appeared as No. 16 of *Parley's Illuminated Library*, published January 6.
3 The booksellers named on the book's wrapper.
4 Vice-Chancellor.

remarks that occur to me. Let us be *sledge-hammer* in this, or I shall be beset by hundreds of the same crew, when I come out with a long story.

Faithfully Always

CD

[Dickens's "few remarks" are added as follows:]

First. To observe the title on the first page of the story under the wood cut, and Secondly the Advertisement on the bottom of the wrapper at the back. [That the story] is precisely the same and the characters the same and the names the same with the exception of the name Fezziwig, which is printed Fuzziwig.

That the incidents are the same, and follow in the same order.

That very frequently indeed (I have marked some of the instances) the language is the same. That where it is not, it is weakened, degraded; made tame, vile, ignorant, and mawkish.

[And] I particularly wish it to be put to the [Judge] and to the Counsel, that this is a [material] part of my damage and complaint. That with the idea (though not, as I think, with the effect) of evading the letter of the law in such matters, my book is made to appear a wretched, meagre, miserable thing; and is still hawked about with my title and my name—with my characters, my incidents, and whole design.

To Lady Holland,[1] 20 January 1844

Devonshire Terrace. | Twentieth January 1844

Dear Lady Holland.

Pray do not think me neglectful, in not having answered your kind note before now. Certain vagabonds have recently produced a flagrant and most audacious piracy of the Carol; and being resolved to put it down, I plunged immediately into *Six* Chancery Suits. One is usually considered very good measure, in respect of irritation and anxiety; but half a dozen at a time have quite a powerful effect, I assure you.

I have come off victorious in all points yet decided, but have been busying myself so much in getting up the case that I have delayed my Monthly Work beyond all precedent, and am now, and have been since the receipt of your note, in the full tide of it. This is the real occasion of my not having seen you; and this prevents me from having the pleasure of accepting your kind Invitation to Dinner on Sunday. I shall not fail to call upon you as soon as I have finished; and I hope to be at large again, on Wednesday.

---

1 Elizabeth Vassall Fox (1770-1845), wife of the 3rd Baron Holland.

Mrs. Dickens begs me to say, that she is much gratified by your enquiries; and that she is as well as it is possible to be. We had some apprehensions beforehand, as she was exceedingly depressed and frightened; but thank God that all passed off before the reality.

I took Serjeant Talfourd out of his own Court, to lead my Chancery cases. Knight Bruce, who was the Judge, understood the matter so perfectly, and appreciated the Piracy so well, that he did not require to hear Talfourd at all. Which I think was a prodigious disappointment to the Serjeant who had made up his mind for a great speech.

I am always Dear Lady Holland | Yours faithfully and obliged Charles Dickens

To John Forster, [11 February 1844]

Such a night as I have passed! I really believed I should never get up again, until I had passed through all the horrors of a fever. I found the *Carol* accounts awaiting me, and they were the cause of it. The first six thousand copies show a profit of £230! And the last four will yield as much more. I had set my heart and soul upon a Thousand, clear. What a wonderful thing it is, that such a great success should occasion me such intolerable anxiety and disappointment! My year's bills, unpaid, are so terrific, that all the energy and determination I can possibly exert will be required to clear me before I go abroad; which, if next June come and find me alive, I shall do. Good Heaven, if I had only taken heart a year ago! Do come soon, as I am very anxious to talk with you. We can send round to Mac after you arrive, and tell him to join us at Hampstead or elsewhere. I was so utterly knocked down last night, that I came up to the contemplation of all these things quite bold this morning. If I can let the house for this season, I will be off to some seaside place as soon as a tenant offers. I am not afraid, if I reduce my expenses; but if I do not, I shall be ruined past all mortal hope of redemption.

To John Forster, [21 February 1844]

....I saw the *Carol*[1] last night. Better than usual, and Wright[2] seems to enjoy Bob Cratchit, but *heart-breaking* to me. Oh Heaven! if any forecast of

---

1 Edward Stirling's musical adaptation for the stage, which he announced as "the only dramatic version sanctioned by C. Dickens, Esqre," produced at the Adelphi in February 1844.
2 Edward Richard Wright (1813–59).

this was ever in my mind! Yet O. Smith[1] was drearily better than I expected. It is a great comfort to have that kind of meat underdone; and his face is quite perfect.

To Cornelius Mathews,[2] 2 March 1844
Address: By The Cunard Steamer. Cornelius Mathews Esquire | New York | United States of America.

London | Devonshire Terrace | York Gate Regents Park.
Second March 1844.
My Dear Sir.

Pray do not suppose for a moment that your letter was suggestive of anything but pleasure and gratification to me. I am in fault not to have replied to it, though even by a brief acknowledgement of its receipt; but my correspondence at home is something so tremendous, that I fall into arrear with my friends abroad, in spite of myself and my desire to retain their good opinion.

I am very glad you like the Christmas Carol. It has been an astonishing success here; and affected me so much in the composition, that if it had been otherwise, I verily think I should have broken my heart.

I do not remember having received the address you speak of, on the subject of Copyright. But I may have done so without being able, now, to call it to mind. For the subject has long since passed from my thoughts. It only dwelt there, when I viewed the influences that make up an American government, through the mist of my own hopes and fancies. When that cleared away, I ceased to have any interest in the question.

Should you ever be in doubt again, relative to the expediency of sending me a Book, pray give me the benefit of it; and believe that I shall, at all times, be glad to hear from you.

My Dear Sir | Faithfully Yours
Charles Dickens

To J.V. Staples,[3] 3 April 1844

Third of April, 1844. I have been very much gratified by the receipt of your interesting letter, and I assure you that it would have given me heart-

---

1 Richard John Smith (1786–1855), nicknamed "O" for having played a character named Obi in a melodrama.
2 Cornelius Mathews (1817–89), a journalist.
3 James Verry Staples, of Clifton, Bristol.

felt satisfaction to have been in your place when you read my little *Carol* to the Poor in your neighbourhood. I have great faith in the poor; to the best of my ability I always endeavour to present them in a favourable light to the rich; and I shall never cease, I hope, until I die, to advocate their being made as happy and as wise as the circumstances of their condition, in its utmost improvement, will admit of their becoming. I mention this to assure you of two things. Firstly, that I try to deserve their attention; and secondly, that any such marks of their approval and confidence as you relate to me are most acceptable to my feelings, and go at once to my heart.

[Source: *The Letters of Charles Dickens*, eds. Madeline House, Graham Storey, and Kathleen Tillotson, vols. 3, 4 (Oxford: Clarendon Press, 1974). Reprinted with permission of Oxford University Press.]

Appendix D: Contemporary Reviews of A Christmas Carol

1. Charles Mackay, *Morning Chronicle* (December 19, 1843)

Mr. Dickens has here produced a most appropriate Christmas offering, and one which, if properly made use of, may yet, we hope, lead to some more valuable result in the approaching season of merry-making than mere amusement. It is impossible to read this little volume though, however hastily, without perceiving that its composition was prompted by a spirit of wide and wholesome philanthropy — a spirit to which selfishness in enjoyment is an inconceivable idea — a spirit that knows where happiness can exist, and ought to exist, and will not be happy itself till it has done something towards promoting its growth here. If such spirits could be multiplied, as the copies of this little book we doubt not will be — if no man would think the happiness of his own festive board complete, unless, as he look round upon the merry faces which encircled it, he could carry his sympathies to some other as affectionate, though more humble circle, which he had made happy with some of the good gifts of Heaven — what a happy Christmas indeed should we yet have this 1843!

Mr. Dickens's "Carol" is divided into five chapters, or "staves." The first stave introduces us to a hard-handed, greedy old miser, Scrooge, who has no sympathy for the sorrows of others, because he cannot even understand what happiness means, except it mean hoarding money bags. The time is Christmas-eve; the scene old Scrooge's office in a dark court. His nephew comes to give him "a merry Christmas," and to invite him to dinner on the next day. The old miser is wrath, calls "Christmas a humbug," and refuses the invitation. It is not without some grumbling that the poor old clerk, Mr. Cratchit, who writes all day on a high stool in a cold little box, or "tank," for fifteen shillings a week, obtains leave to stop away from business on the morrow. A neighbour, who comes to ask Scrooge for his mite towards a subscription for the starving poor "at this festive season," is sent away with a flea in his ear; and the miserable old man goes from his dark office to his dark, solitary home, very angry at everybody for trying to make themselves and one another happy, if for only one day in the year. Arrived at home, and preparing for bed — he is visited by the ghost of his former partner, Jacob Marley (who has left him all his property), who warns him of the evil of his ways, and the heavy chain which he is forging for his restless spirit after death, by his unceasing pursuit of wealth during life. [Extracts from Marley's speech omitted.]

The ghost then promises to send three spirits to the miser, who perhaps may work his reformation whilst yet it is time. The first of the three spirits (occupying stave two) is the spirit of Christmasses past, who, carrying Scrooge back to the period of his earliest childhood, and thence through youth to manhood, re-awakens the softer domestic affections and enjoyments of which he was once susceptible, but which seem to have been smothered with the cares of money-getting. Nothing can be more touching than his solicitous care at school, when all the boys had gone to happy homes except himself,—nothing more joyous than the Christmas-eve proceedings at his first master's, old Fezziwig—a scene so excellently described, that we must extract it, recommending it as a model worthy of imitation. [Extract describing Fezziwig's ball omitted.]

The second of the three spirits (Stave Three), is the spirit of the present Christmas, showing peace and plenty and happiness and comfort and goodwill and congratulation everywhere, in the shop parlour, the humbler "two-pair back," in the cottage, in the mine, in the bowels of the earth, in the light-house, and in the ship at sea. Even Cratchit, who slaves away at Scrooge's office for fifteen shillings a week, is, for to-day, as happy, ay, happier than a king. We wish we could make room for the whole scene; but it is impossible. [Extract describing the Cratchit family at home omitted.]

Breathing a wish (we fear a vain one!) that every Cratchit family may have as good a goose and as good a pudding at the coming Christmas, we must turn over to Scrooge's nephew Charles [sic.] and his wife, an interesting new-married couple, where after dinner, a fine game of romps is performed. [Extract describing the music and games omitted.]

But we must hasten to a close, or we shall be quoting half the book. The last of the three spirits (Stave Four) points out to Scrooge, in appalling truthfulness, the horrors of an old age and death-bed, unassociated with a single object of affection, a single subject for pleasurable reflection. All this is given with Mr. Dickens's peculiar vigour of detail and colouring; until, at last, the affrighted man, upon contemplating his own dark, solitary, unwept gravestone, starts in his sleep and awakes "a wiser and a better man." The transition in stave first is perfectly charming. Scrooge jumps out of bed with alacrity—dresses quickly—sallies out smiling; interchanges "Merry Christmasses" with many happy folk; gives a munificent subscription (to make up for past years' neglect) for the poor, to the neighbour whom he had repulsed but the evening before; sends the largest turkey he can find at the poulterer's to his clerk Cratchit, and astonishes his nephew and niece by dropping into dinner; and the next day goes to the little dark office a cheerful man, and begins business by raising Cratchit's wages.

We need hardly add, after all we have said, that we heartily recommend this little volume as an amusing companion, and a wholesome monitor, to all who would enjoy in truth and in spirit "A merry Christmas and a happy New Year."

2. Anon., *Athenaeum* (December 23, 1843): 1127-28

A tale to make the reader laugh and cry — open his hands, and open his heart to charity even towards the uncharitable, — wrought up with a thousand minute and tender touches of the true "Boz" workmanship — is, indeed, — a dainty dish to set before a King. Smellfungus[1] himself would be puzzled how to cut up this jovial, genial piece of Christmas fare otherwise than lovingly. We shall only pretend to give the hungry, happy reader a slice, by way of staying his appetite till the entire treat smokes with a rich savour on his own table.

The idea of this Ghost-Carol, is simple enough; but we shall leave it to Mr. Dickens to develope the mystery, and content ourselves with a picture or two. The first, a Christmas morning-piece, will make holiday mouths water. [Long extract omitted in which Dickens describes the rich array of holiday food in the shops.]

After this glorious panorama, we must have a cabinet picture. The dinner which follows is laid in the house of a poor clerk. The mother and resident daughter have been too anxiously employed all the morning to stir abroad; another daughter has just come home for her holidays; and the father, come home from church, has laid by his worsted comforter with its long fringe, resolved to have one merry day: [long extract omitted in which Dickens describes the Cratchit family's festive meal.]

We can positively make room for nothing more after such a noble meal. How the sight thereof, and of similar scenes, with sundry ghastly contrasts, works upon the close heart of the miser, Scrooge, and what becomes of Tiny Tim, is more-capitally *carolled* in prose by Mr. Dickens; and will call out, we hope, a chorus of "Amens," in the shape of kindly sympathies and bounteous deeds, from the Land's End to John o'Groat's House.[2]

3. Thomas Hood, *Hood's Magazine* (January 4, 1844): 68-75

If Christmas, with its ancient and hospitable customs, its social and charitable observances, were in danger of decay, this is the book that would give them a new lease. The very name of the author predisposes one to the

---

1 A hypercritical traveler in *A Sentimental Journey* (1768), by novelist Laurence Sterne.
2 Land's End, in the southwest of England, is its westernmost point, and John O'Groat's House, on the northeast coast of Scotland, is considered the northernmost point in mainland Great Britain.

kindlier feelings; and a peep at the Frontispiece sets the animal spirits capering at once along with Mr. Fizziwig [sic.] at his Benthamite[1] Ball, in his warehouse adapted to the greatest happiness of the greatest number. If ever Comfort was personified, there she is, dancing with Hospitality in a white waistcoat, and close beside her the domesticated Robin Redbreast, transformed for the occasion into a little boy. His coat is blue, indeed, instead of brown; but you can swear to him notwithstanding—to the cock of his bill and the cut of his tail, and to the hop that he will give when his turn comes!

It was a blessed inspiration that put such a book into the head of Charles Dickens; a happy inspiration of the heart, that warms every page. It is impossible to read, without a glowing bosom and burning cheeks, between love and shame for our kind, with perhaps a little touch of misgiving, whether we are not personally open, a crack or so, to the reproach of Wordsworth,

> "The world is too much with us, early and late,
> Getting and spending."[2]

Whether our own heads have not become more inaccessible, our hearts more impregnable, our ears and eyes more dull and blind, to sounds and sights of human misery; if our Charity altogether is not too much of a Charity, thinking of home, home, home, and no place but home. In a word, whether we have not grown Scroogey? [There follows a long passage quoting Dickens's description of Scrooge, ending with the following paragraph:]

"But what did Scrooge care? It was the very thing he liked. To edge his way along the crowded paths of life, warning all human sympathy to keep its distance, was what the knowing ones call 'nuts' to Scrooge."

Yes, *screw-nuts*. There was a figure to sit busy in his counting-house, as unmoved as a calculating machine, on the very threshold of Hilarity Term, that is to say on Christmas Eve! On that gracious Eve when knocking at every door and every heart's door in gospel-lighted lands the gentle Spirit of Christianity craves admittance, not to chide or rebuke, but to cheer, to comfort, to pardon, to redeem—to bless the lintel and the hearth, the bed and the board, and to play with the little children! There was a man, to be visited by that divine Spirit, or by Charity and Mercy, who called on him in

---

1 The Utilitarian philosophy of Jeremy Bentham (1748-1832) held that pleasure was the chief end of life and that the greatest happiness to the greatest number should be the goal of society.

2 From a sonnet by William Wordsworth (1770-1850), the first line of which should read "The World is too much with us; late and soon."

human shape. [There follows a long quotation in which Dickens describes Scrooge's rebuff of the men asking him to help provide for the poor and destitute.]

But perhaps by degrees, as the advent of the Holy Day drew nearer and nearer, the miser's misanthropy thawed, his temper mended, and his temperature rose to blood heat: no, not a fibre, or a nerve—not one moral degree, above the freezing point. He kept hardening and stiffening with the weather. [There follows a long quotation in which Dickens describes the dinner at the home of the Cratchit family.]

What a party in a parlour—and all blest! But how did Scrooge the miser spend his Christmas Day?—how did he get over his twenty-fifth of December? Of course in his office, gloating over that gloomy composition, with only half a plum in it, his ledger. Not so: he never even looked into his banker's book to check the balance. He dressed hastily in all his best, and sallied into the street, walking with his hands behind him, exchanging greetings with beggars! patting children on the head!! and smiling blandly and kindly on every body he passed!!! Nay, he actually hurried his steps to meet that very Charity (disguised as a stout gentleman) whom he had repulsed so rudely the evening before. [Quotation omitted.]

There's a change!—a moral trick of metamorphosis as astounding as any mechanical one in the Christmas Pantomimes!—the parish cage into a Refuge for the Destitute—Newgate into the Philanthropic—a Pawnbroker into a Samaritan—a Scrooge into a Samaritan!—a Nero overnight, a Titus in the morning. [There follows Dickens's description of Scrooge's generosity towards Bob Cratchit and their sharing a Christmas beverage, Smoking Bishop.]

If that is not the most wonderful Bowl of Bishop ever promised—the most marvellous promise ever made—there is nothing Extraordinary in this world except an occasional Gazette! How the miraculous change was effected (if not exactly by Faith, Hope, and Charity), by what spiritual Trio (not Gin, Rum, and Brandy) the Worldly Wiseman was converted into a Christian, must be unriddled by the book itself; and haply there shall come a change over the reader also in its perusal. Ours is rather a selfish, luxurious age. "The world is too much with us"—there is a cold calculating utilitarianism, far too much of the hard harsh spirit of the money-grubber, who, being asked if he had ever done a good action in his life, replied, "Yes—he once detected a woman in a sham fit."

[Source: *The Works of Thomas Hood*, IX (London: Ward, Locke, & Co.: 1882-84), 93-103.]

4. Laman Blanchard, "Charles Dickens," *Ainsworth's Magazine* (January 1844): 84-88

[In this essay Blanchard, a Whig journalist and friend of noted writers, reviewed both *Martin Chuzzlewit* and *A Christmas Carol.* Dickens wrote to Blanchard thanking him for "the true spirit of friendship in which you have noticed my Carol." (See Appendix C).]

It was worthy of the wise youthfulness which is a beautiful characteristic of the genius of Mr. Dickens—worthy of the genial purposes which his writings aim so generally at serving—to give the world a little book about Christmas, illustrative of its true spirit, descriptive of its glowing features, and helping to bring closer together hundreds and hundreds of readers—all shaking with laughter, and some sprinkling a few tears over their ripe pleasure—in the enjoyment of a common sentiment. Kindly and wisely it was done; and so much has he had do with the happy ending of the old year, that it is but grateful and honest to begin the new one with an acknowledgment of some of our later obligations.

While we pause, on opening a new year's account with the world, and glance back at the figures which make up the sum of our social profit and loss during the twelve months fled, we often find those figures shaping themselves into the forms of friends and acquaintances lost, drawn nearer to us, or altogether newly acquired, within the year reviewed. We estimate the extent of the damage sustained by death or absence in one case, the gain derived by half a dozen jovial acquisitions in another direction, the agreeable intimacy woven into a web of friendship (fast colours, warranted to wear) in a third quarter; the progress, perhaps, of the little affair of the heart in a fourth. But a monthly visitor, like this "Martin Chuzzlewit," introduces a sad perplexity into the account. Driving a nail pretty deep into the head last January, and giving it a hard hit once a month ever since, he is in many instances the author of a most ridiculous confusion in the brain; which, looking back, no longer separates the fictitious from the real. The literary and the social have become the same. The imagination seizes on some of the favourite characters, and regards them with the same force and entireness of identity with which it recognises the persons we met at Bloomsbury, or in Buckinghamshire, last spring or autumn.

Thus many a reader of a sanguine and impressible turn has already, no doubt, reviewed the losses and acquisitions of the late year, in some fashion of this kind.

★   ★   ★

People fancy, perhaps, that they thank Mr. Dickens enough for his "Prose Christmas Carol," when they buy it; but they do not. They can't be quite thankful until they have learnt all its leading lessons by heart. Those lessons lie deep in laughter and tears, and so commingled are they that sometimes it is very doubtful whether you laugh or cry—it is all a chance. But to read it without emotion, without excitement, without wonder—without putting one's hand up sometimes to feel whether one has a head or without being made conscious, ever and anon, of possessing the luxury of a heart by inward admonitory thumpings, is impossible. It is a little book not to be talked about or written of according to ordinary rules. It is not like the "Turkish Tales," nor "Gulliver's Travels," nor the "Arabian Nights," nor Professor Blank's Political Economy, nor Anybody on Population, that we know of. But it is an excellent play, as Hamlet says, and Hamlet, deep in study at Elsinore, might have read every line of it twice over, and not have thought its warnings much less solemn than were afterwards those of the ghost that visited *him*.

It is easy to say what this ghost-story is not. It is not matter of fact, like the Cock-lane Ghost;[1] it is not super-imaginative, like Blake's famous Ghost of a Flea.[2] It is a Ghost full of solidities. A Dream of Truth.

Most of our readers, perhaps, are in a condition to judge for themselves; others may suppose Mr. Dickens's new performance to be a piece of rapturous pleasantry for the hour, or a German mysticism. Both guesses are wide of the mark. It is in prose, but imagined in a high spirit of poetry. It is in shape high fantastical, but it includes profound meanings, and takes a scope which learned quartos sometimes want.

A sordid money-grasper, one of the task-masters of life, having died and left his partner to the pursuit of wealth by the hardest means, visits him in a ghostly guise one Christmas; and, in explaining the cause of his appearance, "making night hideous," lays bare the whole foundation of the design. "It is required of every man," said the ghost, "that the spirit within him should walk abroad among his fellow men, and travel wide and far; and if the spirit goes not forth in life, it is condemned to do so after death. It is doomed to wander through the world, oh!—woe is me!—and witness what it cannot share but might have shared on earth, and turned to happiness." The evil-

---

1   The Cock-lane Ghost was a hoax conducted by William Parsons, his wife, daughter, and a female ventriloquist during 1760 and 1761 at number 33 Cock-lane, London.
2   A tempera painting by the poet-artist William Blake (1757-1827) depicting a horrific figure carrying a bucket from which to drink blood. Blake may have believed that the souls of blood-thirsty men inhabited the bodies of fleas.

doing and the callous are, in their spiritual condition, condemned to the torture of seeking to interfere for good in human matters, having lost the power for ever.

The ghost of the money-grasper having taught his surviving partner and ex-brother in rascality what he is to expect, introduces to him on successive nights, three spirits of power; Christmas past, Christmas present, and Christmas to come. They in turn conduct the sinner to the innocent scenes of his youth on a Christmas-day; to a contemplation of Christmas as it is, in its infinite diversity, but especially in the excess of its enjoyment; and to a horrible end foreshadowed in the future. The money-loving mortal, wrought upon by these scenes, finds tears running out of his eyes like molten gold — his penitence, his agony, is wrought up to a crisis — and he wakes from a marvellous dream of darkness and light, demon and man, to make everybody happy that comes near him, and enjoy all the year round, yes, everyday of it, a glorious Christmas dinner.

Ah! what misery to tell such a story in this way! But how else is it to be done, unless we copy the book? What are we to do? Can we drag in the Ghost of Marley by the chain of padlocks, keys, purses, and cash-boxes? Can we order in the three spirits, as if they were only rum, brandy, and gin? Can we catch old Fezziwig by one of his calves, that, as he capered, flung a light-about the shop turned into a ball-room, and "shone in every part of the dance like moons?" Can we present him effecting his "cut" so deftly, that he seemed to "wink with his legs," and came upon his feet without a stagger? Can we even secure his fiddler, just in the act of plunging his face into a pot of porter specially provided for that purpose? Is it possible to picture the great Cratchit dinner, the dinner of the joyous family, whose chief earns fifteen shillings a week? Oh, the Cratchits! We could not even squeeze in Tiny Tim upon his crutch, still less the little party scampering off to the wash-house to "hear the pudding singing in the copper;" nor Bob Cratchit, the father, preparing to carve, turning up his cuffs, "as if, poor fellow, they were capable of being made more shabby." Nor the goose — yes, positively, we must give the goose a turn, for it is a *rara avis* indeed.

"There never was such a goose. Bob said he didn't believe there ever was such a goose cooked. Its tenderness and flavour, size and cheapness, were the themes of universal admiration. Eked out by the apple-sauce and mashed potatoes, it was a sufficient dinner for the whole family; indeed, as Mrs. Cratchit said with great delight, (surveying one small atom of a bone upon the dish,) they hadn't ate it all at last! Yet every one had had enough, and the youngest Cratchits in particular, were steeped in sage and onion to the eyebrows!"

But where is the pudding? What is goose without pudding? General

Jackson without America, soy without turbot—for the old order of parallel will not do here.

"Suppose it should not be done enough! Suppose it should break in turning out! Suppose somebody should have got over the wall of the back-yard, and stolen it, while they were merry with the goose: a supposition at which the two young Cratchits became livid! All sorts of horrors were sup-posed.

"Hallo! A great deal of steam! The pudding was out of the copper. A smell like a washing-day! That was the cloth. A smell like an eating-house, and a pastry cook's next door to each other, with a laundress's next door to that! That was the pudding. In half a minute Mrs. Cratchit entered: flushed, but smiling proudly: with the pudding, like a speckled cannon-ball, so hard and firm, blazing in half of a half-a-quartern of ignited brandy, and bedight-ed with Christmas holly stuck into the top.

"Oh, a wonderful pudding! Bob Cratchit said, and calmly too, that he regarded it as the greatest success achieved by Mrs. Cratchit since their marriage. Mrs. Cratchit said that now the weight was off her mind, she would confess she had had her doubts about the quantity of the flour. Everybody had something to say about it, but nobody said or thought it was at all a small pudding for a large family. It would have been flat heresy to do so. Any Cratchit would have blushed to hint at such a thing."

But all this is nothing, unless we could also slip in Scrooge's nephew, just to hear him laugh—and Scrooge's niece, with her little mouth "that seemed made to be kissed, and no doubt was"—and Scrooge's niece's sis-ter, "the plump one with the lace tucker," whom Topper has got his eye upon, even when playing blindman.

★　　★　　★

Wonderfully full of grace and animal spirits are all the scenes thus sketched; and profoundly beautiful is the reason given for playing forfeits. "It is good," says Mr. Dickens, with a seriousness touched with sacredness, though felt in a playful moment, "it is good to be children sometimes, *and never better than at Christmas, when its Mighty Founder was a child himself.*"

After this, which expresses the whole philosophy of the Ghost-story, we shall say no more of it, except that it is a carol not for age or for youth alone, but for both—not for Christmas only, but for every season, whether the sun shines, or the snow drifts. Mr. Leech has illustrated it most happily; his ghosts and shadows are as true as any of the choice corporeal pleas-antries that figure in his brilliant scenes; and nothing could be more like life than these.

5. Anon., *The Times* (January 7, 1844)

This volume, small as it is, will probably add very much to Mr. Dickens's reputation. It is, in fact, an exquisite gem in its way. The whole economy of the work is perfectly delightful, and its moral purpose deserving of the highest praise. Nowhere do we remember to have seen a more cheerful or a more instructive picture of Christmas, or a truer interpretation of the useful purposes to which its festivities may be applied. Generally the tone of the story is sweet and subdued, but occasionally it soars, and becomes altogether sublime. This praise may very possibly be thought extravagant by those who have not read and understood the *Christmas Carol*, but not by one, we are sure, among those who have. The character of the old miser we were, at the outset, disposed to consider extravagant; but when we paused to recollect what has been revealed by the annals of real life, we perceive that Mr. Dickens's fancy had not done any outrage to nature, which has produced monsters quite as hardened, quite as griping and penurious as Mr. Scrooge. That a total change should be effected in the moral economy of such a person is, no doubt, somewhat improbable, but not by any means so improbable as to be past belief. To serve an excellent purpose, therefore, the author was quite at liberty to invent, as he has done, and to dispose of an uncommon character in an uncommon way. The forms assumed by the ministers of conscience in achieving the holy work of repentance are conceived and delineated with poetical beauty, and the idea was singularly felicitous in withdrawing the miser from the influence of Mammon by forcing him to take a retrospect of his former life, and to feel of how much innocent pleasure and manly and elevated happiness the accursed thirst of gold had deprived him. But the master stroke is in drawing aside the veil of futurity.... The task of looking backward inspires the miser with sorrow and regret, but the act of looking forward overwhelms him with the deepest terror. He shrinks in unspeakable horror from the ghastly picture of himself which reasoning consequentially, and listening to the counsel of experience, compel him to draw. He figures to himself his death-bed, approached by no friendly form, but surrounded by thieves and robbers, who plunder his house before he has drawn his last breath, and strip off the linen from his emaciated corpse before it is cold: he follows, step by step, his unloved, unreverenced body to the grave, where Mr. Dickens's profound humanity and charity induce him to stop, neither hinting or suggesting anything of what may lie beyond. But the lesson suffices. The miser becomes penitent, discovers the beauty of benevolence, and strives earnestly, ere it be too late, to make amends to all around him, but still more to his own conscience, for the evil he had done, and the good which he had not done. The whole volume is replete with touching allusions, but none of these is more exquisitely so than that which is made to Him who loved little children, and whose birth hallowed, and will forever hallow, the season of Christmas. The passage in which this thought occurs is brief, exceedingly brief, but it is quite sufficient, we are sure, to reconcile to Mr. Dickens and his manner all those who may have required to be so reconciled. We could, with pleasure, extend this notice, but shall have written to very little purpose if what we leave said does not send every one of our readers to the pages of the *Christmas Carol*. They who do not will deprive themselves of a genuine enjoyment.

6. William Makepeace Thackeray, *Fraser's Magazine* (February 1844): 168-69

[Using the pen name of Michael Angelo Titmarsh (M.A.T.), the well-known author of such novels as *Vanity Fair* and *Henry Esmond* celebrates the fact that Dickens's tale surmounts the snobbery of certain established journals to win wide acclaim.]

As for the *Christmas Carol*, or any other book of a like nature which the public takes upon itself to criticise, the individual critic had quite best hold his peace. One remembers what Buonaparte replied to some Austrian critics, of much correctness and acumen, who doubted about acknowledging the French republic. I do not mean that the *Christmas Carol* is quite as brilliant or self-evident as the sun at noonday; but it is so spread over England by this time, that no sceptic, no *Fraser's Magazine*,—no, not even the godlike and ancient *Quarterly* itself (venerable, Saturnian, big-wigged dynasty!) could review it down. "Unhappy people! Deluded race!" one hears the cauliflowered god exclaim, mournfully shaking the powder out of his ambrosial curls, "What strange new folly is this? What new deity do ye worship? Know ye what ye do? Know ye that your new idol hath little Latin and less Greek? Know ye that he has never tasted the birch of Eton,[1] nor trodden the flags of Carfax,[2] nor paced the academic flats of Trumpington?[3] Know ye that in mathematics, or logics, this wretched ignoramus is not fit to hold a candle to a wooden spoon? See ye not how, from describing low humours, he now, forsooth, will attempt the sublime? Discern ye not his faults of taste, his deplorable propensity to write blank verse? Come back to your ancient, venerable, and natural instructors. Leave this new, low,

---

1 A famous public school, near Windsor, founded by Henry VI in 1440.
2 The crossroads in the center of the city of Oxford, the home of Oxford University. Its main streets radiate from Carfax Tower, in its center.
3 A street in the city of Cambridge, the home of Cambridge University.

and intoxicating draught at which ye rush, and let us lead you back to the old wells of classic lore. Come and repose with us there. We are your gods; we are the ancient oracles, and no mistake. Come listen to us once more, and we will sing you the mystic numbers of *as in presenti* under the arches of the Pons Asinorum."[1] But the children of the present generation hear not; for they reply, "Rush to the Strand! and purchase five thousand more copies of the *Christmas Carol*."

In fact, one might as well detail the plot of the *Merry Wives of Windsor*, or *Robinson Crusoe*, as recapitulate here the adventures of Scrooge the miser, and his Christmas conversion. I am not sure that the allegory is a very complete one, and protest, with the classics, against the use of blank verse in prose; but here all objections stop. Who can listen to objections regarding such a book as this? It seems to me a national benefit, and to every man or woman who reads it a personal kindness. The last two people I heard speak of it were women; neither knew the other, or the author, and both said, by way of criticism, "God bless him!" A Scotch philosopher, who nationally does not keep Christmas-day, on reading the book, sent out for a turkey, and asked two friends to dine—this is a fact! Many men were known to sit down after perusing it, and write off letters to their friends, not about business, but out of their fulness of heart, and to wish old acquaintances a happy Christmas. Had the book appeared a fortnight earlier, all the prize cattle would have been gobbled up on pure love and friendship, Epping denuded of sausages, and not a turkey left in Norfolk. His royal highness's fat stock would have fetched unheard-of prices, and Alderman Bannister would have been tired of slaying. But there is a Christmas for 1844, too; the book will be as early then as now, and so let speculators look out.

As for Tiny Tim, there is a certain passage in the book regarding that young gentleman, about which a man should hardly venture to speak in print or in public, and more than he would of any other affections of his private heart. There is not a reader in England but that little creature will be a bond of union between the author and him; and he will say of Charles Dickens, as the woman just now, "GOD BLESS HIM!" What a feeling is this for a writer to be able to inspire, and what a reward to reap!

M.A.T.

---

1 Asses' bridge.

Appendix E: Notable Film, Television, and Radio Adaptations of A Christmas Carol

1901 Scrooge; or, Marley's Ghost. Great Britain. First filmed version (silent). Cast unknown. Produced by R.W. Paul and directed by W.R. Booth.

1908 A Christmas Carol. Silent film. USA.

1910 A Christmas Carol. Silent film. USA. Thomas A. Edison. Marc McDermott (Scrooge).

1913 Scrooge. Silent film. Great Britain. Seymour Hicks (Scrooge).

1914 A Christmas Carol. Silent film. Great Britain. Charles Rock (Scrooge).

1916 The Right to be Happy. Silent film. USA. Rupert Julian (Scrooge).

1922 Scrooge. Great Britain. Silent film. H.V. Esmond (Scrooge).

1923 Scrooge. Great Britain. Silent film. Russell Thorndike (Scrooge).

1928 Scrooge. Great Britain. Sound film. Bransby Williams (Scrooge).

1934 A Christmas Carol. USA. Radio play starring Lionel Barrymore. Barrymore portrayed Scrooge on radio until the 1950s, an annual event enjoyed by millions of listeners. His performance was largely responsible for bringing Dickens's tale into popular American culture.

1935 Scrooge. Great Britain. Sound film. Seymour Hicks (Scrooge).

1938 A Christmas Carol. USA. Reginald Owen (Scrooge), Gene Lockhart (Bob Cratchit), Kathleen Lockhart (Mrs. Cratchit), and Terry Kilburn (Tiny Tim). Produced by Joseph L. Mankiewiz and directed by Edwin L. Marin.

1940 A Christmas Carol. USA. Gregory Markopoulos (Scrooge).

1947 A Christmas Carol. USA. WABD TV. John Carradine (Scrooge).

1948 A Christmas Carol. USA. NBC TV. Dennis King (Scrooge).

1949 Charles Dickens's The Christmas Carol. USA. Syndicated TV. Vincent Price (Narrator), Taylor Holmes (Scrooge).

1949 A Christmas Carol. Decca records. A sound recording by Ronald Colman.

1950 A Christmas Carol. Great Britain. BBC TV. Bransby Williams (Scrooge).

1951 Scrooge (released in the USA as A Christmas Carol). Great Britain. Alastair Sim (Scrooge), Mervyn Jones (Bob Cratchit), Hermione Baddeley (Mrs. Cratchit), Michael Hordern (Jacob Marley), Glyn Dearman (Tiny Tim). Produced and directed by

Brian Desmond-Hurst. Many critics, and I share in their judgment, consider this to be the best film adaptation of Dickens's story.

1951   A Christmas Carol. USA. NBC TV. Sir Ralph Richardson (Scrooge).

1951   A Christmas Carol. USA. WQXR New York. Radio version starring Alec Guinness.

1952   A Christmas Carol. USA. NBC TV. Malcolm Keen (Scrooge).

1954   A Christmas Carol. USA. CBS TV. Frederic March (Scrooge), Basil Rathbone (Jacob Marley).

1955   The Merry Christmas. Great Britain. Hugh Griffith (Scrooge).

1956   The Stingiest Man in Town. USA. NBC TV. Basil Rathbone (Scrooge), Vic Damone (Young Scrooge), Johnny Desmond (Fred), Patrice Munsel (Belle), the Four Lads (Chorus and Narrators). A 90 minute musical version, broadcast live on *The Alcoa Hour*, December 23.

1957   Scrooge Loose. USA. A short film in which Gumby (a claymation figure) keeps Scrooge from spoiling a children's Christmas.

1957   The Trail to Christmas. USA. CBS TV. Ronald Reagan, host to this western version of Dickens's story, on *The General Electric Theatre*. John McIntire (Scrooge).

1958   The Merry Christmas. Great Britain. Stephen Murray (Scrooge). A musical adaptation.

1959   A Christmas Carol. Great Britain. Frederic March (Host), Basil Rathbone (Scrooge). This 25 minute film was part of Harry Towers's *Tales from Dickens* series, first televised in 1959.

1960   The Andy Griffith Show. USA. CBS TV. The episode entitled "The Christmas Story" was first broadcast on December 19. Ben Weaver, the crusty, Scrooge-like owner of Mayberry's department store, changes his nasty, stingy ways upon seeing Andy, Barney, and friends enjoying a Christmas Eve party.

1962   Mister Magoo's Christmas Carol. USA. NBC TV. Animated film with voices by Jim Backus (Mr. Magoo and Scrooge), Morey Amsterdam (Brandy and James), Jack Cassidy (Bob Cratchit).

1962   A Christmas Carol. Great Britain. Stephen Manton (Scrooge). The first performance of an opera version of the *Carol*. Music by Edwin Coleman.

1964   Mr. Scrooge. Canada. CBC TV. Cyril Ritchard (Scrooge), Tessie O'Shea (Mrs. Cratchit). A musical version.

1964   Carol for Another Christmas. USA. ABC TV. Sterling Hayden (Daniel Grudge), Ben Gazzara (Fred), Steve Lawrence (Ghost of Christmas Past), Eva Marie Saint (Lt. Gibson), Pat Hingle (Ghost of Christmas Present), Robert Shaw (Ghost of Christmas Future), Peter Sellers (Imperial Me), Britt Eklund (Woman). Produced and directed by Joseph L. Mankiewicz and written by Rod Serling, this production argues for the importance of world peace and support for the United Nations. The wealthy and powerful Daniel Grudge, having lost his son (Marley) in a foreign war, has become a rigid isolationist. Under the influence of the visiting ghosts, however, who present him with visions of the aftermath of a devastating nuclear war, and of suffering, starving masses, Grudge comes to realize the importance of international negotiations, of reaching out to others instead of retreating into his right-wing philosophy.

1970   Scrooge. Great Britain. Albert Finney (Scrooge), Alec Guinness (Jacob Marley), Edith Evans (Ghost of Christmas Past), Kenneth More (Ghost of Christmas Present), David Collings (Bob Cratchit), Richard Beaumont (Tiny Tim). Produced by Robert Solo and directed by Ronald Neame. A musical version.

1971   A Christmas Carol. Great Britain. Animated film with voices by Sir Michael Redgrave (Narrator), Alastair Sim (Scrooge), Michael Hordern (Jacob Marley), Diana Quick (Ghost of Christmas Past), Alexander Williams (Tiny Tim).

1973   Marcel Marceau Presents A Christmas Carol. Great Britain. BBC TV. Michael Hordern (Narrator), Marcel Marceau (all the characters).

1977   A Christmas Carol. Great Britain. BBC TV. Michael Hordern (Scrooge), John Le Mesurier (Jacob Marley), Patricia Quinn (Ghost of Christmas Past), Clive Merrison (Bob Cratchit).

1978   Scrooge. Canada. ITV TV. Warren Graves (Scrooge), Drew Borland (Jacob Marley), Ray Hunt (Bob Cratchit), Colin Graves (Tiny Tim). Produced by Joan Krisch and directed by John Blanchard.

1978   The Stingiest Man in Town. USA. NBC TV. Walter Matthau (Scrooge), Tom Bosley (Narrator), Theodore Bikel (Jacob Marley), Dennis Day (Nephew Fred). Animated musical version.

1981   A Christmas Carol. USA. Arts Cable TV. William Paterson (Scrooge), Mark Murphey (Bob Cratchit), Raye Birk (Jacob Marley), Tyson Thomas (Tiny Tim). Televised version of the American Conservatory Theatre's stage production.

1982   A Christmas Carol. USA. Entertainment Channel TV. Richard Hilger (Scrooge), Oliver Cliff (Jacob Marley), J. Patrick Martin (Bob Cratchit). Televised version of the Guthrie Theater's stage production.

1982 A Christmas Carol. Great Britain. Granada TV. Frederick Burchinal (Scrooge), Murray Melvin (Spirit of Christmas), Robin Leggate (Bob Cratchit). An opera version, first staged in America in 1979 by the Virginia Opera Association, presented by the Royal Opera House, Covent Garden, for Granada TV.

1983 Mickey's Christmas Carol. USA. Walt Disney Production. Mickey Mouse (Bob Cratchit), Donald Duck (Nephew Fred), Goofy (Jacob Marley), Scrooge McDuck (Scrooge).

1983 The Gospel According to Scrooge. USA. Christian Broadcasting Network TV. Robert Buchanan (Scrooge), Robert Whitesel (Bob Cratchit), Melanie Burve (Tiny Tim). Points an evangelical theme.

1984 A Christmas Carol. Great Britain. Released in theaters in England and broadcast on CBS TV in America. George C. Scott (Scrooge), Frank Finlay (Jacob Marley), Angela Pleasence (Ghost of Christmas Past), Edward Woodward (Ghost of Christmas Present), Michael Carter (Ghost of Christmas Yet to Come), David Warner (Bob Cratchit), Susannah York (Mrs. Cratchit), Anthony Walters (Tiny Tim). Produced by William F. Storke and Alfred R. Kelman. Directed by Clive Donner.

1986 John Grin's Christmas. Canada. ABC TV. Robert Guillaume (John Grin), Roscoe Lee Browne (Christmas Past), Ted Lange (Christmas Present), Geoffrey Holder (Christmas Future). The first attempt by film or television to present an all-black Carol.

1987 See Hear! Great Britain. BBC TV. A production for the deaf and hearing impaired in which the tale is rendered in sign language.

1988 Scrooged. USA. Bill Murray (Frank Cross), Karen Allen (Claire Phillips), John Forsythe (Lew Hayward), Robert Mitchum (Preston Rhinelander). Murray plays a Scrooge-like television executive who is producing a live broadcast of A Christmas Carol. His cast includes Buddy Hackett (Scrooge), Jamie Farr (Jacob Marley), Pat McCormick (Ghost of Christmas Past), and Mary Lou Retton (an acrobatic Tiny Tim).

· 1988 Blackadder's Christmas Carol. Great Britain. BBC TV. Rowan Atkinson (Ebenezer Blackadder).

1992 The Muppet Christmas Carol. USA. Jim Henson Productions/Walt Disney Pictures. Michael Caine (Scrooge), Kermit the Frog (Bob Cratchit), Miss Piggy (Emily Cratchit), the Great Gonzo (Charles Dickens), Fozzie Bear (Mr. Fezziwig). Produced and directed by Brian Henson.

1993 A Christmas Carol. Great Britain. BBC TV/Arts and Entertainment Network. Jeremy Kerridge (Scrooge), William Walker (Bob

Cratchit), Polly Benge (Mrs. Cratchit). A ballet version choreographed by Massimo Moricone.

1994 Northern Exposure. USA. CBS TV. Episode entitled "Shofar, So Good." Dr. Joel Fleischman (played by Rob Morrow), a disgruntled resident of the town of Cicely, Alaska, longs to be in New York. During the Jewish holidays, the miserable doctor is visited in a dream by his rabbi back home, who appears to him as the Spirits of Yom Kippur Past, Present, and Future, thereby changing the doctor's mind and restoring a more genial mood.

1994 A Flintstones Christmas Carol. USA. The residents of Bedrock stage *A Christmas Carol* with Fred Flintstone as Scrooge.

1994 Bah! Humbug! USA. PBS TV. A reading set in the Pierpont Morgan Library, where Dickens's manuscript of *A Christmas Carol* resides. The program is hosted by Robert MacNeil, the narrator is Martin Sheen, and Scrooge's lines are read by James Earl Jones.

1995 Ebbie. Canada. Lifetime Cable Network. Susan Lucci plays Elizabeth (Ebbie) Scrooge, a hard-nosed businesswoman who runs a department store with ruthless control. Her former partner, Jake Marley, appears on her television set and with his remote control unit dispatches her to three meetings with spirits that help her change her priorities.

1997 A Christmas Carol. USA. Animated version. Voices: Tim Curry (Scrooge), Whoopi Goldberg (Spirit of Christmas Present), Michael York (Bob Cratchit), Ed Asner (Jacob Marley).

1997 Ms. Scrooge. USA/Canada. USA Cable Network. Cicely Tyson (Ebenita Scrooge), Katherine Helmond (Maude Marley).

1998 Ebenezer. USA/Canada. TNT Cable Network. Jack Palance (Scrooge), Jack Palance (Future Scrooge), Rick Schroder (Sam Benson), Albert Schultz (Bob Cratchit). Western version, with Palance as a selfish, greedy villain who, under the influence of visiting ghosts, recovers his humanity.

[For a comprehensive listing of adaptations—film, television, theatrical, radio, and book—of *A Christmas Carol*, see Paul Davis, *The Lives and Times of Ebenezer Scrooge* (New Haven: Yale University Press, 1990) and Fred Guida, *A Christmas Carol and its Adaptations* (Jefferson, N.C.: McFarland, 2000).]

Select Bibliography

Biographies, Letters, and Speeches

Ackroyd, Peter. *Dickens*. London: Sinclair-Stevenson, 1990.

Fielding, K.J., ed. *The Speeches of Charles Dickens*. Oxford: Clarendon Press, 1960.

Forster, John. *The Life of Charles Dickens*. 3 vols. London: Chapman & Hall, 1872-74.

Johnson, Edgar. *Charles Dickens: His Tragedy and Triumph*. 2 vols. New York: Simon & Schuster, 1952.

Kaplan, Fred. *Dickens: A Biography*. New York: William Morrow, 1988.

House, Madeline, Graham Storey, and Kathleen Tillotson, eds. *The Pilgrim Edition of The Letters of Charles Dickens*. 12 vols. (Oxford: Clarendon Press, 1965-2002).

Editions of *A Christmas Carol* and Christmas Stories

Dickens, Charles. *A Christmas Carol. In Prose. Being a Ghost Story of Christmas*. London: Chapman and Hall, 1843.

—. *A Christmas Carol: The Original Manuscript*. New York: Dover, 1967.

—. *A Christmas Carol*, ed. Edgar Johnson. New York: K.S. Giniger Co., 1967.

Glancy, Ruth, ed. *Charles Dickens: Christmas Stories*. London: Everyman, 1996.

Hearn, Michael Patrick, ed. *The Annotated Christmas Carol*. New York: Clarkson N. Potter, 1976.

Slater, Michael, ed. *The Christmas Books*, vol. 1 (*A Christmas Carol, The Chimes*). London: Penguin, 1971.

Studies

Davis, Paul. *The Lives and Times of Ebenezer Scrooge*. New Haven: Yale UP, 1990.

—. *Charles Dickens A to Z: The Essential Reference to His Life and Work*. New York: Facts on File, 1998.

Glancy, Ruth. "Dickens and Christmas: His Framed-Tale Themes." *Nineteenth-Century Fiction*, 35 (1980): 53-72.

Guida, Fred. *A Christmas Carol and its Adaptations*. Jefferson, NC: McFarland, 2000.

Hooper, Linda. *A Little Book About A Christmas Carol.* The Dickens Project, U of California P, 1993.

Pointer, Michael. *Charles Dickens on the Screen.* Lanham, MD: Scarecrow Press, 1996.

Thomas, Deborah A. *Dickens and the Short Story.* Philadelphia: U of Pennsylvania P, 1982.

Wilson, Edmund. "Dickens: The Two Scrooges." *The Wound and the Bow.* New York: Oxford University Press, 1947. 111-34.

Recent Fictional Accounts of Dickens's Characters

Bueno de Mesquita, Bruce. *The Trial of Ebenezer Scrooge.* Columbus, OH: Ohio State UP, 2001.

Osmun, Mark H. *Marley's Ghost.* Corte Madera, CA: Twelfth Night Press, 2000.

Christmas Traditions

Hervey, Thomas K. *The Book of Christmas.* Chicago: Cuneo Press, 1951.

Irving, Washington. *Old Christmas.* Tarrytown, NY: Sleepy Hollow Restorations, 1977. A facsimile of the first edition, with an introduction by Andrew B. Meyers.

Marling, Karal Ann. *Merry Christmas!: Celebrating America's Greatest Holiday.* Cambridge, MA: Harvard UP, 2000.

Sandys, William. *Christmas Carols, Ancient and Modern.* London: R. Beckley, 1833.

—. *Christmastide, Its History, Festivities, and Carols.* London: John Russel Smith, 1852.

Social and Working Conditions

"Children's Employment Commission. First Report of the Commissioners, On Mines; Second Report, On Trades and Manufactures." *British Parliamentary Papers,* 15 vols. (Irish University Press: Shannon, 1968-69).

Engels, Frederich. *The Condition of the English Working-Class in 1844.* London: Allen and Unwin, 1952.